ULTIMATE VERDICT

A Legal Thriller

Michael Winstead

PRAISE FOR ULTIMATE VERDICT

"For lovers of crime novels and courtroom drama, Ultimate Verdict by Michael Winstead delivers an exciting story that moves along without getting stuck in legal humdrum, builds up suspense and intensity, and makes us think hard and feel deeply while we turn the pages. Highly recommended!"

TheColumbiaReview.com

"Winstead has created an engaging cast of secret society members who close loopholes in the legal system using their own brand of vigilante justice. After years on the 'right' side of the law, their compelling arguments for stepping over the line may cause you to struggle with some of your own doubts and demons, as you discover your Ultimate Verdict."

Blair H. Clark, Author
Answers to What Ails You

"Winstead excels at weaving philosophical questions of good and evil into realistic legal, professional and human conflicts. The cast of characters is well developed, alive and very human. The plot is rich with creative twists and blind turns, leading to a satisfying (and surprising) conclusion that ties up closely with the original crime and the initial injustice that propelled the judge and his team into action."

Avraham Azrieli, Author
Deborah Rising

This book is dedicated to my wife and children,
without whom this journey would be meaningless.

This book also is dedicated to the countless victims of crime,
for whom justice has proved so elusive.

A portion of the book proceeds will be donated to victim relief funds.

CHAPTER ONE

On the last day of her life, Hannah Sullivan had a decision to make.

She lay in a heap for a minute, maybe two, her head fuzzy and out of balance. When finally she untangled herself from the bicycle, she hugged her knees to her chest and glanced back at the tunnel. The black ice lurked somewhere beyond the mouth. She hadn't seen it then and still couldn't, transparent as glass.

She assessed the damage, running her hands over her legs, then her arms. Her left knee was raw and red beneath the ripped cloth of her leggings. The hand that broke the fall throbbed with pain. She touched the bruise on her side where she had landed on the handlebar going down. Removing her helmet, she rubbed the marred plastic on the side, evidence her head had collided with pavement.

She glanced at the sky as low clouds infiltrated the valley. A winter front was moving in from the west. The temperature had plunged fifteen degrees since she started to climb. Wind gusts howled through leafless branches and skidded across granite cliffs.

It was time to decide—up or down. She peered toward the summit at Mt. Pisgah. Probably ten miles of steady climbing. Below, the gaping mouth of the tunnel beckoned to her. It would be an easy descent to the safety of her car.

Pulling her shoulders back, she drew a deep breath to clear out the remnants of the crash. With numb fingers she managed to buckle her helmet. The taut strap bit the skin beneath her chin. She rubbed her knee again, thinking vaguely of medical attention and bandages and the scar her wound might leave.

Unzipping the small pack beneath the bike seat, she fished out two painkillers and popped them into her mouth, chased them with water. She slipped the plastic bottle back into an aluminum cage bolted to the bike frame.

Hannah mounted the bike and pedaled once, aiming the wheel neither up nor down, balancing on the pedals for two heartbeats. Abruptly, she

1

turned uphill and began to churn. She clung to the right side of the road as she ascended, snaking around curves, carefully scanning the shadows for more ice, putting distance between herself and the memory of the crash. Less than an hour later, she reached the summit. At this higher elevation, the snow drifted down in big, wet tufts, not yet sticking. To Hannah, the air smelled of triumph. And a hint of something else.

To the west, purple clouds hung like clumps of ripe grapes. She wheeled through the vacant parking lot, toward the bathrooms, confident she could outrace the storm to the bottom. She snapped out of the pedals and leaned her bike against a bear-proof trash can. Closed to vehicle traffic, the Parkway was as abandoned as a dead mine. Unbuckling her helmet, she disentangled long blonde hair and draped the straps of the helmet over the handlebar. As she navigated the path in bike shoes, she wobbled like a horse on cobblestones. The bathroom kiosk was locked. She went around the back for no particular reason, down into a copse of mountain laurel, where she squatted. She saw only a glimpse of the man lunging at her before everything went black.

She awoke on her back. For the second time that day, Hannah craned her head to take stock of her situation. Braided cord bound her wrists and ankles, drawing her arms and legs into the shape of an X. A blanket of snow surrounded her, close to six inches deep. Her breath fogged in small plumes and drifted to the ground. When she let her head drop, it landed on something downy. As she lay back in the snow, now a prisoner, she realized her blunder. What she had seen as courage in heading to the summit alone had been folly in disguise.

"Where am I?" Her voice croaked with fear and dryness.

The silhouette of a man, standing a few feet away, inched closer. He stuck the nipple of a water bottle between her lips, and she took a long swig. She squeezed her eyes shut. Her eyelids were icy.

The man stooped and fiddled with the cord binding her wrists and ankles. She turned her head away from the stench of unwashed body and rotting teeth. For a fleeting moment she thought he might loosen her bindings, but when he finished the cord was tighter. He shuffled away.

Colliding thoughts threatened to burst through to panic. No one knew where she was. The Parkway was closed. Even if someone had been looking for her, they would search the roads, or the parking lot where she left her bike. No one would come looking for her in the woods on a frigid night.

2

"Hey, can anyone out there hear me? Help, Help, Help," she yelped. The wind broke up her voice.

Night came with a hush. A smattering of stars appeared through a tangle of naked tree limbs. The hulk of a steel transmission tower jutted from the mountain before a half moon.

She heard the crunch of boots on snow. He was back. His head lamp threw a dim cone of light toward her. He squatted on a downed tree trunk, well out of reach. The aroma of cooked meat wafted to her through thick air.

He wore an old pair of leather boots, scarred at the toes. The sole of the right boot was beginning to separate. His dirty jeans looked blue-black in twilight. A camouflage hunting jacket covered a gaunt chest. A large knife, with a bone handle, rested in a leather sheath on his hip.

If I can somehow reach that knife, I might be able to cut the tent cord, then I can free myself. Or I could stab him.

"Hey, I need to pee," she said in a pleading voice.

The man stared at her, dark eyes over a grizzled beard not trimmed in weeks. He pinched a piece of meat with bare fingers and lifted it from the metal plate, then worked it into his mouth. He was missing a front tooth on the bottom row.

"Hey, can you untie me so I can go pee? In private? I won't run away. I promise." She could tell she was not far from the parking lot. The parking lot where she left her bike. And her phone. "I don't even know where I am. Where would I go? Untie me, please?"

The man continued eating in silence. His movements were slow and unbalanced. A gust of wind rattled the trees and rearranged the top layer of snow. He tilted his head toward the moon and sniffed the air. Then he left the log and knelt beside her, holding the tin plate low.

She had not eaten since breakfast. The climb had sapped her energy, if not her resolve. There were protein bars in her seat pack—useless to her now. She must eat to survive.

"What is it?" she asked of the lumps of meat on the plate.

"Squirrel," he said. The first word he had uttered.

She had never eaten squirrel before, never even thought about it. "If you'll untie my hands, I can eat something. Thank you."

The man looked at her, canted his head to the side. An amused grin formed in the middle of his beard. He plucked a piece of glistening meat from the plate and dangled it above her mouth.

3

Hannah nodded in understanding, then opened her lips. A chunk of meat dropped into her mouth. The meat was warm and juicy, tasted like the smoke of a campfire.

He wouldn't be feeding me if he planned to kill me, would he? Maybe he's holding me for ransom.

The throbbing in the middle of her forehead intensified, radiating from dull to sharp. She wrinkled her brow, trying to make it stop.

The man fed her pieces of squirrel, followed by a squirt of water each time. She chewed slowly, hoping to give herself time to escape, looking for an opportunity, trying to prolong . . . everything. She was fit and strong; she had proved it that morning. She just needed the slightest opening.

"Hey, my name's Hannah. Hannah Sullivan. What's yours?" she said, hoping to start a conversation.

He ignored the question and dangled the last lump of squirrel above her mouth. The empty plate rested on the snow.

"Give me a minute. It doesn't go down very well when you're lying down," she said, staring into his glazed eyes. "Maybe you could untie me. Then I can sit up. That would make it easier, you know, to swallow and digest the food."

The man returned to the dead tree.

"So, I was just riding up the mountain on my bike. It's nice when there's no traffic. But I crashed a few miles back. Skidded on some ice." The man didn't acknowledge her, so she tried a different approach. "My knee is bloody. You see that, right? And it really hurts. Do you have a first aid kit or something? Something to reduce the swelling in my knee?"

The man ignored her entreaty.

"Hey. I'm injured. Hurt. I need medical attention. Do you have any bandages at least?"

The man shifted his feet in the snow, but he did not move from the log.

She turned inward, trying to remember. The crash was there, but not much afterward. A murky memory of the man lunging at her, hitting in the forehead with . . . something. She tilted her head and eyed the bone knife, still in its sheath.

Maybe that's what he hit me with. What else did he do to me? She lifted her head and scanned her splayed body. None of her clothing had been removed. She wasn't sore in places she shouldn't have been.

"Hey, I really have to pee. I can't wait any longer. Have some decency, for God's sake."

4

At this, the man came closer, squatted beside her. He hovered the last piece of squirrel meat above her mouth.

She opened her mouth yawn wide, and the last chunk of meat tumbled in. She chewed slowly, conserving energy, trying to calm her frenzied mind. Her eyes fluttered closed. *Maybe if he thinks I'm asleep he'll come closer, make a mistake. If I can only get ahold of that knife.* She heard the man shuffle away through the snow.

After a few minutes, Hannah felt a dull warmth seep through her body. Becoming drowsy, she feared falling asleep and missing her chance. She forced her eyes open, imagining she was speeding down a highway in the dark, heading for home, intent on keeping the car between the lane reflectors. In that circumstance, sleep could be fatal.

As she faded, she realized there were no more decisions to make. Her fate was no longer up to her. A turn up the mountain, instead of down, the silly emergence of modesty on an empty mountain, had determined it all. In her foggy state, she did not hear the man approach, did not see him kneel next to her in the snow. She did not see the man raise his arm, could not see what he held in his hand.

CHAPTER TWO

The snow lay almost a foot deep, coating the pines in fresh white fur. The entire mountain range was covered in purity. Glossy rhododendron curled against the cold, ice rimming the leaf edges.

Ranger Arnie Swenson followed the footprints. A boot, perhaps size ten, recent but not fresh. He stopped and pulled binoculars to his eyes, thin rubber eyepieces cold against his sockets. He saw nothing that didn't fit. Trudging up the trail, he passed a thicket of oriental bittersweet strangling a naked hickory tree. A breeze rustled the heavily laden boughs of the pines, dislodging snow in muffled coughs.

He cleared a stand of trees and scanned again. Right to left. Then back. A blotch of something. He refocused. A red spot marred the pristine canvas like expletives from the altar.

He followed the footprints another hundred feet, then two. A better angle. The red blaze was bigger than he thought. Maybe a mountain lion roaming the area had killed a deer. He had seen it before.

Abandoning the trail of footprints, he retraced his own steps to the parking lot and the bicycle. There had been no report of anyone missing in the last few days. But he had what appeared to be a swath of blood, and an abandoned bicycle with the helmet hanging from a drop tine.

Ranger Swenson radioed headquarters for direction and was told to call the county sheriff's office. There, he reached a dispatcher, who patched him through to a detective on call for the weekend. The detective sounded tired, or bored, but agreed to come up and take a look.

That entire section of the Parkway had been closed to vehicle traffic for three days while the storm laid a white blanket over the Blue Ridge Mountains. Ranger Swenson carefully navigated the curvy road on his descent, aiming for the tangents between the hulking granite walls on his left and sheer plunges on his right. He stopped at several pipe gates along the way, unlocked the padlocks and swung the striped poles clear of the roadway.

The snow layer dissipated to a thin crust as he descended three thousand feet. At a gate just west of the river, he met Detective Rick Underwood. They shook hands. Underwood shouldered a police blue duffle bag.

"You got any boots in there? The snow is about a foot deep on the trail," Swenson said, staring at the detective's loafers.

"No. I forgot those. Didn't realize I'd need them."

"Well, I've got a pair of rubber boots in the back if you want them."

"I appreciate that."

They left Underwood's car at the overlook below the gate and climbed the mountain in Swenson's Suburban. Swenson leaned forward over the steering wheel, trying to stay in the tracks left from his descent. Narrow traces of black pavement showed through the snow until they passed through the first tunnel, and then the tracks became almost indiscernible depressions. The vehicle lurched and slid in a few places, but Swenson kept a steady pace and his foot off the brake to prevent an uncontrollable skid.

Detective Underwood gripped the handle above the passenger door and squeezed the duffle bag between his calves. When they finally arrived at the summit, they were greeted by a low-angled sun glaring off the whiteness. They tromped across the parking lot to the bicycle, the red frame peeking from under a ridge of snow. No lock. A blue and white plastic helmet dangled from the handle bar.

"How long has it been here?" Detective Underwood asked.

"I'm not sure. It wasn't here on my last patrol before the storm, on Friday morning," Ranger Swenson said.

They started down the trail, following the footprints. Ranger Swenson led the way. Underwood unslung the duffle from his shoulder on occasion to take pictures of the boot prints, the trail, the snow-laden bushes. A breeze carried nothing but clean. A faint scent of pine. At the point on the trail where the red blemish was first visible, they stopped.

"Is this all you?" Underwood asked, pointing at the disturbed snow.

Swenson eyed the other boot prints, a single track leading away, toward the peak of the mountain. "Yes. The other person never stopped, as far as I could tell." He offered Underwood his binoculars.

Underwood peered through the binoculars, adjusted the focus, then let the binoculars fall to his chest. "I'd say it's blood," he muttered. "I can't think of anything else that would stand out like that in this landscape."

"I agree."

"Let's go. I'll plant these little orange flags along our route," Underwood said, pulling a bundle of plastic flags from the duffle.

Hiking through the snow, they navigated a tangled thicket of rhododendron, worked their way around fallen trees. In sunken spots the snow exceeded Underwood's rubber boots. They paused upon a granite outcropping. The detective confirmed with a glance through the binoculars that they were encroaching upon a crime scene.

"Let's go slow. Let me lead so I can take pictures of the path in front." Underwood handed the bundle of neon flags to Swenson. "Place these as we go."

They crept up to the spot as if stalking game. A young woman lay in the snow. Her face was a bluish pallor, her lips frozen together. A yellow jersey was punctured with dozens of holes, each marked with a red aureole. Dark leggings covered her to the ankles. There was a tear on the left knee, exposing the skin. Splotches of red roughly outlined her torso, as if drawn there with a dripping pen.

"Based on what she's wearing, I'd say this is the person that bike belongs to," Underwood said, angling his head toward the parking lot.

Swenson allowed himself to breathe. "Looks that way."

So obvious was her demise that neither officer thought it necessary to check for a pulse. The men stood for a few minutes over her body, looking and listening. Scanning the woods for any sign of anything. Underwood pulled out his cell phone. "Four thirteen," he said. "I don't see any footprints leading to or away from the body."

"Depending on how long she's been here, the snow could have covered up any prints. It's been snowing on and off up here for two days. Stopped sometime around noon."

Underwood nodded. "What have we got, an hour 'til dark?"

Swenson looked off to the southwest. "If that."

"All right. We came in from that direction. Let's head off this way and see what we find."

They wound through the trees, ducking branches bereft of leaves, occasionally looking back over their shoulders at the twisting line of fluorescent orange marking their route. Nothing stirred except the snow squeaking softly beneath their boots. At the edge of a granite boulder they spotted a green, nylon tent. With his gun aimed at the tent, Underwood called out.

"Sheriff's office. Is anyone in there?" No one responded.

They stationed themselves on opposite sides of the tent opening. As the breeze stirred, a whiff of charred wood rose from a fire pit. Acrid.

The detective peeled aside the tent flap and discovered a man encased in a sleeping bag. With his gun trained on the bag, Underwood prodded the man awake with a boot and identified himself, showing his badge.

The man sat up and rubbed his eyes. After looking around the tent several times, he said in a slurred voice, "You're here about that girl."

Swenson and Underwood pulled him upright, then bound his hands in handcuffs. Underwood frisked the man for weapons. Then he unbuckled the man's belt and slid off the leather sheath containing a Bowie knife. He carefully pulled the gleaming knife from the sheath, examined it for blood, then slipped the knife back into the sheath and placed both in a plastic evidence bag.

Ranger Swenson began to ask a question, but Underwood stopped him with a raised hand. "Wait, wait," Underwood said. "Miranda. We've got to Mirandize him."

"Sorry. Of course," said Swenson. He was trying to maintain his composure in the macabre atmosphere in which he found himself. Then in his tenth year as a Ranger, he had never encountered a corpse on the job, had never investigated a murder.

Underwood pulled a card from his wallet and squinted to read the Miranda warning in the dim light. "Do you understand your rights?" he finished.

The man responded with a cough.

"What's your name?" Underwood asked.

No response.

"Did you do that to that girl over there in the woods?" Swenson pointed down the curling path from which they had come.

Dried blood caked the man's ears and stained the shoulders of his camouflage jacket. He stared off in the direction of the woman's body, ignoring the officers.

Swenson searched the tent, finding a wallet in the folds of the sleeping bag. The wallet contained a few bills and a hunting license. No driver's license, and no credit cards. The hunting license was three years out of date. "Henry Lawter," he read from the tattered license.

He continued searching the small tent and uncovered a rifle buried beneath a pile of clothes in the back corner. He emerged from the tent holding the .22 caliber rifle in front of him. "Still loaded. And it looks like he's cooking meth up here."

Underwood stuck his head inside the tent to confirm the paraphernalia of a low-budget meth lab. "Is your name Lawter, Henry Lawter?" the detective asked, looking directly into the man's bloodshot eyes. "There are lots of Lawters around here," Underwood said absently.

The man stared back at the detective with eyes void of emotion.

Swenson led the way down to the girl, the snow duly trampled. Behind, Underwood prodded the silent man along with the barrel of the rifle, aimed squarely at the base of the prisoner's lurching head. The man stumbled several times as they stepped over and around decaying trees.

They arrived at the woman's body and stood silently over her, as if not wanting to disturb a sleeping child. The frozen blood stains contrasted sharply with otherwise white surroundings. As they looked down, contemplating a life taken, the handcuffed man began to talk. His words came out in a mumble, his speech tainted by dilapidated pronunciation. He spoke with his chin pressed to his chest, his shoulders hunched against the cold. The officers moved closer so they could hear his voice in the whispering winds.

"She came down the trail there." The man nodded his head toward the path that led to the top of the mountain. "She squatted down to pee behind some bushes. She had blood all over her leg, like from a accident or something. I snuck up on her and grabbed her and stabbed her in the forehead." He shrugged, as if this burst of violence was a natural reaction to the encounter. "Anyhow, just stunned her. Front part of the brain, you can have a frontal lobotomy and still survive."

"What do you know about lobotomies?" Underwood asked, clenching and unclenching his left fist. "Did you know this woman?"

The man ignored the question. "I dragged her down here and tied her up. She was unconscious most of the time. When she woke up she said she was hungry. I gave her some squirrel meat. Gave her some Oxy for the pain. I put it in the squirrel meat. She didn't know it was there. She passed out again. That's when I stabbed her. A bunch of times."

Ranger Swenson looked down at the bright red pinpoints covering the woman's torso. This blunt confession of murder felt like dirty fingers scrabbling into his throat. He retched as he imagined what the woman, still without a name, had endured. How long had she been tortured at the hands of this madman? The pain she must have felt each time she was stabbed. Over and over again. Dozens of times. Had she tried to scream?

Underwood resumed the interrogation. "You said you did it. Were you high? Was there anybody else here? Are you alone in these woods?" The rapid-fire questions left little room for an answer. Underwood stepped in front of the man so he could watch his eyes. "What are you doing out here? Why did you do it? She wasn't threatening you, was she? She was totally innocent. Why man? Why did you kill her?"

The man blinked, but he remained silent, his hands clasped behind him, ringed by shiny steel.

Underwood grabbed the prisoner by his dingy collar and shook him. "Why?" he shouted into the man's face.

The man's head wobbled, but he said nothing.

Detective Underwood knew of ways to make the man answer, but he had what he needed: a murder-scene confession, witnessed by a Park Ranger, an officer of the United States of America. He didn't want to do anything to taint that confession.

As darkness began to fall, the men began to shiver. The killer among them unconsciously shifted his legs to generate warmth. Long shadows crept onto the murder scene.

"Why is the blood still red?" Swenson asked. "I thought it was supposed to turn a rusty brown color."

"It's frozen," Underwood said. "Otherwise, you probably would never have seen it from the trail. We need to head back to the car and call the crime scene team."

They trudged through the snow to the parking lot, following the trail of neon flags. Swenson's bobbing flashlight led the way. Underwood stowed Lawter in the back of the SUV and called the crime-scene investigators.

Underwood leaned against the side of the running vehicle, smoking a cigarette. The darkness had closed in on them, the only light an eerie green from the dashboard. A steady plume of exhaust rose into the cold, framed by the darkness. "We've got him. A solid confession. We need to write it up."

Swenson adjusted his hat. "Looks that way. Open and shut, I'd say."

Underwood gazed at the orange glow at the end of his butt, then flicked it away into the snow. "I don't mind telling you, it took all my self-control not to put a bullet in the back of his head."

CHAPTER THREE

Henry Lawter killed Hannah Sullivan on a narrow strip of land owned by the National Park Service. Federal soil. As a consequence, it fell to federal prosecutors to decide whether to prosecute Lawter, or to allow the State of North Carolina to take over the case.

Caroline Bannister, United States Attorney for the Western District of North Carolina, shook hands with each of the men assembled around the conference table. She had summoned them all to her office in Charlotte for this conference. She settled into the lead chair. Her navy suit was pressed and creased, her pleated white blouse neatly tucked beneath the jacket.

"Good morning, gentlemen, and thank you for coming. As you know, this case has been plastered on television, and the front page of the newspapers, for almost a week now. Very high profile. It certainly looks like a murder case, and from everything I've heard, it appears we have the murderer in custody and a rock-solid confession. But I want to make sure we have an ironclad case. Robert, will you take us through the evidence?"

Assistant United States Attorney Robert Crenshaw laid out the evidence gathered to date, the highlight of which was Henry Lawter's uncoerced confession to two law enforcement officers. "The confession is the key to the case," he concluded. "And Ranger Swenson and Detective Underwood can tell you what they heard in their own words."

"Before we get to that," Caroline said, resuming control, "I have a few questions. Number one, were there any footprints leading to or away from the body?"

"No footprints, other than those made by the officers and Lawter when they led him to the body," Crenshaw said.

Caroline glared at her underling. The pupils in her green eyes were narrow, vertical slits, a small bulge at the bottom, giving them a teardrop shape. A condition called Schmid–Fraccaro syndrome. She could have an entire conversation with those cat eyes. "Ranger Swenson, since you will be testifying, and Mr. Crenshaw will not, did you notice any footprints around the body?"

"No ma'am. I did find some footprints along the trail that leads to the top of the mountain, but nothing near the body when we first found her."

"And what do you make of that?"

"I'm not a forensic scientist, ma'am, but I think it means that Lawter killed her during the middle of the snow storm, and because it kept snowing, his footprints were filled in by the snow."

"And the footprints you found along the hiking trail, why weren't those filled in by snow?"

"They had to be made later, probably that morning."

Caroline bored in, testing how the star witness would perform on cross-examination. "Were they Lawter's footprints, or was someone else on that mountain when Hannah Sullivan was killed?"

"I don't know, ma'am."

Caroline leaned back in her high-backed chair and refocused her attention on a ceiling light. "Does anyone know whether the footprints along the trail match Lawter's?"

The men remained silent.

"All right. Who *is* in charge of the crime-scene investigation?"

"That would be me," said FBI Agent Damien Porter. "And we haven't checked the boot prints."

"Why not?"

"Well, for one, until this moment I wasn't aware there were any footprints on the trail. It's more than 200 yards from the crime scene, and at least that far from Lawter's campsite."

"So, you haven't spoken to Ranger Swenson or Detective Underwood about what they did or saw on the mountain that afternoon?"

"No, I haven't," Agent Porter said curtly. "I've read their reports."

"Ranger Swenson, Detective Underwood, there's no mention of those footprints in your reports?"

Both officers shook their heads.

"But I did take some pictures of the footprints on the Pisgah trail," Detective Underwood offered. "I haven't . . ."

Caroline interrupted. "You can be damn sure that Lawter's defense counsel will know there were footprints on that trail. Robert, who is Lawter's defense attorney?"

"Joseph Washington, public defender."

Caroline stood up and stalked the room, stopping at a colorful print of a landscape, her back to the conference table. She stared at the art but didn't see it. "Guys, this shouldn't be news to you. We have to turn over the photographs in discovery. And Washington will know that we can't identify those footprints as belonging to Lawter. And that means there could have been another person on the mountain when Hannah Sullivan was murdered."

She moved to the door and leaned her back against it. "What was the time of death, Robert?"

"I don't know."

"Time of death, anybody? Detective Underwood?"

"We found her on Sunday afternoon. The ME estimates she died late Friday night, possibly early Saturday morning," the detective said. "But the autopsy report isn't finished yet."

"Do we have an official measurement of the snowfall on Mt. Pisgah during that time frame?"

Ranger Swenson raised his hand. "There is a weather station up there, but we don't have the official data just yet. I can give you an estimate."

"All right Ranger Swenson, what is your estimate?"

"The snow started falling around noon on Friday, and approximately six inches fell before midnight. On Saturday, another four inches or so fell, and on Sunday another two inches. The snow stopped Sunday around noon."

Caroline strode back across the room and folded her arms on the top of her chair. "So, the fact that six inches of snow may have fallen between her death and the discovery of her body would explain why there were no footprints from the body to or from Lawter's campsite," she said. "It also could explain that the footprints on the trail were irrelevant, because they must have been made long after Hannah was stabbed to death."

"Yes, ma'am," Ranger Swenson ventured, even though not asked.

"Question two: Where's the murder weapon?"

Crenshaw wrung his hands under the table. "We haven't found it yet. Agent Porter has the details of the crime scene investigation."

"Agent Porter, no murder weapon?"

"Not yet. We're still looking for it. The snow just melted, so we've brought in cadaver dogs in hopes they can find it."

"Any idea what kind of weapon was used to kill her?"

"Thin, stiletto blade," Agent Porter said. "Like an icepick."

"An icepick? Or like an icepick?" Caroline asked. She pursed her lips as she waited for a response.

Agent Porter traced his finger down a report. "A rounded, non-serrated blade, possibly an icepick or similar instrument. Forty-seven stab wounds."

"She was stabbed forty-seven times," Caroline repeated. "Why that many?"

Agent Porter shrugged. "No idea. Our psychologist just received the file. No opinion from him yet."

"All right. Question three: Why wasn't the confession typed up and signed by the accused?"

"I can answer that," Detective Underwood said. "Immediately after we got back to the SUV, Ranger Swenson made notes of the confession. When the crime scene investigators arrived, we transferred Lawter to a squad car and transported him to the station. Once there, he wouldn't talk. I typed up his confession, put it in front of him, but Lawter wouldn't sign it."

"And what did you use to type up the confession?"

"Ranger Swenson's notes, and my excellent recollection of his confession."

"Let me get this straight. We have no murder weapon. We have no witnesses. We have no footprints leading from Lawter's campsite to the body. We have mysterious, unidentified footprints on a trail two hundred yards away. And we have an oral confession, but nothing in writing." Caroline sat back down at the head of the table and laced her hands behind her head. "That's anything but ironclad. Let me hear about the confession. Ranger Swenson?"

"I was on routine patrol when I pulled into the Mt. Pisgah parking lot, the one on the north side of the Parkway. The Parkway was closed because of the snowstorm. I saw a red bike leaning against a trash can. I walked around a little and saw some footprints on the path that leads to the top of the mountain and the observation deck."

"What day was it?"

"Sunday, February 13."

"Please continue," Caroline said.

"I followed the footprints along the trail. I stopped every once in a while and looked up and down the mountain with my binoculars. That's when I saw a splotch of red in the snow."

"Could you see a body?"

"No ma'am. Not from there."

"How far away were you?" Caroline asked.

15

"Approximately 200 yards or so. It was down the slope."

"Did you go down the slope?"

"Not at that time. I called it in. Then I drove down the mountain to meet Detective Underwood."

"Where?"

"On the Parkway, down near the river. Then we drove back up the mountain."

"And once you got back to the parking lot, what did you do?"

"We went over and looked at the bike for a minute, then I showed the detective the footprints in the snow."

"Was it still snowing when you were out on the trail?"

"No ma'am. It had stopped. That's when I started my patrol."

"Okay, please continue."

"I showed Detective Underwood where I saw the red, gave him my binoculars to see it better. Then we walked down the hill toward the scene, placing markers as we went."

"What kind of markers?"

"Little orange flags."

"Then what?"

"We came to her body. She was lying in the snow, and there was a little snow on top of her also. She was a light blue color, and the color had gone out of her lips. She was splayed out."

"Splayed out how?"

"In an X shape," Ranger Swenson said, making the shape with his arms.

"Did you check for a pulse?"

"No ma'am. It was pretty obvious she was dead, and we didn't want to get that close to her body, didn't want to disturb the crime scene."

"Did you see any wounds on her body?"

"Yes, we did. A lot of wounds. And what looked to me like a lot of blood in the snow around her body."

Caroline took all this in, gauging how Ranger Swenson told the story as much as the content of his statements. Dressed in his olive uniform, she thought he would make an excellent witness before a jury.

Ranger Swenson recounted their circuitous search and discovery of Lawter's tent, how they crept up to it, that Detective Underwood drew his gun as they approached the tent.

"Did Lawter say anything at that time?"

"The first thing he said was: 'you're here about that girl'."

"Those were his exact words?"

"Yes ma'am."

"And he said that without any prompting at all, before anyone even talked to him?" Caroline continued, already planning the direct examination of the ranger.

"That's correct. Up to that point, the only thing we'd said, well Detective Underwood said, 'sheriff's office' and asked if anyone was in the tent."

Caroline nodded for him to continue.

"Right after Lawter said 'you're here about that girl,' Detective Underwood read him the Miranda warning. It's a good thing he did, because I was about to ask Lawter some questions."

"Have you ever arrested anyone before, Ranger Swenson?"

"No ma'am. I've given out citations and such, but never an arrest. We usually leave that to the sheriff's office."

"So, when did Lawter first tell you anything about stabbing Hannah?"

"We handcuffed him and marched him back over to the body. It was getting dark, and we followed the neon flags we'd laid out on the route from her body to his tent. We got back over there, and nobody said anything for a long while. We were all just looking at her. We didn't even know her name. That's when it hit me, that she was really dead. That a day or two earlier she'd probably been riding that bike on the mountain, and then she was just dead. And I was picturing it in my mind, what might have happened to her, when Lawter just started talking."

"Did he start talking in response to any questions from you or Detective Underwood?"

"No ma'am. He just started talking. He just blurted it out, like as we were standing there he suddenly realized that he'd taken someone else's life."

"Did he seem remorseful at all?"

"Not really. He seemed more stunned than anything. I guess we were all stunned. Well, I can't speak for Detective Underwood. Lawter told us he tied her up with some kind of cord. We couldn't really see the cord or the stakes in the snow, but Detective Underwood went over closer to her body and scraped some snow away from her foot and revealed the cord and a tent stake."

"Which foot?" Caroline asked.

"She was laying like this," Ranger Swenson gestured, "so it was her left foot."

"And then?"

"And then he told us he stabbed her a bunch of times. That was pretty obvious, us standing there."

"Did he tell you what he stabbed her with?"

"No, he didn't. He didn't say what he used to kill her."

"You found a big knife on him when you handcuffed him, a Bowie knife."

"We did. It didn't look like that's what he used, but I'm no expert. The wounds were kind of small. I can't imagine what it felt like, to be stabbed so many times like that. All over her body. Her chest, her neck, her arms and legs. It had to be incredibly painful. Who does that? Who just stabs someone who's on the ground like that, and so vulnerable?" Ranger Swenson bowed his head and wiped his eyes.

"I don't know Ranger Swenson," Caroline said. "You made notes, yes?"

"I wrote all this down afterward, as I sat in the car waiting for the CSI team."

"And you saved your notes? They're in the file?"

"Yes ma'am."

When it was Detective Underwood's turn, his account was almost identical to that of Ranger Swenson. Any departures were insignificant. He stressed that he read Lawter the Miranda warning from a card he kept in his wallet before any interrogation had begun.

As Caroline sat with her eyes closed, picturing the scene, visualizing the three men standing over the body of Hannah Sullivan while Henry Lawter confessed, Agent Porter placed a photo array in front of her.

She opened the indexed binder and scanned the pictures: Hannah's body at the crime scene; autopsy photos; a disheveled Henry Lawter in handcuffs standing outside a police car and at the station as he was booked into jail. The photographs of Lawter depicted a youngish man who bore no outward traces of evil. From the images alone, he could have been guilty of public drunkenness or petty theft. Caroline had hoped to see the cold eyes of a killer, a man she could easily portray as a butchering villain. It wasn't there.

"Do you want to hear more about Hannah?" Crenshaw asked.

"Sure, Robert. Tell me what you know."

Crenshaw summarized the information from his interview with Hannah Sullivan's parents. "She graduated from Chapel Hill three years ago, with a degree in Business Entrepreneurship. She took a job with a hotel in Asheville, where she was working as a night manager. She was on a local cycling team, training hard and racing, hoping to join the US Cycling Team. That's why she was climbing the mountain that day."

"Boyfriend? Or girlfriend?"

Crenshaw shook his head. "Her parents told me that with her career and cycling, there was no time for anyone else."

"So why was she riding up the mountain in a snowstorm, alone?"

"I talked to her cycling coach. He said they were planning a team ride that morning to the top of Mt. Pisgah but called it off because of the weather report. Hannah either didn't get the message, or she ignored it. He said he wasn't surprised she went alone. She was that dedicated."

"So, we portray her as a budding cycling star, brutally murdered before she could realize her Olympic dreams," Caroline said with a sanguine smile.

"It's not a stretch. Her parents certainly see it that way," Crenshaw said. "They are pretty shaken up but willing to talk to you at any time."

"Not yet," Caroline said. From three years as an Assistant District Attorney prosecuting domestic violence cases in state court, she knew how persuasive the relatives of crime victims could be. She wanted to focus objectively on the physical evidence, not on the emotion. "I'm concerned that we don't have a videotaped confession, or a written confession from Lawter himself. Does that seem odd to anyone?"

"Not really," Detective Underwood said. "I've seen it before. Sometimes when the perp sees what he's done, the blood and everything, he just blurts it out. Then when he gets to the station, he shuts up. I don't see that it makes much difference in this case."

She turned to Underwood. "The difference, detective, is that we don't have a confession in his own words. Didn't you think to record his confession on your cell phone?"

"No, I didn't." The detective folded his arms over his chest. "We weren't interrogating him. He just blurted it out when we got back to the body."

"And once you got him to the station?"

"Of course, once we got him to the station we put him in an interview room and turned on the video. Standard operating procedure. But he didn't say anything. Didn't even ask for an attorney."

"Agent Porter, I'm sure the FBI interrogated Lawter. What did you get?"

"Nothing. We Mirandized him again. Then he asked for a lawyer."

"Anything else I need to know?"

19

Detective Underwood spoke up. "The District Attorney would be happy to take this one off your hands. He's prosecuted quite a few murders. Seventeen or eighteen I think. All convictions."

Caroline engaged the detective's eyes.

He shifted in his seat. "What's with your eyes?"

"Is that where you want to go with this conversation, detective? You want to talk about my eyes?" She continued to stare until he glanced away. "Now, detective, I presume Mr. Anderson is aware that the Justice Department has preemptive jurisdiction in this matter. Ms. Sullivan was murdered on federal property. Please report to Mr. Anderson that when I decide whether the federal government will prosecute Henry Lawter for murder, I will so inform him." She looked at each of the men in turn to punctuate the point. "We're done here, gentlemen."

CHAPTER FOUR

After the three law enforcement officers shuffled out of the room, Caroline gently closed the conference room door. She remained standing, her hands knitted behind her back.

"Do you want this case?" she asked Robert Crenshaw.

Crenshaw smiled for the first time. "Absolutely. Don't you?"

"Absolutely."

"Even without the murder weapon?"

She nodded. "Even without the murder weapon. Do you know how rare it is for a federal prosecutor to try a murder case? I know a lot of US Attorneys who have never tried a murder case. What do you think the odds are that you or I will see another murder case in our careers?"

Crenshaw shrugged. "Maybe a drug murder or two. But a case like this? Slim to none."

"It's a way to make my mark on this office."

Crenshaw hesitated. "Not to mention that we would be securing justice for Hannah Sullivan."

"Of course, Robert. Do you think I don't care about her? I do care. I care deeply. Lawter has to be brought to justice."

"But?"

"Our prosecution can't be about emotion. Emotion is the reason the footprints on the trail weren't checked. Emotion is the reason neither Detective Underwood nor Ranger Swenson recorded the confession on their cell phones. Emotion is the reason I don't want to meet with Hannah's parents until I make a decision. Of course, the case would have been better had they recorded Lawter's confession, or if he'd signed something."

"Agreed, Caroline. But under the circumstances, I don't think it will be difficult to explain why they didn't record his confession while they were standing in a foot of snow and it was getting dark."

"Think there's any chance that Underwood and Swenson concocted the confession?" she said.

Crenshaw shook his head. "I don't. You?"

"Not after hearing them tell it."

"There's another good reason to take the case."

"And that is?"

"Judge Westlake wants it."

"How do you know?"

"He told me," Crenshaw said.

Caroline walked around the long, oval table. "He told you?"

"Remember, I was his law clerk for two years. We still have lunch occasionally. He told me he wanted the case in his court. He's never tried a murder case."

"But you didn't talk about the evidence or anything, did you?" Caroline asked hesitantly.

"Of course not. We both know better than to cross that line. Everything he knows he saw on television or read in the newspapers." Crenshaw flicked a tuft of hair off his forehead and back into place.

"Good."

"So, are we taking the case?"

Caroline nodded. "Start putting a case together for the grand jury. We'll wait for the final forensic reports before submitting, but I want to be ready to go to the grand jury once those results are in hand."

CHAPTER FIVE

A federal grand jury already was in session, reviewing the evidence in various cases far less sensational than the Hannah Sullivan murder. Once the forensic evidence had been fully compiled and analyzed, Crenshaw presented the Hannah Sullivan case to the grand jury. Ranger Swenson and Detective Underwood both were brought in to testify, and their testimony was impeccable. The grand jurors were riveted by their recitations of Lawter's confession as he stood over Hannah's frozen body.

The forensic evidence established that Henry Lawter's hunting jacket had blood on it, but the blood did not match Hannah's blood type. The grand jurors did not seem concerned about this. Nor were they concerned that none of Lawter's DNA was found on Hannah's clothes or body, or that the weapon used to stab Hannah had not been found. At the conclusion of the one-sided presentation, the grand jury deliberated for less than an hour before returning a true bill of indictment—their unanimous conclusion that Henry Lawter had probably murdered Hannah Sullivan.

In the wake of the grand jury indictment, Caroline Bannister had to decide whether to seek the death penalty against Henry Lawter. Given the circumstances of Hannah's death, the utter brutality of the stabbing, Caroline concluded there was no other rational choice. In reaching this decision, she was swayed by Lawter's murder-scene confession and the autopsy photographs of Hannah's body, which highlighted the small dark holes in her skin where Lawter had stabbed her repeatedly. As Henry Lawter waited in prison, Caroline decided that a lifetime locked away in a prison cell would not be a fitting punishment for such a man. Or justice for Hannah.

Caroline met with Hannah's parents, who drove to Charlotte from their home on the coast. Sean and Rosalind Sullivan had been informed of their daughter's death two months earlier, and they had not recovered. Perhaps they would never recover. Rosalind Sullivan's wan skin and hollow eyes had stripped away any vibrancy, and in her grief she had almost attained her daughter's post-mortem pallor. Sean Sullivan weakly grasped Caroline's hand when offered, as if the burden of shaking the hands of hundreds of mourners had permanently injured his fingers. In response to Caroline's offer of condolence, Mr. Sullivan responded, "she was our only child."

She told the Sullivans about the evidence that had been gathered, Lawter's confession, and that a grand jury had indicted Henry Lawter for the murder of their daughter on federal property. Caroline spared them the more gruesome details of the autopsy and post-mortem photographs, though one of them would have seen Hannah's corpse when they identified their daughter's body at the morgue. As Caroline spoke, Sean Sullivan remained attentive. Throughout the meeting, Rosalind Sullivan stared blankly at the wooden table or at the walls.

Pausing so she could frame the issue without revealing her own opinion, Caroline said simply, "I need to know whether you want me to seek the death penalty." In response, Hannah's mother bowed her head and leaned forward, as if the weight of this question had landed squarely on the back of her neck and pushed her down.

Sean Sullivan, hands clenched together in his lap, sat open-mouthed for a moment. He nibbled his lower lip. "This is our decision?"

Caroline had invited no one else to the meeting because she did not want anyone from the prosecution team to overtly or inadvertently express any enthusiasm for seeking the death penalty against Lawter. She did not want the Sullivans' preference biased in any way. As she scanned Sean Sullivan's face and the collapsed form of his wife next to him, Caroline realized the couple had been asked to make too many decisions, to contemplate far more consequences in a short time than they were capable of enduring. She absently wondered if they had been able to navigate the long drive from the coast without incident.

It was Caroline's nature to take charge, to solve the problem at hand, and she could have informed the Sullivans of her strong preference for seeking the death penalty for their daughter's murder. If she did that, the Sullivans would quietly nod their assent, and the matter would be decided. But she wanted to learn the Sullivans' unvarnished opinion of the matter. "I want to know your wishes," she said.

Sean Sullivan looked to his wife for an avenue of escape, but she had collapsed onto the table and was quietly sobbing. "We haven't talked about it," he said.

"Have you at least thought about it?" Caroline asked, seeing the need to lead Mr. Sullivan out of the murky shadows of indecision.

He looked down at his hands. "Every day," he said. "At least I have."

"And?"

Sean Sullivan looked up, his jaw set. Eyes rimmed with red stared piercingly into Caroline's green eyes. "He's an animal. He deserves what Hannah got. Anything less would be an abomination."

"I agree," Caroline said. She sat back in her chair at the head of the table, rubbed her hands along the chair arms. "Thank you for making the trip. A decision of this magnitude needs to be made face to face."

Sean Sullivan nodded, stood up, and coaxed his wife from her chair. They trudged out of the conference room as if trekking through thick mud.

As required, Caroline submitted to the Department of Justice her request to seek the death penalty against Henry Lawter. Accompanying the request were the most probing and poignant pieces of evidence, including videotaped interviews of Ranger Swenson and Detective Underwood. She also included a short letter, signed by both of the Sullivans, imploring the Attorney General to authorize her to seek the death penalty against Henry Lawter for killing their daughter. Historically, the death penalty has been pursued by federal prosecutors in fewer than twenty percent of the eligible cases, so Caroline knew there was a substantial chance her request would be denied. But in a relatively short time, the Attorney General approved the request. As she drafted the notice declaring the United States of America's intent to seek the death penalty against Henry Lawter, she could feel the adrenaline surging.

CHAPTER SIX

While one side was trying to execute Henry Lawter, the other endeavored to save his life. As Lawter's court-appointed attorney, Joseph Washington's first legal maneuver was to file a motion to have Lawter's confession excluded. The confession was damning. If the jury heard the confession, even though it wouldn't come from Lawter's own lips, a conviction was almost a certainty. Without the confession, Washington thought he had a solid chance of getting Lawter acquitted.

Caroline Bannister received the motion like a punch in the gut. After reading the motion through for the second time, she stood before the floor-to-ceiling windows in her office, arms crossed, watching rain splatter the glass. This motion to exclude the confession was that very unpredictable development that could derail her first murder case. She slid behind her desk and hit the speed dial on her telephone console. While the phone cycled through three rings, she drummed her fingers on the walnut desk.

He picked up before the fourth ring.

"Robert, have you seen the motion to exclude?"

"Just scanning it now."

"You know I've been worried about something like this, but this is a bombshell. The confession *is* our case."

"I know. Lawter was deaf? I wouldn't believe it if I didn't have the audiologist's report right in front of me."

"Can we win this motion? If the confession gets tossed, we've got nothing left to go to trial."

"I think we can win it."

"You think? The confession is the linchpin of the case. There's no murder weapon, no eye witnesses, basically no forensic evidence."

"Caroline, I've had all of fifteen minutes to digest this and work out a strategy. I know how important this is to you, to me, to the whole office."

"And to Judge Westlake," Caroline ventured.

"I'm sure it's important to him. It's the most significant aspect of the case until we get to trial."

"Then you argue it, Robert. He knows you. You have to argue the motion. And you have to win it. This isn't just an ordinary case. This may define your career. And mine."

* * * * * *

The players gathered in the ornate federal courtroom, paneled dark wood with a mosaic ceiling and maroon carpet. Windows that looked out upon the Pisgah mountain range to the west were concealed by heavy velvet drapes.

Caroline Bannister and Robert Crenshaw sat at the prosecution table next to the jury box. Although Crenshaw would argue the motion *in limine*, Caroline wanted to be present to show Judge Westlake that the US Attorney's Office was fully invested in the case. Crenshaw nervously shuffled papers, feigning last-minute preparation.

Joseph Washington sat alone at the defense table, a single accordion file before him, staring at something or at nothing high on the wall behind the Judge's bench. A few minutes before nine o'clock, his client was escorted into the courtroom by two United States Marshals and seated unceremoniously in the chair beside him. Lawter was dressed in an orange jumpsuit, the uniform of county prisoners. The marshals remained close.

Judge Raleigh Westlake entered his courtroom from a door to the side of the bench and ascended three steps to his high-backed chair with some haste. At the marshal's announcement of the Judge's entrance, the attorneys and Lawter rose from their seats.

"Please be seated," the Judge said. "Good morning, counsel. Are we ready to proceed?"

Crenshaw and Washington both answered up.

"All right. I have read the motion *in limine* and the government's response, as well as all the exhibits attached thereto. Mr. Washington, you may proceed."

Washington's argument to exclude the confession was based on the fact that Henry Lawter had been deaf when the officers interrogated him at the murder scene. To support this assertion, Washington presented an audiologist's affidavit, which stated that Lawter's eardrums had been pierced, probably by a sharp implement, before the officers found him in the tent. The audiologist had tested Lawter's hearing on two occasions, and both times Lawter exhibited severe hearing loss. Based on these tests, the audiologist concluded in his professional opinion that Lawter could not have heard the Miranda warning read to him by Detective Underwood, even if the detective had shouted the warning. "Based on this evidence, Your Honor, Mr. Lawter was not properly apprised of his constitutional rights to remain silent and to have counsel present during the interrogation. As a result, his confession is therefore inadmissible."

Crenshaw rose from his chair, buttoning the top button of his jacket. "May it please the Court. Preliminarily, Your Honor, the officers were not aware when they arrested Henry Lawter that he was hearing impaired. And the US Attorney's Office was not aware of this fact until Mr. Washington filed his motion. Now, the law requires that a suspect be advised of his constitutional rights before a custodial interrogation is commenced," Crenshaw argued. "If the defendant did not hear the Miranda warning, he also could not have heard any of the questions asked of him by the officers. Because the defendant could not have heard the officers' questions, from the defendant's perspective there was no custodial interrogation and thus no legal trigger for the Miranda warning. There are dozens of appellate cases that hold that the custodial interrogation is the trigger requiring the Miranda warning. In effect, because the defendant was deaf and could not have heard the officers' questions, the officers asked no questions at all. No interrogation took place. As such, the defendant's confession was not a response to the officers' questions or any interrogation, but a voluntary confession, an excited utterance if you will. He only confessed once he saw Miss Sullivan's body lying in frozen blood. Then he blurted out what he had done to her. That's the very definition of an excited utterance."

"He was in handcuffs," Washington replied. "That's the very essence of being in custody."

"But if he couldn't hear the detective's questions," Crenshaw said, "there was no interrogation. The defense can't argue that no Miranda warning was given because the defendant was deaf, while at the same time arguing that he was interrogated even though he was deaf. There is absolutely no evidence that the defendant's confession was given in response to any of the questions asked by either Detective Underwood or Ranger Swenson."

"Mr. Washington," the Judge said, "is there any indication that Mr. Lawter's statements were in direct response to anything that the detective or the ranger asked him?"

"Not that I'm aware of, Your Honor. But the custodial interrogation began *before* Mr. Lawter said anything."

"Well, that's incorrect counsel," Judge Westlake said. "According to the government's affidavits, your client said, 'you're here about that girl' before he was handcuffed, or Mirandized, or asked any questions."

"I agree," Washington said. "I misspoke. But that statement isn't inculpatory."

"It's at least evidence that Mr. Lawter was aware of Miss Sullivan's body, is it not?" the Judge countered.

"I concede that's an inference the jury could draw, Your Honor."

"Mr. Washington, do you have any evidence to present to the Court about how Mr. Lawter's eardrums were damaged?"

The government doctor who examined Lawter and later repaired his eardrums concluded that Lawter's eardrums had been pierced by an object consistent with an ice pick, and the wounds were unhealed and therefore recent. The blood on the collar and shoulders of Lawter's hunting jacket was his own. Washington had intentionally not asked his client how his eardrums had been damaged. It was quite clear that Hannah Sullivan had not attacked him.

"I do not have any evidence to offer the Court on that point," Washington said.

Judge Westlake had been studying Henry Lawter during the hearing. Lawter had remained almost motionless, with his head down or his eyes averted. When the Judge first read the motion to exclude the confession, the most poignant question that came to mind was whether this defendant was smart enough to have planned all of this. Had Lawter stabbed his ears with the same weapon used to kill Hannah Sullivan precisely so that his attorney could argue that the Miranda warning was not effectively given? Was Lawter that smart? At one point during the hearing, the Judge thought he detected what might have been a smirk cross Lawter's face, but he couldn't be sure.

When he'd remarked to Robert Crenshaw, his former law clerk, that he "wouldn't mind" if the Lawter murder case were prosecuted in his court, the Judge had anticipated that circumstances could arise that would make a conviction less than certain. He knew that because the confession was so potent and damning, there was a substantial likelihood the confession would be challenged on some ground. No decent defense lawyer could let that evidence be heard by a jury without employing every conceivable effort to have the confession thrown out.

The Judge had carefully analyzed the legal briefs submitted by each side. One of his law clerks provided him with a bench brief setting forth what little case law could be found on the issue, and because the legal issue was so unusual and significant, Westlake had done his own legal research, hoping to unearth some authority the lawyers and his clerk had not found. The case precedent provided no clear answer to whether self-inflicted deafness constituted a ground for excluding an otherwise voluntary confession.

The prosecution's brief made it clear the confession was the crux of the government's case. If he excluded evidence of the confession, the government might dismiss the case because the remaining evidence was not sufficient to prove Lawter guilty beyond a reasonable doubt. A confessed murderer would go free. On a technicality.

The Judge scanned the briefs in front of him for a few minutes to exhibit the weightiness of the issue before he ruled. There were no other sounds in the courtroom, as if the lawyers were holding their collective breath.

"Anything else, Mr. Washington?" the Judge finally said.

"No, Your Honor."

"Anything else from the United States, Mr. Crenshaw?"

"No, Your Honor."

"All right then. Thank you both for preparing such good briefs and for making cogent and illuminating arguments to the Court on the motion. Given the absence of binding precedent mandating the confession is inadmissible, I'm going to let the jury decide whether Mr. Lawter's confession was voluntary. The confession is admissible. The motion *in limine* is denied," he pronounced.

CHAPTER SEVEN

Eight months after Hannah Sullivan was murdered on the mountain, trial day dawned crisp and clear, promising a deep azure sky. A bevy of death penalty protestors gathered in front of the federal courthouse in Asheville, their growing number spilling off the sidewalk and into the street. Death penalty proponents countered them. Most of the demonstrators carried signs extolling their respective positions, and they soon began to parade up and down the sidewalk and street.

Caroline Bannister, in a navy suit with cream blouse, and rolling a black briefcase, waded into the throng.

"Justice for Hannah," chanted a group of protestors, marching in a tight circle that almost touched the bottom step of the courthouse.

"No More Killing," shouted a larger group, whose elliptical march turned away upon reaching the outstretched hands of two federal marshals.

Without comment, Caroline ascended the granite steps and passed through the metal detector. She waited as her briefcase was X-rayed. "Interesting protest going on out front," she remarked.

"We don't see that very often," the marshal said. "Are you on that case?"

"I am," she smiled and walked down the hallway to the elevators, her steps echoing.

In the upstairs attorney lounge across from the main courtroom, she joined Robert Crenshaw and defense counsel Joseph Washington as they looked down upon the demonstrators. Trial was scheduled to start in forty-five minutes, yet the courtroom remained locked. As they watched from an upstairs window, some of the demonstrators began to scuffle. Marshals tried to keep order, but it became clear they would need reinforcements.

"I had no idea the case would generate this much public interest," Caroline said.

"This is Asheville," Washington replied. "If those demonstrators are any measure, looks like the citizenry is against the death penalty about two to one. My plea offer is still on the table, Ms. Bannister. He'll plead guilty in exchange for life imprisonment."

31

Caroline turned to her adversary. "That's already been rejected, Mr. Washington. Given the confession and the circumstances of this brutal murder, I will not take the death penalty off the table."

"Okay, I tried." Washington shrugged.

"You don't think he's innocent, do you Joseph?" Caroline asked.

Washington didn't answer.

They waited in silence for a time as the clamor outside became loud enough to breach the closed windows. Police cars from the City pulled up, accompanied by a flatbed truck loaded with striped barricades. Two workers began unloading the barricades, establishing a small perimeter around the courthouse entrance as police officers gently pushed the crowd back.

"I heard there were some demonstrators out front," Judge Westlake said as he entered the lounge. He stood in shirt sleeves and a tie, his black hair perfectly controlled. The lawyers stepped aside so he could get to the big window. "What would you say—a hundred, hundred and fifty?"

"That looks about right," Crenshaw said.

"If this continues, we might have to arrange an alternative ingress and egress for the jurors. We certainly don't want them to be harassed walking from the parking lot to the courthouse. Think about that for a bit and we can discuss it at the lunch break. I'll also ask the marshals to carefully screen any courtroom visitors to make sure there are no disruptions. But my courtroom is open to the public."

"Looks like about two to one against the death penalty out there," Washington said. "I expect the local media will cover the trial heavily."

Judge Westlake looked at the defense attorney, a comment on his lips. He held that comment. "I'll ask the marshals to open the courtroom now."

As the attorneys sat patiently at their tables in the courtroom, Westlake stood before the mirror over the sink in his private bathroom and adjusted his robe to center his striped tie in the gap. He wiped a handkerchief across his high forehead. This was his first murder trial, and he had spent considerable time rehearsing what he was going to say to the jury, going over the jury instructions he would give at the conclusion of the evidence. He assumed an expression of judicial integrity, fair but firm, and stared back at himself. He was ready to go.

The Judge entered the courtroom to the ceremonial announcement from one of the bailiffs and ascended the bench. His eyes darted across the courtroom to ensure that all who needed to be present were in attendance.

He noted the presence of a gaggle of local reporters, and scanned a few other gallery faces he did not recognize, but to his disappointment most of the spectator pews were empty. The Judge asked Marshal Cunningham to ensure no one had brought in a camera or cell phone. The marshals manning the security checkpoint downstairs had already performed this task, but Cunningham reconfirmed that no one had breached the Judge's standing Order.

The trial officially began when twelve jurors and two alternates sidled into the jury box. The jury was comprised of seven men and five women. One alternate was male, the other female.

For the lawyers, it was like the curtain peeling back on opening night. As the attorneys stood for the jurors' entrance, tiny creases of tension appeared on the lawyers' faces.

Once the jurors were seated, Judge Westlake gave them a summary of the case. All the jurors had heard snippets of evidence forecast by the lawyers during jury selection two weeks earlier. They had been told by Caroline Bannister that the defendant had confessed to two law enforcement officers and that they would be asked to impose the death penalty on Henry Lawter. All the jurors had acknowledged that in the right circumstances they could vote for death—otherwise they would have been excluded. Today's summary of the case by Judge Westlake was not new information for most of them.

"You may also have noticed the gathering of demonstrators out front. Our First Amendment at work," the Judge smiled. The faces of some of the jurors relaxed. "I will assure you they will not become a problem for you, or for this Court." He spoke now to those in the gallery. "If there are any disruptions in my courtroom, from any source, of any kind, you will be taken into custody. Period." He turned back to the jurors. "Now, if any of you are approached by anyone outside of this courtroom, or feel uncomfortable in any way about what is going on outside, let one of the marshals know, and we will address your concerns." The Judge nodded in finality, then sat back in his chair. "All right. Mr. Crenshaw, the United States may proceed."

Caroline Bannister stood. "If it pleases the Court, I'll make the opening statement for the United States."

"Yes, of course Ms. Bannister."

Caroline walked over to the two easels placed strategically between the jury box and the Judge's bench and turned to the jurors. "Hannah Sullivan is dead because Henry Lawter brutally murdered her," she began, standing between the easels. "Because she obviously can't tell you what happened to her, we want you to be able to see her as the vibrant young woman she was." She peeled an opaque plastic cover from a head shot of Hannah Sullivan not long after her graduation from the University of North Carolina. "This is the daughter her parents loved and remembered. She was twenty-four, a competitive cyclist, and she was cut down in the prime of her life. Why? Because she had the gall to pursue her dream of riding with the US Cycling Team. On the day she was murdered, she was training. She rode her bike up the Blue Ridge Parkway, a solo ride, and had just reached the summit at Mt. Pisgah. She propped her bike against a trash can in the parking lot, and because the Parkway bathrooms were closed for the season, she walked down a trail so she could go to the bathroom. Something each of us do, multiple times, every day. She was a modest young woman, and she walked down the trail a little way so she could relieve herself privately behind some bushes. That's when the defendant brutally attacked her with an icepick. And this," Caroline peeled away the plastic cover from a photograph on the other easel, "is what Henry Lawter did to her."

In the jury box, hands covered mouths. Several jurors looked away.

The picture was an autopsy photograph of Hannah's lifeless body, the image so sharp that it was almost as if Hannah's corpse had been placed within a few feet of the jurors. She was tinged blue, with dozens of spots of dark blood on her torso, arms, legs and neck. Her closed eyes formed the base of a triangle, the apex of which was a prominent stab wound on her forehead. A piece of metal had broken off, and its black tip poked sharply from her pale skin, a gruesome reminder of how the young woman had survived the first attack before Lawter killed her some hours later.

After giving the jury some time to ponder the photographs, Caroline resumed. "You will hear evidence from Arnie Swenson, who is a Park Ranger, that the defendant confessed to killing Hannah Sullivan by stabbing her multiple times. You can see the stab wounds on her body in the autopsy photograph. Those dark holes are the puncture wounds, with dried blood surrounding them. There are forty-seven holes, forty-seven stab wounds. Forty-seven times he plunged a weapon into Hannah's body. And when the defendant admitted the murder, Ranger Swenson was standing right next to him, looking at Hannah's dead body in the snow. Detective Rick Underwood also was there. Detective Underwood gave the defendant the standard Miranda warning before the defendant confessed. There is no dispute about that. And Detective Underwood was also standing right there, next to the defendant and Hannah's body, when the defendant admitted to killing her. There will be no contradicting testimony. There was nobody else on the mountain that day, and the Parkway was closed to vehicular traffic. The defendant admitted to killing Hannah Sullivan, no one else could have done it, and he is guilty of murder beyond a reasonable doubt. Thank you." Caroline strode back to the counsel table and sat down.

Defense attorney Washington reserved his opening statement until the commencement of the defense evidence.

"The Government may call its first witness," the Judge intoned.

Ranger Swenson stood before the witness chair and was sworn in. He testified meticulously about the confession Lawter had given voluntarily as they stood over Hannah's body. Swenson helped the jurors visualize the crime scene, describing the freckles of snow in the creases of Hannah's clothing, the defendant's disheveled campsite, the tent cord wrapped around Hannah's left ankle, and the frozen blood surrounding her. He even mentioned the blue pallor of her skin when they discovered her. His account was punctuated with crime-scene photographs introduced into evidence by Robert Crenshaw and shown on the computer screens in the jury box. Together, they successfully re-humanized the young woman Henry Lawter had so brutally destroyed. The jurors no longer had to imagine Hannah's face, or the partially opened lips that exhaled her final breath, or the blood that slowly seeped from her body into the snow.

Joseph Washington, having little to work with, started his cross-examination of Ranger Swenson by asking about the weather conditions. "According to wind data taken from the tower on top of the mountain, just above where you were standing, the wind peaked at 36 miles per hour that day. That's pretty breezy, especially blowing through all those trees where you were standing. Are you telling this jury that with that wind, you heard my client speak with crystal clarity?"

"Yes," Ranger Swenson said. "There was a slight breeze in the late afternoon, but I did not consider it to be windy. With the snow insulating everything, and the Parkway closed to traffic, it was as quiet as . . . well, it was as quiet as a cemetery up there."

Washington winced, instantly realizing his mistake. "Isn't it true that you could have easily recorded everything that my client allegedly said on your cell phone?"

"That is true."

"And if you had done that, then our jury would be able to hear everything he said in my client's own voice, and not have to rely on your memory of what he said?"

"That is true. But I'm not just relying on my memory. I've also re-read, over and over, the notes that I wrote in my vehicle as we waited for the forensics team to arrive."

"You said 'we.' So Detective Underwood was in the car with you when you wrote the notes, true?"

Ranger Swenson leaned forward. "No sir. When I said 'we' I meant the defendant and myself. The defendant was in the back seat of the SUV, in handcuffs, as I wrote my notes in the front seat."

"Where was Detective Underwood?"

"At first, he was outside smoking a cigarette. I stood out there with him for a bit, and then I got back in the vehicle because it was freezing outside."

"And what was Detective Underwood doing outside, besides smoking?"

"He was pacing back and forth in the parking lot. He had my flashlight, and it looked like he was examining the bicycle we found. Once the forensics team arrived, he went back to the scene with the investigators."

"Did my client say anything at all when he was sitting in the vehicle with you?"

"No sir, he did not."

"And what did you do once the forensics investigators arrived?"

"I handed off the defendant to a deputy, and then I went home to kiss my children goodnight."

Judge Westlake offered Robert Crenshaw the opportunity to redirect the witness.

Caroline leaned over and whispered: "Don't ask any questions, Robert, you can't do any better than that."

"No further questions," Crenshaw announced.

Crenshaw next called Detective Rick Underwood to the witness stand. Detective Underwood buttressed Swenson's account with almost identical testimony, none of it contrived or embellished. When asked to re-create on the stand the Miranda warning he had given as they stood next to Lawter's tent, Underwood pulled a card from his wallet and read the warning to the jury in a slow, clear voice.

"Was there anything that would have prevented the defendant from hearing you read the Miranda warning, detective?" Crenshaw asked.

"Not that I'm aware of. Everything was very quiet up there."

"Now, I anticipate the defense will call a witness to testify that the defendant's eardrums had been punctured and he was at least partially deaf at the time you advised him of his constitutional rights. At the time, did you have any indication that was the case?"

"No sir. The defendant didn't do or say anything that indicated he could not hear everything that I said to him."

"So, you did not know he had a hearing impairment at that time?"

"No sir."

On cross-examination, Washington got Detective Underwood to admit that he could have recorded both the Miranda warning and everything that Lawter said that afternoon.

"But you didn't do that, did you detective?"

"I did not record your client because I didn't think it was necessary. I was planning to interview your client on video once we got to the station. While we were up on the mountain, there was no doubt what was said, or what happened, and I had Ranger Swenson as a witness to everything. You're trying to make something out of nothing."

Washington sparred with the witness. "No, detective. I'm simply pointing out that there were better ways to document what was said up there that evening, so we wouldn't have to guess about anything. That was your duty. Now, after you put my client in the SUV, did he say anything else to you."

"No, he did not."

"When you interrogated him at the station, on video, did he say anything at all?"

"No, he remained silent."

"So, the video of the interrogation is just my client sitting there silently, and you asking him a bunch of questions that he didn't answer?"

"That's correct."

"And didn't you think it was odd that he didn't say anything during the interrogation at the station?"

"I didn't think it was odd. I just thought that he figured he'd already confessed to us and didn't need to do it again. We believed him."

Washington objected. "Motion to strike as to what anyone other than Detective Underwood believed, Your Honor."

"Granted," Judge Westlake said, turning to the jury. "Members of the jury, you are to disregard Detective Underwood's statement as to what other people believed or were thinking."

Washington pressed ahead. "Detective Underwood, do you recognize the possibility that my client did not answer any of your questions or respond to you at all because he was deaf and could not hear you?"

"I do not recognize that possibility."

"You don't detective? You don't recognize the possibility that my client was deaf when you found him in the tent?"

"No sir, because when I asked him at the station if he wanted something to drink, he asked me to bring him a soda. He could hear then. I think he could hear the entire time."

CHAPTER EIGHT

The next two days of the murder trial were consumed with forensic evidence from government experts, who testified about puncture wounds, and blood volume and loss, body temperature, rigor mortis and lividity, and how Hannah Sullivan slowly bled to death. On cross-examination, Washington did his best to create holes in the government's evidence—primarily the absence of the murder weapon and the lack of Henry Lawter's DNA on the decedent's body. Washington asked the medical examiner whether the absence of Lawter's hair, blood, skin or saliva on the victim's body created any doubt in his mind that she had been killed by the defendant.

"We did not find any other person's DNA on Miss Sullivan's body or clothes. But finding DNA on dark clothing, like the tights Miss Sullivan wore, is notoriously difficult, and the weather also could have spoiled any DNA. Our not finding other DNA on Miss Sullivan certainly doesn't mean she stabbed herself. Somebody obviously killed her."

"Sir, no one is disputing that Miss Sullivan was stabbed and that she died. All I'm asking you is whether you found any of Mr. Lawter's DNA on Miss Sullivan or on her clothes."

"No sir. We did not."

"Thank you. And did you find any of Miss Sullivan's DNA on Mr. Lawter or on his clothes?"

"We did limited testing of the defendant's clothes. There was blood on the collar and shoulders of his hunting jacket . . . I think it's Exhibit 22. That blood was the defendant's."

"Now sir, if the victim was lying on the ground and her wrists and ankles were bound, wouldn't, in your opinion, someone have to crouch down or even kneel next to the victim in order to stab her? In other words, could someone have stabbed her in that position while standing up?"

"I think it's highly probable that your client . . ."

"Sir. You don't have any forensic evidence that my client was anywhere near Miss Sullivan, isn't that correct?"

"No, that's not correct."

"It isn't?"

"No sir. We tested the cord that bound Miss Sullivan's wrists and ankles and found two things."

Washington interrupted the medical examiner. "I want to take you back to my previous question."

Crenshaw rose from counsel table. "Your Honor. The witness has the right to answer the question that he's been asked and explain his answer."

"Mr. Washington," the Judge said, "you did ask the question. The witness is entitled to answer that question, and then you can circle back if you want to."

"What was the question again?" the witness asked.

The court reporter reviewed her computer screen, which was recording the testimony in real time to the Judge and the attorneys, but not to the jurors. She recited the previous colloquy. "Question: Sir. You don't have any forensic evidence that my client was anywhere near Miss Sullivan, isn't that correct?"

"Answer: No, that's not correct."

"Question: It isn't?"

The medical examiner answered. "As I was saying, we tested the cord that was tied around Miss Sullivan's ankles and her wrists. It was braided cord, what you might think of as parachute cord. On that cord we found some skin fragments, and we tested those fragments for DNA. The DNA of the skin fragments on the cord matched the defendant's DNA."

Washington rubbed his forehead. "To what degree of error?"

"About one in 600,000. And, the cord tied to Miss Sullivan matched a small roll of the same cord found in the defendant's tent," the medical examiner said with satisfaction.

Washington tried to recover. "But no DNA from my client was actually on Miss Sullivan or on her clothes?"

"As I've already stated, none of Mr. Lawter's DNA was found on Miss Sullivan or on her clothes."

"Now please listen carefully to my next question. If a person had to kneel down next to Miss Sullivan in order to inflict the stab wounds, isn't it likely that person would have some blood splatter on his hands or clothes?"

"The weapon would likely have blood and minute pieces of tissue on it, but it's doubtful there would be any blood splatter."

"No blood splatter?"

"No. Because Miss Sullivan was fully clothed, the blood splatter likely would have been absorbed by her clothing."

The government rested its case at the end of day three, and Judge Westlake dismissed the jurors. After the jurors departed, the Judge asked Washington how many witnesses he planned to call for the defense. Washington said he would call two witnesses—an audiologist to testify that Lawter was deaf when he allegedly confessed to killing the victim, and a forensics expert to testify about the absence of Lawter's DNA on the victim's body. The Judge also asked whether Washington planned to call the defendant as a witness.

"I don't know," Washington responded. "Game day decision, Your Honor."

"Your Honor, may I be heard," Crenshaw spoke up.

"Yes, Mr. Crenshaw."

"The anticipated testimony from the defense witnesses is either cumulative or irrelevant. As for the defendant's degree of deafness, the United States already has stipulated that the defendant was deaf when he was arrested, and Your Honor already has ruled the defendant's confession is admissible. Any additional testimony about the defendant's deafness is irrelevant and cumulative. As for the absence of the defendant's DNA on Miss Sullivan's body, there is no dispute about that, and the government's witness just testified about that." Crenshaw continued his tack of nullifying Lawter's human traits by referring to him simply as the "defendant."

Washington began to reply, but Judge Westlake held up his hand. "Mr. Crenshaw, are you moving to exclude the prospective witness testimony as cumulative or immaterial?"

"Yes, Your Honor. That's what I'm asking."

The Judge nodded his head minutely. "I understand your points, Mr. Crenshaw. But I'm going to allow Mr. Washington to mount a defense. His client is on trial for his life, and he's entitled to call witnesses in an attempt to establish reasonable doubt. Although the confession is admissible, the jury will be allowed to consider evidence on the issue of voluntariness of that confession. The jury also is entitled to hear about the absence of the defendant's DNA on Miss Sullivan's body. The oral motion to exclude the testimony is overruled."

"I want to make a motion for judgment of acquittal under Rule 29," Washington said.

"Go ahead, Mr. Washington," the Judge said. "We're still on the record."

"Your Honor, there is none of my client's DNA on the victim's body or clothes, and none of the victim's DNA on my client. There are not witnesses. We have no murder weapon, and certainly no forensic evidence indicating that my client killed or harmed Miss Sullivan in any way. Therefore, there is insufficient evidence to support a conviction on the homicide charge beyond a reasonable doubt."

Crenshaw was prepared to respond, but Caroline abruptly stood up to address the Court. "Your Honor, Mr. Washington has conveniently omitted the fact that two law enforcement officers testified to the confession that the defendant made at the crime scene. The defendant said, in clear and unequivocal language, that he stabbed Miss Sullivan repeatedly. The medical testimony is unrefuted that she bled to death from those stab wounds. The defendant's confession is overwhelming evidence of his guilt. Moreover, the defense has glossed over the evidence that the defendant's DNA was found on the cord that held Hannah down while she was stabbed. He tied her up, and then he stabbed her to death. That is strong evidence of kidnapping and murder."

"I agree, counselor. The motion is denied, Mr. Washington. All right, if there's nothing else, I will see you at 9:00 a.m. sharp. Perhaps we can submit the case to the jury by Friday."

Caroline and Crenshaw met for dinner and reviewed the progress of the case. They had put on an entire murder case in only three days, and even though the presentation had been quick, it also had been powerful. They agreed that the evidence of Lawter's guilt was overwhelming and that, up to that point in the trial at least, there was no reasonable doubt.

"I'm just a little concerned that the jury might expect more," Caroline said. "If just one of them thinks that three days of evidence isn't enough to vote for the death penalty, we could be in trouble."

Crenshaw tilted his head. "Maybe. But I've seen a lot of studies that say jurors think cases take too long anyway, that the evidence is repetitive, and they get bored. We ended on a high note. If we add more witnesses, it would just be cumulative evidence anyway, and maybe weaker."

Crenshaw chewed a forkful of pasta. "Did you catch what Judge Westlake said at the end, about the defense *attempting* to establish reasonable doubt? He also said he agrees that the evidence is strong. He's sending a signal that the case is a lock."

Caroline frowned. "Frankly, I thought his ruling allowing Washington's witnesses to testify was the only thing he could do. He couldn't exclude them without inviting an appeal."

"It was a signal," Crenshaw countered. "Remember, I spent two years with Judge Westlake. I know him pretty well. He doesn't throw out something like that without being very careful about the words he chooses."

"We'll see," Caroline said. "It's way too early to celebrate."

CHAPTER NINE

The next morning, Joseph Washington gave a brief opening statement and then called his first defense witness. The audiologist testified that Henry Lawter had been legally deaf when he was examined in prison not long after his arrest. At Washington's urging, the audiologist expanded his testimony to state that Lawter was experiencing severe hearing loss at the time the law enforcement officers arrested him on the mountain. His testimony was almost identical to the affidavit that had been submitted in the unsuccessful attempt to have Lawter's confession excluded.

"So," Washington said, "given the state of his eardrums, could Mr. Lawter have heard people speaking to him? Either at the crime scene or at the Sheriff's office afterward?"

"No sir, he could not have heard people speaking to him."

"Even if they were yelling at him?"

"If someone had been yelling very loudly, he might have been able to hear sounds, but not words. Not given the serious damage to his eardrums."

"So assuming for the moment that a detective read him a Miranda warning in a normal tone of voice, could Mr. Lawter have heard that constitutionally required warning?"

"No, sir."

Washington passed the witness to the government.

The prosecutors had long ago decided who would cross-examine each defense witness. Because Crenshaw had immersed himself in the forensic evidence so he could intelligently conduct the examination of the government's own expert witnesses on those topics, Crenshaw also would cross-examine the forensic witnesses for the defense. In the unlikely event Henry Lawter testified, Caroline would conduct his cross-examination, a prospect she relished.

The voluntariness of Lawter's confession was the sole issue on which the defense had a chance of escaping a guilty verdict. Crenshaw trod carefully.

"So, from your examination you can determine exactly when the defendant became deaf?"

"Not with exact precision," the audiologist admitted.

"If you cannot determine precisely when the defendant became deaf, how do you know he was deaf when he was arrested?" It was an open-ended question, not the type normally used in cross-examination.

"I connected the dots," the witness said.

"What dots are you referring to?"

"The fact that the blood on Mr. Lawter's ears and neck was his own blood." The audiologist said.

"So you are concluding that the defendant's own blood on his ears and neck came from his ears?"

"Yes. From what I could tell, there were no other wounds on Mr. Lawter from which his blood could have come. It had to come from his ears."

Crenshaw reverted to a leading question to better control the witness. "This fact was not something you personally witnessed, was it?"

"No, sir."

"This fact was gleaned from the forensics reports concerning the blood on the defendant?"

"Yes."

"You don't know when the blood got on the defendant's hunting jacket, do you?"

"Well . . ."

"It's a yes or no question, sir. You either know when it happened, or you don't," Crenshaw said, seizing control.

"No, I don't know when that happened," the witness admitted.

Crenshaw paused so he could formulate the next question precisely. "So, doesn't your conclusion that the blood on the defendant's body and clothes came from his ears necessarily indicate that the defendant stabbed himself in the ears with a sharp instrument?"

The witness hesitated.

Crenshaw pushed ahead. "You can't have one without the other, can you? You can't conclude that the defendant was deaf at the time of his arrest, without also concluding that the defendant's deafness was self-inflicted, can you?"

"Well, someone else could have done it to him," the witness offered.

"You don't think that's plausible, do you?"

The witness shook his head. "I don't know."

"Do you think Miss Sullivan stabbed the defendant in his ears to pierce his eardrums?"

"No, I don't see how that's plausible."

"Sir, you don't have one shred of evidence that would lead you to believe that someone else pierced the defendant's eardrums, do you?" Crenshaw said with a tone of incredulity.

"No. I'm just an audiologist."

"In your opinion as an audiologist, were the injuries to the defendant's ears consistent with the damage that would be done by a sharp object such as an icepick?"

The witness looked down at his hands. "Yes, Mr. Lawter's eardrums were pierced with a sharp and slender object such as an icepick."

"Both eardrums?"

"Yes."

"And how badly were the eardrums damaged?" Crenshaw asked.

"Enough that both eardrums needed surgical repair."

"So the defendant stabbed himself in the eardrums with a long sharp weapon such as an icepick, is that what you are saying?"

"That is the most probable conclusion."

"Did the defendant tell you that he stabbed himself in the ears so he didn't have to listen to Hannah Sullivan scream?"

Washington jumped from his chair. "Objection."

"Overruled," Judge Westlake said. "You may answer the question."

"He did not tell me that," the audiologist testified.

"His hearing has been restored, correct?"

"Yes. A doctor operated on both eardrums, and additional testing revealed his hearing loss is about twenty decibels."

"Twenty decibels," Crenshaw said. "Is that considered minor?"

"It's on the low end of what we call mid-hearing loss."

"So the defendant can't clearly hear people speaking in noisy places, is that right?"

"That's correct. And he can't hear soft sounds."

"But he can hear me asking questions right now?"

"He should be able to hear you asking questions."

Crenshaw turned to face Lawter.

The jurors' heads swiveled in the same direction.

"And he can hear your testimony, correct?"

"There should be no reason he can't hear my voice from this distance."

"Your Honor," Crenshaw said, "could you instruct the defendant to nod if he can hear our voices?"

"Objection," Joseph Washington stood from his chair. "May we approach the bench, Your Honor?"

Judge Westlake beckoned them forward, then clicked off his microphone. Once the three attorneys were standing at the Judge's bench, they continued in hushed voices.

"Your Honor," Washington began, "whether Mr. Lawter can hear our voices or understand the questions at this juncture, here at the trial, is irrelevant to whether he was deaf when the Miranda warning was allegedly given. Plus, it violates his Fifth Amendment right against self-incrimination."

"Mr. Crenshaw, isn't your request essentially compelling him to testify?" the Judge asked.

"Not to any material facts. All it establishes is whether he can hear or not."

"Your Honor, if I may," Caroline interjected. "I think it would be significant to determine for certain, on the record, whether Mr. Lawter can hear the testimony and the proceedings to make sure that he doesn't later claim that he couldn't participate in his own defense because he couldn't hear the testimony."

The Judge absently rubbed his chin. "I tend to agree with that. Although the expert witness has already testified that Mr. Lawter can hear the proceedings."

"The defense will stipulate that Mr. Lawter can hear and understand the proceedings," Washington said.

"But with all due respect to Mr. Washington, that doesn't solve the problem," Caroline said. "Lawter could still claim that his own attorney made that stipulation without his consent and that he couldn't contest the stipulation because he couldn't hear."

"It does present a conundrum," the Judge said. "All right. Here's what I'm going to do. Mr. Crenshaw, finish your examination of the witness, then I'll send the jury out, and then, on the record, we will determine whether Mr. Lawter can in fact hear the proceedings." He clicked his microphone back on.

The lawyers returned to their tables.

Crenshaw continued to stand, flipping through pages of a legal pad, not sure whether to venture further. He had read the audiologist's affidavit, carefully crafted by the defense attorney. He did not know what information had been withheld from the affidavit, so he decided not to gamble. "No further questions."

The Judge folded his hands on the bench. "Now, ladies and gentlemen, we're going to take a short recess, probably only fifteen or twenty minutes, then you'll come back in and hear any remaining witnesses in the case." Judge Westlake tapped his fingers lightly on the bench as the jurors filed out.

"Mr. Lawter," Judge Westlake said in a slightly louder voice, "the issue of your hearing capabilities has been brought to my attention. Mr. Lawter, can you hear the testimony that's being given from the witness stand, and the questions the lawyers have been asking? Nod yes if you can hear me."

"Yes, Your Honor, I can hear you," Lawter said in a soft voice. It was the first time he had spoken in the courtroom.

"And has there been any part of the trial, whether opening statements, or testimony, or objections, or my rulings, that you have not been able to hear completely?"

"I could hear pretty much everything."

"All right, pretty much everything. Was there any part of the case, a particular witness, that you could not hear completely?"

"The ranger, I think. He spoke softly sometimes."

"Very well. Mr. Washington, are you still prepared to stipulate that Mr. Lawter has been able to hear and understand the proceedings? Confer with your client, please."

Washington conferred with Henry Lawter, then entered the stipulation on the record.

The trial resumed once the jury returned to the courtroom. Washington called next a former coroner from Tennessee who, upon retirement, had become an expert for hire.

"Was there any DNA whatsoever from Mr. Lawter on the victim's body?" Washington asked.

"No, sir. None." The expert spoke in a slow, deliberate fashion, making sure his words were precise.

"Was there any of the victim's DNA on Mr. Lawter or his clothing?

"No, sir."

"Does that surprise you?" Washington said.

The coroner shrugged. "It's unusual, not unique."

"No further questions."

Using suggestions from the government's medical examiner, Crenshaw asked on cross-examination whether the dark clothing that Hannah Sullivan wore that day could have impeded the discovery of Lawter's DNA on her clothes.

"That could have been a factor," the former coroner admitted.

"And couldn't the absence of the defendant's DNA on Miss Sullivan be explained by the fact that it was a cold winter day and the defendant wore a hat and coat?"

"That might explain the lack of hair, for example, but I would have expected some DNA from him to be found on her. Saliva. Skin fragments. Something."

"Well his DNA was found in skin fragments taken from the parachute cord tied around Ms. Sullivan's wrists and ankles."

"It was," the coroner nodded.

"And the fact that Miss Sullivan did not have any of the defendant's skin under her finger nails, could that be explained by the fact that she did not fight back because she was tied up and because the defendant had drugged her?"

"It could be."

"Sir, can you say with medical certainty that anything from the crime scene exculpates the defendant, or proves that the defendant did not kill Hannah Sullivan?"

The ex-coroner smiled. "I've been doing this a long time, Mr. Crenshaw. And I'm pretty sure that it's not my job to prove anyone innocent or guilty. I just give you the evidence. It's the jury's job to determine whether the defendant is innocent or guilty, right?"

Crenshaw looked down at his legal pad, scrambling for a new line of attack. "You didn't answer my question, sir. Can you say within a reasonable degree of medical certainty that anything from the crime scene establishes that the defendant did not kill Hannah Sullivan?"

"No, I cannot testify to that."

"Miss Sullivan had opioids in her body, did she not?"

"The victim had opioids in her bloodstream."

"You called her the victim. Do you even know her name?"

The witness turned to the jury. "That's what we are trained to do. The body lying on our table is a victim or a subject. It makes us focus on the objective evidence instead of the emotion. And yes, I know her name. She was Hannah Sullivan."

"How did Hannah die?"

"From blood loss."

"Hannah died from being stabbed?"

"Yes, sir."

"How many times was Hannah stabbed?"

"Forty-seven times."

"Have you ever seen a stabbing victim with so many stab wounds?"

The witness shook his head.

"Sir, you have to answer out loud."

"Sorry. No, I haven't."

"And how many years did you serve as a coroner in Tennessee?"

"Twenty-eight years."

"Thank you for your testimony," Crenshaw concluded. He looked over at the jury, attempting to gauge whether anything had swayed them toward a not guilty verdict. He settled back into his chair, uncertain.

Henry Lawter did not testify, depriving Caroline of the chance to grill him in front of the jury about his confession on the mountain. She didn't disagree with Washington's decision. Had she been in his position, given the facts of the case, she would not have called Lawter to the stand.

CHAPTER TEN

Caroline Bannister stood before the jury in a black suit and an azure-colored blouse, an American flag pin on the lapel of her jacket. It was essentially the same uniform she had worn throughout the trial, a tactic designed to subliminally suggest to the jury that nothing had changed. The strength of their evidence had not been diminished one iota by the defense.

Her closing argument focused on Lawter's confession and the unrefuted testimony of Ranger Swenson and Detective Underwood. The defendant had spewed forth his heinous deeds voluntarily, without coercion, and after having received the standard Miranda warning, Caroline said. The defendant had not been forced to say one word.

"We all have doubts in our lives," she said. "But there is no *reasonable* doubt that Henry Lawter tied Hannah Sullivan up and savagely murdered her. His skin cells were on the parachute cord. The parachute cord was in his tent. There was no one else on that mountain that day."

As she stood before the larger-than-life photograph of Hannah Sullivan, Caroline looked each juror in the eye and implored them not to let a murderer go free because he had caused his own deafness with the same icepick with which he had stabbed Hannah Sullivan to death. "She deserves at least that from you."

Joseph Washington focused on the absence of the murder weapon and what he called the "unconstitutional confession." Washington told the jury that reasonable doubt existed because both the ranger and the detective had failed to record either the Miranda warning or the confession, a simple task with cell phone technology.

"Ladies and gentlemen, you should find Mr. Lawter not guilty because my client's confession was not voluntary. To find that it was would create a slippery slope in which the police could chip away at the constitutional rights belonging to all of us. A confession cannot be voluntary if the confessor can't hear the Miranda warning, and Mr. Lawter's deafness was not disputed."

Four and a half days after the murder trial began, the case went to the jury. Judge Westlake excused the two alternate jurors because there was no need for them to participate in the deliberations, but told them they were welcome to stay. They opted to remain in the courtroom to hear the jury's verdict.

After the jury filed out, the attorneys shook hands, congratulated each other on a well-fought battle, and settled in the attorney lounge across from the courtroom to wait. Only a handful of protesters remained outside. Their numbers had dwindled each day of the trial, and the remaining few sleepwalked their way along the sidewalk beneath tired signs.

Waiting was the hardest part. That's when the second-guessing began. A trial lawyer could not stop rummaging through those things that had been missed, those questions that could have been tighter, the witness who veered slightly from the script. Did they choose the most powerful evidence? Did they overwhelm the jury with scientific explanations or arcane terminology?

"What could we have done better?" Caroline asked Crenshaw.

A marshal stuck his head in the door of the conference room. "They're back."

"Thirty-nine minutes," Crenshaw said, checking his watch. "That has to be a good sign."

Back in the courtroom, Judge Westlake took the verdict sheet, glanced quickly at the jury's handwritten answers, and handed the pages back. The marshal returned the verdict sheet to the jury foreman.

Giving no outward sign of the verdict, the Judge cleared his throat: "Ladies and gentlemen, I want to remind you that there will be no outbursts from anyone when the verdict is delivered. Marshals, please make sure that anyone who makes any disturbance is removed from the courtroom. Now, Mr. Foreman, have you reached a unanimous verdict on all of the counts before you?"

The jury foreman, a man with three children of his own, rose from the first row.

"We have, Your Honor."

"On count one of the indictment, for kidnapping a person in federal territory, how does the jury find?"

"We find the defendant guilty."

A rumble went through the gallery. Judge Westlake scowled, and the noise extinguished like a wave hissing into sand. "And on count two of the indictment, for murder in the first degree on federal land, how does the jury find?"

"We find the defendant guilty," the foreman said without hesitation.

Judge Westlake polled each juror, asking each of this was in fact their verdict, securing official confirmation that the verdict was unanimous. "Thank you for your service, ladies and gentlemen. Please remember not to discuss the case among yourselves or with anyone outside the courtroom. The media may seek to talk to you, but you should politely decline, as you will need to be back here on Monday morning for the sentencing phase of the case. I fully expect everything to wrap up by the end of next week."

As the marshals handcuffed Henry Lawter, Caroline Bannister turned to Hannah's parents, who were sitting in the first row. "Round one goes to the good guys," she said, offering her hand to Sean Sullivan.

"Thank you. Thank you and Mr. Crenshaw for everything you've done," Hannah's father said.

Rosalind Sullivan, her eyes wet, could only manage a nod.

"Next week it gets a little harder for you," Caroline said. "You'll need to be strong when you testify. You need to be able to tell the jury everything you can about Hannah, what a great young woman she was, what she meant to you."

"We can do that," Sean Sullivan said. "The jury only has two choices, right? The death penalty or life in prison?"

"Not exactly," Caroline said. "The jury will answer a series of questions about intent, and aggravating factors, and mitigating factors. It's a long list, a long jury charge, and essentially a recommendation to the Judge. The Judge actually imposes the sentence: either the death penalty; or life in prison without the possibility of parole. But the Judge can't impose the death penalty if the jury votes for life in prison."

"Then let's hope the jury sees that monster for what he truly is," Sean Sullivan said. The Sullivans walked from the courtroom, his arm around her shoulders, their backs straighter than they had been since they were informed that their daughter was murdered on the mountain.

The courtroom now empty, Caroline ambled to the jury box. Something had changed since the verdict. Air that had been dense and tainted was now clear and crisp, as if a rain shower had washed through the courtroom. Her fingers slid gently down the length of the smooth, wooden rail that encased fourteen juror chairs. She looked at each empty chair and wondered whether each occupant had the strength to sentence a man to death. She came to Hannah Sullivan, her portrait resting on an easel tucked in the front corner. She imagined Hannah's last hours, lying in a blanket of snow, no one nearby to offer a kind word or a caress. Or hope. What does it feel like to be stabbed forty-seven times? Does the pain go away after ten, or twenty, or not at all? What do you think about as your blood slowly seeps into the snow?

CHAPTER ELEVEN

Catherine Bannister's grave was unkempt. Brown weeds encroached upon the white marble headstone, a headstone marking her as twenty years old when she died. The earth surrounding the plot had been rumpled by squirrels digging shallow holes to store acorns. Moldy leaves dotted the plot, smelling wet and dirty and old.

Caroline knelt beside her sister's grave and replaced the withered flowers with a fresh set of chrysanthemums she had cut from her garden that morning. She filled the stone vase with water from a plastic bottle, watching dirt and decayed leaves float to the top.

"Good morning Cat," Caroline said quietly, noting how different her voice sounded from the voice she had been using in the courtroom for the past week. "The weather is sunny today. Just a hint of fall, and the sky is Carolina blue."

Catherine Bannister had been killed almost twenty-five years earlier. Her body had been found strung up on a metal fence along a major Charlotte thoroughfare. Evidence of torture marred her. Her beautiful face had been slashed with a razor, one of her arms broken. Her life had ended with a bullet to the face.

The killer had never been caught, and Caroline did not know why her sister had been killed. There had been speculation of gang reprisal, or a drug dealer sending a message, but nothing concrete. The case went cold, and then into the frozen file, archived and unlikely to be revived.

Caroline plucked an acorn from the grass and tossed it away. Then another. "I'm in the middle of a murder trial, Cat. My first one. It's thrilling and frightening all at once. The defendant killed a young woman, a woman not much older than you."

She leaned over to sniff the fresh mums. "But we caught him, and now he's been convicted. And next week we're going to ask the jury to sentence him to death. He deserves it." She pulled absently at a tall stalk of weeds. "I'm sorry to say I haven't made any progress in your case. I haven't found them yet, Cat. But I'm still looking. I'll never stop looking."

Caroline leaned back against the headstone and listened to the birds chatter, watched squirrels dart from limb to limb. The sun warmed her face. There had been a time when she imagined she heard her sister's voice, leaking from somewhere, as she re-lived the highlights of their youth, sharing their secrets, discussing what went wrong. But that time had passed long ago. She had no answer for why Catherine had wandered down one path in life, and she another. It was a proposition she had debated on innumerable occasions, but she had found no answers. The emptiness she felt over the loss of her sister had not abated much over the years. Her sister's death had shaped her, formed her, like deft hands transforming a lump of clay.

After another few minutes of silence, she chided herself for being lazy, for lingering about when so many other things needed to be done. Her desk would be piled high, her email inbox overflowing. And she needed to prepare for next week. She had to convince the jury to give Lawter the ultimate verdict. Anything else would constitute failure. She stood up and brushed off her jeans. Then she kissed the smooth top of her sister's gravestone and left the cemetery.

CHAPTER TWELVE

The demonstrators were back in full force in front of the federal courthouse, opponents and proponents now roughly equal. The guilty verdict, splashed upon the front page of the local paper over the weekend, had galvanized the pro-death penalty crowd, and many of them stood on the sidewalk with rifles slung over their shoulders, a blazing endorsement of North Carolina's open-carry law. Some held signs that read, "He Should Die." Another sign said, "Volunteer Executioner."

Law enforcement had closed a section of the street to automobile traffic. Caroline ambled through a narrow corridor leading from the parking garage to the courthouse, barricades on either side. Her photograph had accompanied some of the stories in the newspaper and on television announcing the murder verdict, and many of the protestors recognized her. Some applauded and shouted congratulations, while others chided her.

A woman with long braids and a chiseled face, jeans and sandals, paralleled Caroline outside the barricades, and when Caroline stepped up on the sidewalk, the young woman beckoned to her. For a reason she could not explain, Caroline stepped over. The young woman thrust a folded note into Caroline's hand. Caroline nodded and walked away.

As she waited to clear security, a ritual she had to endure even though the marshals knew her well, she unfolded the note. In a flourishing hand, the young woman had written that she also was deaf, and would she please consider sparing Mr. Lawter's life because it would not be right to sentence him to death because of his disability. Caroline wandered to the glass doors of the courthouse and looked out upon the throng. The young woman stood still as the demonstrators circled around her like an awkwardly placed tree.

Caroline read the note again, held it up to the glass, then placed it in her pocket. Until that moment, she had not considered Henry Lawter to have a disability, especially given that his deafness was self-inflicted. And she didn't see why it mattered. He had murdered Hannah Sullivan, and his disability had played no part in that act and certainly didn't absolve him of the crime. It was highly likely that he had made himself deaf only after he had killed Hannah, though there was no way to be sure. His hearing had been mostly restored by surgery while he awaited trial. That she knew. Caroline wondered if the young woman who had written the note was truly disabled, or whether she might be a relative of Lawter's seeking to garner some sympathy for her kin.

Lawter's extended family sat behind the defense table, spread out among the wooden pews. They had come out of the shadow of the mountains to testify in the penalty phase and to provide moral support for their convicted brother. Many of them, having lived for generations in the area, lacked trust in their government, and it was evident in the clothes they wore to court and the prattle that continued even after Judge Westlake took the bench and bade them all to sit.

Hannah's parents sat in the first row behind the prosecution table, anchoring that side of the gallery. A smattering of friends joined them, most planning to testify about who Hannah Sullivan had been, the promise she brought to their world, and the grief they would forever endure. In contrast to Lawter's supporters, Hannah's group was respectful and subdued. They wore on their faces the solemnity of a Sunday congregation.

Though an uneven battle, the guilt phase of the trial had pitted lawyer against lawyer, expert against expert. Evidence and law and science carried the day, providing firm guidelines for the jury's deliberation. In contrast, the penalty phase shifted the issues to a different plane, one filled with emotion and overcast with an unwelcome obligation to condemn or to forgive. The families of the victim and the guilty, thrown together, exhibited an almost primal attitude, one seeking to kill, and the other desperately trying to protect a weakened member of their pack. Family pitted against family. The sour odor of fear and sadness permeated the gallery.

Throughout the penalty phase of the trial, Henry Lawter slouched in the chair beside his attorney, listening to Hannah's friends and relatives tell about the life he had taken. The person they described bore little resemblance to the woman he had attacked, perhaps because he had been in a drug-addled state during the entire ordeal. The young woman had screamed in agony with each plunge of the icepick. That he did remember. And after he walked away from her, leaving her bleeding and dying in the snow, he had thrust the icepick into his own ears repeatedly so the screaming would stop. He had never revealed this to anyone.

The testimony from his relatives did not move him until his nephew testified that he would miss his uncle Henry if he went away to prison for a long time and couldn't take him hunting or fishing for a while. The boy apparently didn't understand that the government wanted to execute his uncle. The other defense witnesses testified without poignancy of his childhood and his lack of education, how he turned to drugs as a teenager. Their words were all true but lacked the power to redeem his actions.

He and his defense attorney had to decide whether he should take the witness stand to plead for his life. Washington told him the jury would want to hear from the man they had just convicted of murder, and any humanity he could show them might just save his life. Although he understood the gravity of the proceedings, he viewed the trial, as he viewed his life, as a preordained storm sweeping over him, wielding a power he was unable to rebuff. He had long ago resigned himself to helplessness. He believed his fate was sealed at birth, so that no good or evil deed would alter the ultimate outcome. He had lived this way for thirty-four years, with little attempt to control his thoughts, his decisions, or his actions. In the small country church in which generations of Lawters had worshiped, they were told to put their faith in God, that everything that happened to them, for better or worse, was God's will. Within this cloak of predetermination, he viewed his actions as not wholly his, actions for which he was legally responsible but not, in some sense, fully accountable. He didn't want to face the jury, or face the Sullivans. He wanted to say he was sorry, but he knew that wouldn't be enough, that it would fall short of everyone's expectations, just like the rest of his life. At a break in the proceedings, he told his defense lawyer he didn't want to take the witness stand.

After the last witness testified, Caroline Bannister rose and delivered an impassioned speech, simultaneously sympathizing with the burden placed upon the jurors while stressing their oath and civic responsibility.

"We cannot, as a civilized society, without the safeguards and protections of a courtroom and a trial and a judge and a jury, allow any man to act on his own as judge, jury and executioner. That's what Henry Lawter did." Pointing at the defendant, Caroline said, "*He* decided to kidnap Hannah and force her to beg for her life. *He* decided that she should die. *He* wielded the weapon that ended her life. He plunged that icepick into her forty-seven times. And what did she do wrong, ladies and gentlemen? What did she do to deserve any of this? Her crime was the simple pursuit of a dream – to be an Olympic cyclist."

Caroline sidled next to the portrait of a smiling Hannah Sullivan, which had been pulled closer to the jury. "There are some crimes so brutal, so heinous, so outrageous, that the criminal cannot be allowed to continue to live among us. They cannot be allowed, even while in prison, to inflict fear upon us, to terrorize our lives, to disturb our sleep. To teach others how to do what they have done, perhaps even to brag about it. Such a criminal has forfeited that right. Henry Lawter is such a criminal. Life in prison is not a fitting punishment for him. Life in prison is not justice for Hannah Sullivan. Thank you."

Joseph Washington rose slowly, silent as he walked to the rail at the front of the jury box. He could not ask the jury to focus on his remorseful client. He could not ask them to forgive the man too cowardly to face them.

"My colleague, Ms. Bannister, did not mention the death penalty in her closing argument. She didn't want to use that term because it is so blunt, so final, so irreversible. Instead, she focused upon what she doesn't want you to do, which is find life imprisonment without the possibility of parole. What good would it do to sentence my client to death? What if you are wrong, and Mr. Lawter did not kill Miss Sullivan? Your verdict of death would be irreversible. Two deaths from one terrible, tragic incident would be too much to bear. A death sentence won't bring Miss Sullivan back, it won't erase what happened. I ask you to sentence my client to life imprisonment, which for him will be four or five decades of sitting in a cell thinking about what he has done. That's the most fitting punishment for Mr. Lawter."

In a tone bereft of inflection, Judge Westlake read to the jury the instructions for their determination of the sentence to impose upon Henry Lawter. Twenty-one pages, meticulously prepared, that took almost an hour to read.

Given his predicament, Henry Lawter was not sure which sentence he wanted the jury to impose. A part of him preferred death, though his lawyer had told him only three federal inmates had been executed in the past twenty-five years. His lawyer had promised to appeal, but that prospect brought no comfort to him because the District Attorney had announced over the weekend that he would be prosecuting him for murder under North Carolina law. Lawter wasn't sure how much longer he wanted to battle, or whether any of it would make any difference in the end. A lifetime in prison, away from the outdoors, probably without the drugs and alcohol that had sustained him for the past twenty years, did not appeal to him.

The jury deliberated the penalty longer than it had the determination of guilt. The seven men and five women spent the better part of three hours in debate, emotions rising and falling, the evidence almost forgotten as they wrestled with their personal doubts. The steady voice of the jury foreman reminded them they all had sworn an oath, and all had acknowledged they would vote for death if the right circumstances were presented. If the murder of Hannah Sullivan did not justify the death penalty, he said, he could not envision any circumstances on earth that would.

The jurors re-assembled in the courtroom, their faces etched with burden. Some of them looked down as they shuffled the few short steps from the jury room to their swivel chairs. One female juror wiped tears from her cheek. Not one of them looked at Henry Lawter.

"Ladies and gentlemen, have you reached a verdict on sentencing?" the Judge said, breaking the prolonged silence.

The jury foreman rose from the first row, resolute.

"We have, Your Honor."

"Hand your verdict sheet to the marshal, please."

Judge Westlake took the folded sheaf of papers and reviewed the jury's answers to the multiple sentencing questions, making sure all questions had been answered and that the jurors had signed in the appropriate places. He handed the verdict sheet back to the marshal, who returned the document to the foreman.

The Judge guided the foreman through the verdict sheet, question by question. The jury unanimously found Henry Lawter intentionally killed Hannah Sullivan on federal land and that there were aggravating factors to his actions. Not a single juror decided there were mitigating factors that might save Henry Lawter.

"And with respect to section four, what is your sentencing verdict?"

The foreman's voice quavered as he read from the verdict sheet.

"We, the jury, vote unanimously that Henry Lyman Lawter should be sentenced to death."

There was a brief outburst from Lawter's supporters that quickly abated as the marshals approached the gallery.

Judge Westlake banged the gavel and regained control of his courtroom. "This is a difficult time," he said, "but anyone who disrupts these proceedings will be removed. Is that understood?" He paused for a moment to let his message sink in. "All right. Mr. Foreman, were the jury's findings on all of these questions unanimous?"

"Yes sir. All twelve of us."

At the request of defense counsel, Judge Westlake polled each juror, and each confirmed aloud their assent to the death penalty and that they all had signed the verdict sheet willingly and without any coercion. Then Westlake released the jury, thanking them for their service and reminding them that they were under no obligation to speak to anyone about the trial or their verdict. They moved from the jury box in a quiet procession befitting the gravity of their decision.

As the sentencing verdict was read in the courtroom, Henry Lawter alternated his attention between the Judge and the jurors. He didn't fully understand the aggravating factors or the mitigating factors, or what they ultimately meant. Even though he thought he had prepared himself to hear the jury's verdict about death or life imprisonment, to accept either one, he still winced when he heard the foreman say it out loud. They voted to kill him. All of them. Not even the mothers on the jury could find any reason to keep him alive. He couldn't really blame them. They had children, too. And they heard all the evidence. That's more than he had given to that girl.

As he stood up, the marshals buckled a leather belt around his waist and shackled his hands and ankles. He figured that when they killed him he'd be strapped onto a table or a chair, with his hands and ankles bound, probably a hood over his head.

"All right," Judge Westlake said. "Formal sentencing will take place the first week of December. I'll have the clerk notify you of the precise time and date."

Lawter looked at his lawyer, then at the Judge. He raised his chin. "There ain't no need, Judge. I already know what you're going to do."

CHAPTER THIRTEEN

ONE YEAR LATER

Judge Westlake hurled a case book across his chambers. It landed with a thump and a rattling of pages in a far corner. The Court of Appeals opinion lay on his desk. The appellate court had just reversed Henry Lawter's murder conviction, deciding he had made a grave mistake by admitting the confession into evidence, finding fault with a Miranda warning read in a normal voice to a man who was deaf. It was undisputed, the court wrote, that Henry Lawter had been deaf when Detective Underwood advised Lawter of his constitutional rights. The fact that neither law enforcement officer knew the accused had been deaf was irrelevant, the court ruled. The three higher judges concluded that under those circumstances, Lawter had not been properly advised of his constitutional rights to remain silent and to have counsel present. Therefore, the confession was inadmissible. The appellate opinion did not mention Hannah Sullivan by name, referring to her either as "the deceased" or "the victim."

Judge Westlake spun his chair around to face the windows in his chambers. Mt. Pisgah stood in the distance, its transmission tower like a pin pricking a blue balloon sky. Hannah Sullivan died on the western slope of that mountain. Her killer had been safely locked away in prison for the past year. He reeled with the possibility that Henry Lawter might go free.

He punched a button on his phone. "Robert, have you read the Fourth Circuit opinion?"

"No sir, I'm preparing for a deposition. Opinion in what case?"

"The Lawter case."

"No."

"Well, let me save you the trouble. They reversed the conviction. The confession is inadmissible."

"Shit."

"When can we meet?"

63

"Tonight?"

"In my chambers at six."

"Yes, sir."

They perched on the edge of comfortable chairs in the Judge's chambers. Soothed by dark bourbon, they commenced an uncomfortable conversation.

"We have to re-try him," the Judge implored. "We cannot just let a murderer go free."

"It's not my decision. I'll talk to Caroline, of course, but she might dismiss the case for lack of evidence. Remember, there's no physical evidence linking Lawter to the murder. None of his DNA was on Hannah's body, and none of hers was found on Lawter. Without the confession, what else is there?"

"Robert, you have to convince her. There's no doubt Lawter is guilty. He wasn't coerced or beaten into confessing. He's not even making that argument. The reversal makes me look like a fool. This was my first and only murder case."

"It was our first murder case, too. We don't get that many chances as feds. But that's why Caroline might be against a second trial. Her reputation has been sullied. I'm sure she's concerned that without the confession, the jury might find him innocent. That would be much worse."

"Then maybe I should talk to her."

"Judge, do you want that to come out, that you had a conversation with the US Attorney about pushing forward with a criminal case?"

"I see your point, Robert. I'm just wound up about this. You will just have to use all of your persuasive powers to convince her then," the Judge insisted. "We can't let Lawter go free."

*   *   *   *   *   *

Caroline Bannister, trying to contain the damage inflicted by the reversal of Lawter's conviction, stood with her arms folded over her chest, gazing at the Charlotte skyline.

"There's too much risk, Robert," she said. "We don't have the evidence. If we re-try him and lose, then we're viewed as twice prosecuting an innocent man. He could sue us. That would prolong this cluster another two or three years."

"There's no doubt he murdered Hannah Sullivan. The confession wasn't coerced. This is not a situation where the cops overstepped. This is ridiculous."

"Sometimes the law is an ass, Robert." She paused for a moment, raking her finger tips beneath her chin. "Go talk to the local DA out there, see if he will take the case. He was itching to try Lawter in the first place."

"And what if he doesn't bite?"

Caroline shrugged, feeling the burden the Lawter case had suddenly become. "Maybe find the murder weapon."

District Attorney Michael Anderson was an elected official, which made him a political animal first, and a prosecutor a distant second. Serving his sixth consecutive term, Anderson had, for the first time in years, drawn an opponent in the primary. His record as a prosecutor sparkled, for all seventeen murder cases during his long tenure had garnered guilty verdicts, including three death sentences. All of his convictions had withstood the appeals.

"Let me get this straight," Anderson said. "You warned me off the case originally, essentially threatening to use the weight of the federal government to keep me from prosecuting Lawter, and now you want me to come in and clean up the federal government's mess?"

"Not to clean up our mess. To do justice for Hannah Sullivan," Crenshaw offered.

"What justice can I do for her?"

"Once Lawter was convicted, you were very quick to announce you were going to try him for murder. Maybe a local judge won't toss the confession."

"The defense now has a federal appeals court telling us all that the confession violates the Fourth Amendment. Tell me how a state judge ignores that?"

"It would be tough, I agree."

"Not just tough. Impossible. Ask for an *en banc* hearing, or appeal it to the Supremes."

"We're looking into that."

"Good luck. I'm not going anywhere near this one," Anderson said.

Over a series of meetings, Crenshaw convinced Caroline to appeal the case to the United States Supreme Court, but in a relatively short period of time the Supreme Court rejected the application for writ of *certiorari*. This ruling left the court of appeals' decision intact, with nowhere else to go.

They lingered over coffee in the small conference room next to Caroline's office.

"We've got nothing left," Crenshaw muttered.

"How about the murder weapon? A witness? Something on forensics?" Caroline said.

"The FBI has been over all of it again. Agent Porter's had a team working frantically, going over all of the photographs, the autopsy, scouring the mountain side for additional evidence. Nothing. He's just as pissed about this as we are."

"What about the footprints on the trail leading to the viewing platform at the summit? Did anybody ever figure out who those prints belonged to?"

"Not that I'm aware of."

"Then figure it out. It's a loose end. Maybe somebody saw something."

"What do you want me to do Caroline – stand in that parking lot and ask every visitor if they happened to be on that trail when Hannah was killed?"

"If that's what it takes."

After another week without progress, it fell to Crenshaw to inform the Sullivans that the man who had murdered their daughter was going to be freed. He drove to the coast to deliver the message. As he sat in the Sullivans' comfortable living room, he borrowed the method doctors often use to deliver fatal news, meandering through the missing evidence, resorting to arcane jargon and legal precedent at various points, circling back to the powerful confession, before finally arriving at the conclusion.

"Unfortunately, we can't try him again. There is nothing else we can do. I'm sorry."

Sean Sullivan, not prone to hyperbole or drama, said in a low voice, "Hannah did not die in vain, sir. She was murdered. Something must be done about that."

These failed efforts were merely prelude to the inevitable outcome that Henry Lawter would walk out of prison a free man. On a windy afternoon, with a chill blowing off the mountain peaks, Judge Westlake signed the order releasing Henry Lawter back into the world. Westlake signed the order with the fountain pen his wife had given him when he was confirmed as a judge, rather than using the electronic stamp that marked the everyday decisions of the federal judiciary in undistinguished fashion. Having no choice but to set Hannah's killer free, the Judge signaled his discontent in a flourish of ink.

CHAPTER FOURTEEN

It was the strangest of courtrooms.

There were no official trappings: no portraits of retired jurists; no government seals; no court reporter; no jury box. No microphones or computers or broad wooden tables for the lawyers. No Bible for swearing witnesses.

The courtroom, hastily constructed in a semitrailer, measured a mere eight feet wide by twenty-eight feet long.

Judge Westlake scanned the small room. An American flag draped a brass pole in the front corner. Maroon carpet concealed a pitted plywood floor. Brown sound-dampening panels lined the walls and ceiling of the trailer. Elevated insignificantly above the proceedings, the Judge nestled behind a small desk in a black nylon robe. Not his official robe, but one purchased at a costume store, complete with a white wig reminiscent of those worn by English barristers or constitutional statesmen. The Judge had discarded the wig, and his dark hair shimmered slightly under the fluorescent lights.

With hands clasped on the desk, he leaned forward. Steamy air inside the metal box, heated from a day in the sun, smelled of aftershave and sweat. And fear.

"The Court calls for trial the case of United States of America versus Henry Lyman Lawter." His voice was too loud for the small space. By habit, he glanced at the court reporter, who wasn't there.

"Would the defendant please stand?"

Two United States Marshals, out of uniform, pulled Henry Lawter to his feet.

"Mr. Lawter, you stand accused of the murder of Hannah Sullivan on federal land."

Disheveled from a night of carousing, Lawter wore a confused expression. The waist of his denim shirt hung over his belt, and his black jeans had a tattered hole on the right thigh. A three-day beard shrouded his mouth. His tennis shoes were untied, the laces frayed. A thick zip tie encircled his wrists, which dangled in front. He shook his head almost imperceptibly, as if anything more spirited might draw a physical rebuke from one of the guards.

"How do you plead, Mr. Lawter?"

Lawter shrugged. "I'm supposed to be a free man."

"And Hannah Sullivan is supposed to be alive, Mr. Lawter." The scowl that had marked the Judge's face for a month quickly returned. "No response to that, I see. You are quite adept at holding your tongue, when it suits you."

The Judge glanced at the enlarged photograph of Hannah Sullivan, tacked to the side wall of the trailer. Blond hair, gently curled, rolled to her shoulders. Clear blue eyes shone above an unblemished face. It was the same photograph that had stood as a reminder at the first trial.

"Look at her, Mr. Lawter." The Judge's voice boomed.

Beneath hooded eyelids, Lawter glanced at the photograph. "I'm really tired Judge. I'm a free man. You signed the order releasing me."

The Judge looked down at an empty legal pad. "Well, I had no choice but to release you Mr. Lawter. The court of appeals overturned the jury verdict. But that was just a technicality, not a finding of innocence. You have to atone for what you did. Isn't that right, Mr. Crenshaw?"

Robert Crenshaw rose from a small chair, securing the top button of his jacket. "That is correct, Your Honor," Crenshaw said with a hint of quaver in his voice.

"All right, Mr. Lawter. You don't want to enter a plea. But we all know you are guilty."

Lawter shrugged his shoulders again. "Maybe so, maybe not," he muttered.

"Mr. Lawter, it appears you have been a busy man in your few months of freedom. A couple of drunk and disorderly charges, suspicion of stealing narcotics from a pharmacy, and theft of a bicycle from a student." Westlake laid the pages on his desk. "What do you have to say for yourself?"

In the insipid heat of the trailer, sweat trickled down Lawter's forehead and nose, beading in his whiskers. "My lawyer is already working on the lawsuit against you for violating my rights. We'll just add this to it."

"Mr. Lawter, you don't seem to understand your predicament," the Judge said. "You are on trial, right now, for the murder of Hannah

Sullivan. Mr. Crenshaw is prosecuting you on behalf of the United States of America, and the other gentleman to your left is your new attorney."

"I already had my trial. And I don't know who this guy is." Lawter tilted his head toward a man he had never seen before that evening. "My lawyer said you can't try me again. Double jeopardy, or something."

"Well, that's not correct," the Judge responded. "You can be tried again, per Miranda v. Arizona. Miranda's confession was excluded by the Supreme Court, and the jury still found him guilty in the second trial. In any event, I'm not going to argue with you about legal precedent. Mr. Johnstone, does your client have a plea to enter?"

David Johnstone rose slowly from a folding chair along the side of the trailer. He had never met Henry Lawter, had never conferred with his new client. Johnstone looked at Lawter, just a few feet away. He had last seen Lawter from the gallery as a spectator during the federal trial in Asheville, there by happenstance because he had another case in the building at the time. He had lingered in the courtroom longer than his duty demanded, out of the morbid fascination with which one watches murder trials.

In the voice he used to project an air of confidence across the expanse of a vacuous courtroom, Johnstone said, "Given the irrefutable confession, which this Court has ruled admissible, Mr. Lawter pleads guilty."

Henry Lawter vigorously shook his head. "No. I don't plead guilty."

The marshals on either side of Lawter gripped his arms hard enough to silence him.

"Mr. Lawter, any further outbursts and the marshals will tase you. You know what that's like. Now, I accept your guilty plea, Mr. Lawter. It seems we do not, after all, need to have a second trial. Mr. Crenshaw, does the United States have a recommendation as to sentencing?"

Robert Crenshaw smoothed his tie. It was his prosecution that had been derailed by the appellate court, and despite his efforts to secure a second trial, and his scrupulous re-examination of the evidence, he had come up empty.

"Yes, Your Honor. As we did at the first trial, the United States requests a sentence of death."

"Very well. Any evidence to submit on sentencing, Mr. Johnstone?"

Johnstone hesitated for a moment, unsure how to respond. Even in cases where his clients had been convicted of murder, he had always fought to avoid the death penalty.

"Mr. Johnstone?" the Judge said.

"Yes, Your Honor?"

"Are you with us here?"

"Yes, of course, Your Honor. It's just that a sentence of life in prison is an option."

The Judge adopted a softer tone. "David, we can't exactly hold the man in a secret prison for the next three or four decades, can we?"

"No, sir. I don't see how that would be practical."

"So, the United States has requested a sentence of death. How does the defendant respond?"

Johnstone cleared his throat, returning to the small courtroom, once again resuming the journey to its most certain destination. "The defense has no objection to the proposed sentence."

With unfeigned satisfaction, Judge Westlake folded his hands atop the wooden desk. "Well, this has been so much easier the second time around. No need for additional evidence, or a jury, or a trial when you have such a solid confession and a guilty plea."

The Judge paused to compose his thoughts, thinking back to the first trial. He had been fully prepared then to impose the death penalty, had rehearsed each statement carefully. This was different. Here, he was free from the constraints of the Constitution or the federal code. This was outside of the law, this was outside of . . . everything. On the wide boulevard of lawlessness, there are many exit ramps, but Judge Westlake refused to take one. He inhaled the heated air, taking no refreshment from it, and the words came back to him in an authoritative voice.

"Mr. Lawter, the Court does find you guilty of the murder of Hannah Sullivan, on property owned by and under the custody of the United States of America. Such an offense is punishable by death or life imprisonment under Title 18 of the United States Code, section 1111. The Court finds the existence of aggravating factors, in that the actions of the defendant were heinous, cruel and depraved, and Miss Sullivan was particularly vulnerable under the circumstances. I find no mitigating factors. Under the law, I have no choice but to impose a sentence of death. Now Mr. Lawter, you may address the Court. In a quiet voice."

"Okay, Judge. Look, I don't want to plead guilty."

"Your guilty plea is already entered and has been accepted by this Court. The issue here is not about the nuances of Miranda warnings, or about whether you want to enter a guilty plea or withdraw it. These are all just legal technicalities that, in many cases, like yours, have gotten in the way of justice. They keep our judicial system from getting to the truth. They keep our system from operating efficiently. The issue here is whether you killed Miss Sullivan. Did you, Mr. Lawter, kill Hannah Sullivan?"

"I don't want to say."

"All right. You may remain silent. But a trial is about seeking the truth. You know what you did. We know what you did. The question is whether you want to admit the truth, just like you told the investigators that afternoon on the mountain. You've never claimed that you didn't tell those officers that you killed Hannah. You've never said you didn't do it. You've never said you are innocent." He paused as a wave of anxiety passed through him. "Now, I can tell you there is considerable research that admitting your guilt can make you feel better, perhaps even pave your way into the afterlife, if you believe in things like that."

"What if I say nothing?" Lawter said in a somewhat challenging tone. "What if I keep quiet this time?"

Judge Westlake leaned forward in his chair, internally questioning his decision to allow this murderer to address the Court. He wanted the truth, unadulterated and from the killer's own mouth, but he wanted no part of a debate with this defendant over the intricacies of constitutional law.

"Mr. Crenshaw, would the defendant's silence at this juncture change the verdict, the sentence, or anything at all?" Westlake asked.

"No sir," Crenshaw said without rising.

"Mr. Johnstone?"

"No, Your Honor. The defendant's silence would not alter the outcome of this proceeding."

"You see, Mr. Lawter," Westlake said, as if Lawter's ordained fate were now entirely out of his hands, "silence is not a virtue in this particular situation. Your own attorney has acknowledged that you are guilty. You told both Detective Underwood and Ranger Swenson what you did, and how you did it. A federal jury found you guilty. There is no doubt about your guilt. You know it, I know it. Everybody in this courtroom knows it. Even the court of appeals knows it, but they decided to elevate form over substance. Now, you don't have to tell us what you did, if you don't want to. However, we have several choices about how your sentence can be carried out. So acknowledging to us your crime, and perhaps showing some remorse that you brutally took someone else's life with no justification, might just persuade us to choose a method with a more . . . pleasant effect."

71

Lawter hung his head for a moment. "Either way, I'm doomed. That's what you're saying? Whether I admit what I did or not?"

"That is correct, Mr. Lawter," the Judge said.

Lawter looked down at the carpet and nodded. "Okay. I never expected to get out of prison anyway, not after what I did. I figured I'd get convicted the second time around. I was surprised when they let me walk right out of that prison."

"Signing the order releasing you was one of the most difficult things I've ever had to do," the Judge said.

"Well, I guess I got a few months of freedom. Anyway, I wanted to testify at the trial, tell what I did, apologize to her family, but my lawyer said no." He paused for a minute, working his jaw. "Okay. If I admit what I did, will you do it on the beach, where I can see the sun come up over the ocean? I never seen that before."

The condemned man's last request was uttered in a tone anticipating denial. The Judge wondered if Hannah had made any last requests to her captor, whether she had known what fate awaited her, and whether this man had shown her any mercy at all before plunging the icepick into her prone body dozens of times. Even so, an odd need to oblige the condemned man tugged at him.

"Marshals, assuming Mr. Lawter admits to my satisfaction his heinous crime, can we accommodate his request?"

Marshal Cunningham, the more experienced of the two, though never in these circumstances, spoke up. "I am sure we can get that worked out, Judge. If that's what you want. We might need a little time to plan the logistics. Not how we had planned it."

"I understand, and I appreciate your flexibility and professionalism. I'm sure Mr. Lawter appreciates it as well. Mr. Lawter, do you understand that your request is a difficult one to satisfy and that the marshals will do their best to carry out your last request?"

"I guess so."

"All right then. Mr. Lawter, we must be completely satisfied with your allocution. You have to tell us everything. Are you prepared to tell us that you murdered Hannah Sullivan?"

"Wait, I don't want to be electrocuted."

The Judge shook his head. "You misunderstand, Mr. Lawter. I did not say electrocution. I said allocution." The Judge drew the word out.

"Allocution means you have to not only admit what you did, but tell us the facts so that we know you are telling the truth."

Lawter shifted his feet and nodded slightly. "Oh. All right. I thought you was going to hook me up to some car batteries or something. I don't want that. I think I understand what you mean. Okay. I murdered that girl. I didn't know what her name was or anything about her. She was a perfect stranger to me."

"Just so we are clear, Mr. Lawter. You murdered this girl, this girl in the picture?" The Judge pointed to the photograph of Hannah Sullivan.

"Yes, I killed her. That girl."

"Please continue."

Johnstone, who had dutifully played his part in this charade of a trial, shifted in his chair. "Is this necessary, Your Honor? Can't we move to the next step?"

The interruption surprised the Judge. "Mr. Johnstone, let's be patient, shall we? Mr. Lawter didn't testify at his first trial. Perhaps there is some mitigating circumstance of which we are not aware. Perhaps Mr. Lawter can enlighten us on that point. And besides, I am intensely curious to know why such things happen in a civilized society, and what our system of justice can do about it. We can all learn from this experience."

"Yes sir. I understand. It won't change anything though."

"Let's at least afford Mr. Lawter the opportunity to enlighten us on his motives. Mr. Lawter, will you favor us with an explanation for your actions?"

"You mean . . ."

"Why you killed Hannah Sullivan."

"Well . . . I don't know, you know. She came down into the woods there. Maybe she saw I was cooking meth or something. Maybe she was going to tell somebody. I was high anyway. When I did . . . you know."

"When you stabbed her?"

"Yeah. When I stabbed her."

The Judge probed the logical alternatives Lawter could have chosen instead of murder, the ease with which he could have escaped. "But if you were worried about being caught, why did you stay there? Why didn't you just pack up your campsite and move on? There was no one else around. The Parkway was closed because of the snowstorm. If you had just moved on, or ignored her, Hannah would still be alive."

Lawter paused for a moment, as if he'd never considered that question. He gnawed on his lower lip. "I don't know. I got high on meth."

"That is not a satisfactory answer," the Judge said loudly. "Did Hannah say something to you? What random thought entered your head and suddenly turned you from a petty criminal into a murderer? Please tell me why you did it."

"I don't guess you've ever done meth Judge, but it makes you forget reality, or changes it. That's why people do it."

Judge Westlake had never sampled an illegal drug, had never taken prescription medication that wasn't prescribed for him, wary that someone would discover his transgression. His world did not comprehend murder without reason. Unconvinced by this flimsy explanation for killing an innocent woman, he dragged a handkerchief across his forehead, concluding that no matter what Lawter told him, he would never fully understand why he had killed Hannah Sullivan. "I will move on then. What about the icepick, what did you do with the icepick?"

Lawter smiled for the first time that night, showing teeth wrecked by methamphetamine. "I disposed of it, you might say."

"Well, of course you did. The FBI search teams never found it, even with metal detectors and dogs."

The Judge and Crenshaw had themselves searched the area a few days before Lawter was released, hoping to find an additional shred of evidence to support a second trial. They had combed the dirt at the campsite and where Hannah had been found and beyond, down into the thick woods and the vines and the decaying leaves, searching for a murder weapon that had vanished like Houdini's elephant. He and Robert had both worked feverishly for an entire afternoon, covering the same terrain the FBI had methodically searched, scrabbling through soil that still held the remnants of Hannah's blood. They had found nothing.

"How did you dispose of it?"

"Easy. Climbed a tree. Drove the icepick down in the crotch of a branch with my hammer. Broke off the wooden handle. Burned the handle in my campfire."

"So if anyone ever found the metal part, there would be no fingerprints, no DNA on it," the Judge said. "And you burned the wooden handle." The Judge rubbed the stubble emerging from his chin, noting its rasp and scrape. "Now, Mr. Lawter, did you pierce your own eardrums with the same icepick you used to kill Hannah Sullivan? That's what everyone has suspected."

"Yeah, I did."

"And did you do that because you knew you would be caught and wanted to argue that you could not have heard the Miranda warning because you were deaf?"

"I ain't that smart Judge."

"Then why did you puncture your own eardrums?"

Like a child called to the principal's office, Lawter looked down at his dingy shoes. "I did it so I couldn't hear her scream no more. She was screaming really loud. I knowed she was in pain. So I stabbed her a bunch more times. A bunch more. But she wouldn't stop. She kept screaming. So I dug the icepick into my ears. It didn't work though. Even after I did it, she was still screaming inside my head. That's when I went back to my tent and took a bunch more meth. To knock me out."

"How did you . . . It doesn't matter," the Judge said, now feeling the exhaustion of their endeavor. "Mr. Johnstone is quite right. There is no point to further discussion. Mr. Lawter, I thank you for your honesty. It is helpful to the Court in determining the truth about what happened to Miss Sullivan. It may help her rest in peace. I hope it will help you too. I will grant your last request to die on the beach. May God have mercy on your soul. Marshals, please carry out the sentence forthwith."

The Judge looked about for his gavel, pulling out the wide drawer in the desk, but the drawer was empty. It was perhaps the lone detail they had forgotten in hastily building the courtroom. This omission deprived him of the ability to punctuate his declared sentence with the rap of a wooden mallet. Instead, he slapped the table twice with the palm of his hand. "Court is adjourned."

Stepping down from the dais, he moved to the metal door specially installed in one side of the trailer. He did not look again at the man he had just sentenced to death. He had seen enough of Henry Lyman Lawter, and the man's case had now been closed, permanently removed from his docket. The prosecutor and defense attorney fell in behind him while Marshal Cunningham checked the video monitors and unlocked the door.

"You guys will keep him here for a while?" Westlake asked.

"Yes, sir. We need to alter the plan a bit. We weren't planning to carry this out in such a public place as a beach."

"Well, I understand Marcus. But I gave him my word." The Judge patted Cunningham on the shoulder. "Do justice for Hannah."

"Yes sir. It's not a problem."

Judge Westlake turned back toward the door, ready to leave the chamber.

"Do you want to leave your robe here, Judge?"

"Yes, of course. Thank you for reminding me." The Judge unzipped the black robe and handed it to the marshal.

A moth fluttered into the trailer and lit on the wall next to the door. The Judge trapped it in his right hand and, once outside, he released it into the night.

The trailer door closed behind them, its rasp less satisfying than the clang of iron prison bars. The air outside was much cooler than the thick air inside the trailer, and scented with pine. The Judge inhaled deeply, as if to purge something from inside.

"That was intense, gents," the Judge said, mopping his forehead. "I thought everything went smoothly. Robert, your thoughts?"

"Everything according to plan, Judge. Lawter got the sentence he deserved. Too bad we had to go through a trial and a lengthy appeal. Two years and a lot of money wasted."

"Not wasted, Robert. There was a chance the system would work, but it didn't. We had to step in. How about you, David, what do you think?"

Johnstone lit a cigar with a shaking match. He exhaled deeply, blowing a cloud of blue smoke away from the others. "About what I expected." He offered nothing more.

The Judge nodded. "You are both to be congratulated for your roles in seeing that justice has been done. It wasn't easy for anybody, but we had to do this for Miss Sullivan. Thank you for that."

They shook hands. The adrenaline created by their mutual endeavor had not yet been replaced by the need for reflection. For several minutes they stood about in their suits and ties, out of place on a sandy road in the darkness. With hands thrust in pockets, the Judge gazed at the murky sky and the skinny Florida pines in silence, wondering what he had just done.

CHAPTER FIFTEEN

Raleigh Westlake, United States District Judge, ignored the mandate of an appellate court and instead imposed the ultimate verdict upon Henry Lawter. In making that decision, he invoked natural law and morality, relying on Absolute Truth to support his conclusion that if one person is undeniably guilty of killing another, the body of laws which have been ordained by men should stand as no impediment to his execution. An eye for an eye. The ends justify the means. Something along those lines. He was less clear in his rationale for the verdict than he was its imperative.

The five members of the cabal were as points of a star, none more important than another, each performing tasks necessary to maintain the balance of their endeavor. Lieutenants Crenshaw and Johnstone, because of their roles in the day-to-day imprisonment of guilty men, easily agreed to the idea of a clandestine trial. Somewhere within them lay deep-seated frustration with the institution to which they had devoted their lives.

Cunningham and Perez, charged with the responsibility of fulfilling the Judge's order, needed no loquacious argument to understand why Henry Lawter should die. They had served in Iraq together. Marines. They had seen men and women torn apart by bullets and bombs. Some of the bullets had come from their own triggers, the gentle pull of the last joint of the index finger releasing a fusillade of projectiles, turning bodies into dripping bags of parts. Both of them, sometimes independently and often in tandem, had witnessed countless lives seep away into the sand. They did not question their orders; nor did they count their kills. They had attained a certain level of detachment that most men cannot acquire.

Marcus Cunningham, who had served on Judge Westlake's court detail for ten years, was a big man, broad across the shoulders. He could manhandle any prisoner with whom he was entrusted, though this skill had not been recently utilized until they were called upon to snatch Henry Lawter from a St. Augustine street.

Ignacio Perez, smaller in stature but large in courage, had once rescued a family from a burning apartment building after a drone strike, even though their platoon commander had called them off. This measured his sense of justice, if not his capacity for remorse. He had been assigned to the federal courthouse in Asheville for six years.

Cunningham and Perez were different people, but not different men. As they guarded Lawter in the trailer courtroom, the US Marshals spoke in clipped tones. Their movements were efficient, calculated, their eyes frequently downcast, searching the ground. Hardship was not a condition they recognized, and the lines between right and wrong, legal and illegal, had long ago blurred into clouds of swirling sand. They made no distinction between the execution of Henry Lawter and termination of targets they had been assigned in a desert land overseas.

Cunningham monitored a video feed on his laptop. Four concealed cameras mounted atop the two trailers gave a 360-degree view of the area surrounding the rig. The only place the cameras couldn't capture was beneath the trailers.

"It's just after oh two hundred, so we've got a few hours Iggy. Why don't you get the prisoner secured? I'll start re-vamping the mission."

Perez checked the zip tie binding Lawter's hands and the security of the gag, then cinched a long plastic tie around the prisoner's ankles. The chair on which the condemned man sat rolled easily to the rear of the trailer, stopping next to the large cargo doors. With a ratchet strap, Perez secured his prisoner and the chair to two steel rings bolted to the side of the trailer.

Cunningham searched Google Earth for a spit of beach where they could take Lawter to die. The original plan had been to inject the prisoner with a large amount of heroin and dump his body on an isolated street in Jacksonville, a short drive up the interstate. He would be deemed just another accidental drug overdose on a long list in a city that was inured to such things. Once the cops identified the body and checked Lawter's record, they would find previous arrests for possession of controlled substances and paraphernalia, petty theft, as well as the murder of Hannah Sullivan. With this history, an accidental drug overdose would seem a natural way for a man like Henry Lawter to die. It should raise no suspicion. There would be no crime, no investigation. But that plan had to be scuttled.

Vilano Beach, just north of their location, had good access from Highway A1A, but was cluttered with houses. The risk of detection would be high, even though most residents would be asleep. After a few more minutes on the laptop, Cunningham discovered Anastasia Island, just south of the city, and Anastasia State Park. The park covered a large swath of the peninsula, which meant there would be no waterfront houses, no people gazing out of windows at the ocean as a suspicious trio walked down the beach in the middle of the night. A paved road ran from the highway almost all the way to the sand. The road was approximately a mile and a half long and followed the contours of the salt run that separated the park from the ocean. If the entrance gate was closed, which he concluded was a high probability, they would have a long walk with a prisoner along an open road. Not ideal, but the conditions never were. They had made many long treks with prisoners in the open Iraqi desert, with no more than a dry *wadi* for cover.

Opening the street-view window, Cunningham virtually navigated the park road all the way to the beach. There were no houses or campsites along the route. There would be little traffic, but without the opportunity for recon, he had no way of knowing whether the park was patrolled at night.

"Looks like Anastasia State Park is our best bet. About a half hour from here," Cunningham noted.

"A state park. Think they have night patrol?" Perez mused.

"I would assume not."

"My mother told me that when you assume, you make an ass of u and me."

"Your mother was a smart woman."

"What's the cover along the road?" Perez asked.

"Nothing's well defined. Looks like thick brush most of the way. Probably swampy."

"Swampy. That could mean snakes. I don't like snakes."

"Rattlers and moccasins. Gators too. So we stay dry."

"Well, if we see any snakes, maybe we just push him in the swamp and let the serpents take care of him."

"Interesting idea," Cunningham said. "Save that one for later."

"Camouflage and face paint?"

"I'm thinking khakis, sweat shirts and ball caps," Cunningham said. "If we run into anybody, might be better for us to look like three drunks coming home late to the campsite. Forgot the gate would be locked. Had to park the car and walk in."

"I like it," Perez said. "I'll get the smack ready. No weapons except for the stun guns. Travel light."

Cunningham checked again the route along which they would be on foot, pausing several times to get the 360-degree view at key locations where the road neared the campsites or there was an intersection. He plugged the park address into an app on his cell phone, then closed the program.

"Should we leave the rig here?" Cunningham asked.

Perez leaned against one wall, arms folded. "Let's transfer the prisoner to the car here. I'll drive the rig to a rest area. Fits in better. You follow in the car. Then we take the car over to the park." Perez was the only member of the group who had a commercial driver's license, and he had driven the tandem rig down from North Carolina the night before.

The split-screen of the video feed captured the Judge and the two lawyers still standing outside on the road, physically less than ten yards away, but miles distant in terms of their continued responsibilities. The lawyers were silent, possibly in shock. Perhaps they suddenly realized they had become death's constituent.

"Think they'll sleep?" Cunningham said.

"Doubt it. They're just boots, not used to this sort of thing. You remember when we were boots."

"I do. Nervous as a whore in church. That first mission, man . . ."

"I don't see any difference between this and hunting down targets in Iraq. Bad guys are bad guys, even if you find them on American soil. Those guys didn't get a trial before we took them out. This guy did," Perez said, tilting his head at their dozing prisoner. "At least one trial."

"No difference," Cunningham agreed. "At least not one I'm going to worry about. Judge knows what he's doing. A little unorthodox, but I trust him."

"Me too," Perez said.

"All right, you get a little shut-eye Iggy. You've got to drive the rig back tomorrow. I'll watch the prisoner. Sunrise is 7:24. Depart at o'four hundred?"

"Sounds like a plan. I haven't slept in two nights. Don't want to get sloppy." Perez checked the video monitors a final time. The lawyers had gone to bed in Alpha trailer. He slipped out the side door, ensured that the cab was locked and the generator was still humming, then joined the lawyers in the sleeping quarters.

At 4:24 a.m., Perez and Cunningham pulled out of a rest area along the interstate and began the short drive toward St. Augustine, their prisoner in the trunk. They said nothing. They were used to silent missions. They turned off US 1 and passed the quiet police station on King Street, then zigzagged through the small downtown area and drove across the Bridge of Lions. Fortunately, the drawbridge was down. The water in the bay chopped as the pre-dawn wind began to grow. Cruising down A1A through a sleepy Anastasia Island, they passed an alligator farm.

"We could take him there," Perez suggested.

"You have a reptile fetish?"

"Don't think so. I just want to be rid of this guy."

Turning off the highway onto the park road, they pulled the car onto the sandy shoulder just in front of the unmanned guard shack. It was 4:51.

While Cunningham remained in the car with their prisoner, Perez spent a few minutes patrolling the woods for campers and early morning runners. Finding no one about, he returned to the car, opened the trunk, and they pulled a groggy Henry Lawter out into the open. In case they happened upon someone along their route, they removed the tape and gag from the prisoner's mouth, then cut the plastic ties that bound his hands and feet.

"Say a word," Cunningham whispered, "or utter any sound at all, and I'll tase you. You understand?"

"I'm hungry," Lawter said.

Cunningham wrenched Lawter's arm behind his back. "I said not a word."

Flanking the prisoner on both sides, the marshals ushered Henry Lawter around the locked gate and began his death march. They did not realize the gate was similar to the pipe gate Hannah Sullivan had circumvented on her ride up the mountain.

A new moon provided little illumination, and there were no street lights. Once adjusted to the darkness, they could see just well enough to stay on the concrete sidewalk that followed the road. Their pace was brisk. Perez frequently turned around to look for headlights coming up the road from behind.

Lawter stumbled along between them, a result of still being under the influence from the night before and stubborn legs that did not want to take him to the end. The marshals pulled and prodded him down the path, and they had completed about half their journey when Lawter said he needed to pee.

Cunningham checked his watch. 5:07. "It's probably been six hours or so," he said with slight resignation.

"All right," Perez agreed.

They maneuvered Lawter off the path onto a sandy slope and stepped back so he could take care of his business. It took a minute. He zipped up. And then he bolted around them and started to run back up the road, heading toward the car or some glimmer of escape, screaming "help" at the top of his lungs.

CHAPTER SIXTEEN

The marshals were caught off guard. Lawter had seemed barely able to walk only a moment earlier, and now he was almost twenty yards away, veering into the road, still yelling. Out of Taser range, they had no choice but to pursue their fleeing prisoner. After chasing him a hundred yards or so, they hadn't closed the gap.

"Shit," Cunningham said, gasping for breath. "Get him Iggy. I don't think I can catch him." The bigger man slowed to a jog, then a walk, then stopped and put his hands on his knees, watching the prisoner merge into the darkness ahead.

Perez kept running at a steady pace, not sprinting, hoping Lawter's burst of adrenaline would soon subside. It had been years since he'd been forced to chase anyone. Sometimes a man running for his life can go a long way. And fast. He needed to pace himself.

The escaping prisoner, now struggling for breath, stopped yelling. But he kept running. His shoes slapped loudly against the asphalt. The humid air clung to him.

As Perez ran away from the beach, away from their destination, he knew they were losing valuable time. The mission schedule didn't include extra minutes for chasing down the prisoner. If he didn't catch Lawter soon, the sun might be up before they could get down to the beach. That would infinitely increase the risk of detection. A disaster. He slowly gained ground, closing the gap to fifteen yards, then ten. He reached to his hip for the Taser, but wasn't sure if he was close enough yet. If he missed Lawter from this distance, he would have to re-load, losing more valuable time. He decided against it. Unless Lawter started shouting again.

Lawter suddenly swerved off the road and turned onto a narrow path through a thicket of low palm plants. Out of sight. Perez rounded the corner at full speed before realizing Lawter had stopped and was standing directly in front of him, staring him down, preparing for battle. He was too close to use the Taser now, so he barreled into the prisoner, launching them both into the palm thicket. They wrestled in the underbrush, Lawter

83

wiry and terrified, flailing his arms and legs at everything. Perez allowed the condemned man to heave and thrust, to wear himself out, and then Perez was on top, his right forearm pressing against Lawter's throat.

"Stop struggling or I'll crush your windpipe. Right here," Perez said, breathing heavily. "No beach, no sunrise, no heroin."

Lawter released his grip on Perez's shoulders, holding his palms skyward in surrender.

After regaining his breath, Perez dragged Lawter to his feet, then pulled him clear of the thicket. Still on the narrow path, he wrapped Lawter's wrists with a zip tie, then stepped back and delivered a right hook to the prisoner's jaw, dropping him to the sand. "Asshole."

Lawter lay on his side, trying to shake off the blow and the exertion of his escape. "What did you expect? Just let you take me down to the beach and kill me?"

"You don't even deserve that courtesy. Not after what you did to that girl. But that's what the Judge ordered."

Lawter began yelling for help again but only said it once before Taser probes struck him in the torso. His body convulsed on the ground for half a minute.

A few yards away, Cunningham stood in firing position, his legs apart, the charged leads dangling from the gun. "No choice," Cunningham said.

"Maybe he'll die of a heart attack," Perez said.

They stood over Lawter for a time as the tremors stopped and he began to breathe regularly again. They gagged him and waited a few minutes at the edge of the road to see if anyone had heard the shouts or the scuffle and had come looking for the source. The area remained quiet and still. They saw no lights at the campsites across the way. No cars came up the road. When they were convinced their chase and Lawter's shouts had gone unnoticed, they headed back toward the beach. Lawter gave them no further trouble.

At 5:28 they arrived at the closed concession stand and bathhouse at the end of the park road. Traversing the short boardwalk, they half dragged Lawter through the thick sand onto the beach. The Atlantic Ocean rumbled in the near distance. They walked north for a few minutes, away from the lights of the pier jutting out into the water off St. Augustine Beach.

"There," Perez said, pointing to a series of large dunes separating the beach from the backwater salt run.

They nestled into a dune, their khaki attire almost blending into the sand. It was passable camouflage. If caught in the dunes, they could be fined, but that was the least of their concerns. It was quieter here, out of the wind. The new moon revealed vague shapes of their surroundings. From this vantage, the ocean boundary was defined only as a curving outline of light sand. They stared off into the ink, the surf pounding as the tide seemed to rise. At that hour, the line between ocean and sky was indistinguishable. Thousands of miles separated them from the next land to the east, water stretched to infinity. Sea oats stood above them like brown-helmeted sentinels. Though encased in a seemingly secure cocoon, the rest of the world oblivious to the night's escapades, the marshals remained vigilant.

Perez brushed debris from his pants and checked himself for scratches and bruises. He pulled several thorns from his right bicep and plucked a cluster of sand spurs from his socks.

Lawter fell asleep to the rhythm of crashing waves, resigned to his fate.

As six a.m. approached, the light began to change. The once inky ocean took on a pewter hue, then became the silver of fish scales, the sun itself still a furtive longing. Minute by minute their surroundings began to emerge, which meant someone might be able to see them against the dunes.

Just after the first jogger passed by, Perez announced it was time. "Let's do it."

Cunningham shook Lawter awake. "This is it, Lawter. Be still. This is your moment." Cunningham pointed toward the ocean. "The sun will be up in a few minutes."

Perez pulled on latex gloves. He rolled up the denim sleeve covering the prisoner's left arm, closed Lawter's hand into a fist and squeezed the forearm and bicep together for about a minute. Then he drew a syringe full of liquified black tar from a glass vial and stuck it in a vein slightly pulsing on the inside of Lawter's left elbow. Perez pushed the plunger home.

Between them, Lawter tottered on the sand. In seconds his eyes became murky with bliss.

Perez refilled the syringe with heroin and stuck the needle back in a vein snaking down Lawter's left bicep. It jiggled with the pulse of the prisoner's heartbeat.

As seagulls began to chatter, the sun signaled its arrival in a glitter of pink and purple that spread like liquid across the horizon. Everything took on the striated, fleshy color of pink grapefruit.

Cunningham grabbed the prisoner's chin as Lawter began to fade. "This is it Lawter," he whispered. "This is how your life ends."

Lawter opened his eyes to take in the orange disc peeking over the horizon. He said something unintelligible through the gag.

Perez pulled Lawter's right arm across his body, placed Lawter's right thumb on the syringe, and depressed the plunger on the second dose. He held it there for a few seconds, until Lawter's head dropped as the heroin took him under. When Lawter's body slumped against Perez, he released his grip on Lawter's hand, letting the prisoner's arms hang limp.

The marshals silently watched the sun rise over Anastasia beach as the heroin shut down Lawter's breathing. His breaths became shallower and soon ended with a last, desperate heave for air. Perez put his ear to Lawter's nose and heard nothing. He checked Lawter for a pulse and found none.

"It's done," Perez said. "6:04." He removed the gag from Lawter's mouth and clipped the zip tie binding his hands, stuffing both in his own pocket. With his shirt tail, he wiped the vial that had held the heroin and slid it into Lawter's sock. Then he scattered a metal spoon and a plastic lighter on the sand between Lawter's legs. He slipped the latex gloves off his hands.

They sat there for a moment, waiting for finality. The dead man was wedged between their rigid shoulders. When they finally wriggled out of the dune and stood up, the body slumped to the side, the needle still dangling from its left arm, resting awkwardly upon the sloping, pocked sand.

The marshals left the beach as silently as they had come, not looking back at the killer. Their footprints would soon be erased by wind and water, their presence there forever unrecorded.

CHAPTER SEVENTEEN

Judge Westlake wanted to run. From the moment he stepped out of the courtroom trailer after delivering the death sentence to Henry Lawter, he had an urgent impulse to take off down the sandy road that might in fact lead to oblivion. As David Johnstone puffed smoke from his cigar, Westlake could think of nothing but escape. To escape the cloying confines of the trailer, to escape from this group of men who had engineered the death of Henry Lawter. To escape his own mind.

Though he had steeled himself for the mental strain, he could not simply shrug it off. Physical exertion seemed the answer, but in these trailers, on this mission, he was boxed in by the very things he had carefully constructed to conceal their operation. To be spotted running in the stark middle of the night would draw attention, attention that would raise questions and suspicion. It would be reckless, both to himself and to the men who trusted him.

Instead, he tried to sleep. But sleep would not come. Even after a series of bourbons. The bunks of the living quarters in Alpha trailer were spartan, only a slight upgrade from thin prison mattresses. That was intentional. There were three bunks, two beds per, coarse sheets and a thin blanket. Limp pillows had to be pounded into the shape of comfort. The Judge did not want any of them to sleep well on the night they had condemned a man to death. As he rolled and twisted in the bunk, he remembered. The night hum of the air conditioner was punctuated by the sounds of men turning and sighing.

He stared at the springs of the bunk above, shaking his head slightly. The trial went exactly as scripted, and everyone played their parts well. Their undivided loyalty to each other was critical to the endeavor, to ensure secrecy, without which they all would be doomed. One uncertain man could send them all to prison, or worse. What he could not forecast was how the others would deal with the repercussions of what they had done. When they emerged into the light of the next morning, how would they react? Would anyone panic?

Westlake had known Robert Crenshaw for a decade. The plan they had most recently set in motion had been incubating for years, cultivated during their frequent weekend gatherings at the Judge's house at Lake Fontana. As Westlake recalled it, Crenshaw made a stray remark, tossed in the midst of a poker game among inebriated competitors who were trying to hide their tells under the influence. Robert was bemoaning the fact that one of his convictions in a white-collar-fraud prosecution had been set back by the court of appeals.

"Six years of investigation, grand jury, trial, conviction, then appeal. Now back to square one," he said, scanning his cards. "No telling what a re-trial will cost the taxpayers. Ridiculous waste of resources. Maybe you guys could just take care of it," he nodded toward Cunningham and Perez, sitting across from him. "One of you was in the Marine Corps, right? You know how to do that sort of thing."

They stared back at Crenshaw in unified silence.

"That's just the liquor talking," the Judge said. "Although sometimes it speaks the truth. I'll take two cards Iggy," Westlake said to Perez. "By the way, they were both in the Marine Corps."

"What?" Crenshaw said.

"Iggy and Marcus. They are both Marines."

"In combat?" Crenshaw said, looking back and forth at the two.

Cunningham nodded. "Iraq. Two tours."

"You guys have seen some shit, I'll bet," Crenshaw said.

Perez dealt two cards face down to the Judge.

"You killed some people while you were over there?"

This is how the initial seeds were sown. From liquor-coated bravado. If the judicial system failed, as it often did, there was another way to ensure that guilty men would be punished. It was only a fledgling idea, flitting in out of their conversations like a firefly. Westlake wasn't sure that any of them, including himself, would ever act on it when the time came. *If* the time came.

And then the murder of Hannah Sullivan entered their lives like a locomotive careening around a sharp corner. A young woman stabbed to death, a crime-scene confession, the guilty verdict, and reversal of the conviction on appeal. Judge Westlake had vigorously encouraged Crenshaw to seek a re-trial by either the US Attorney's Office or the State District Attorney. When both prosecutors declined, he and Crenshaw had taken matters into their own hands, scouring the mountain for the murder weapon that might be enough evidence to convict Henry Lawter a second time.

Exhausted and defeated, they sat on their haunches on the mountainside, looking out at a valley of muted color. Absently tossing acorns over the edge of the rocks, the Judge had broached the idea of a secret trial, a lawless concept which, if he were honest with himself, had been lurking within him for quite some time. Hannah Sullivan's murder made it real. Lawter's impending release made it necessary. Out of choices within the system, this lawless option took shape.

"We are re-trying Henry Lawter for the murder of Hannah Sullivan," he said to Crenshaw. He let the pronouncement sit for a few seconds. "But not in my federal courtroom. He will be put on trial in a specially designed mobile courtroom. In secret. And you will put Lawter away for good. This time there will be no chance of reversal," Westlake said.

The men sat side-by-side, the knees of their pants muddy and stained. The cool, clear air did nothing to deter them. Crenshaw listened while the Judge explained.

"Years ago, I purchased a used tractor-trailer rig with tandem trailers through an offshore company I set up while I was in private practice. I've leased it out to shipping companies, a legitimate business venture that can never be traced back to me. Iggy and Marcus will outfit one trailer as a courtroom, and the other as living quarters. We can dispense justice on the road."

"Wait . . ." Crenshaw said.

"He who hesitates is lost, Robert. You want a second trial, I want a second trial, and we're going to have one. I'm not setting Lawter free so he can kill someone else. Now, Marcus and Iggy will take care of logistics, including extraction, transportation, security, and carrying out the sentence. I'll give them time to put the mission together before I release Lawter, and we'll need to be ready to move soon thereafter."

"So Cunningham and Perez are already committed?"

"Not yet. But they will be."

"How can you be so sure?"

"I know them. I know about their personal lives. I know what they did in Iraq, and not all of it was legit." He eyed Crenshaw, waiting for an objection. "I'll preside, and you'll prosecute. The only thing missing is a defense attorney."

"Why do we need a defense lawyer?" Crenshaw said. "It's not as if there's a chance of acquittal, right? We're not doing this . . . thing . . . putting ourselves at risk, with an idea that somehow Lawter is *not* guilty."

"Due process. Even a guilty man has a right to counsel," Westlake said. "And I think I've already found our man."

During his tenure on the federal bench, the Judge mentally catalogued the lawyers who appeared in his courtroom in criminal cases, sorting the attorneys by skill level, experience, and courtroom presence. At first, the list had no defined purpose, simply a subjective compilation of area lawyers by a bored Judge. But when the court of appeals reversed Lawter's conviction, the Judge ranked the candidates. David Johnstone topped the list. Johnstone had both prosecuted and defended murderers, and because he lived in Charlotte, his physical distance from the other team members would provide a geographical buffer and make it unlikely they would be seen together except on rare occasions.

"What do you think of David Johnstone?" the Judge asked.

Crenshaw tossed a few acorns over the side, listening to them rattle on the rocks before answering. "Good lawyer. I've had him on a few cases. I know he was once a prosecutor, but he defends the Constitution like it's his sister's reputation. Why do you think he would agree to do this?"

"He's going through a nasty, drawn-out divorce. His wife is cavorting with his law partner, now ex-law partner, and I think he wants to kill somebody." The Judge chuckled.

"Seems risky."

"He attended a good part of the Lawter trial in my courtroom," the Judge said. "I tried to get a read on him. He seemed almost pleased when Lawter was convicted."

"So if you're set on having a defense attorney, how do we approach him?" Crenshaw said.

"I think we should set up a meeting with him in Charlotte. The two of us. Under the guise of asking him to serve as an officer in the local chapter of the Federal Bar Association."

"What if he says no?"

"If he says no, and this ever comes back on us, then we have two credible witnesses with impeccable backgrounds who will say the conversation never happened. Johnstone was under a lot of stress because of the divorce and parting ways with his law partner, started to see conspiracies in every corner. Misunderstood us."

They found Johnstone a boiling cauldron of anger and frustration, with no place to direct the coming eruption. Surrounding a table in a corner booth at a restaurant in downtown Charlotte, and after several rounds of stiff drinks, they had to coax Johnstone very little before he admitted he had often contemplated ways to solve legal problems beyond the boundaries of the judicial system. He just couldn't bring himself to go beyond the stage of wishful thinking. Johnstone had read the appellate opinion reversing the Lawter conviction, and though he thought the court might be right on the law, he also thought it would be a perversion of justice if Lawter were to go free. Johnstone signed on to the team before their steaks were finished.

Back in Alpha trailer, Westlake slowly adjusted to the thin mattress, and sleep overtook him. There were no windows in the trailer to let in light. He dozed for a couple of hours until he felt a rumble, whether from within or without he could not tell. Then he felt the acceleration of the rig, the gentle swerve onto the highway.

They settled around the small oval table they used as a workspace and for meals. After an uncomfortable length of silence that led Westlake to fear the mission had been aborted, Cunningham spoke. "Mission accomplished. No civilian interruptions. No collateral damage."

"No collateral damage?" Crenshaw asked.

Cunningham turned his head to the voice. "We didn't have to hurt anyone else. I had to use the stun gun on him. He ran off for a few minutes. But no one spotted us, and we got him down to the beach without further incident. We left Lawter in the dunes with a needle sticking out of his arm. Looks like a drug overdose. He'll be found soon, if not already."

"So Lawter is dead?" Crenshaw said. "You're sure. Because if . . ."

"He's dead," Cunningham confirmed.

CHAPTER EIGHTEEN

Detective Jordan Summerhays presided over the gathering of evidence on the beach. The detective watched an evidence technician working within a cordoned area at the base of the dunes on the edge of Anastasia State Park. Though Saturday was his day off, he would probably have been at the beach that morning anyway, a little further south, either surf fishing or playing bocce ball with friends.

Two uniformed officers kept the public at bay, and though the evidence tech was still taking photographs of the body reclined against the dune, the detective's preliminary conclusion was that the man had died of a drug overdose. The needle sticking out of the man's arm was a telltale sign, and it would not have been the first accidental overdose Detective Summerhays had seen that year. Most of the junkies had the good sense to take their drugs in the comfort of the indoors, but perhaps this man had been camping in the park, or had simply wandered up the beach from one of the nearby hotels or rental houses, for the previous evening had been a mild one.

The evidence tech stood up and waved him over. Summerhays ducked beneath the ribbon of yellow tape and traversed the shifting sand, pitted with indentations, but not revealing any clear imprint of a shoe or foot.

"What do you think, Beth?"

Detective Summerhays had worked a few cases with Beth Roberts. They were both young, and the detective wondered whether she was attached.

"The guy's probably in his mid-thirties. No ID that I could find." She stripped off her rubber gloves. "Found a spoon and a lighter between his legs. Needle still in his left bicep. A vial of what looks like black tar heroin was stuffed in his sock. I'd guess a heroin overdose, but we won't know without a tox screen. No signs of foul play."

"How did he get here?"

"Still expecting miracles, I see. This sand's no good as evidence of anything. Ten seconds from now it will reveal different clues. A few hours ago, who could say? He's been dead a few hours, if I haven't mentioned that. If you haven't found an unattached car, or a bike, or a boat, I'd have to say he probably walked here. No way to tell whether he was alone or not."

"Anything peculiar about the body?"

"Peculiar? Not really. He's got a few tattoos, a couple that are common in prisoners. His teeth are in bad shape. Could be evidence of long-term drug use. Looks like he pissed himself at some point, but that would be consistent with an OD."

"All right. If you're done collecting evidence, I'll let the EMTs pick him up and take him to the morgue."

She snapped closed her evidence kit. "Done."

While two paramedics strapped the anonymous body to a stretcher, Detective Summerhays walked north up the beach. To his right, the Atlantic Ocean methodically played with its waves, and on his left stood windswept dunes that concealed the placid salt run. As ideas emerged, he made notes in his pocket-sized spiral notebook:

- Who is the decedent? Is he a local?

- If not a local, where was decedent staying?

- Did he buy the drugs here, or did he bring them in?

- Are there any signs of foul play?

- State Park. Call state investigators?

His stroll up the mostly deserted beach brought him to the northern tip of Conch Island. On a map, the island profile looks like a man staring at the mainland, a sharp nose and high forehead casting an accusatory glare. Summerhays stopped at the forehead and gazed across the inlet at Vilano Beach, peaceful and calm. Waves rolled into the Matanzas River, so named for the Spaniards' slaughter of French settlers four and a half centuries earlier. The detective absently wondered how much blood had spilled onto these shores. Nature, in her incessant remediation, seemed to have wiped away all traces.

By the time he arrived back at the dune where the man had been found, the detective was tired. Beth had cleared the scene and wrapped up the crime tape, her search for evidence fully concluded. She had left a small red flag at the base of the dune to remind him of the place the body was discovered, for without it, the man could have died one or two dunes over, in either direction. The detective's long trek up the beach had altered the position of the sun, and he now doubted the man had walked in from the north because it was a very long distance. That left only two other directions, unless the man had come in on a boat that had disappeared.

Summerhays sat down on the beach, facing the dunes. As he picked absently at his shoelaces, he noted a considerable amount of sand had worked its way into his running shoes. He checked his notes and the scant list of evidence unearthed so far. It still made no sense to him that a man would walk out onto the beach to shoot up, unless he had met a dealer out here late at night to purchase the drugs. That was certainly a possibility, especially if the dealer had come by boat.

As the sun began to drop from its apex, the detective smiled to himself and wrote down one more question – **Where did he get the spoon?**

CHAPTER NINETEEN

Judge Westlake walked across the green lawn to the seawall of the harbor and stood there for a long time gazing out at the tip of Conch Island, not far from the spot where Henry Lawter's life ended. The precise patch was hidden from his view by stretches of houses and sand, but not hidden from the view of his mind's eye. He pictured Lawter slumped against the dunes, his head lolled to the side, with a needle sticking out of his arm. Then he visualized the photograph of Hannah Sullivan lying in the snow, with forty-seven holes marring her body.

The Judge's Catholic upbringing and loyalty to the judicial oath battled with his sense of justice despite the system, all set against the backdrop of a Cherokee heritage that fought to understand and balance good and evil. Westlake did not believe Lawter was evil, but Lawter had certainly done evil things. So had he.

As he walked along the harbor, he justified himself with the excuse that he was fixing a flaw in the system. He pondered the notion that the Constitution was drawn by men at a time when the tyranny of a king was fresh in their blood, and how those protective shields of the law had often been beaten into swords by crafty lawyers and naive judges. For when the framers adopted the Constitution, they approached it as victims in need of protection from an oppressive foreign government. Nothing about the Lawter case involved an oppressive government. Why then, Westlake asked himself, should the rules not simply be adjusted as circumstances changed? He did not believe that breaking the rules in isolated cases would lead to chaos, especially when those very rules perpetuated the injustice in the first place. And as for taking the law into his own practiced hands, that is exactly what he had been selected to do, as confirmed by ninety-seven members of the United States Senate.

And yet, as he walked around the Castillo de San Marcos, where the Spaniards fought British invaders in an effort to maintain control of a sunbaked stretch of land when there were so many sunbaked stretches of land, he wondered whether the laws of the land had ensured any human progress at all. He stood before the fort's execution wall, some thirty feet high, craters from musket balls pocking its surface. He wondered how many men had been executed there, all without the luxury of a trial. With the shimmering bay off to their left, what had they thought about as other men aimed muskets at their chests? How much crimson blood had soaked into the coarse sand?

He crossed the street at the Bridge of Lions and walked through a throng of tourists to the Basilica Cathedral. The St. Augustine Catholic parish is the oldest in the country, and while the church is perhaps not as elaborately adorned as others, it has an old-world heft and a traditional feel, giving it undeniable gravitas. Westlake stood in the aisle, looking at crucified Jesus. He was trembling, so he knelt, crossed himself, and sat down in a pew. He bowed his head and closed his eyes.

It had been a long time since he'd gone to church, or prayed. Growing up in Atlanta, his father tried to raise him Catholic, while his mother secretly taught him the religion of the Cherokee Wolf Clan. He took communion in the morning, and at night his mother told him Cherokee legends. His favorite was the Wolves Within. She often sat on the end of his bed, her long dark hair braided, and told him the story in a deep whisper that could not be heard beyond the closed door.

"A young Cherokee brave was nearing manhood, and he had noticed the conflict that raged within him. Night and day the battle ensued, and he was in turmoil," she said. "So he went to the Tribal Chief for advice. As they sat around a campfire, the Chief, who was old and wise and had seen many battles and almost a thousand moons, said to the young brave – 'what you are feeling inside you is the battle between two wolves. One of the wolves is evil, filled with bad feelings such as anger, envy, jealousy, revenge, and false pride.' And the young brave asked, 'this wolf is inside of me?' And the Chief nodded, 'yes, this wolf is inside all of us. The other wolf inside of us is good. It is joy, peace, love, justice, truth, compassion and faith.' The young brave thought about this conflict for a time, wondering whether this battle between the wolves was causing his sleepless nights and the tumult in his belly. As they stared into the fire, the young brave asked: 'if these two wolves are fighting inside of me, which wolf will win this battle?' And the Chief turned to him with his lined face and said, 'the battle will be won by the wolf you feed'."

As he sat in a pew remembering his mother's voice, Raleigh Westlake realized that some time ago he had decided to feed both wolves. Each had to exist for the other to survive. There could be no good without evil; no love without hate. No justice without injustice. His renegade punishment of a man who had savagely ended the life of an innocent young woman epitomized the conflict. He knew it would never end. At least not for him.

Finding his way into a confessional booth, he crossed himself. "In the name of the Father, and of the Son, and of the Holy Spirit. My last confession was more than one year ago. Forgive me Father, for I have sinned. I have committed a mortal sin." Westlake did not look up as he knelt in the confessional with his eyes closed. No cushion for comfort, he knelt on a wooden rail, worn smooth by the knees of other repentant sinners. The wood bit into his shins.

"Last night I committed a terrible sin, but I did so out of virtue, to avenge a tragedy that this person had visited on a helpless girl." He paused then, remembering Bible passages taught in his Sunday school classes. *Judge not; that ye be not judged.* "I did this . . ." he could not bring himself to utter the word 'murder' in the church, "because the system that is supposed to be responsible for these things failed, and justice had to be done." *Vengeance is mine, sayeth the Lord.* "This was not vengeance at all, it was justice, pure and simple. Truth prevailed. I am sorry for this and all the sins of my past life." Westlake said three Hail Marys, then crossed himself again.

He left the confessional, allowing the door to remain open. He hurried from the church with his head bowed. The priest's side of the confessional was empty.

CHAPTER TWENTY

Caroline Bannister hung up the phone and swiveled her chair to look through the floor-to-ceiling windows at the Charlotte skyline. Night was falling, and the windows reflected her like a mirror. She swept the auburn hair from her forehead and adjusted the collar of her cream blouse, which had become canted over the course of the day.

She had just been notified, by a detective in St. John's County, Florida, that Henry Lawter had died of a drug overdose. Jordan Summerhays, whose voice sounded young, told her that Lawter had been found on the beach five days earlier with a needle sticking out of his arm. Given his criminal history, the detective was not surprised that Lawter had reached the end in this way, and neither was Caroline Bannister.

"So the ME has determined the cause of death as an accidental heroin overdose?" Caroline had asked distractedly.

"Not exactly. The ME has concluded he died of cardiac arrest, caused by a large amount of heroin in his system."

"Doesn't sound like much of a distinction. I appreciate you letting me know."

"There's something that's bothering me though," the detective said to prolong the conversation. "The ME found two marks on the deceased's chest that may have been caused by stun gun probes."

"Okay. Why is that interesting? He could have received those wounds from a prison guard or a whole host of other people."

"The wounds were fresh. I've already talked with the prison warden, and they have no record of Lawter being tased or being unruly at all during his prison stay, especially over the last month or two before his release. A bartender at the bar where he was drinking the night before says there was a scuffle involving Lawter, and he thought maybe they had taken the fight outside."

"Why are you telling me this, detective?" Caroline said in a bristly tone. "These marks on his chest, if they were made by a stun gun, could have been inflicted by these guys who he fought with. It seems like half the population has a Taser these days. I bought one myself. And if the ME has ruled it a drug overdose, what is there to investigate?"

"I don't know that there *is* anything to investigate. It's just that his body was found a few miles from the bar where he was drinking and a couple of miles from his hotel."

"So you're thinking why walk, or take a cab, or hitch that far if you're just going to shoot up?"

"Exactly."

"Maybe that's where his dealer was."

"That's certainly possible," the detective said. "There are a few known heroin dealers out on the island."

Caroline paused and pulled out the second drawer of her desk, on which she propped her bare feet.

"You know what Lawter did, don't you detective?"

"I've read some of the court file online. It looks like he got away with murder."

"Indeed. He killed a young woman up on Mt. Pisgah after she'd ridden her bike up there in a snowstorm. He confessed right there at the murder scene, but unknown to the two law enforcement officers, he was deaf at the time, probably because he punctured his own eardrums with an icepick. He was tried and convicted in federal court. It was a novel legal issue on the confession, but it ultimately was excluded by the court of appeals. There wasn't enough evidence to try him a second time around, so we had to dismiss the charges. He literally got away with murder."

"I'm just wondering if someone was bent on revenge," the detective said, a reach in his voice.

"You mean Hannah Sullivan's parents? I've met them and spent quite a bit of time with them, but I don't see either of them following Henry Lawter to . . . where did you say it was?"

"St. John's County. St. Augustine Beach."

"Atlantic side, right?"

"Right. About an hour south of Jacksonville."

"Anyway, I don't see Hannah's parents doing something like this. And I thought you said it was a heroin overdose."

"It was."

"So why would anybody kill someone in a method as elaborate as that, given that there are so many other ways to do it? Have you ever had a murder case where the deceased was killed by a drug overdose?"

"No, I haven't."

Caroline leaned back in her chair. She had become disinterested in the conversation. Detective Summerhays, whose average day probably involved stolen bicycles and drunk and disorderly conduct on the beach, seemed like he was stretching for something that wasn't there.

"I've got to let you go, detective. If you find something concrete, and your superiors or your DA thinks there's something to it, please let me know." She disconnected the call without waiting for a response. She had wanted to say that Lawter got what he deserved, that the forces of karma had converged at just the right moment over St. Augustine and had seen to it that justice was done, but it would seem beneath her office to make such a comment aloud.

The red lights atop various downtown buildings were blinking, and she allowed herself to fathom for a moment whether Sean and Rosalind Sullivan could have put together such a scheme. Certainly, they had motive. But she couldn't envision them doing it, or even hiring someone to do it. The whole thing was too elaborate.

Caroline vividly remembered the meeting with the Sullivans about whether she should seek the death penalty for Lawter. Rosalind Sullivan had been inconsolable and unresponsive for most of the meeting. Sean Sullivan told her that Lawter deserved the punishment his daughter had received, but what parent wouldn't say that? Caroline had not seen that fire in Sean Sullivan since, and she doubted he had the stomach for exacting revenge on anyone. In the moments after the jury's guilty verdict, Sean Sullivan had merely shaken his head in sadness. He had taken no pleasure from the pronouncement. And where would a man like Sean Sullivan find heroin? Or the cunning to kill someone?

CHAPTER TWENTY-ONE

Caroline presided over the weekly staff meeting, attended by all of the Assistant United States Attorneys in her district. Since the last meeting, she had her hair cut and re-styled, and a dash of color covered a few strands of gray. Starting with the AUSA on her left, each attorney summarized the cases for which they had primary responsibility. The briefings included prosecutions of drug trafficking, a human smuggling ring, bank fraud, and the civil cases to which the United States was a party.

Robert Crenshaw discussed an environmental pollution case he was prosecuting against one of the country's largest utilities, in which the United States of America was unfortunately outmanned and underfunded. He asked for three additional paralegals to help review and manage the hundreds of boxes of documents the utility company defendant had just delivered in a document dump. Caroline gave him one, to be re-assigned from the Charlotte office.

Satisfied she was up to speed on the major cases in her office, Caroline ended the meeting before noon. "We're done. Thanks for your hard work, everyone. Robert, please stay behind."

Once the conference room cleared, Crenshaw moved over to sit in the chair next to Caroline.

She flipped to a page in her almost-filled legal pad. "I had a conference call with a detective down in Florida yesterday. He told me Henry Lawter died of a drug overdose, on the beach no less."

"Interesting. I didn't know he'd gone down to Florida," Crenshaw said.

"Apparently. Anyway, I thought I'd give you my notes on the conversation. You can handle anything that comes up." She carefully tore out two pages of notes and handed them to Crenshaw.

"What do you mean if anything comes up?"

"Well, the detective, who seems very young, doesn't think everything adds up. For one thing, the body has some marks on it that look like maybe the guy was hit with a stun gun, and they found him a mile or two from his hotel, so the detective is trying to figure out how he got there and why he went so far just to shoot up."

Crenshaw clenched his hands under the long, rectangular table. "I don't know, maybe that's where he met his dealer or something."

"That's what I said," Caroline replied, pushing a lock of hair behind her ear. "Junkies do strange things. They don't follow predictable patterns. But I don't remember anything in Lawter's past about heroin use. I thought he was a meth addict."

"He was a meth addict. Maybe he graduated to heroin while in prison."

"Could be. The detective even asked me if I thought the Sullivans could have done this out of revenge, or hired someone to do it."

"The Sullivans?" Crenshaw chuckled. "I don't see them as being capable of killing anyone, much less doing it so it looks like a drug overdose. Do you think the Sullivans would even know where to get heroin?"

"No. Of course not. It's a ridiculous theory."

"Do you want me to look into this, Caroline?"

"No. I told the detective that if his superiors or his district attorney thought there was something worth investigating, to give us a call. I'll tell Doris to route any calls from Detective . . . What's his name?"

Crenshaw looked at her notes. "It looks like Summerhays."

"From Detective Summerhays to you."

"Okay."

Caroline appraised her top lieutenant for a moment. She knew he had been devastated by the reversal of Lawter's conviction. As a form of penance, she had made him draft the press release announcing that the US Attorney's Office would not be re-trying Henry Lawter for Hannah Sullivan's murder.

"How are you doing Robert? Personally, I mean."

"I'm fine. Everything's going well at home. It's just that this environmental case has got me hopping. We're outgunned about ten to one on this thing, and we've got 782 boxes of documents to review, analyze and organize."

"When did those come in?"

"Last week."

"And the company is claiming none of these documents is electronically stored?"

"You got it. These are mostly design and construction documents from when the retention ponds were built decades ago. Nobody was storing documents on a computer back then."

"We know the trick. It's an old one. I used it myself when I was in private practice. Ship the opposition truckloads full of crap when there's only about a shovelful of important information to be found. If you bury it deep enough, maybe it will never be found."

"That's why I need more paralegals," Crenshaw said, reviving his earlier request.

"I can see that. All right. I'll give you the authority to hire two more, but only on a temporary basis."

"Thanks. That will help."

"And on this Lawter thing. Don't worry about it, Robert. I know I was tough on you when the appellate court reversed his conviction. It wasn't your fault. It's a case of first impression, and it could have gone either way. And I know you worked your ass off trying to put the case back together again. I'm sure it wasn't fun going to the DA with hat in hand."

"No, especially given that we wrestled the case away from him the first time."

"I remember. So, was Anderson a smug son of a bitch when you asked him to take a look at it?"

"Smiled like the Grinch. I laid everything out for him, even took the Sullivans with me, but he didn't let me get very far before he shut it down."

"Can't blame him," Caroline said. "But he doesn't need to rub our noses in it."

"Yeah, and he's running for re-election, so he doesn't need the flak."

"Well, guys like Lawter, they live on the edge. Something like this was bound to happen. Maybe he got what he deserved after all."

CHAPTER TWENTY-TWO

Jordan Summerhays sat in a rocking chair on the front porch of the Sullivans' house, sipping a glass of sweet tea and gazing out at the marsh. "So tell me about your daughter," he said.

"She was a wonderful girl," Rosalind said. "Bright, pretty, ambitious. Everything you could ever hope for in a child. She was our only one." Rosalind dipped her head to hide tears.

"She was training to become a professional cyclist," Sean added. "That's what she was doing up there on the mountain that day, before . . . before that animal killed her. She rode up there by herself, to test herself. She was always doing that. Testing her limits."

"So how did you feel when Henry Lawter was set free?"

"How do you think we felt?" Sean said with irritation. "That there's no justice in this world. Certainly not for our Hannah. This guy killed her, admitted it, and a jury convicted him. Then he just walks, with no repercussions. I was mad as hell. I'm still mad as hell that he's walking around free while our daughter is in the ground."

"It's not fair," Rosalind managed.

"Detective, you were a little cryptic on the phone about why you wanted to see us," Sean said. "Something about another investigation involving Lawter?"

Summerhays scanned their faces. "That's right. I'm just tying up some loose ends. Henry Lawter died down in St. Augustine. About two weeks ago."

"He's dead?" Rosalind asked. "You're sure?"

Summerhays nodded. "Yes, absolutely certain."

"Good," Sean said. "He didn't deserve to live."

A few moments passed in silence.

"How did he die?" Sean asked.

"Drug overdose, it appears," Summerhays said. "I can't say too much, because it's still an ongoing investigation."

"Investigation? What is there to investigate?" Rosalind said.

"As I said, I can't disclose very much. But it's possible that someone killed Henry Lawter. There are just some things that don't add up."

"If that's what happened, whoever did it deserves a medal," Sean said.

Summerhays rocked slowly, watching white birds flutter above the marsh grass. He decided there was nothing else he needed to ask. "Well, thank you for your time. Again, I'm very sorry for your loss."

He shook hands with the Sullivans, then walked down the short brick path to his rental car. His captain had given him approval to interview the Sullivans in person, the only potential lead in a possible homicide that didn't look like a homicide to anyone but Jordan Summerhays. The medical examiner had officially listed the cause of death as a heart attack due to a heroin overdose. The burns on Lawter's torso may have come from a stun gun, probably inflicted sometime in the forty-eight-hour window before death, but could not be conclusively related to his death, the autopsy report said.

As he drove toward the airport, he reviewed the short conversation in his head, not just the words, but the expressions on the faces of Hannah Sullivans' parents. Rosalind Sullivan was still incapable of anything but grief. Sean Sullivan was stunned when he told them that Henry Lawter was dead. Genuinely stunned. Although Hannah's father showed obvious anger, Summerhays was convinced he had nothing to do with Henry Lawter's death. He wound his way along the road on the edge of the marsh, certain he had reached a dead end in his investigation.

CHAPTER TWENTY-THREE

In between, killers live like the rest of us. They adopt normal lives to hide in plain sight. And so it was for Judge Westlake after he returned from killing Henry Lawter. He resumed his duties on the federal bench, a routine he found increasingly monotonous and unrewarding. From the lawyers who appeared before him, arguing esoteric points of law, the arguments sounded more and more like blather. Everything took on a hue of mundane gray.

He found some solace at the lake house on Fontana, a house he and Heather had purchased while they were still living in Atlanta. The house was surrounded by five acres, mostly wooded. At first, they spent the occasional weekend there, but after moving to Asheville they stayed at the lake house more frequently. Heather had loved the house and the lake views, and when she was diagnosed with breast cancer, it was the place she had gone to convalesce. She died on the screened porch watching the water and listening to the lonesome cry of the loons.

The Judge sat in a rocking chair, staring out at the mist rising from Lake Fontana.

"You would love this morning H," he said to a ceramic urn holding Heather's ashes. "The sun is just peeking over the ridge, and the fog is hovering over the water like a movie set on the English moors. Trout season is just around the corner. I need to get out my gear and check over it. I bet there are some big ones down deep just waiting for warm weather." He sipped from a mug of coffee and scanned familiar surroundings. He felt comfortable in the lake house, a blend of wood and stone that brought nature inside.

With Heather gone and Lawter dead, he needed something to do, something to distract him from what he had done. A project, a big project, a months-long project he could throw himself into with vigor. He got up and ambled into his den. The enlarged photograph of Hannah Sullivan anchored one corner. He knew he should return it to the courthouse, but he hadn't been able to let her go. He slid into the high-backed chair behind

106

his desk and gazed at Hannah, her blond hair and blue eyes, the dazzling smile of promise. The daughter he and Heather lost to a miscarriage would have been about Hannah's age.

The Judge rubbed his right shoulder, realizing how out of shape his muscles had become. The hours of sitting, reading briefs or staring into his computer, had turned him old. He needed to go for a run.

He set out on a trail at the Tsali recreation area, a trail that wound through the woods, emerging at points along the water's edge. The air was crisp, and a gentle breeze swirled the mist off the water, revealing its smooth, grey surface. His gait was steady, if not springy, as he glided down a path still covered with a dusting of last fall's pine needles and leaves.

The hour sped by as he navigated the woods, and he returned to the parking lot with an accelerated burst. With hands on hips he warmed down and then walked to his car, where he found a man breaking into his Mercedes. The man, wearing a dirty trench coat, had wedged a wire coat hanger between the window and the rubber weather seal and was trying to trip the door lock. The Judge stopped about thirty feet away.

"You might want to stop that," he said.

The man turned around. The hanger remained in the door. He had a medium length beard, unkempt, and a black watch cap covered his head. "This your car?"

"It is. But whether it's my car or someone else's, you're about to get yourself into a bit of trouble."

The man didn't move.

"What are you doing? Looking for money, or were you going to steal it?"

"Money. You left your wallet on the seat." The man thrust both hands in his coat pockets and tilted his head toward the car beside him.

Westlake eyed him, wondering if the man had a gun or other weapon concealed in his coat. He glanced around to pick an exit route in case the man threatened him. He had read a recent report on de-escalation and remembered that keeping an intruder engaged might prevent violence. "You from around here?" Westlake said.

"No, I ain't. What's it to you anyway?"

"Well, you were obviously trying to break into my car. Just wondering if you know who I am."

"Not a clue," the man said.

"People know me around here. I'm a judge."

"That so?"

"It is. Listen. I'd be happy to give you a little money. It might help you out a little, save me the trouble of having to fix a broken lock or a broken window. Might even save you a trip to jail."

The man's shoulders slumped a little. "How much?"

"How about twenty dollars. I don't carry cash usually, but I've probably got twenty handy."

"You've probably got a lot more than that handy. How about fifty dollars?"

Westlake took a step toward the man and his car. "Look. This isn't a negotiation. You could be in a lot of trouble here, and I'm offering to help you out. Now step away from my car. I'll see what I've got in my wallet."

The man moved off a few steps but remain fixed on the car.

Westlake went around to the passenger side, putting the car between himself and the vagrant, then unlocked the door with the metal key. Keeping an eye on the man, he looked inside his wallet and saw that he had about seventy dollars in bills. He took out two twenties and folded them in one hand. He closed the passenger door and looked at the man over the roof.

"I'll give you money, but first I need you to take your hands out of your pockets."

The man complied immediately.

Westlake stepped around the back of the car and over to the man, whose hands were still hanging by his sides. As he came within a few feet he could smell the mixture of sweat and grime that emanated from the man's body. He reached out a hand with the folded bills. "Here, take it."

The man reached out one hand and took the bills. "Thanks," he said, then turned and walked away into the woods.

Westlake watched him trudge down the path. When the man had walked out of sight, Westlake removed the wire hanger from his car door. He considered calling 911 to report the encounter, but quickly dispensed with the notion. There was no point.

As he drove home, he felt compelled to visit his mother for the first time in weeks. Joyce Littlefield lived in a small house on the Qualla Boundary. Since Heather had died nineteen months ago, he had been seeing less of his mother. He didn't know why. He was no busier than anyone else's son.

Maybe it was the Reservation, the feeling it gave him. The strips of businesses catering to tourists, bracketed by run-down houses, reminded him of roots he was unwilling to fully acknowledge. Since the casino and the twin hotel towers had been built, Cherokee had flourished. The gambling enterprise generated a lot of money for the Eastern Band of Cherokee Indians. Half of the gambling bounty was distributed in semiannual payments to tribal members, including Judge Raleigh Westlake and his mother.

He turned onto Old Mission Road and stopped at his mother's house, a modest modular home set back from the road amid towering trees. He went through the unlocked front door and found his mother in the living room, watching the news on a flat screen television.

He bent down to hug her in her recliner. "Well son, it is so good to see you. I just knew today you would come to visit."

"Did someone call you to tell you I was in the village?"

Joyce smiled. "Just a mother's intuition."

"Just your intuition, right."

"No. Dorothy called me a few minutes ago. Said she saw your car over by the casino."

"I figured. Well, I haven't been out this way very much in the past few months. I've been very busy." In fact, he had been spending almost every weekend at the Fontana house, not thirty minutes away.

"It's okay Raleigh," I understand. "Unless you're coming out to gamble, this ain't exactly a destination for most people."

"I wish I could get you to move into the lake house. It's much bigger and has a great view of Fontana."

"You've got too many floors for an old woman to navigate," she said. "I've got everything I need here." She spread her arms.

"All right. I've been trying to persuade you for years, and I can see I haven't made any headway."

"Besides, you don't want your old mother moving into your house."

It was true, but he rebutted her contention nonetheless. "Not at all. I wouldn't insist if I didn't want you to do it."

"Okay, I'll do it. I'll move in with you."

His eyes widened in surprise.

She pointed a finger at him and laughed. "See. It's right there in your face. You think you can fool your mother. You don't want me to live with you."

His face turned red. "All right. All right. You got me. How about I take you to lunch?"

She pushed a button on a remote and her chair tipped up and forward, making it easy for her to stand. She was seventy-three and recently had her left hip replaced.

"How is your hip?" he asked.

"Stiff, but it doesn't hurt. I'm still going to physical therapy about once a week."

As his mother straightened, he was struck by how frail she looked. Her long hair, once lustrous and dark, had turned grey years earlier but now had an unhealthy, wiry consistency to it, like a nest of steel wool. Raleigh remembered how his father had been enamored with his mother's hair, buying her brushes, combs and barrettes. She had lost more weight since he had seen her last. Her blouse and skirt hung loosely from her frame. Her face was a younger face, high cheekbones covered with rust-colored skin, not yet fully consumed by wrinkles. Dark eyes had retained their brightness.

She noted his examination. "Yes son, I'm getting old. Beats the alternative."

"Are you still going to church?"

"Not much these days. It doesn't do much for me anymore."

"Okay. I'm just concerned that you're isolating out here, all by yourself."

"That's what old people do, isn't it? Especially after they've lost their family."

"You haven't lost your family. Well, father is gone, but that was thirty years ago. I'm still here."

"Rarely," she said. "And Heather's gone. I miss her."

"I miss her too, mom."

"I used to talk to her almost every day. She didn't much like living out at the lake, so far from everybody else."

"What are you talking about? She loved the lake."

"No, she didn't," Joyce said firmly. "She loved you. You don't know everything about your wife."

He began to respond but knew that he, a well-trained and seasoned lawyer, could not win this argument with his mother. He held the door open for her as she struggled into the car. He slid into the driver's seat, turned the ignition, and was greeted with a beep announcing the passenger seat belt was not engaged. Pulling the seatbelt across his mother's torso he said, "You have a death wish?"

"No such thing. I just assume my son is a safe driver."

"Well, let's just say we did it to stop the infernal beeping from the dashboard."

"We can say that."

Raleigh looked at his mother, who stared straight ahead through the windshield. "Are you still driving, mom?"

"Sometimes. If I need something from just down the street. Madeleine or Dorothy drive me if I need to go further."

"How's your eyesight? Without your glasses?"

"Keen as an eagle's," she said.

"Uh-huh."

They had been like this, mother and son, for as long as he could remember, or at least since they had both moved to the area almost twelve years earlier. It was good-natured jousting that rarely turned acrimonious. They had been through the tribulations of Harleigh Westlake's long, slow decline, a period over which Raleigh's admiration for his mother had grown. She had stayed in the vast, empty Atlanta house for almost twenty years after her husband died, continuing in earnest the charity work that her husband had endured only because it was good for his business. After Raleigh and Heather left Atlanta for the federal bench in Asheville, Joyce became lonely, and Raleigh moved his mother back to the Qualla Boundary. He tried to persuade her to move to Asheville so they would be closer, but she had insisted upon living by herself.

On the Rez, Judge Westlake was still viewed as a transplant from Atlanta. On the other hand, his mother had merely returned home after a forty-year journey.

"The election's coming up," she said.

"Election?"

"Tribal Chief."

"I thought that was in September."

"It's the primary. Patrick's running again, and Keith Blackstone."

"Okay."

"You could throw your hat in the ring."

"I'm not eligible. You have to live on the Rez for at least two years."

"Sell your condo in Asheville and move back."

"Mom, I've got a full-time job in Asheville. I'm a federal judge, remember?" He was not willing to trade his lifetime federal appointment for a position overseeing bickering clans of the Cherokee nation. Some of the inter-clan disputes originated hundreds of years earlier, before the

Europeans settled in the area, before more than half of the Cherokee were forced to march west before the Civil War. Many of the long-simmering disputes centered around land ownership, though there was a bit of racism between the full-blooded Cherokee and those whose native blood had been spoiled by the Europeans. Raleigh was of Cherokee and Irish descent, though he carried more of the aquiline features of his father's family. His skin was considerably lighter than his mother's.

They pulled into the parking lot of Granny's diner. "This okay?"

"Sure, been eating here once a week for most of my life."

"You lived in Atlanta for forty years, more than half of your life," Raleigh countered.

"It seems like a small blip in the history of time," she said. "A time I'd like to forget. Except for you, son." She patted his leg and smiled.

The owner greeted and seated them. "Joyce, good to see you. Judge, an unexpected treat to see you this afternoon." He held out his hand, and Westlake shook it. "I'll bring you some water and utensils. Buffet? The roast beef is exceptional today," he said, scurrying off.

"I think he has said the roast beef is exceptional almost every time I've come in here," Raleigh said.

"And it usually is," said his mother.

Raleigh helped her navigate the buffet, heaping mashed potatoes, green beans, creamed corn and roast beef on her plate. It was enough food for two days. Raleigh circumnavigated the salad bar and loaded his plate.

"The roast beef is exceptional today," she said between bites. Pointing her fork at his salad, she said, "You're ain't ever going to build muscle if you don't eat some red meat, get some protein."

He put down his fork. "Mother, I'm fifty-three years old, and I don't think I could build muscle if I ate nothing but protein. Moreover, I don't want to build muscle."

"You could if you ordered that muscle milk."

"I see. I like my body trim. I'm very fit. I run three or four times a week, you know. Went for a run this morning, in fact. I'm training for a marathon."

"Your father was disappointed that you never played football or baseball."

"Yes, he told me that. Quite often as I recall," he said.

"He was proud of you for what you did accomplish. College, law school."

"He never told me that."

"No, probably not. He wasn't that kind of man. Stingy with the praise. Kept things inside mostly. Probably what caused his heart attack."

"Oh, his heart attack couldn't have been caused by the heavy drinking, his weight, his lack of exercise, or his cigar smoking?" Raleigh said, rolling his eyes.

"Maybe that contributed. But people who keep things bottled up, increases their cortisol level, and that stresses the heart."

"I see. Have you been reading the New England Journal of Medicine?"

"No. Saw it on television. And don't say it ain't true just because it was on television."

"I wasn't going to say that. In fact, I know it's true, but that doesn't mean it's what killed him."

"Confession's good for the soul. Psalms."

"John Wesley said that," he corrected her. "Look, let's not argue about this, or anything else."

"Who's arguing, Raleigh? We're just talking here. A mother and her son, who she hardly sees anymore."

"Look, I've been . . ."

She cut him off. "Busy. I know you've been busy. So tell me, Mr. Busy, about some of these cases you're working on that keep you so busy in Asheville."

"You know I can't discuss any of the cases with you. At least until the case is over."

"Then tell me about some of the ones that are over."

"Do you really want to hear about those? It's boring stuff. A lot of drug cases, and civil cases with people suing each other over money."

"And murder," she said with a mouthful of food.

"I don't handle murder cases. Well, only one in my entire career."

"And he got off, didn't he?"

He looked up from his salad. "He was convicted, but his conviction was reversed on appeal. How do you know about that?"

"People out here ain't stupid, Raleigh. We have the internet you know. People watched that case pretty closely. It was terrible what that man did to that young girl."

A waitress appeared to refill his mother's glass with tea. She had long, strawberry-blonde hair and green eyes.

"More tea?" she asked.

"Yes, sweet tea, please."

Westlake watched her walk away.

She glanced back over her shoulder, a look of something on her face. What was it?

"Where were we? Yes, the Lawter case. It was terrible. And people around here were following the case, you say?"

His mother nodded.

"Really. That's surprising. They know the jury verdict got reversed?" He chewed a fork of salad.

"They know you got reversed. Looks to people out here like that murderer got off because you made some kind of mistake. They still talk about it."

He stared at his mother for a few seconds, a chill working down his spine. He glanced around the restaurant. Their waitress must have gone into the kitchen. He could not see anyone obviously looking at him. No one appeared to be eavesdropping.

"But I guess he got his in the end," she said.

"What do you mean?"

"He's dead. Drug overdose. In Florida. About three or four weeks ago."

He stopped chewing. His ears seemed to fill, and he no longer heard the clink of silverware or the gabble of conversation from nearby tables or the clatter of dishes. The long silence became uncomfortable. "I didn't know that."

"You didn't know, Raleigh? You'd think that a bigwig like you, and a machine as big as the federal government, would know all about something like that. A criminal you set free, and you didn't know?"

"Well, I didn't know." He repeated the lie to his mother. "How did you hear about it?"

"Someone told me about it. I don't know who. Found it on the internet, I think."

"I see. Well, I'm finished with my salad."

"I'm done too. It's all I can eat." Her plate was less than half-finished. "I'll take the rest home for dinner."

He dropped her off at the house, helped her as she limped through the front door. He made an excuse as to why he couldn't spend the afternoon with her. He drove back to the lake house, stunned that his mother had been following the Lawter case, that she knew Lawter was dead. Though their team was still operating in secret, minor connections were being made at random. Apparently, the general public now knew that the confessed killer he had set free was dead. He hoped the suicide story would stick, that no one would investigate. He could not shake the look his mother had given him when he lied to her. He had no reason to believe his mother knew anything other than what she told him, but he had no confirmation she had told him everything she knew about Lawter. Mothers know their sons.

CHAPTER TWENTY-FOUR

The five of them gathered around the poker table at the lake house, chips neatly stacked on the green felt. They played Texas Hold'em, attempting to bluff each other while a placid lake shimmered the moon.

David Johnstone held two jacks. He scanned the faces of the others, looking for tells. Through the months he had grown to know them all better, their facial expressions and mannerisms, the subtle eye movements. Furtive talk of secret trials and executions could expose a man's thoughts. Marcus Cunningham was the most difficult to read. Perhaps he had learned to mask his emotions and thoughts while on tour in Iraq. Crenshaw, on the other hand, frequently revealed the strength or weakness of his cards. When he bluffed, his eyes searched and darted, and his hand flitted about his forehead, either stroking his eyebrows or fiddling with a strand of hair. When Crenshaw's hand was good, his countenance became more relaxed as he stared off into the distance. Right now, Crenshaw was bluffing.

"Robert, your bet." The Judge broke the silence.

Crenshaw looked at the growing pot of poker chips. "It's . . ."

"Two dollars to you. David raised."

Crenshaw stared at a nothing hand, his left index finger running along his eyebrow. "I'll see your two bucks and raise you five."

Perez, Cunningham and Westlake folded in quick succession. Johnstone scanned the five cards upturned on the table. There was nothing there, four cards from different suits, except for the Jack of Spades, giving him three of a kind. He tossed a five-dollar chip into the pot and called.

Crenshaw turned over his cards, revealing a pair of threes, seemingly surprised that Johnstone had the better hand.

Johnstone raked the small pot of chips toward him. "Look," he said, "I don't know how this is supposed to work, but I'm assuming we're sitting here playing poker, enjoying our host's liquor, because at some point we're going to—how should I put this—conduct another trial?"

"It's only been six months since Lawter," Crenshaw said.

"There's no timetable, Robert," Judge Westlake said. "It could be six weeks, six months, or longer. It all depends on when we identify someone who has committed a heinous crime and eluded punishment. It's all about dispensing justice. It doesn't matter how long in between, as long as we're careful. Anybody disagree?"

Nobody said anything.

"Iggy, Marcus, you guys are in charge of logistics. What do you think?"

Perez started. "It all depends on the target. Who is it? Where is he? Circumstances. Defenses. Well, maybe defenses. Depends. Best to vary the MO so we don't establish a pattern."

"Vary the MO. Like do it a different way?" Johnstone said.

"Yeah," Marcus said. "People get into routines. We don't want to establish a routine for our missions. When my team was given a target in Iraq, sometimes we knew the target's daily habits, sometimes we didn't. Everybody has a routine, and once we knew the established routine, the guy was toast. So we don't want to get into a routine. The where, when, and how, those need to be different in each case."

Westlake nodded. "I agree. We vary our routine, so there's no pattern. We don't go to the same geographical area more than once. We carry out the sentence in a different way. Without a pattern, each one is just a random, unsuspicious, accidental death."

"Right, Judge. Different place, different method of execution. Everything made to look like an accident," Cunningham confirmed.

"All right," Johnstone said. "I have a case for us to consider. This crime was every bit as heinous as Lawter."

"Close by?" Crenshaw asked.

"Eastern part of the state, near New Bern."

"So tell us about it," Westlake said.

Johnstone told them about a parent who had made pornographic movies of the children when they were still in their adolescent years. Some of the movies involved sex with adults, some involved sex with animals. The parent sold the videos for drugs, or money for drugs.

"One of the kids lives in Charlotte now. I recently represented him on a drug possession charge. He's all screwed up from what happened to him as a kid."

"And his father did this to him and his siblings?" Crenshaw asked.

"No, not his father. His mother."

"The mother. Jesus Christ," Crenshaw said. "The things people do to their kids."

"Terrible things," Perez said. "Some buddies told me that in Afghanistan parents would send their kids out to play soccer in a suspected minefield because the Taliban wanted the field cleared. Threatened to kill the whole family if they didn't comply. The parents promised the kids that if they got blown up they would go to heaven for doing Allah's will."

"There are a lot of bad people in the world," Westlake said. "We can't avenge everything. Tell us more about the mother. Did she get prosecuted?"

"Not according to the son. This porno ring was part of a bigger gang, and she rolled over and testified against the gang. Cut a deal in exchange for her testimony, and in return they cut her loose. Served some probation on a drug possession charge, but that was it. She was never prosecuted for child abuse, statutory rape, exploitation of a minor, nothing like that."

"So some defense attorney like you got her off," Crenshaw said with a bit of venom.

"Yeah, I guess so Robert. And some prosecutor thought her testimony was valuable enough to get probation for her," Johnstone shot back. "So anyway, after her release she stayed clean for a while. Odd jobs, that sort of thing. Her son says she's back into the drugs, maybe selling again. And get this. The son says she's babysitting neighbor kids at her house while their parents are at work."

"Holy shit," Cunningham said.

"And the son is worried she's going to do it again?" Westlake said. "This time not to her own kids."

"Right."

Westlake spoke again. "You may be right, David. She may be worse than Lawter. He killed one person, though a vibrant young woman. This one you're talking about, she wrecked the lives of her own children. Probably others as well. There's no telling how far this goes."

"One of the daughters killed herself last year," Johnstone added. "Left a note saying she couldn't live any longer with what her mother had done to her."

Perez said, "Plus, if the mother is dealing drugs, no telling how many of her customers may have died from overdoses, or hurt or killed somebody to get money to support the habit."

"I don't know about all that, but I think she's a candidate for a trial," Johnstone said. "The sexual abuse went on for almost three years. The oldest child, my client, is nineteen now. The sister who is still alive lives with foster parents."

"Hold on," Crenshaw interjected. "Isn't she a likely target for a hit by the drug gang she turned on? Somebody's bound to get her even if we don't lift a finger."

"You're not getting cold feet, are you Robert?" Westlake asked.

"No. It's just, as a prosecutor, I've got some questions."

Johnstone responded. "Well, could be. But the drug gang was in Charlotte, prosecuted and convicted awhile back, and she's changed her name and moved down east. Maybe somebody's after her, maybe not. I can certainly gather more info on her and put together a file."

"I'm interested," Cunningham said.

Perez nodded agreement.

"But no files, David," Westlake said. "No paper trail. No links. Will your client suspect your involvement if his estranged mother suddenly winds up dead?"

"I thought about that. To make it safe for all of us, maybe I should stay out of it."

"You can't stay out of it, David. Everybody has a role to play. Robert prosecutes, I judge, and you have to defend her."

Johnstone rubbed his jaw. "I figured it would have to be that way. That's what I signed on for. But to keep suspicion off the entire group, I was thinking that if I'm physically somewhere else, then that allays suspicion since I'm the only link."

Nobody said anything for a time. There were no rules for their endeavor, only that loyalty was imperative.

"Let's put it to a vote," Westlake said, breaking the silence. "It has to be unanimous, or we don't do it. That's the rule from now on. Robert, you first."

"Look," Crenshaw said, "I don't want to be the guy to say no. But this case is different than Lawter. Lawter confessed. We know he did it. He didn't even deny it. We don't know anything about this woman. Her son could be lying about the whole thing. Nineteen-year-old kid might have an axe to grind with his mother over something she did that's far less heinous than what he's accused of. Maybe he told you this stuff so the judge would go easier on him on the possession charge. What proof do we have other than his accusation?"

"I've seen one of the tapes." Johnstone got up from the poker table, retrieved a video tape from his overnight bag, and set it on the table. "I've already watched it, and I don't care to watch it again. But if you guys want proof, the mother is on the tape. With the kids."

"Pass," Crenshaw said.

Westlake took control. "No, Robert. We have to watch it. Aside from the allegations of the son, who can't testify, it's the sum total of our evidence, pure and simple. This video either establishes her guilt beyond question, or we don't prosecute her." Westlake picked up the videotape from the table. "Which one is she, David?"

"Blonde. Big woman. You'll know."

Westlake slid the tape into the VCR, and they watched. The scenes, apparently filmed with a home video camera on a tripod that swiveled, were graphic. Even Perez and Cunningham, who had seen some of the worst atrocities that one human can inflict on another, watched in stunned silence and frequently averted their eyes.

"I've seen enough," Crenshaw said after only a few minutes. "Turn it off. Turn it off." When the screen went black, Crenshaw said, "I vote to put her on trial. She does not deserve to be walking around with the rest of us."

The vote was unanimous.

CHAPTER TWENTY-FIVE

Elise Rutherford sat on a plastic chair. She had a gag in her mouth and a dark hood over her head. The gag tasted like new cloth. Both her hands and her feet were bound with zip ties. There were two irregular holes in the back of her camouflage-patterned tee shirt where the Taser leads had struck her, and two rough burn marks on the middle of her back. The burns looked like partially healed bullet holes. They felt like cigarette burns.

Though an air conditioner hummed steadily, a steady stream of sweat ran down her brow. She jerked her hands and feet in a futile effort to free herself. No one had spoken in her presence since she had been abducted. She did not know where she was, or who had kidnapped her. She did not know why. Her black sweat pants were dirty. She may have soiled herself. Beneath the hood her eyes were wide with terror and fury. As she kicked her feet, the chair on which she was sitting, overburdened with her weight, tipped up off the floor. She felt a heavy hand push down on her shoulder. She stopped kicking. She growled through the gag and hood, but it came out unintelligible, a feral grunt. A hand pinched a nerve running up the side of her neck. A sharp pain shot up the back of her head.

She heard metal creak and a door open somewhere nearby, and then close again. Hard-soled shoes thudded across a thin carpet covering a wooden floor, the sound hollow. She guessed the shoes belonged to two people, four feet. Chairs rolled and then sighed with weight. A wisp of cologne seeped through the cloth into her nostrils. Then silence. She rotated her head to see if any light could penetrate a loose thread in the hood, but she remained in utter darkness.

She heard the scrape of the metal door again, and then a man's voice next to her said, "All rise." It was a deep voice, an official voice. She felt two strong hands lifting her up under each armpit. To keep from falling, she shuffled forward, keeping her feet under her. The wounds on her back stung. The thump thump of heavy feet, of intentionally heavy feet, came from somewhere in front of her.

"All right, be seated." His voice was higher, a hint of raspiness.

121

The strong hands moved from her armpits to the front of each shoulder and gently pushed her back into the chair. She was being maneuvered by strong men accustomed to handling people such as her.

"Any trouble, gentlemen?"

"No sir," two voices said in unison. The cadence was clipped, maybe military.

"Before we remove her hood, let me remind everyone that no names other than the defendant's name should be spoken during this proceeding." There was a slight pause. "All right, remove her hood."

Two of the hands released the cord lock at the back of her head that kept the hood cinched around her neck. The hood came off slowly, and the light from bright fluorescents forced her to close her eyes. She blinked several times until her pupils adjusted. With the gag still tight in her mouth, she looked at her surroundings. She saw two men seated at identical small tables, six or eight feet in front of her, against the side wall. Both men were wearing suits and rubber masks. They had their heads turned away from her. At the front of the room sat a man in a black robe. He perched behind a large desk on a platform a foot or so above the floor. He also wore a dark mask that covered his entire face. The walls and ceiling of the room were covered with a dark material ridged with tiny pyramids. The carpet was thin and the color of blood.

"Now, Ms. Rutherford," the man at the front said with some level of dignity. "I am the Judge in this trial. The man closest to me is the prosecutor." The man turned slightly so that she could see he was wearing an identical black mask. She saw around the sides of the mask that the man was white, and his hair was a nondescript brown.

"The man seated closest to you is the defense attorney, your lawyer, who has been appointed by the court to represent you in this case." The second man turned so she caught a glimpse of his identical black mask. There were tiny slits at the eyes, but she could not see the man's eyes.

Elise Rutherford tried to shout through the gag, but no real words came out. Even to herself she sounded like a squealing hog about to have its throat slit. She didn't understand what this man was talking about. *A trial. How could there be a trial? I haven't even been accused of anything.*

"Before we get started, we have a couple of ground rules. First, I will have your gag removed if and only if you promise not to yell or scream. If you yell or scream, then the gag will be replaced, and if you cause a disruption of any type in my courtroom, the stun gun may be used on you again. Do you understand? Nod your head if you understand."

She stared back at the Judge and nodded her head.

"Second, no matter what is going through your head, you will at all times show respect for all of the people in this courtroom, including me. No outbursts. You will speak only when I ask you a question. You will not use any foul language. You will direct your responses only to me. Nod if you understand."

She nodded.

"You may remove the gag, but be ready to subdue Ms. Rutherford at the first sign of disruption or disrespect."

A man stepped from behind her and tugged down the gag. She caught a momentary glimpse of his black mask and dark skin beneath.

"Now Ms. Rutherford, I will ask you to stand up while the charges against you are read. The officers will assist you."

She was pulled to her feet, and she caught the whiff of excrement soiling her pants. "My back hurts," she said.

"Well, Ms. Rutherford I am sorry to hear that. But I asked you not to speak unless I ask you a question. And you agreed to that, didn't you?"

"Yes, I agreed."

"All right. Let's stick with the simple rules I laid down, or the gag will be reinstated."

"Ms. Rutherford, you are charged with endangering your three children, sodomizing your three children, exploiting your three minor children for sexual purposes, statutory rape, child abuse, child neglect, child abandonment, and engaging in the making of and distribution of child pornography. There are probably other charges that could be brought, but those are all I need to mention at the moment."

How could they know about that? How could anyone know about that? The charges were dropped. I was given immunity. The prosecutor told me the file would be sealed. Not to protect me, but to protect the kids.

"Now, I am going to ask you how you plead in response to these charges, but before you say anything, I want you to know that we have a videotape showing you engaging in these acts with your minor children. All three of them. Think about that before you answer. Now, how do you plead Ms. Rutherford?"

"I don't know what the fuck you're talking about up there." A thumb pressed hard into one of the wounds in her back. "Ow, shit man."

"Watch your language," one of the black masks admonished her.

"How do you plead, Ms. Rutherford?"

"I don't want to plea at all. All those charges were dropped years ago. I can't be persecuted for them things anymore. The DA of Charlotte told me that, personally."

"Well, this is a different day and a different court. If you don't want to enter a plea, then I shall receive a plea of not guilty, and we will proceed to the evidence. Is that what you want, Ms. Rutherford?"

"What do you mean by 'evidence'?"

"That will be up to the prosecution, but I know that one very compelling piece of evidence of your guilt is the videotape I spoke of earlier. We've all seen it."

"Where did you get that tape? All of them copies was destroyed."

"Apparently not," the Judge said, holding the tape aloft for her to see.

She looked down at her dirty tennis shoes as the reality of her situation began to sink in. "Look, I know what I done is wrong. I know my kids is totally fucked . . . I mean messed up, by everything their mama has done, but I got immunity for all this."

"Your immunity was given to you by the State of North Carolina. Not by this court. We are aware that you are babysitting young children in your home, children from your neighborhood, and God knows what you are doing to them."

How does he know I'm babysitting neighbor kids? How does he know what I've been doing with them? Nobody knows about the hidden cameras in the bathroom or the bedroom. Nobody knows.

"I presume from your silence that you are pleading not guilty, so . . ."

"No wait. Are my kids gonna testify? I don't want them to see their mama like this. This is degrading, me being here all chained up and having messed my pants. I don't want them to see me like this."

"Well Ms. Rutherford, if you plead not guilty, then the evidence has to be presented, and your kids may have to testify. And, of course, they would see you just as you are, and they would likely testify against you. Given what you did to them, can you blame them?"

The man they called the prosecutor shifted in his seat and turned to look at her.

"Okay. I may as well do the time. I did the crime. I know that. I got lucky I had a hell of a good lawyer the last time. Not like this 'defense attorney' you say." She thrust her head toward the table. "He's just sitting there like a bump on a log."

"Are you pleading guilty to all charges, Ms. Rutherford?" the Judge asked.

"Yeah. I plead guilty. To all of it."

"Well, all right," the Judge said. "Is the prosecution satisfied with the guilty plea?"

"Yes, Your Honor," said the man. It was the first time he had spoken. Unlike the others, his voice was not commanding, but contained a hint of doubt.

"Is the defense satisfied with the guilty plea?"

From her assigned lawyer, "Yes, Your Honor. And I see no need for allocution in this particular case."

"Very well, then. Ms. Rutherford, you have pleaded guilty to all of the charges, and I accept your guilty plea. Do you have anything to say before I impose sentence?"

She stared at the man in the black mask who said he was a judge and was probably staring back at her through the narrow slits. She was a disheveled woman who was thirty-six but looked fifty-six. The ravages of drugs and a hard life were etched in the creases around her mouth and eyes. Her body was bloated by a life lived always on the edge of non-life, and the abuse to which she subjected herself and her children. In addition to the Taser burns on her back, she had multiple scars on her arms and legs from cigarette burns. She wondered how much she should say to this judge, how much she should show him. She wondered if any of it would make any difference. She had done it. All of it. She was guilty of everything they accused her of.

"I got something to say." She stared at the floor a few feet in front of her. "Look. I got pregnant when I was sixteen. I was raped by my stepfather. I had Caleb when I was seventeen. The other two, the girls, I don't know who their daddies are. I did what I did because it's what I had to do for money to buy food, to pay rent, to take care of my kids. I did it because that's what I thought I had to do to keep from getting beaten by my boyfriend. He beat me anyway. I got scars. I got scars all over my body. I got scars in my brain. I don't know if that makes any difference to you. I ain't proud of it."

There was a prolonged silence in the courtroom. She thought that might be a good sign. Maybe the judge would be lenient.

"One of your daughters killed herself, about a year ago, is that correct?" The Judge said.

"Yeah, she did. Shot herself."

"And she left a note blaming you, is that correct?"

"She did. And there ain't a day gone by that I don't think of her and blame myself."

"Do you understand, Ms. Rutherford, that when you bring a child into this world, it comes with a critical responsibility to take care of that child, to protect that child?"

"I do now. I probably didn't back then. I wasn't much older than a baby myself."

"And yet you didn't protect any of your children. You harmed them. You caused them damage. You damaged one of your children so severely that she shot herself rather than live with the shame of something you did to her, that she could not prevent, that wasn't her fault."

"Yes, that's probably the case of it."

"So you are responsible not only for the things you've admitted to, but you basically murdered your own daughter. Isn't that right?"

"I didn't kill her. She shot herself. But maybe what I did drove her to it. I can't deny that. I was messed up back then. Messed up all the time." Tears ran down her cheeks. "I carry a picture of her with me. She was so pretty. And so smart."

"All right, is there anything else you want to say Ms. Rutherford?"

She shook her head and sniffled.

"You imposed a great weight of guilt on your children, a weight so heavy and burdensome that your daughter killed herself at fifteen for something she didn't do and for which she was not to blame. You've ruined countless lives. You're a predator. Here's what I'm going to do. I'm going to let you live with that same guilt for a time, maybe a very short time, and maybe a little longer. Maybe just a few hours, maybe a few days. You are going to think about what you did. And then we are going to come for you. When you least expect it. And when we come for you, we are going to execute you."

"You're going to kill me? I thought I was going to jail for a while, but you're going to kill me? That ain't right. I got immunity . . ." Before she could say anything else, one of the men at the rear of the trailer slipped the gag back into her mouth. She kept talking, but it was no use. She'd been relegated to a grunting animal again.

The Judge nodded, and the hood went back over her head and was cinched tight in the back. She was again blind. She heard the shuffle of chairs and footsteps, the scrape of the metal door on un-oiled hinges.

"We've got to get that fixed," someone said quietly.

CHAPTER TWENTY-SIX

"Get up," the official voice said. Rough hands grabbed her and pulled her from the chair. Before, as the accused, Elise Rutherford had been handled firmly, but without malice. Now, as a convicted criminal, she was being pushed and prodded roughly. They spun her halfway around. "Stand still." She felt a tug on the zip tie binding her feet, and then the tie released. "Step down." She did. "Step down again." She took another step and was on solid ground. Her hands were still bound, she was still gagged, and the hood was over her head. She could hear nothing but the sound of crickets and other night insects.

There was a man on either side of her, moving her forward. "Walk." The same voice. She took several steps. "Stop." She heard a car door open. Someone pushed her head down and to the side. "Get in." She flopped sideways onto the back seat. Someone pushed her legs and feet, and a different man pulled her shoulders from the other side, sliding her into the car. She couldn't tell how many of them there were. She was lying on her side. Someone swung both doors closed. Then she heard the front doors of the car open and at least two people got in the front seat. Seat-belt buckles snapped. The car started. The car did not smell new or old. The radio was not on. It was like these people were trying to conceal every sign of who they were, even about the music they might listen to. She hadn't seen their faces and had no way of identifying any of them. She thought that was a good sign. She rubbed the seat with a finger of her bound hands and realized she was lying on some type of a plastic sheet, maybe a tarp.

They traveled over smooth roads of dirt or sand, then hit pavement. There were stretches where the tires hissed over asphalt, with cars occasionally passing them, and long stretches where the only sound was the hum of their own car. She was unaware of time. She had no idea how long she had been in the courtroom, or how long she had been in the car. She assumed it was late at night because she didn't feel the heat of the sun, and the car was not hot when they pushed her inside. Her stomach growled. She could not tell if it was from hunger or fear.

From the front passenger seat came the official voice. "The last time we did this, we asked the prisoner how he wanted it done. We're not going to ask you. You don't deserve a choice. We thought about putting a garbage bag over your head and throwing you into the river. But it would take only a minute or two for you to drown. You'd panic for a while, but it would be over too quickly for you. You need to suffer."

The driver spoke. His voice was not as deep as the official voice, and from that clue she thought the driver might be a smaller man. "Another option is to slice you up, not enough to kill you, but enough that you'll bleed a lot, and then throw you out on the mud flats for the gators. I've seen what they do. If it's just one, he'll drag you under and drown you, then stuff your body in a hole somewhere and eat you a little at a time while you rot. But if it's a bunch of gators, they'll fight over you and tear off your arms and legs."

This man's voice was more menacing. It was like he had killed before and would not hesitate to do so again. He spoke again, at a lower volume. "If we do it that way, we have to make sure there are lots of gators around so they rip you apart."

Her body shuddered as she imagined alligators tearing at her limbs.

"Or," the official voice said, "we'll tie her behind a truck, her own truck, and drag her through the woods and thickets for a few miles. Then when she's really beaten up, we'll tie her legs to a tree with a chain and inch forward until we pull her in half. That's how they used to lynch blacks in the South decades ago."

She detected a faint accent in his voice. Definitely from the South, but she couldn't tell the man's race.

The official voice again. "I wonder where she'll break. Arms first, or the spine? Either way, that's the way to do it. That's the most painful. Agonizing. I sure wouldn't want to die that way. Any way but that."

"I agree," the driver said. "We'll let her stew for a while, think about what she did to her kids. Think about her dead daughter. Think about the pain and fear she caused them. Then we'll come for her. And we'll take her to the woods. And that's how we'll do it."

They drove in silence for what seemed to Elise Rutherford an interminable time. All she could think about was what she had done to her children, what she was doing to the neighbor kids. She couldn't help herself. It was a compulsion. An addiction. She needed the money, and the videos she sold on the internet brought in good money. And Sophie, her youngest, whom she had allowed to be defiled by men who didn't give a shit about any of them. Poor little Sophie couldn't live with the shame of it, couldn't bear the burden of keeping it secret any longer. She had killed herself when she was just in the ninth grade. It was all her fault. These men were right. It was all her fault.

The car slowed, and she felt the familiar bump leading up the sandy driveway to her house. She lived in a small farmhouse about ten miles from New Bern. Her closest neighbor was a half mile away. The car stopped, and the men got out. She heard the back doors open and they pulled her from each end, one tugging her wrists and the other her ankles.

"Feel that," official voice said. "That's about one percent of the force of a truck pulling you apart." They pulled harder, as if in a tug of war. She could hear them grunting with the effort. She felt her knee pop and screamed through the gag. Then they let go. She was sweating harder than she had in the trailer, and the stench of her own body almost overwhelmed her as they dragged her out of the car and to her feet. "Take two steps forward." She complied, and someone slammed the back door of the car. "Forward." She walked several steps until she was at the front stoop of her house. "Up two steps. You know the way." She climbed the steps and shuffled through the front door. They turned her and pushed her down on what felt like the rumpled sofa in her den.

"Now, here is what's going to happen." The official voice again. "Listen carefully. We are going to put you in your bedroom closet. Then we are going to cut the zip tie on your hands. We are going to leave on the hood and the gag. Do you understand? Nod your head."

The guilty woman nodded.

"We have cut your phone line and have destroyed your cell phone. We've also disabled your truck. We are coming back soon. It might be an hour, or a day, or a week. And when we come back we are going to do exactly what we talked about in the car. Somebody is going to find the two halves of your body out in the woods somewhere. Or maybe they'll never find you. Nod your head if you understand."

She nodded again.

They heaved her up from the couch and pushed her into her bedroom and into the closet there. They shoved her down on the floor among her shoes and boots. Someone cut the zip tie on her hands and slammed the closet door. She could hear the scrape of furniture, maybe a dresser or a bed, being pushed across the floor and against the closet door. Then she heard receding footsteps and the slam of the front door.

Her breath heaved. She was exhausted. She hadn't eaten in a long time. She reached behind her head to undo the hood, but stopped. She wasn't sure she wanted to take the hood off just yet. She sat for a few minutes until her heart slowed and her breathing became more regular. Then she took off the hood. The closet was pitch black, but there was a dim strip of light at the bottom of the door. She pulled the gag out of her mouth, letting it dangle from her neck. The gag was wet. Her mouth was dry. Her right knee throbbed. She couldn't stretch out without standing up. She grabbed the doorknob and pulled herself into a sitting position, then stood up slowly. Then she turned the knob and pushed against the door. The door was not locked, but the furniture holding the door was heavy. She heaved against the door with her shoulder and the furniture moved an inch or two. Enough to let in some fresh air and to see that dawn was breaking. A dirty gray light entered the closet from her bedroom window.

"Hello, is anybody there?" No one should be there, but she wanted to make sure the men had actually left. They were cruel, and they might be standing just outside the door to take her away and do . . . what they said they would do. No one responded. She heaved against the door again and moved it enough to get her left foot between the door and the jamb. She twisted her leg into the gap and pushed against the door with her shoulder. The door wedged open another few inches. She was able to get her hip in the crevice, and eventually her entire body. With heaving effort, she shoved the door open enough for her to wriggle out. Once out of the closet, she could see that her dresser had held the door shut.

She sat down on the bed and took stock of herself. Her senses were acute with the adrenaline of what just happened. She ran her hand through her hair, which had become greasy with sweat. She stank of sweat and the shit in her pants. Her mouth had the gummy feeling of exertion and unbrushed teeth. She got a cup of water from the bathroom without looking in the mirror. She drank another. She turned on the tap in the bathtub, noticing the tile was slimy, and the grout was dark with mold. She disrobed, throwing her underwear in the trash and leaving her tennis shoes, pants and grimy T-shirt on the floor. She eased herself into the hot water, her hefty body nearly filling the tub. Water sloshed over the side, but she let it run. She could hear it splashing on the tile and she didn't care. She rubbed her swollen knee and wondered what it would really feel like to be dragged behind her truck and then tied to a tree and pulled in half. She grimaced and started to sob again. Her thoughts swirled quickly in and out of her head. She had no doubt they would do it. She just didn't know when. But they would probably be back that night, to work again in the dark. If they had really disabled her car, they had done it so she wouldn't run. She'd have to check that. Even if she ran, they'd find her again. They had already found her living out in the country even though she'd changed her name and moved. She reached up and turned off the water and laid in the tub, hoping the hot water would cleanse her body. And her soul. She slid down so her head was underwater, her feet pressed against the tile above the faucet handles. She stayed that way for a few seconds, until she remembered the threat of a trash bag over her head and being drowned in the river.

After she toweled off she put on fresh clothes, grabbed the keys to her truck, and went outside. Clouds hung low, spitting rain. The dirt driveway had not yet turned to mud. When she opened the truck door the overhead light did not come on. When she turned the key in the ignition, nothing happened. She popped the hood and saw that the battery had been removed and that the battery cables were missing. The rain became cold and the wind picked up a bit. Elise Rutherford looked up at the sky and let the rain lick her face for a minute or two until she started shivering. She closed the truck hood and went back inside her house.

She made a breakfast of scrambled eggs and bacon on the rusting stove and took her plastic plate to the living room couch. She grabbed the remote and switched on the television. Her VCR whirred to life. On the television screen were images of her having sex with her children. She picked up the VCR remote and pushed the off button, but nothing happened. She tried again. Nothing. Her youngest daughter Sophie, about nine at the time, said from the screen, "No mommy, I don't want to do this anymore." Sophie started to move out of the frame when a naked man picked her up and tossed her back down on the blanket and told her to stay there or he would hurt her.

Elise Rutherford jumped up from the couch, knocking the plate of eggs to the floor. She scrambled over to the wall and pulled the VCR plug out of the wall socket. It was the only way she could make it stop.

She had not seen Sophie, or any of her children, in more than four years. That was part of her immunity deal. She couldn't see her kids again, ever. She couldn't go within 300 feet of them. She was allowed to talk to them on the phone, but only the eldest, her son Caleb, would ever talk to her. Elise Rutherford slumped back into the couch and covered her face in her hands. She couldn't force the tears to come. She mewed like an injured cat. There was nothing she could do to make this go away now. They knew where she was. This recent ordeal, the trial in the middle of the night, had brought all those terrible memories right to the surface. From now on, every heartbeat would be filled with the sound of Sophie's voice. Every breath would be tainted with the stench of what she had done. She was rotting from the inside, had been rotting from the inside for most of her life.

The men would be back soon, and she did not want to be in their clutches ever again. With more resolve than she had ever shown in her life, she got up from her couch, got her pistol from her bedside table, put the barrel in her mouth, and ended her life. In the briefest of interludes between squeezing the trigger and ceasing to exist, Elise Rutherford felt a shadow of peace.

CHAPTER TWENTY-SEVEN

Elise Rutherford's death was reported in the newspaper as an apparent suicide. There was no suicide note. Neither of her children showed up to claim her body. She was unceremoniously cremated, her remains to be dumped from a plastic bag and scattered at sea.

"No one seems to care," Crenshaw said. "The article says she died of an apparent self-inflicted gunshot wound to the head. The information I received is that the sheriff has concluded, at least preliminarily, that it was suicide."

"Why are we talking about this in my chambers, Robert?" Judge Westlake said with irritation.

"Where else should we discuss it?"

"Not here."

They left the federal courthouse as the sun dipped below Mt. Pisgah, casting them in deep shadow. With tourist season yet three months away, the Asheville streets were uncrowded, and they walked briskly to a vegetarian restaurant, where they were ushered to a corner table.

Westlake leaned forward and spoke in a low voice. "Robert, we all agreed we would not have any conversations about our cases except when we were all together. You remember that discussion, that agreement, don't you?"

"I remember. But I'm concerned that Marcus and Iggy . . ."

"No names."

Crenshaw continued. "I'm concerned that they may have taken matters into their own hands and . . . done something they weren't supposed to. She's dead. We all agreed that we were only going to scare her straight, not actually . . . you know."

"That's not what we agreed to. We agreed that as a first step we would attempt to put the fear of God in her, and then escalate matters if that didn't work."

"Yeah, but she's dead the very next day."

"We should not be having this conversation in a public place," Westlake said, his ire apparent. "It's reckless. I'll convene a meeting at the lake house, this weekend. Now, *let's* order dinner."

* * * * * *

David Johnstone, Marcus Cunningham and Iggy Perez arrived at the lake house, joining Westlake on the wooden dock that jutted twenty feet into the water. Shiloh, an apricot-colored Labradoodle the Judge had recently rescued, lay at the Judge's feet, her nose on his left shoe. A round, metal fire pit threw off just enough warmth to stem the morning chill. Wisps of mist hung above the still, black water.

"I understand Ms. Rutherford has passed away," Westlake began, rubbing his hands together over the fire.

"Confirmed," Cunningham said in the official voice.

"No problems with the re-delivery, I take it?"

"No, sir."

"So tell me what happened."

Cunningham sipped from a mug of hot chocolate. "We drove around for quite a while, doubling back a few times so she couldn't trace the route back to where we'd parked the rig. We told her we would be back and what we would do to her when we came back."

"Which was?"

Cunningham shot a glance at Iggy Perez, then continued. "We told her we were going to drag her through the woods behind her own truck, then tie her legs to a tree and pull her apart."

Westlake grimaced. "Is this something you guys picked up in Iraq?"

"I saw it happen there once, but they did it with camels," said Perez. "It's an old form of execution used by a lot of different cultures. The Persians, Spaniards."

"It was also practiced by the Romans against Christians," Westlake said. "Second or third century, I think. But that's beside the point. Were you actually going to do that to her?"

"No," Cunningham said. "It might leave too many clues, too much evidence. No way to make *that* look like an accident. We said it just to scare her."

Perez jumped in. "We had already disabled her truck and her phone line, destroyed her cell phone. We took her back to her house and put her in a bedroom closet. We'd rigged the house with microphones. We were listening to her from a spot just down the road."

"She didn't see your faces?" Westlake asked.

"No sir, kept our masks on the whole time."

"Did she kill herself?"

"Confirmed," Cunningham said. "We didn't actually see her do it because she was in the bedroom, but we heard a single gunshot over the microphones. And nobody else went in the house after we left."

Westlake nodded. "All of the evidence points to her killing herself. Suicide." He leaned back in the deck chair. "So what do you think made her do it?"

Johnstone had been quietly listening. He had been the one to suggest that they put Elise Rutherford on trial. Going in, he had been absolutely convinced she should be severely punished for what she had done to her children, even though she'd been given immunity by state prosecutors. There was no possibility of reforming a child molester. But news of her death brought him no elation. "Maybe she died of guilt. And maybe the threats," he said quietly.

"And probably the fact that we left that videotape in her VCR. When she turned on her TV that's what she saw. Her and her kids. That could have driven her to it," Perez said.

"Death by shame," Westlake said. "Well, she's dead now. I can't honestly say that's an undesirable result."

They sat in silence for a few moments, contemplating the water. Judge Westlake thought about the two secret trials, the two lives they had taken.

"You did get the tape back, right?" Johnstone asked. "I mean, my client gave it to me, so if you left the tape behind, that might implicate him in some way."

"We got it," Perez said. "And the microphones." Perez removed the videotape from the pocket of the canvas bag he seemed to carry everywhere. The tape was encased in a plastic bag. He handed it to Johnstone.

"By the way," Westlake said, "did you find any other videotapes in her house? Any evidence of her with other children?"

"We didn't look, Judge," Perez said. "Remember, we didn't know what she was going to do after we left, so we didn't want to remove anything from the house."

"And we didn't search her computer," Cunningham said. "We couldn't run the risk of leaving a trace of her computer being used after she was dead."

"Right, right," Westlake nodded. "Well, it sounds like you guys covered everything, as usual."

"You said you cut her phone line and disabled her car," Johnstone said. "I assume you fixed those things? Sorry for asking. But I'm the one who got this started with her, so I just want to make sure."

Perez nodded. "That's what we do. We didn't actually cut the phone line, just detached it from the house. That's been fixed. We reinstalled her battery and cables in the truck. Didn't leave a trace there."

Cunningham said, "If there is an investigation, it will look like a suicide, pure and simple."

"Wait. Shit," Johnstone said. "Her son said she had some secret video cameras. Did you find those?"

Cunningham nodded. "One in the living room. One in the bedroom. Both concealed. They were off when we entered the house both times. Made sure of that."

"But you can't be sure she didn't turn them on once she got out of the closet, right?"

"No, we can't be sure, but if she did all it would show would be her in the house alone. Might even show her shooting herself. That would put the whole issue to bed," Cunningham said.

"You're sure they weren't motion-activated cameras?" Johnstone asked.

Cunningham scraped the sole of his boot across the head of a raised nail on the dock. "No, we can't be sure of that. We didn't check," he said, his head down.

As the sun rose above the ridge, the mist began to burn off the dark water. Westlake stood and fiddled with the fishing rods stored on hooks underneath the dock roof. Shiloh followed her owner, sniffed at his feet.

"Where's Robert?" Johnstone asked. "He's late."

"Not late," Westlake said over his shoulder. He came back to the group and re-settled in his chair, leaning forward with elbows on knees. "I invited you guys out early. He's not supposed to be here for another hour or so. We may have a problem. I stress the word 'may.' Don't jump to any conclusions. He came to my chambers earlier in the week to tell me Ms. Rutherford was dead. Innocuous enough, except that he read me the newspaper report of her death from the internet, which means there may be a digital trail on some computer that he searched for her name."

Perez and Cunningham looked at each other.

"He may also have called the sheriff's department down there to check on whether there's an investigation. He didn't admit to that. Just said he had some information from the sheriff's department. If he did call, hopefully he made the call from a cell phone and not from a landline inside the US Attorney's Office."

Westlake gazed up at the sun peeking over the ridge that surrounded the lake. "I think we might have a chance to get out on the lake and do some fishing this afternoon, gentlemen."

"Is that a metaphor for something, Judge?" Johnstone asked.

Westlake smiled. "No, just an observation that Fontana is inviting us to enjoy her bounty."

Perez spoke. "Uh, Judge, do you want us to do anything about Crenshaw?"

"No. Of course not. No. I just wanted to let you guys know that he's obviously feeling the pressure. It's baffling to me because this whole thing has been in the works for years. He was the first one to mention it, I recall. And it was an intriguing idea, not that I hadn't thought about it before. I don't know if we were just joking or not. You guys were here, playing poker with us, when he started talking about that case he had that he was so frustrated with. You remember—Iggy, Marcus—the one he spent six years on and had to tee up for a second trial. But maybe it was just talk for him. Maybe he thought it would never really happen. But then along came Lawter, and it became very real. Maybe I misread Robert. Maybe he's not fully committed to this mission."

"So how do we handle his . . . lack of commitment? Johnstone asked.

"Well, I don't have a silver-bullet solution. I've known Robert for a dozen years. He was my law clerk. When you work that closely with someone for two years, you get to know them pretty well. He'll be loyal."

"What do we do to ensure his loyalty, and discretion?" Johnstone asked.

The Judge leaned back in the deck chair, his hands knitted behind his head. "I have no idea," he said.

CHAPTER TWENTY-EIGHT

While the others met on the dock at the Fontana house without him, Robert Crenshaw spied on them through binoculars from a stand of trees on the other side of the cove. The Judge, Johnstone, Cunningham and Perez were all there, huddled on the dock around a fire pit. From that distance, Crenshaw could not hear what they were saying. It was enough that they were meeting well before he had been told to arrive. He was right to be suspicious. He guessed they were talking about Elise Rutherford's death. There would be no other reason for them to meet early. Unless they were talking about him.

He dropped the binoculars, revealing eyes rimmed in red. Beneath were dark circles too large for a man so young. Since the trial and execution of Henry Lawter, he had a constant anxiety coursing through his body, sometimes so acute that he felt electrified. At times, especially when dulled by alcohol, the feeling was subdued and faint. At other times, like now when his teammates were discussing something in secret, his nerves flashed and his muscles vibrated. A churning stomach, tingling limbs. Sleepless nights. He had always been an anxious man. The fear of the unknown affected him more acutely than it did others. And in his line of work, there was a lot of unknown. More variables than constants. In the past, he'd tried to channel the anxiety into something positive, recognizing it as a signal to be vigilant and wary. It made him more cautious as a prosecutor, more prepared.

Despite his misgivings, he knew that Lawter's death was the right outcome, had perhaps even been necessary. He was not as decisive as the Judge. He had learned that during his two-year clerkship, before becoming a prosecutor. Prosecuting criminals was not in his blood. But when the Judge mentioned he would support him for a position in the US Attorney's Office, had lobbied him to apply for that job and no other, Crenshaw had seen it as the right move. And he didn't want to disappoint his mentor. Crenshaw liked the black and white aspect of it. For him, crime and punishment were not matters of right or wrong. It was much simpler than that. Legislative bodies passed laws. Those laws had to be enforced to avoid chaos. Whether a law was just or not was irrelevant to him. The Rule of Law was paramount. Lawter broke the law when he killed Hannah Sullivan. Crenshaw could not allow that transgression to go unpunished.

He did not want to admit that he, Judge Westlake, and the others had broken the law when they subjected Lawter to the secret trial in the mobile courtroom. But they had broken the law. They had befouled it. It was an irreversible act. And therein lay the conflict that churned his stomach. To enforce the law, they had to break the law. Unlike the others, he could not dim the turmoil of that night by returning to a routine and pretending nothing had happened. He did not feel guilty that Lawter was dead. He felt guilty because he had violated the law and his solemn oath to uphold the United States Constitution. And yet he had survived it, somehow. His health was deteriorating, and to cope he besieged his body with alcohol and anti-anxiety medication almost every night. He was seeing a therapist.

Through the binoculars he watched the Judge get up and examine the fishing rods resting on hooks under the dock roof. The dog followed him. He had often fished with the Judge from that dock, talking about the law, and life, Heather Westlake's cancer, and the aftermath of her death. The other men were drinking steaming mugs of coffee. He wished he'd thought to bring a thermos of coffee with him.

Crenshaw had regained something of a balance in the months after the Lawter case by throwing himself into other cases. Working harder than he had since taking the bar exam, he had little time for thoughts of Henry Lawter. But then along came the Elise Rutherford trial. There had been another way. They had options. The Judge was wrong about that. With Lawter they'd had no choice because he couldn't be re-tried successfully without the confession.

Admittedly, Elise Rutherford was a terrible person and had done heinous and unforgivable things to her children. Someone else had determined, however, that she should not be prosecuted for those acts. That decision, in and of itself, would not have dissuaded Crenshaw from prosecuting her under federal law. The immunity agreement was a different issue. The immunity agreement was a promise by the government not to prosecute her for those crimes. For her part, Elise Rutherford had given the government what it demanded in exchange for the agreement not to put her in jail. She had provided the government with the evidence it deemed more important than prosecuting an ignorant, downtrodden woman and incarcerating her for a period that would consume the prime of her life. Crenshaw and the others had violated that contract. They had broken the promise that another agent of the government had made to Elise Rutherford. To Crenshaw, it didn't matter that the agreement had been made by a state prosecutor and was not legally binding on the federal government. If anyone ever found out what had happened, that the immunity agreement had been violated upon the whim of a federal judge and a renegade prosecutor, witnesses would refuse to cooperate, even when they were guilty of a crime. The system would collapse into chaos.

He pulled the binoculars to his eyes again. They were done talking and were leaving the dock, heading toward the house. Crenshaw checked his watch. He was not scheduled to arrive for another hour. To avoid suspicion, he had to wait. As he watched them walk toward the Judge's house, he wondered whether the marshals killed Elise Rutherford, or whether she committed suicide as the New Bern Chronicle had reported. Cunningham and Perez could have killed her and made it look like suicide, just as they had with Lawter. He should not have called the District Attorney about Elise Rutherford. He could see that now. The DA's surprise at the call had been evident in his voice, but Crenshaw had made up a thin story that the feds were tracking her as a material witness in a federal investigation.

"Was she in witness protection?" the DA had asked.

"No. The investigation was in the preliminary stages. I can't tell you more than that at this point. But I need to know. Did she kill herself?"

"Looks that way," the DA said.

"You sound unsure."

"Well, you know how this works. It's only been two days. From the crime scene itself, looks like a suicide. Though there were some odd things about the scene."

"Odd things. Like what?"

"She had video cameras in her house. I'd rather not say more than that until forensics are back. Maybe a little *quid pro quo* would ease the flow of information," the DA suggested.

Crenshaw had pondered that for a moment. He couldn't know how valuable the information from the DA would be. His thin cover story about a federal investigation could easily unravel. He should be able to get from Perez and Cunningham everything he needed to know about Elise Rutherford's last hours. If they were honest with him.

"Wish I could share something else with you at this point, but I can't. If the United States Attorney's Office needs anything else from you, I will let you know. Thanks for your help." With that, he had hung up.

His call to the DA in New Bern was risky. It was critical not to leave a trail that could somehow connect Elise Rutherford to any of them. Yet he made that call because his trust in the Judge had begun to slip. Until recently, he had held the Judge in high esteem, even revered him. Almost from the moment they met. Crenshaw interviewed for a judicial clerkship in his third year of law school, submitting his application to Judge Westlake as something of a lark. Having grown up near Philadelphia and gone to law school at Temple, Crenshaw knew little about the western corner of North Carolina that comprised Westlake's judicial district. He needed a respite from the grind of law school, and spending the summer biking and hiking in the mountains would be fun. If he got the job, there were a few modest ski slopes nearby for winter activities.

He had been ranked in the top twenty-five percent of his law school class. It was a rank that would not guarantee him a plumb position in a prestigious law firm or a clerkship with a well-respected judge after graduation, but it got his foot in the door to a few places. Crenshaw couldn't define the nature of their chemistry, but from the very first lunch interview it was evident that the Judge had a different take on the law than Crenshaw had ever heard before. In law school he and his classmates were inundated with legal theory, the important role of the law and the judicial system in civilized society. Westlake saw it differently, describing his role not merely as the decision-maker passing judgment from on high to uphold the law, but as someone who could help guide the people who appeared in his courtroom to a better way of life.

He took the job. Even though Westlake had another law clerk at that time, the Judge showed more interest in Crenshaw. He was invited to sit in on every hearing, every attorney conference, and all of the trials. His counterpart was not. During his clerkship, Crenshaw checked around with other federal law clerks he had met, and few of them received the attention that Judge Westlake gave him. Their relationship matured from employer-employee to that of mentor-protégée, and Crenshaw flourished. Frequent fishing trips on Fontana and nearby streams in the Smoky Mountains had grown their relationship and provided them with an opportunity to debate deeper issues in the law. And Crenshaw sought to become an Assistant

United States Attorney in large part because he wanted to continue working with the Judge.

That was nine years ago. And while he had absorbed the Judge's philosophy of the law, and had been permanently shaped by it, something had recently changed. In both of them. He had trouble discerning the precise catalyst for the Judge's change of heart. Perhaps it was Heather's death, a long and tortuous death by cancer, which would make anyone hard and bitter. Heather Westlake had died about six months before the Lawter case had landed in the Judge's court. Maybe it was the infamy of being reversed by the Fourth Circuit Court of Appeals in his first and only murder case. Whatever the reason, the Judge had veered over the line and had taken four other people with him. Crenshaw didn't know the other three that well. Given their backgrounds, he wasn't surprised that Cunningham and Perez followed the Judge's every dictate. Loyalty coursed through their veins. Johnstone, however, was a different sort. Johnstone's agreement to join the team seemed an odd move at a stage in his career when his reputation was solid and untarnished. But the Judge was persuasive, and Johnstone quickly agreed to join them. As he watched the Judge's back recede through the binoculars, Crenshaw wondered whether something like that lurked in everyone.

Crenshaw was bitter about the precarious position in which he found himself. He and the Judge had worked together a long time, and he could not forget how rewarding that had been. A deep friendship had developed between them. But the Judge had dragged him into this mess. Put him at risk. He could not forget that either.

143

CHAPTER TWENTY-NINE

Crenshaw drove around the mouth of the lake to the Judge's house. At the front door, the dog greeted him by sniffing his shoes, tail slowly wagging. He held out an open palm. The dog sniffed and licked his palm.

"You got a dog, Judge?"

"I did. Just this week. A rescue dog. She's a Labradoodle."

"She seems nice." Crenshaw lightly patted her head. "What's her name?"

"Shiloh."

"Who is going to take care of her when you're in Asheville?"

"I might take her with me to the condo sometimes. Otherwise, I guess my housekeeper will take care of Shiloh."

"You have a housekeeper?"

"Sure, hired her a few weeks ago. She comes a couple of times a week, cleans, cooks meals, etcetera."

"You're just full of surprises," Crenshaw said.

"Did you bring your fishing gear, Robert?"

"I did. Out in the car."

They spent the afternoon fishing on the Judge's pontoon boat, trolling the shallows. The group reeled in enough bass to fill a small cooler. The placid waters eased Crenshaw's tension, and the idle banter and jokes almost made him forget that his cohorts had been secretly meeting without him just that morning.

The Judge fried bass in corn meal in an iron skillet on the grill. Crenshaw made rice. Cunningham cooked a plate of biscuits. They settled around the metal table on the screened porch and re-lived the fishing trip, the lunker Crenshaw caught, the ones that escaped by tangling themselves in the weeds or zigzagging under the boat. After dinner had been cleared and drinks poured, they gathered around the poker table in the great room. A fire crackled with seasoned hickory and oak. Keeping with tradition, the Judge dealt the first hand of five-card draw.

"So, what happened to Elise Rutherford?" Crenshaw ventured before the first round of betting began. He had refrained from asking that question during the fishing trip, not wanting to seem too eager or accusatorial. He hoped now his tone did not sound confrontational.

"She killed herself," Cunningham said.

"Really? So, this wasn't you guys doing it and disguising it as suicide? Like with Lawter?"

Cunningham stared across the table at Crenshaw. "No. Like I said, she shot herself. Plain and simple."

"Robert," the Judge intervened, "we all agreed to the sentence that would be given to Ms. Rutherford. No one should be naive. We all knew that the way we handled her might result in her taking her own life. It seems simple to me. After being confronted again with what she'd done, and what might be in store for her, the guilt consumed her."

"But she had been given immunity," Crenshaw said.

"Immunity by the State of North Carolina," the Judge said. "Not immunity by the US Justice Department. How many times have you prosecuted someone under a federal law when the accused got an immunity deal from the DA?"

Crenshaw shrugged his shoulders. "It's happened."

Johnstone spoke up. "All the time. Early in my career, still wet behind the ears, I got a plea deal from the DA for a guy who was running video poker machines. I didn't know there was even the potential for federal charges. Not a month after my client allocuted to the state court judge, the feds came in and charged him with federal racketeering crimes. Used his own allocution to make their case. The client was none too happy. But I was stupid, and it stuck."

"The difference is, we . . . this group, are not the federal government," Crenshaw replied. "We could have done this differently. We could have investigated this properly and we could have brought charges against her under federal child pornography laws. We could have done this by the book."

"Is that what this is all about, Robert? You wanted another feather in your cap for prosecuting a child pornographer?" the Judge asked.

"No. It's not about that. I wouldn't have been the AUSA prosecuting the case anyway. Somebody else handles those crimes."

"And how is it that the US Attorney's Office would have even known about Elise Rutherford?" Johnstone said. "The only evidence, and the tape, came from me. She changed her name, even."

"I don't know," Crenshaw said. "It just feels wrong. With Lawter, we knew he was guilty. He confessed, and the system failed because of a technicality. Elise Rutherford was different. Someone who knew all of the circumstances made a reasoned decision not to prosecute her. Whether we like it or not, we should be satisfied with that. We should respect that decision."

"Then why not respect the decision of the Fourth Circuit Court of Appeals in the Lawter case?" The Judge asked.

"Well, this is different."

"It's different because Lawter was your case? Is that what you're saying?" Johnstone said.

"You guys are ganging up on me. Look, I don't want to argue about this all night. I just wanted to let you know how I felt about it. That's all." Crenshaw took a long gulp of whiskey.

The Judge adopted a more consoling tone. "Robert, I know you're scared. I know you're worried that someone might investigate and find out what we are doing. There's always the risk of being caught."

"I won't let that happen to me," said Crenshaw.

The Judge peered at Crenshaw's face, his pallid complexion, his bloodshot eyes. "It's natural to be scared, Robert. I was literally sick to my stomach for a couple of days after Lawter and after Elise Rutherford. That just confirms we're human, that we're not psychopaths. I feel for these people. I really do. But they made the choices that led us here."

"Hell, I used to throw up before almost every mission," Perez said. "A lot of the guys in the unit did the same thing."

"You?" Crenshaw said. "I didn't think you had a nervous bone in your body."

Perez continued. "You've got to understand. None of us took lightly what we were doing. The guys on the other side may have been wearing a different uniform, and some of them did some really horrible things, but most of them were just acting on orders from some officer in a concrete bunker. They were all human beings. We had reasons. They had reasons. Who really knows who was right?"

"Robert, the law is a wonderful thing," the Judge said. "In theory, it's perfect. Every case is fully vetted, and the objective unvarnished truth comes out where everybody can see it. The problem is that when you interject people into the equation, people with bias and self-interest, the truth becomes contorted. Twisted. Put lawyers into that equation and it gets even worse. My view, and you know this, is that the truth is paramount. Truth has to win out, every time. And sometimes truth and justice are not the same thing. Sometimes truth and justice are enemies."

"I know that." Crenshaw swirled the amber liquor in his glass. "You guys get scared, too? All of you?"

"Terrified," Johnstone said. "I was afraid if I said anything during Elise Rutherford's trial, I would vomit into my mask."

"Everybody has doubts, everybody has fear, Robert," the Judge said. He got up from the table and went to the wet bar. "Anybody else?" he said, holding up a crystal decanter of bourbon.

To a man, they topped off their drinks. As they stood around the table, the Judge raised his glass. "To fear and self-loathing," he said. "It keeps us all human."

CHAPTER THIRTY

Judge Westlake sat in the high-backed chair behind his desk in chambers, his fingers steepled beneath his chin. Nancy Framingham, one of his law clerks, settled herself in a burgundy leather chair on the other side of the mahogany desk.

"Nancy, did you know today is the one-year anniversary of the appellate court's reversal in the Lawter murder case."

"I did not know that," she replied.

"That's right, you weren't here when we tried Lawter. Have you read the appellate opinion?"

"I have."

"Have you read my opinion on the motion to quash the confession?"

"I have not."

"Do you agree with it? The appellate opinion, I mean?"

"That's a revolver with five bullets loaded," she ventured nervously.

"Indeed it is. And yet it is a legitimate question about which legal scholars may disagree."

Nancy paused, gathering her thoughts. "Well, as I see it Judge, there is the diplomatic answer, in which I point out the merits and flaws of the counterposing arguments, a completely transparent effort not to take a position either in favor of or contradicting my boss. And then there is the direct answer, in which I risk alienating you because I disagree, or risk looking like a toady who will always agree with you because you are my boss."

"And yet with ample loquaciousness you still have managed to dodge my question. Pick a sword."

"If I must pick a sword, I happen to agree with the court of appeals."

"Why? Justify your position."

"All right," she said. "Simply put, there needs to be a bright line. The question cannot be whether Lawter may have understood his rights despite his loss of hearing. There is a constitutional guarantee here that must be adhered to. Knowledge without due process doesn't satisfy the constitutional mandate. Accommodations must be made in this situation much the same way that disabilities are protected under the ADA. If hearing is a major life activity, which is undisputed, then the loss of it must require an adjustment in the way constitutional warnings are provided to the deaf. The officers could have avoided the entire debacle by simply handing the accused a card that had the Miranda warnings on it."

"What if Lawter couldn't read?" the Judge asked.

"Is that really an issue, in this day and time?"

"Could be. There are still pockets of illiteracy in the coves and valleys of these mountains."

She paused. "And the officers wouldn't know for sure whether Lawter could read because he wouldn't respond to questions because of his deafness."

"They didn't know he was deaf. Probably wouldn't know if he could read. So we elevate form over substance, and a murderer goes free."

"It's the necessary price of ensuring the Constitution protects everyone," she said.

"Well put. That's why I hired you. You look a bit like her, by the way."

"Like whom, Your Honor?"

"Like Hannah Sullivan. Lawter's victim."

"Okay.

"I'll see you before the end of the day." He dismissed her.

Westlake swiveled his chair to look at Mt. Pisgah, shimmering in the sun. Hannah Sullivan had died there two and a half years earlier, and Westlake wondered whether anyone else was, at that very moment, thinking of her. Had Hannah's parents found any peace in the wake of Henry Lawter's death?

What would Heather think? He had no person to blame for the death of his wife. Cancer didn't have a face. It erupted and killed from within, and it did so without mercy. He thought of Heather in a way he had not for some time, a longing for her calming presence. They had met in his first year of private practice and married a year later. His mother had come to the wedding. His father had died from the bear hug of alcoholism during the short engagement, an inevitable event he considered something of a wedding gift from his dad, for it removed from the ceremony the specter of Harleigh's unpredictable, drunken behavior. No one spoke of his father during the wedding or at the reception, and no one ventured that the groom must be sad that his father was not alive to see him married. In the glee of his matrimony, it was easy for him to forget his father ever lived.

Heather had been a teacher at a private school on the north side of Atlanta, a job she loved. Despite his demanding schedule, he made a priority of having dinner with his wife every night he was not traveling. He had insisted that their dinner conversation not be about his work, for even though client confidentiality prevented him from revealing much about his cases, even to his wife, he considered her successes and challenges in educating a select slice of the city's youth to be far more interesting. They had tried to have children of their own, but the repeated efforts didn't take, and while they never stopped trying, neither cared enough to have fertility testing or suggest another way. Heather was fond of saying she had about twenty-five children, who rotated out each school year, and perhaps she didn't have the time or patience for more. For his part, Raleigh had no ardent desire to raise children, for he feared that his father's lack of parenting skills and lack of empathy had buried itself in his own genetic code.

Heather had been diagnosed with breast cancer not long after they moved away from Atlanta. An initial double mastectomy had proved promising, but the cancer came back, invading her nodes and her soul. She had dutifully submitted to rounds of radiation and chemo therapy, but her cancer marched on unabated, and she ultimately declined further treatment. He moved her from the Asheville condominium out to the lake house on Fontana, a serene place where she found contentment watching ducks and geese playing on the water. He stayed with her when he could, commuting to Asheville when he could not re-schedule proceedings to the courthouse in nearby Bryson City. And then she died. They had said all they could say well in advance, and he thought he was prepared, but he realized when he held her cold hand and nuzzled her cheek an hour afterward that he was not prepared at all. He could not list all the ways he missed her.

Though it was midafternoon, he decided to leave the office early and go for a run. He stopped by his condominium and changed into running clothes, then made the short drive out to the forest. He parked in the same gravel lot where Hannah Sullivan had left her car the day she died, perhaps in the same space. While she had hopped on her bike and taken a short route to the Parkway via pavement, Westlake, starting slowly, headed down a dirt trail that led in the general direction of Lake Powhatan. Named for the Indian chief who was the father of Pocahontas, the small lake was encircled by a root-filled path that ultimately curled down alongside the picturesque Bent Creek.

He had become bored with the daily routine of being a Judge, deciding motions that had little impact. There were more important matters to be addressed. Henry Lawter had been executed to avenge the death of Hannah Sullivan. Elise Rutherford's suicide, although not predetermined, had probably kept other children from becoming her victims. There was good in that. But to the outside world, one looked like an accidental drug overdose, the other a suicide. The vigilantes accomplished justice in the dark. He did not shy from the word "vigilante," for he knew its Latin root meant watchful. And he was proud of being watchful.

He meandered through a tunnel of rhododendron, now out of bloom. The trail was soft beneath his feet. He tried without success to listen to the babble of the creek, but it told him nothing. Its voice was overpowered by the howling of the two wolves inside his head. It was exhausting work feeding both of them. He was trying to do the right thing, but they kept up their incessant dissonance. They snarled at one another, or one snarled at him when he favored the other. Knowing there was no way to quiet them by reason alone, he turned up the Hard Times Trail and began a steep ascent. The prospect of an easy jaunt in the woods on a sunny afternoon had been sullied, and this run had turned into a mission. He would exhaust himself and the wolves. As he chugged up the hill of the forest road, the need for pain inculcated from a multitude of unnamed sources, his arms punched the air wildly, not merely pulling his body to the top, but striking out at something else. He neared the top with ragged breath and aching thighs, each step an attempt to advance the stone of his disaffection. The wrenching effort left moisture in his eyes. At the top he slowed but did not stop, and soon he reached a trail to his left. He had not planned to run this far, or this hard. He allowed the gravity of the descending trail to pull him down, and he released control, his feet thudding hard into the path without restraint, his arms gyrating wildly to maintain a semblance of balance. He gave into it for once, the plunge, releasing all control. He plummeted to the bottom with surprise that he had not fallen or tripped or tumbled on his way down. Here, the trail leveled out among the pines, the clear path coated with decaying pine needles that provided respite for his aching legs. If one could not find peace in that setting, then peace was unattainable. He came to a narrow gate and was forced to slow as he sidled through. Once on the other side, he chugged along the rocky path worn by footsteps and bike tires and thousands of rains. A place where wolves once roamed and howled. His head down, his feet barely left the ground, shuffling in the dust. And inside, the wolves began to howl again.

CHAPTER THIRTY-ONE

In a courtroom in Savannah, Tyler Becksdale stood before a judge, awaiting his sentence. He nervously smoothed a red tie that was slightly askew, then thrust his hands in the pants pockets of his navy suit. Becksdale was charged with involuntary manslaughter for plowing his SUV into a crowd of people. He had been drinking. Five of them died. He pleaded guilty to all five counts.

Judge Hal Manning peered over his spectacles at the defendant. "Mr. Becksdale, I have pondered the appropriate sentence to levy in this case, considering all of the factors here. It has been a very difficult decision. On the one hand, five innocent lives were taken away by you that evening. Their loved ones will never see them again. On the other hand, you are by all accounts a promising young baseball star, and you were barely eighteen when this happened. Just a kid really. I know you were celebrating being drafted and your new major league contract. I know that you have a drinking problem. Your blood-alcohol level that night was more than twice the legal limit."

Judge Manning paused as the reporters in the gallery scribbled notes. "I could sentence you to a very long prison term. Per the sentencing guidelines, you could be in prison until you're a middle-aged man, at the very least. You are a young man, and you could spend a considerable part of your life behind bars, where you'll be thrown in with a bunch of thugs. I don't think you are a thug, Mr. Becksdale. You made a mistake – a serious mistake – but a mistake nonetheless. I hereby sentence you to time served, plus thirty days in a court-approved alcohol rehabilitation center."

The courtroom erupted in fury. The husband of one of those killed jumped up from the gallery, shouting. "This is ridiculous. An abomination. No justice for my wife or the other victims. You're crazy . . ."

Three bailiffs grabbed the man and began to shove him toward the double doors and out of the courtroom.

"Stop," the Judge shouted over the din. "His wife was killed. Leave him alone. Get the defendant out of my courtroom."

A cadre of bailiffs surrounded Tyler Becksdale and ushered him toward a side door that led to a back hallway, away from the prying questions of the media and the outrage of his victims' survivors.

Judge Manning did not try to regain order. He allowed the crowd, mostly reporters and family members of the victims, to have their outrage. They were entitled to it. Once Becksdale left the courtroom, the reporters began shouting questions from behind the railing. They were good questions, legitimate questions. But he wasn't going to answer any of them. He wasn't going to respond, or hold a press conference, or issue a statement. His sentence was one that could not be objectively explained, a sentence that was beyond lenient given any rational view of the case.

CHAPTER THIRTY-TWO

Judge Westlake folded the newspaper and placed it on his desk. He rested his chin in cupped hands. He had just finished reading a story, in the national section, about the Tyler Becksdale case. The Savannah judge who had imposed no sentence on the drunk driver had been his law school classmate at the University of Georgia. The competition between himself and Hal Manning, who had bested him by a spot in the final class rankings, had been friendly but fervent. Westlake found it hard to believe that Manning could be the judge who had essentially relieved an eighteen-year-old drunk driver from all culpability for his crimes.

Westlake and Manning had shared more than study time and a competitive bent to excel at the law—they had shared, in quiet whispers among the cubicles in the law library, the story of their lives, the tales told by children of alcoholic fathers. At first, they had downplayed the wild unpredictability of their addicted dads, preferring not to reveal in full the dysfunctionality of their childhood and its impact on their lives. After a time, the deflections and bravado diminished, and honesty prevailed.

Harleigh Westlake had started with little but through hard work built a small real-estate development empire in Atlanta. As his mother had said on many occasions, only then did Harleigh Westlake feel confident enough to move them out of a cramped apartment and into the huge house he had built as a trophy to himself. The house had seven bedrooms on three acres inside the perimeter in Buckhead, a glittering, outsized message that Harleigh Westlake had arrived. But the big house and the buildings with his father's name on a plaque in the lobby were external trappings, for Raleigh knew his father was almost empty inside. It was as if the alcohol had eaten away anything other than anger and resentment. Raleigh could not remember a time, even as a small child, when his father had hugged him. Instead, his father greeted him with a handshake. When Raleigh was six, his father had squeezed his right hand so aggressively, to "show him how a man properly shakes another man's hand," that the ligaments in Raleigh's right hand were sprained. Afterward, his father would not let his mother take him to the doctor.

Raleigh and his mother wanted for nothing material. His father took them on occasional vacations to exotic places like Hawaii and Fiji, but his father was a businessman first, and fatherhood and husbandhood seemed to elude him. Even in his teens, Raleigh looked up to his father. Time with his father was still a cherished opportunity. He was sometimes invited on fishing trips, mostly when his father was courting a new client, sometimes a professional athlete or entertainer who had moved to the area and had millions to spend on a new Harleigh Westlake home. More often than not, Raleigh was abandoned to the boat captain while his father drank and talked business.

On one trip off the eastern coast of Florida, when he was fourteen, Raleigh hooked into a trophy-sized kingfish and battled it for the better part of an hour, with the aid of the first mate. The captain recorded it on video, Raleigh heaving the big fish toward the boat, his thin muscles groaning, his back aching with the effort of bringing in a fish that weighed more than he did. Sweat poured off his face, and his hands turned raw. Yet finally he won the battle and hauled the fish to the side of the boat, where the first mate waited with the gaff. Raleigh leaned over the side, beaming at his trophy, still heaving with effort, when a shark bit into the tail half of the fish. The shark thrashed and chewed the king into an unrecognizable piece of bloody carrion. Raleigh plopped back into the swivel seat, defeated. His eyes bulged with tears he fought hard to restrain.

His father, who had been sitting in the shade of the boat canopy, drinking and trying to convince a newly minted basketball star to agree to a new build, walked over and clasped a meaty hand on his shoulder. Raleigh spun around in the swivel chair, wiping away tears, hoping his father would think it was sweat. His father leaned down and whispered, almost seething. "Don't you dare cry. Not here, not in front of the client, not in front of me, not ever." Then his father stood up, stretching his six-feet-four body, and said, "well that's a lesson to us all boys. The sharks always win." He laughed big and patted his son on the shoulder. Then Harleigh Westlake went back to the client.

His father used his big body, his physical preeminence, to intimidate his wife. At first, intimidate was all he did, but as Raleigh's mother survived the oral lashings and threats, even seemed to grow stronger from it, his father's grip on her weakened. Then, his tactics changed. Money had always been the currency of his communication, and as long as Joyce remained a loyal servant to his grand plan, the money kept flowing. She had two fancy vehicles, one for herself and one for hauling Raleigh around to endless soccer games and track meets that his father rarely attended. She had two walk-in closets filled with designer clothes, and a house filled with furniture chosen by one of the city's most prominent interior designers. All the trappings of a contented wife of a successful property developer.

But Joyce Littlefield of the Cherokee Wolf Clan had never belonged to Harleigh Westlake. She had never belonged to anyone. And when this realization overtook Harleigh one night in a sultry southern summer, he retaliated for what he firmly believed was her direct disloyalty. The perceived slight from his wife was trivial, a raised eyebrow or frown over a new construction project perhaps, and Harleigh's tirade had been disproportionate and vicious, ending with him throwing the better half of her carefully constructed wardrobe out of their bedroom window and into the pool below. While Raleigh stood on the diving board attempting to catch a stray dress or shoe hurled toward the pool by his father, his mother stood silently in the bedroom, arms crossed, and watched her husband destroy things that meant nothing to her. The designer wardrobe was his idea, a way of packaging a wife he could show off at charity functions and groundbreaking ceremonies. As the clothes flew out the window, Harleigh screamed that if he had not rescued her from the impoverished Reservation and transformed her into the woman she was, she could never have afforded the clothes, or the house, or any of it. When finally his burly body tired from the effort and he plopped down onto the bed in sweaty frustration, Joyce stepped to the window and tossed into the pool the left leather shoe whose counterpart her husband already had discarded.

Harleigh's days began with orange juice and vodka, or coffee with Kahlua. If the ill, foreboding feeling of the day before did not subside, he took a nip or two at midmorning, then two or three drinks at lunch to fuel his addiction. Raleigh learned this on the rare days his father was sober and repentant, in a mood for confession. Yet his drinking progressed, and this sullen mood became constant, wrapping him like a second set of dank clothes. There were no reprieves. Raleigh could not remember a day in the last ten years of his father's life when he had not taken a drink.

Then he turned violent. Raleigh, who by this time was in his mid-teens, was no longer the easy target. But Joyce, with her petite and slender body, offered little physical resistance to her husband. At first, he took it out on her sexually, forcing her when she didn't want to. Her husband outweighed her by more than 150 pounds. She often took the pounding in silence, for reasons she did not fully understand. Yet she would not bend to his will, whatever that will demanded.

Harleigh, unable to control his own life, unable to tame his addiction, desperately tried to assert control over something, over anything. He imposed ridiculous curfews on his son, for a time forbidding him to stay out past eight o'clock on any evening, weekends or otherwise. Raleigh had done nothing to justify the restriction, and when he disobeyed his father's mandate, his father took away his car. It had been his father's plan to force him to ride the bus to high school, a penitence, and to embarrass him through the pulled privilege. His mother intervened and drove him to school each morning, until his father found out. Once he learned of his wife's transgression, Harleigh took away the keys to both of Joyce's cars. Undeterred, Raleigh began running to and from school each day, often with a backpack.

His father lived each day in a fog, peering out from it as if from an unlit lighthouse, trying to gain some purchase on anything outside himself. One Sunday afternoon, he and his father were watching their beloved Falcons fritter away yet another football game, when Harleigh slipped into a drunken rage. His mother made the mistake of politely inquiring about the progress of the game, and in response his father threw a half-full scotch bottle at her, hitting her on the cheek. While she lay on the carpet, her cheek swelling with redness, his father kicked her in the side. Raleigh had enough, and while his father loomed over his mother, cursing her because she had dared to exist that day, Raleigh delivered a roundhouse punch to his father's right temple. His father crumpled and went down in a lump. In his stupefied state, he stayed down. While his father's rage did not end after that, it remained, for the most part, embedded within his own body.

The last days of Raleigh's time at home were filled with tired trepidation. His father had become a caged animal, only this animal knew how to unlock the gate and roam freely throughout their lives. His mother had moved out of the marital bedroom and now slept in a guest room down the hall from Raleigh's room. There were days, sometimes strung together five or six at a time, when his father did not emerge from his bedroom at all. Alcohol stashed in various hideouts throughout their home became his father's constant and reclusive companion. He could sometimes hear his father through the bedroom door conversing with the entity, sometimes pleading with it, sometimes cursing it. The master bedroom took on the stench of the unwashed, became a darkened cave with a colorless pallor, lifeless as anything other than a cell.

Raleigh's reprieve came when he escaped to college, leaving behind a mother he both feared for and admired. In the early days of college, Raleigh traveled home frequently. To comfort his mother, or to spell her, he knew not which. He begged his mother to leave Harleigh, to perhaps go back to the Reservation, where she had people, loving people who could help restore her comfort and faith in other human beings. But she would not leave her husband, even though he had long ago left her. His father rarely left the house, except for trips to the liquor store. He had become a hospice patient of sorts, craving and consuming the very thing that was killing him. His mother, the discomfited caretaker, had absorbed some of his father's bitterness. How could she not? She too had succumbed to the disease and become its victim even though she did not drink it. Raleigh watched from afar as the poison invaded her slowly and began to cloud her eyes. The light from her dimmed considerably, and Raleigh thought of her as a dying star, even though she was not yet halfway through her life. At forty, she looked fifty. The luster of her once-sleek raven hair had evaporated, and she carried herself like a blanket that had become tattered and torn.

The physical separation Raleigh gained while away at college did not fully insulate him from his father's demise or his mother's dejected plight. As graduation neared, he became consumed with a spreading dread, a dread that circumstances might propel him home again, and he knew he had to find another destiny. He did not want to join his father's real estate firm, though both father and company needed an infusion of fresh blood and energy.

Law school became for Raleigh not a destination in itself, but a way station where he might bide his time and delay his arrival to wherever. The challenging first year classes and the inquisitive professors who demanded dedication overtook Raleigh's brain and permitted little room for thoughts of his family. Visits home became rare. He took an apartment at school and stayed there through the summers. Though he spoke to his mother on the phone with some frequency, the conversations were often bleak. On the occasional holiday for which Raleigh trekked home, meals were a gloomy affair consisting of mother and son dining alone, shoulders hunched in apprehension of the threatened appearance of the man they now referred to as "him." With his desire to live gone, the man Raleigh once looked up to, whose touch Joyce had once coveted, had lost his identity and his name. To his son and wife, he had become a shapeless entity who roamed at night, noticed but unseen, whose trail could often be detected in half-eaten sandwiches in the kitchen or doors left ajar in the night. During those times, his mother did not want to talk about Harleigh's health, or his tirades, or the business that was failing in his absence.

Raleigh's future, which had once appeared to him as a murky grey shape dominated by his father, had begun to clarify, as if through some miracle of alchemy. No longer known solely as the son of real-estate developer Harleigh Westlake, a tether he had longed to snap without realizing it, Raleigh began to see a future separated from his past. He excelled at the learning of the law, earning a third-place class rank after his first year, and became a sought-after first year law clerk.

During job interviews, he was often peppered with the question: "Are you related to Harleigh Westlake?" He struggled to answer. He at first admitted Harleigh Westlake was his father, but that answer inevitably led to a series of other questions transparently designed to determine how much of his father's legal business Raleigh could bring to the firm. So his answers gradually became vague and, ultimately, lies in which he claimed that Harleigh's brood was a different branch of the family tree. Scrupulously honest up to that time, even to himself, it was the first time Raleigh could remember overtly lying to someone else who mattered. And he liked it. He liked the way it blocked further inquiry and turned the attention back to his grades, his classes, his qualifications. And this brought him out from under the dome of his father.

Some of these stories he shared with Hal Manning, who had similar tales. By comparison, Raleigh's father seemed like a hapless boxer whose punches rarely landed. Hal Manning had suffered the loss of a leg and internal injuries when his father drove them into a tree while drunk. The wreck ended Manning's college football career. The elder Manning had died, and his son, now a state court judge, had endured a lengthy period of rehabilitation that delayed his entry into law school by two years.

Raleigh had not seen Hal Manning in at least a decade. As he thought back on their history, the dark stories shared with downcast eyes in the late hours, Raleigh pondered how Hal could have let off a drunk driver who had mowed down five people in a crosswalk.

160

CHAPTER THIRTY-THREE

Tyler Becksdale stumbled from a bar on Bay Street, fumbling for his car keys. He was still celebrating the Savannah Sand Gnats victory that evening, a game in which he had struck out the final three batters to preserve the win. His fast ball had been consistently clocked in the 93-94 mile per hour range, and he had allowed no hits in two and a third innings. Several scouts watched him put on a sterling performance. He just knew his chance was coming to be called up to the big leagues.

He opened the door to his yellow Hummer and angled his six-feet-five frame into the driver's seat. He started the car and checked his texts for the address of a party someone had told him about on Wilmington Island.

A black man slipped quietly into the passenger seat and pressed a stun gun against his right hip. "Drive," the man said. "Over the Talmadge Bridge."

Becksdale looked down at the gun.

"Mister, you've got the wrong guy . . ."

"Shut up and drive," the man said, shoving the gun harder against his side. "Everybody knows who you are, Tyler. The kid who struck out the side tonight."

Tyler drove across the long bridge spanning the Savannah River and into South Carolina, then turned onto a sandy road that wound between cypress trees and live oaks. He parked behind a tractor-trailer rig idling on the shoulder. The man in the front seat with him snatched the car key from the ignition. Another man pulled open the driver side door and showed him a second stun gun.

"Out," the second man said.

Tyler unbuckled his seat belt and slid out of the Hummer.

The back doors of the trailer were opened, and the two men prodded him up the step and into a chair. The metal doors swung shut, and the bolt was jammed into the floor, locking him inside. While one of the men held a stun gun against his neck, the other buckled a cargo strap around his torso

161

and arms, and a second strap around his calves. He was completely immobilized.

"I am Judge Raleigh Westlake," a man said from behind a narrow desk at the front of the trailer. "You are here to be sentenced for the deaths of the five people you killed last fall, Mr. Becksdale."

"I've already been sentenced and served my time for that," Tyler said.

"That was in another courtroom and another day, I'm afraid. Your lawyers argued that you should be sent to an addiction clinic and given probation because you suffered from a heretofore unrecognized condition called 'privilege syndrome.' You were given too much to work with, it seems. By your parents and by God. The judge, who you might want to know was a law school classmate of mine, apparently found this syndrome made it impossible for you to discern right from wrong. I don't recognize that condition or that legal defense, Mr. Becksdale. Do you have anything to say for yourself?"

"Wait. This is crazy." Tyler looked about at the faces staring at him. Besides the two who stood beside him with Tasers, there were two other men, in suits, who looked like businessmen or lawyers.

"Do you want to perhaps apologize for what you did?" The Judge said.

"Sure," Tyler sniffed. "I'm sorry. Sorry for all of it."

"One of the people you killed was an eight-year-old girl who was on her way to trick or treat with a friend. Do you even know her name, Mr. Becksdale? Do you know the names of any of the people you killed?"

"I didn't see her, or any of them. I was drunk."

"At seven p.m. on a Wednesday night, you were drunk?"

"That's the truth."

"Your estimated speed was fifty-four miles per hour on a downtown street with a speed limit of twenty-five."

"Like I said, I was drunk."

"That is exactly the point. Do you think that being drunk is an excuse? Do you think it is a defense to your actions? It may be a cause of what you did, but it's certainly not a justification or a legal excuse. Do you understand that?"

"I don't know."

The Judge rubbed his chin, his mouth slightly ajar. "Did you learn anything from rehab? I've received a report that you were at least partially inebriated when you were picked up this evening, driving a new Hummer I might add."

"I learned some stuff."

"But you didn't quit drinking?"

"I quit for thirty-one days."

"So you stayed sober for the grand total of one day after you were released from rehab?"

Tyler nodded. "You know, some friends picked me up from rehab. They were partying the next night. I wanted to party with them."

The Judge gripped the arms of his chair. "Again, do you even know her name? The eight-year-old little girl?"

Tyler shrugged his broad shoulders. "I did know their names, but I forgot. You have to believe me."

"You forgot. You forgot the names of all of the people you killed?"

"I blacked out. I don't remember anything about that night. The crash, or anything."

"Well let me remind you, Mr. Becksdale. Casey Miller was just eight years old when you killed her. She was in the second grade. She wanted to be a nurse. So not only did you deprive Casey of her life, but you took away her parents' child. Say her name, Mr. Becksdale."

"Casey Miller," Tyler whispered.

"Louder, dammit."

"Casey Miller," Tyler shouted.

"Say 'I killed Casey Miller'."

Tyler shook his head.

The Judge bolted up from his chair. "Say it or I'll come over there and kill you myself."

Tyler raised his head and stared with rounded eyes, as if realizing for the first time how this would end.

The Judge's voice grew louder. "Mamie Thompson, 66, Casey Miller's grandmother. Say her name. Joanne Nelson, 29, taught middle school. Say her name. Herbert Davidson, a dentist and father of three. Say his name. Mickey Livingston, 41, a truck driver. Say his name!"

Tyler shook his head at every word.

The Judge leapt down from the desk and rushed over to him.

The big man standing beside him intercepted the Judge. "No, Judge. You don't want to do this."

Tyler said in a shaky voice, "I paid good money to get out of it. To my lawyers and to the judge. They took my whole signing bonus."

"No way Hal Manning took a bribe from you," the Judge said.

"It's true," Tyler said. "All of it. My bonus was $1.25 million. The judge got a million. Two-hundred thousand for each victim. The lawyers took the other two-fifty."

Judge Westlake retreated a step, holding up his right hand. "You must be mistaken, Mr. Becksdale. The million was what it cost you to settle the civil cases."

"No, sir. The million went directly to the judge. My insurance company paid to settle the other cases."

"You're saying you paid Judge Hal Manning one million dollars to let you off?"

"My lawyers did. They handled it. It's the absolute truth."

The Judge took a deep breath. He held up his palms, then stepped away from the teenager bound to the chair and resumed his position at the bench.

"That's right. I have almost nothing left," Tyler pleaded.

"You have led a sorry life, Mr. Becksdale. You're a drunk. And you killed five people. What a waste. For them, and for you. I'm not going to let you get away with it. I'm not going to let you get away with murdering five people, including a little girl. What kind of message would that send to the world?"

"I don't know," Tyler sniffed. "Maybe that everyone gets a second chance."

"You had a second chance, Mr. Becksdale. And a third chance. You squandered it. You were sent home from school for being drunk on your high school campus, at least twice. What is it you want a second chance to do, get behind the wheel and kill more people?"

"I was going to cut back, eventually."

"We're doing you a favor. Believe me, Mr. Becksdale. It would have killed you eventually. That's what it does. I've seen it." The Judge leaned back in his chair, looking at a flickering ceiling light. "Does the prosecution or the defense have anything to add?"

"No, Your Honor," the two men in suits said.

"Mr. Becksdale. I am going to give you the one thing that you really seem to have craved over the past few years. We're going to let you get drunk."

Tyler opened his mouth but couldn't think of anything to say.

The Judge and the two men in suits left the trailer through a front door he hadn't noticed before.

Tyler tilted his head to look at the smaller man to his right. "Guys, I'll give you my Hummer. Just let me go. It's fully paid for."

The man pulled two bottles of liquor from a canvas bag on the floor. He unscrewed the cap from one and held the bottle in front of Tyler. "Open up."

Tyler shook his head. "I don't want to. This has scared me straight. I will never, ever touch another drop. I promise."

"Look. There are two ways we can do this, kid. This is the easy way."

"What's the other way?" Tyler said, hoping to keep the man talking. Maybe prolonging things would give him a chance to escape.

"You don't want to know."

The cell phone in his jeans pocket chimed with a text. The larger man fished in his pocket and withdrew the phone.

"Who is that?" Tyler said. "My friends are expecting me at a party, right now. They'll come looking for me. Come on, let me go. Please."

"One last time," the smaller man said. "Open up or I'll knock your teeth out and pour it in."

"All right. All right." Tyler swallowed hard, then opened his mouth. He felt a surge of burning liquid pour in, then swallowed. "Damn, that burns. What is that shit?"

"Myers Rum 151. Open."

Tyler Becksdale opened his mouth again and again until his head swam. Thoughts of escape evaporated, replaced by a soothing warmth. He eventually passed out sitting in the chair bolted to the floor of the trailer.

Perez lifted the prisoner's left eyelid. The prisoner did not flinch. "I thought the Judge was going to punch him," he said. "Lucky you stepped in."

"Yeah, he lost his cool. Think the kid really bribed that Savannah judge?" Cunningham asked.

"I don't know. Could be. It would explain a lot."

"Yeah, but it doesn't change the fact that the kid is guilty. Showed no remorse whatsoever," Cunningham replied, pulling on leather gloves.

They carried Tyler Becksdale to his vehicle and plopped him in the passenger seat. At 3:37 in the morning, long after the bars had closed, Highway 17 had become a deserted path through the trees. Cunningham drove Becksdale's Hummer toward the lights of Savannah. During the short journey, Becksdale remained unconscious, zip ties binding his hands and feet.

As he came up to the causeway that spanned the tidal basin separating South Carolina from Georgia, Cunningham slowed the car and lowered the front windows. He revved the engine and angled the right front wheel up onto the narrow curb of the concrete barrier that protected drivers from plunging into the Little Black River. Then he turned the steering wheel to the right and nosed the right front bumper up against the bridge's concrete railing. He put the SUV in park and got out. He wrestled Becksdale's long, limp body across to the driver's side, and buckled him in. With a box knife he cut the straps binding Becksdale's hands and feet. He screwed the cap off a half-empty bottle of rum, splashed a little liquor on Becksdale's chin and shirt, then tossed the bottle on the floor mat. From Tyler Becksdale's phone he sent a reply to the last text message, saying he had gotten distracted by a girl and was sorry he hadn't made the party. Then Cunningham set the phone on the center console. He looked around the vehicle, noticed a gym bag in the back seat. A black, left-handed baseball glove lay on top. He could smell the freshly applied glove oil.

"You had some promise, kid," Cunningham muttered. "Pissed it all away." He put the transmission in drive again, then closed the front door. The car nosed against the concrete barrier, but could go no further. It had taken less than three minutes for Cunningham to set the stage.

Perez waited in the rig, at the entrance to the bridge. If anyone came upon them now, Perez and Cunningham would merely be two Good Samaritans who had stopped to help a vehicle in distress.

Perez eased the truck onto the bridge, stopping a few feet from the rear bumper of Becksdale's Hummer. Cunningham retrieved an old piece of carpet from the cab and stuck it to the front bumper of the rig with double-sided tape. Perez put the truck in gear and nudged the rear bumper of the Hummer, just above the vanity plate that read "BB Star." The Hummer scraped along the bridge railing for a few feet. Perez accelerated, using all the torque of the big diesel engine, pressing hard against the other vehicle. With the engine revving, the concrete railing snapped, and the Hummer went through the railing and plunged into the river.

Cunningham looked down both sides of the highway and saw no other vehicles. He stood at the bridge railing, watching the car go down. The taillights emitted a dim, red glow. While the rig idled, Cunningham removed the piece of carpet from the front bumper of the truck and climbed into the passenger side of the cab.

"Not the first time a car has gone off this bridge," Perez said.

The tide lapped just a few feet below the surface of the road. They waited a couple of minutes to make sure Tyler Becksdale did not miraculously escape and swim to the surface. Then Perez put the big rig in gear and drove across the huge suspension bridge into the lights of Savannah.

CHAPTER THIRTY-FOUR

As Judge Westlake laced up his shoes on the cold hearth, he eyed the clay funeral urn on the bookshelf next to the fireplace. The urn, made by a local Native potter, had a reddish-brown caste, with streaks of fire on it. It contained his wife's ashes. He could not pinpoint the exact date on which he had stopped talking to Heather, stopped seeking her counsel and solace. Part of him wanted to tell Heather what he had been doing, why he had been doing it, but whenever he tried to bring it up, to say it aloud, the other wolf shut him down. The internal battle over the mission of the cabal, once raging within him, had all but ceased. He knew which wolf was winning, and he had no intention of starving that wolf.

Shiloh wandered into the den, her nails clicking softly on the hardwood floor. He reached down to rub her head. "Hey, Shiloh. I know you want to go running with me this morning, but I'm going on a long run. It's too far for you. You'll have to work up to it." He scratched gently behind her ears as she panted. Then he led her to the crate in the utility room and latched the door. As he left the house, he could hear Shiloh's lonesome howls.

The fifteen-mile loop wound past the closed federal courthouse in Bryson City. The town, near the head of Lake Fontana, had about 1,700 full time residents. The courthouse was located in a nondescript brick and concrete building near the center of town. Less grandiose than befitted any federal judge, yet Westlake had liked his courtroom because of its quaintness and lack of pretense. Its spare, simple furniture had been the model for the trailer courtroom he had designed, although in miniature due to the trailer's restrictive size. The building was still in use, with federal agencies housed there. While television trucks and media vehicles had once occupied the parking spaces in front of the building, those spaces were mostly unoccupied now, except on Sundays, when the congregation of the church next door parked there. In the age of security necessitated by terrorist threat, the Bryson City courthouse stood as a beacon of unterrified existence near the mouth of the Tuckasegee River.

168

As Westlake ran past the building, he recalled his last trial there, an odd prosecution of a group of men for conspiring to secede from the United States of America to form their own government. The men, who hailed from deep recesses of the mountain fabric around towns such as Robbinsville and Murphy, had stopped paying their taxes years ago because they claimed the income tax system was voluntary. According to their not-guilty plea, the men had simply decided to stop volunteering their money to the government. Similar claims by tax protesters had landed a lot of people in prison. In addition, the men already had begun printing currency for their new country, tentatively called Nantahala Nation after the Nantahala River Valley that ran through the area. In Nanta Nation, the US Dollar could be exchanged for Nanta Coin, all freshly minted and containing an aluminum core plated with a thin layer of gold or silver. Though the forefathers of this new nation had designed a rudimentary economic system that relied heavily on bartering, they also set the currency exchange rate at a level where the metal in the coins was worth far less than corresponding values in US Dollars. The Nanta Coins were to be dispensed by, and the US Dollars supporting the currency were to be held in, the Nanta National Bank. It was a twist on the abandoned gold standard. The plan was quite elaborate, but both the State of North Carolina and the United States Comptroller of the Currency declined to issue a charter for the Nanta Bank.

The defense in the trial of the Nanta Nine, as the defendants came to be called, centered on two distinct but interrelated legal theories. The first argument was that if the Cherokee Nation could exist slap in the middle of the western part of the state and could operate as an independent sovereign in the same way that Germany and Japan were independent nations, Nanta Nation must be treated equally. The second defense theory, which Westlake thought had a bit of traction on the legal side, was that the men had been exercising their First Amendment right to petition the government by threatening to form a new country whose boundaries would include all the land whose owners agreed to be annexed into it. The theory was crudely modeled on the Declaration of Independence and its reliance on natural law. After a several-week trial in which all of the defendants testified, an unusual scenario for most criminal trials, a jury of their peers, selected from nearby towns and villages, found the Nanta Nine not guilty on all charges. In all his years as a practicing attorney and judge, Westlake had never seen a jury that better represented a cross-section of the people of the area, and some of them were distantly related to the defendants. These relationships, outside of the degree of consanguinity that would have disqualified the jurors from serving, were a bane to the prosecutors' case and something about which they complained incessantly.

Westlake had accepted the jury's not-guilty verdict with some resignation and a wry smile. The verdict was an unsubtle form of frontier justice. After the jury had been dismissed and the media had gone home, Westlake granted the United States' motion for a judgment notwithstanding the verdict on some of the charges, effectively nullifying the jury's decision of acquittal. On those charges upon which he found the defendants guilty as a matter of law, he imposed relatively minor sentences that ranged from probation to a few months in prison. He also ordered forfeiture of the Nanta Coins remaining in the Nanta Nation Treasury and the US Dollars, a sum of several hundred thousand dollars. Most of the defendants had thanked him, for they knew the very public trial had given them a pulpit from which to press their protest against a government that had proved unworthy of their support. Those who had received Nanta Coins in exchange for US Dollars were entitled to reclaim their US currency. Few made such a claim, either because they did not want to acknowledge their association with the founding fathers of Nanta Nation, or because they were proud of it. Westlake found a way to have the seized funds distributed to various charities throughout the area, including an animal shelter and a couple of charities whose philanthropy benefitted citizens of the Cherokee Reservation.

This replaying of the trial in Westlake's mind ended about the time he reached the Road to Nowhere. The six-mile road represents an unrealized promise by the federal government many decades earlier to build a road on the north side of Lake Fontana, as compensation for taking land necessary for creation of the lake and the Great Smoky Mountains National Park. The valley, once dotted with fertile farms, is flooded. The highway that once connected those communities to the outside world is now at the bottom of the lake. The promised road that would allow natives to access the area and old family cemeteries has never been built. Judge Westlake himself had joined the effort to persuade Congress to appropriate the funds to finish the road, but the effort proved unsuccessful. The federal government made a monetary settlement instead. A few years later, the federal courthouse in Bryson City was closed. From a budget perspective, closing the courthouse was a wise move, but many of the locals saw it as one more governmental act that was designed to ignore them. Now, with the closest federal courthouse in Asheville, those in the farthest reaches of Western North Carolina had to travel several hours when they had business in federal court.

His warm-up now complete, it was time for the serious portion of the training run. Westlake had studied a plethora of articles, and a few books, devoted to the physical demands of the marathon and the training of the body. He had borrowed from several training regimens to construct his own program. But he found few resources on the training of the athlete's mind. In interviews published online, he'd read about athletes who described their state during monumental performances as "being in the zone" or "seeing the game in slow motion." Westlake did not find these vague descriptions particularly helpful. He was more interested in how to get there. He had experienced the runner's high, that state of euphoria encased in a natural release of dopamine, on a handful of occasions. Yet, there seemed no concrete path to achieving that state. Through years of running he had developed his own theory, which basically involved an effort to not think about anything and focus on his breathing. Heather had called it meditation on the move, and Westlake could not deny the accuracy of that description. By no means was his theory a novel one, though clearing his mind proved difficult for a man who made his living with his brain, analyzing complex fact scenarios and legal problems. To shut if off was neither a basic instinct nor an easy task.

As he inclined his body into the first serious hill, he wondered if Hannah Sullivan had used a similar technique as she climbed the mountain on her road bike the day she was killed. What was she thinking about, if anything, as she pushed up the mountain? A part of him believed a subdued mind would lead to additional blood and oxygen for the muscles that carried his body along the path, yet he also thought the mental energy necessary to subdue his mind might negate the benefit. He pondered all of this as he crested the first hill, his heart monitor beeping to announce he had exceeded eighty percent of his maximum heart rate. His mind was not at peace, and this unrest reflected in his elevated pulse. Westlake eased onto the plateau, and his heart monitor alarm went silent a minute later.

He passed another runner who was on his way out of the park, and they exchanged silent waves. Training hard had never been a problem for Westlake. His problem was the opposite—giving his body the rest it needed. From his first run to school when his father had forbidden him to drive the car or hitch a ride with another student, he had pounded the pavement as if pounding evil back into Hell. Perhaps he was. Those early runs were not merely a crude form of transportation, they were escape. In the escape, at least in the beginning, euphoria reigned. Anger receded as exhaustion emerged, and as a youth he made it his goal to exhaust himself almost every day. His high school track coach in Atlanta subscribed to the hard-easy approach and prescribed at least two workouts a week in which the team ran at a pace where they could talk comfortably without gasping. These easy runs were designed to keep from over-taxing the body, especially before a race. Westlake ignored his coach. He could race faster only if he trained faster, he maintained.

And maybe enveloped in this drive was another factor, one on which he had no handle and could not name. Something other than the inexorable degrading of his body's resiliency to life was driving him back to the roads, back to the challenges to which he wanted to submit his entire being.

He came to the dark tunnel, a form of echo chamber, and his footfalls became those of dozens of other runners plowing through the tunnel with him. In those echoes he could hear Heather's voice, urging him along as she had at so many finish lines before the cancer took her breath away. He emerged from the tunnel into a bright sun that caused him to shield his eyes. Stopping to look around, he scanned the trees, the granite boulders ascending into a forest whose leaves had begun to turn. He expected to see something there, revealed in that blaze of sunlight, but nothing revealed itself. He took a deep breath, turned around, and plunged back into the dark tunnel.

CHAPTER THIRTY-FIVE

Westlake drove to Cherokee, with Shiloh asleep on a blanket in the back seat of the Mercedes. On a leash, he walked her onto the porch of his mother's house and rapped lightly on the front door. It took a bit for his mother to get to the door. He could hear her shuffling about in the living room.

She swung the door open and stared at him through the mesh of the screen. "You could have walked on in, Raleigh. I don't keep it locked."

"Yes. Well, I wanted to introduce you to someone." He held up the leash, then pulled open the screen door. "Mom, this is Shiloh. Shiloh, this is my mother, Joyce Littlefield."

They came around the screen and his mother bent to pat Shiloh's apricot head. "She's beautiful. Is she trained?"

"She is. An accident every now and then."

"This is a surprise. I wasn't sure you were ever going to allow me to meet her."

"I know."

"Where did you get her?"

"At the animal shelter over in Asheville."

"Interesting," his mother said, her knuckles under her chin. "Anyway, come on in. To what do I owe this unexpected visit?"

"I came to take you to lunch. First Sunday of the month. Remember?"

"I didn't know this had gotten to be a regular thing," she said.

"Sure, we talked about it last time. Anyway, do you want to go to lunch at the diner?"

"Okay. Let me get my coat."

They sat at a window table, Westlake glancing furtively at the car, where Shiloh lay on the back seat. He had cracked the windows even though it was cool outside, but the sky was clouding up, so he worried about rain dripping in and spoiling the leather seats. They ate hurriedly and walked back out to the Mercedes.

As he withdrew his key to unlock the doors, a man approached from the rear. He wore a long beard of grey wool, and he appeared neither threatening nor nonthreatening, though he walked with the deliberate stride of a man on a mission. Westlake opened the passenger door for his mother first. Shiloh perked up in the backseat. The man stopped near the rear of the vehicle.

"Do you remember me?" the man said in a soft voice.

To Westlake this was a volatile question. Remembering this man could be good or bad. He took the noncommittal approach. "You do look familiar."

The man hesitated, and Westlake assumed a wary pose. He gently closed the passenger door, shutting his mother inside, and stood poised beside the car. Shiloh sniffed at the crack in the rear window and pranced on the leather seat, emitting a low whine.

When the man reached inside his coat pocket, Westlake took a step backward. The man removed his hand from his pocket and produced a business card. "I'm Jack Newland. You sent me to prison a few years back. Remember?"

Westlake regained his breath. "I do remember you, Mr. Newland. You were one of the Nanta Nine." For the briefest of moments Westlake pondered the notion that his earlier reminiscence of the trial had magically produced Newland's appearance that very afternoon.

"I was. Anyhow, you mentioned that if you ever needed firewood, you'd give me a call. With fall coming on, I figured you might be in need."

The two men stepped toward each other. "That was what, six or seven years ago?" Westlake said.

"Eight."

Westlake reached out and took the business card. "As a matter of fact, I was just noticing that my wood pile is dwindling. I'm probably in need of another cord or two. What have you got?"

"Good oak, seasoned two years now. And some hickory too."

"Oak or hickory sounds good. How much for a cord?"

"One fifty, split. Two fifty for two cords."

"I think you've got yourself a deal, Mr. Newland. Two cords will be great." The two men shook hands. "How have you been getting along since . . . you know, since you got out?"

"Just fine, Judge."

"You know where I live, Mr. Newland?"

Newland smiled and spit a stream of tobacco out to the side. "Judge, I know where you live. I expect everybody around here knows where you live."

Beneath the cap and woolly beard, Westlake was not sure if he saw menace or amusement.

"And we're real proud of you, too. One of our own has made it big."

"'One of our own?' Oh, are you a tribal member too?"

"Yes sir."

"Which clan?"

"Bird clan."

"I'm Wolf myself," Westlake said.

"Yes, sir. I know your mama." Newland waved at Joyce, who was looking at him in the side mirror. She opened the passenger door, nudging her son out of the way.

"Is that you, Jack Newland?" she said, moving forward to give him a hug. "How's your mama doing?"

"Pretty good. She's ailing, ain't we all. But she's getting by."

"I don't see her much anymore."

"No ma'am. She's not driving anymore. We take her to town every now and then, but she doesn't get out much."

"Well, tell her I said hello and I hope to see her soon."

"I will, ma'am." Jack Newland tipped his cap and walked away.

The Judge called after him. "When might you be delivering that firewood?"

Newland stopped. "I'll drop it off in a couple of days."

"Okay," Westlake said. "What about payment?"

Newland pointed to the card in Westlake's hand. "Address is right there on the card. Just mail me a check when you get around to it."

Westlake sidled around the car, watching Jack Newland get into a dilapidated grey pickup truck on the other side of the lot. He stared at the truck, hoping to commit it and the license plate to memory.

"That Jack Newland is a good man," Joyce said. "Sweet to his mama."

Turning the key, Westlake said, "You know I sent him to prison a few years ago."

"Everybody knows. His mama was not your biggest fan for a while. Thought Jack might die in prison, but you gave him such a light sentence he was back home before he'd hardly been missed."

"A good deed?" Westlake ventured.

"You get it right every once in a while, son. Listen, let's go over to the casino."

"The casino?"

"You know where it is, don't you?"

Westlake screwed up his mouth. "Of course I know where it is, mother."

"I sure hope so. It's why you get that check twice a year."

"I am aware of that as well." In fact, the semiannual check he had received as a member of the Cherokee Tribe was largely responsible for paying his law school tuition. "Are you saying you want to give some of it back at the casino?"

His mother shrugged her shoulders. "If I do lose, it won't be much. I just play the slots."

"What about Shiloh?"

She shrugged. "Well, I guess you can leave her in the car with the windows down, or you can drop her at my house."

"It looks like it might rain."

"They have a parking garage, Raleigh."

"We'll drop her at your house. Put her in the bathroom with her pallet. I don't think she'll chew on anything, but I'm not one hundred percent sure."

"That's fine. There ain't nothing in the bathroom she can chew up anyway."

With Shiloh secured in the small bathroom of his mother's house, they drove back to the casino. Westlake left his mother at the quarter slots, the machines emitting flashing lights and computerized chimes. He weaved through the casino to the blackjack tables. The crowds were light on Sunday afternoon. Most of the tourists had already headed home. He took an empty seat at a table with two others, a table designed for eight. He passed his fingers over the green felt. It felt new. Although he played poker on many weekends, they played for small stakes. It was rare that anyone won or lost more than $20 at his weekend poker games. He changed a $100 bill into chips and quickly lost two rounds. Playing at a casino, where the house had the odds, was not a comfortable endeavor for the Judge. Winning or losing at blackjack was largely a matter of luck, with bluffing a non-issue. He won a couple of hands but was soon down to $50 in chips.

His mind wandered, still thinking about what Jack Newland had said: *I expect everybody around here knows where you live.* After a dozen years on the bench, he knew he would make some enemies, mostly those he sent to prison or ruled against in civil cases. Staying out at Lake Fontana most of the time, he was isolated. He had no security other than an alarm system, and maybe Shiloh. Maybe he should install a security system, with motion detectors and outdoor cameras. He vowed to check the revolver he kept in the top of his bedroom closet. He didn't even know if it was loaded. An intruder could break into his home without him knowing it. Someone could slip across the lake in a boat, undetected, and with an easy escape route. Break-ins happened at Lake Fontana, but rarely. If the homeowners of the fancy houses on the lake were a target, they were usually a target of gossip, not crime. He might be imagining it, but there was something almost sinister in the way Newland had approached him, the ease with which he had conversed with the man who had sent him to prison. Though admittedly it was a light sentence. In imposing a minimal sentence, had Westlake engendered good will, or had he created enemies because he overturned the jury and found the defendants guilty despite the judgment of their neighbors? He couldn't clearly read the situation. He did not think of himself as one of them and knew he was considered an outsider. Despite what Jack Newland had said. He worked for the federal government, which had been the arch enemy of the Cherokee Nation for eons. Maybe he had earned some favor because his mother was born on the Reservation and had come back to live out her life there, but he was not one of them, and never would be. Unless he was wrong.

He looked around the casino. The only faces he thought familiar were members of the staff—dealers, waitresses, pit bosses standing by like stoic totems. Everyone else was a visitor from another place.

He lost another few hands of blackjack, then scraped up his remaining two $10 chips. He got up from the table, pushed the chair in and started to walk away. Then thought better of it. He stepped back to the table and slid the chips back across the felt to the dealer. "Thanks man. It was fun," he said awkwardly.

He found his mother, who was up a few dollars playing the slots. She had a cupful of quarters. "You ready to go?"

"What, have you lost all your money, already?"

"No, just ready to go."

"All right. This machine's turned cold anyway."

They exited the casino, and Westlake gave the valet his ticket. When the young valet hopped out of the Mercedes, Westlake tipped him $10. As he drove off, he eyed the grand building in the rearview mirror and vowed he would never go there again.

CHAPTER THIRTY-SIX

Lyle Walker was a Texas oil man, and that made him a gambler. He made it big before fracking became a vast, polarizing industry. Starting out as a wildcatter, he brought in a few wells that enabled him to start a regional drilling company that bought up a vast number of oil and gas leases in the Permian Basin. The Permian Basin covers about 75,000 square miles in West Texas and New Mexico. When prices were high, the company was extremely profitable, but a few dry wells and a glut of Saudi oil changed the cycle once again.

Walker made a lot of money, but he never learned how to keep much of it. A bad investment here, an unsatisfied wife there, and cash gushed out of his bank account. In response to his dwindling reserves, Walker went back to the banks for loans. The banks, once friendly when oil prices were high, refused to lend additional money for oil and gas drilling. Many of the banks were still suffering the shock of the latest financial meltdown from toxic mortgages. Those that survived were stashing their lending capital in safe government bonds, earning more than they paid out to depositors, strengthening their balance sheets. In that climate, no one was lending to the likes of Lyle Walker.

To remain afloat, Walker started seeking investors. At first, he secured small investments from members of his church, his neighbors, teachers and administrators from the district where he was on the school board, and from his fellow Rotary Club members. All legal, fully vetted by lawyers. One investor in his limited partnerships, who got in early with $25,000, was the president of a local bank. The banker was willing to risk his own money, but with regulators hovering about he couldn't push through a bank loan for Lyle Walker.

As oil prices recovered, profits soared, and Lyle Walker was able to pay a nice return to his early investors. Word spread, carried on the West Texas wind, and soon Walker had investors clamoring to get in. His friends and former business partners were already invested on the ground floor. Walker began selling limited partnership interests to the unwary and unsophisticated. Those souls thought they had missed out on the latest oil boom, until Walker opened a fund in which they could invest, sometimes a little, sometimes their entire life savings, on the promise of higher prices for limited oil. Walker's enterprise rebounded from bust to boom, and he was once again thought of as a Texas oil baron.

But there was a problem. Lyle Walker didn't have any more land to drill on, and he couldn't find additional oil leases at a reasonable price. Most of his wells were at full capacity. He failed to tell his investors these important facts. When oil prices sank again because OPEC eased production limits in the inevitable cycle, the profits dried up, and Walker began using the money from new investors to pay dividends to keep his original investors satisfied. This scheme worked, for a little while. New investors were harder to entice because oil prices had dropped, so Lyle Walker began to fabricate his financial results. He cooked the books. He touted his successes, and hid his failures. Walker told potential investors he had predicted an oil glut and expected the decline in prices and, in a stroke of genius, he had invested substantial sums in iron mines in South America and gold mines in Africa. These investments weren't real, but most investors never looked behind the gleaming Lyle Walker smile or the glossy brochures he gave them. Even if they had looked behind the facade, they would have been able to find only scant information about the shell companies in foreign countries that supposedly owned a piece of mines no one could have found on a map.

When business was good, Walker made money on the front end through the drilling company, and on the back end in managing the limited partnerships. Yet, as oil prices dropped and drilling activity subsided, he became less of an oilman and more of an investment manager, taking his two percent management fee even as clients' account balances plummeted. Walker had a lavish lifestyle to support. He had more than a dozen fancy and antique cars at his homes in Texas. He was a member of three golf clubs even though he didn't play golf. He used the memberships merely as an introduction to affluent, potential investors. He had just built a vacation home north of Palm Beach, Florida and was in the process of purchasing a fishing lodge on a lake in western Canada when the complaints began rolling in. Walker's scheme began to unravel.

Walker had wisely used his money to purchase relationships. He contributed heavily to a multitude of politicians and charitable causes, and he became something of a confidante to the Governor on energy issues.

He was appointed to the Board of Trustees of a major Texas university, his *alma mater*, where he had been a sensational running back for three college years. The Texas Tornado, a nickname given to him in high school for his whirling, slashing style of running, had no trouble developing high-powered friends as his oil drilling business grew. He was viewed as the quintessential Texas entrepreneur: tough, generous, and not afraid to take a risk. His connections and money, his physical stature and athletic reputation, made him an easy winner of a seat in Congress.

When the White-Collar Crime Task Force of the Justice Department received word of a potential Ponzi scheme involving oil and gas limited partnerships in Texas, they learned quickly what they were up against. That Lyle Walker was well-liked and well-connected was but one of the hurdles in the path of the investigation. The other was that the President himself had anointed Walker as the new face of the party. The power of the politic could not be ignored, especially in Washington.

The Task Force also discovered that Walker had been well-advised in constructing his criminal enterprise. His scheme did not easily fall within the purview of federal securities' regulators. Each of the 511 oil and gas partnerships was limited to forty-five investors, and Walker never solicited or accepted investors from outside the State of Texas. None of the shares in any of the partnerships was solicited or sold on any stock exchange. On its face, the enterprise wasn't a federal issue.

As a consequence, Texas securities' regulations, known as Blue Sky laws, were the only protection for the investors who had been defrauded. The Task Force investigated the possibility of indictment under federal money-laundering laws, but the evidence was slim, and an effort on that front would look like a weak swing.

Caroline Bannister was a member of the Task Force. As a member, she delivered periodic updates of Task Force investigations to her local team in Charlotte, which was at various times conducting its own investigations of white-collar crime in the western half of North Carolina. Robert Crenshaw and two others were responsible for leading prosecutions of crimes that included bank fraud, wire fraud and real estate fraud. Gathered in the large conference room next to Caroline's office, she told her team about Lyle Walker. Her frustration was evident.

"Not only is this guy incredibly well-connected, it looks like he has masterminded a crime that the feds won't touch."

"Why not?" said one of her AUSA's.

"The AG's staff is hiding behind the United States Attorneys' Manual. The manual says a federal prosecutor should decline prosecution if no substantial federal interest would be served, the accused is subject to effective prosecution in another jurisdiction, or there is an adequate noncriminal alternative to prosecution. So, someone high up in the Justice Department, undoubtedly close to the Attorney General himself, has made the decision that the federal government will not prosecute Lyle Walker. It's all political, and transparent as hell. Everybody wants to be seen as tough on crime, but nobody wants to touch the heir apparent to the throne."

"What's the scope of the financial loss?" one of the other prosecutors asked.

"Five hundred million and climbing," Caroline said. "Most of the late investors, the ones who got stung the most, were school teachers, political contributors, retirees. In other words, people who can ill-afford to lose their life savings in this Ponzi scheme."

"How many investors have lost money?" Crenshaw asked.

"About two thousand."

"Hard to believe the Justice Department has decided not to pursue prosecution for a crime of that magnitude," said Crenshaw.

"Believe it, Robert. What's worse is that we can't be sure the Texas AG or any of the local prosecutors are going to do a thing. They could use the Texas securities' laws to prosecute, but we've made some discrete inquiries about their intentions and had the door slammed on us. The statute of limitations is going to run out on these claims. Apparently, the investigation has been limping along for five or six years," Caroline said. "This guy is a prime target, but it looks like he's going to get away with a Ponzi scheme the likes of which we haven't seen since Madoff. There's nothing we can do at this point," she shrugged.

* * * * * *

Crenshaw reported all of this to the team when they met again at Westlake's house on Lake Fontana. Since Tyler Becksdale had drowned in the river, their mission had become stagnant. Crenshaw had been receiving not so subtle hints during their frequent poker games that it was time for him to suggest their next target. He felt the pressure. He had other potential targets to present: a drug dealer with a burgeoning network in

Charlotte; a fledgling online gambling concern that had cropped up. But Westlake wanted to hear more about Lyle Walker.

"I'm intrigued," Westlake said. "Are you sure the feds aren't going to indict Walker?"

"Not certain, but according to what I hear from my boss, the investigation is being closed."

"And the Texas AG?"

"Doubtful. The Texas AG was one of Walker's teammates on the football team, and Walker is connected to every important Texas politician, state and federal. The Task Force even discovered that Walker's enterprise contributed heavily to the local district attorney's re-election campaign. Apparently, none of them wants to shine a light on this at all, because it would reveal their association to the guy."

"Maybe the House Ethics Committee will investigate," Johnstone suggested.

"Even if that were true," Westlake retorted, "it would drag on for years, and all Walker would probably get is a censure."

"What happens if we do nothing?" Johnstone asked.

Crenshaw twisted his mouth. "Well, my guess is that the class actions against him will succeed or be settled, bleed him dry, and he'll file for bankruptcy. A year or two from now he'll be all cleaned up. Maybe he'll be dinged a little, politically. But these kinds of scandals tend to fade quickly."

"Yeah, he'll be dinged all right, and rise from the ashes." Cunningham said. "The Texas Tornado will be dubbed the Comeback Kid, and the public will love him right through it all. There's precedent for that."

"Here's another reason we should be interested," Crenshaw said. "The drug dealer I told you about, he's under investigation for killing another drug dealer. It's a murder case sure, but nobody sees that as a poster prosecution. Some of us privately think the drug dealer did a good thing. Now contrast that with Walker. He's ruined hundreds, if not thousands, of lives. A lot of people lost their life savings. Most of them will never recover, will have to live off government subsidies for the rest of their lives. In some ways, Walker indirectly made them wards of the federal government, which will cost the taxpayers millions of dollars. Plus, now get this, according to what Caroline told us, as many as ten people may have committed suicide because of the bad investment in Walker's Ponzi scheme. They lost everything, became destitute. A few of them left suicide notes directly blaming Walker."

"Like Elise Rutherford's daughter," Johnstone commented.

"Exactly," Crenshaw said.

"Have the suicides been verified?" Westlake asked.

"The Task Force has proof, but I haven't seen it," Crenshaw said.

"And you can't examine the files for fear of leaving a paper trail," the Judge said.

"Right."

"So if Lyle Walker's financial scheme caused ten people to commit suicide, isn't that worse than what Elise Rutherford did, as a whole?" Johnstone said. "Elise Rutherford molested all three of her children, but only one of them killed herself."

"Are there alternatives to our special form of justice?" Westlake asked.

"We could leak it to the media. Maybe that will put pressure on the feds to prosecute," Perez offered.

Crenshaw shook his head. "That might be traced back to me, somehow. Plus, it sounds like the political machine is ready for that. Caroline says she heard a rumor, probably more than a rumor, that Walker and his party already have a team of libel lawyers lined up to sue anybody who runs a story about it. And the AG has already threatened to fire anybody even suspected of a leak. Apparently, Walker has friends all the way to the top. He's a US Congressman. Those guys don't topple easily, and this one is very smart and savvy."

"To recap," Westlake said, "we have a criminal mastermind who put together an incredibly complex investment scheme, with the help of lawyers and accountants, to defraud thousands of people out of their life savings. He thought about it, planned it, executed it, and because he's monied and connected politically, no prosecutor will touch him for fear of getting burned and being relegated to a backwater judicial district. He gets away with it, rises quickly through the ranks, gains power in Congress, and who knows how much influence he wields."

"That's the gist of it," Crenshaw said. "But remember, he hasn't killed anybody, not directly. Lawter killed Hannah Sullivan. Elise Rutherford was responsible for her daughter's death, and we didn't even execute her for it. She killed herself. Tyler Becksdale killed five people."

Westlake rested his elbows on the table. Somewhere between Elise Rutherford's assisted suicide and Tyler Becksdale's forced drowning, he had felt this become a part of him. Inculcated into his daily thinking, it was no longer a project or an endeavor that would one day end. The trial and execution of bad men had become a permanent fixture in the fabric of his daily life. And not one that he wanted to banish.

"Marcus, Iggy, what do you guys think?" Westlake said.

"Same old story. Rich guy wins," Cunningham said.

Perez: "Us peons, we figure this happens all the time. It's the way the world works."

"Are you suggesting we do nothing?" asked Westlake.

"No," Perez said. "I'm just saying this guy is at the top of a long list, and most of them won't ever be touched."

"Here's why I think this one's different," Westlake said. "Lawter and Elise Rutherford, and most of the people locked up in our prisons, they did what they did because they were on drugs, or impoverished, or just plain stupid. Most of their crimes are isolated. Mostly they've hurt themselves, sometimes another person or two. As Robert said, one drug dealer kills another one. A big loss to the deceased obviously, maybe to his family, but limited. Society doesn't give a damn about the death of another drug dealer."

"Yeah, but what about Sophie Rutherford? She killed herself because of what her mother did to her," Johnstone said.

"And we dealt with that," Westlake said, displeased at the interruption. "Lawter killed Hannah Sullivan while high on meth. Elise Rutherford pimped out her kids while on drugs. Tyler Becksdale kills five people while drunk. Addiction is not an excuse, but it's a circumstance. Lyle Walker – this is a guy that thought about what he did, knew full well the potential consequences, knew full well how it would hurt people, a lot of people, and he did it anyway. He planned it, implemented it, got rich off it. He's cunning. That makes him more dangerous than any of the others. He's an apex predator."

"Judge, you're thinking this sets a bad example," Cunningham said. "If no one prosecutes Walker, everyone sees the system is broken. The smart guy gets away with it. There will be copycats. Someone's got to send a message to him and others that this type of shit won't be tolerated."

Westlake pointed at him. "Exactly, Marcus."

"Wait a minute," Crenshaw said. "Lawter, Rutherford and Becksdale all look like accidents or suicides. No one is investigating. But you're thinking of something different with Walker, aren't you? If you're thinking of sending a message, you don't want this to look like an accident or suicide, do you?"

Westlake smiled. "No. I think Lyle Walker's fate should be public, very public, and we should send a strong message that someone is out here watching the rest of the crooks. Anonymously, of course."

The men remained silent for a moment. Perez swirled the ice in his glass, then said, "Doesn't that put everything at risk, Judge? Right now, no one even knows Lawter, Becksdale and Rutherford were murdered. Nobody has spotted the link. We do what you're suggesting, everybody knows there's a vigilante group out there."

"The FBI would get involved," Crenshaw said. "We're talking about a US Congressman here." He thumbed the five cards in his hand.

Westlake argued the point. "We need to send a message. These white-collar crimes, they're thinking crimes. The guys who come up with these schemes, they're analyzing risk/reward. They know the odds are small that they'll get caught. They steal millions of dollars, maybe hundreds of millions of dollars, and the odds that they ever get caught are infinitesimal. And if they do get caught, they go to jail—Club Fed—and they get out after a few years. If they've been smart, they've stashed the money in the Caymans or someplace offshore, and they get to enjoy a good part of that criminal bounty once they're free again. And this guy Walker, he has political power. If he keeps ascending, then when word gets out about his scheme, and it will get out, people will see that crime pays. That crime pays handsomely."

"Jail time is just part of the business plan," Johnstone said. "I've heard some of my clients talk about it. If the scheme is big enough, it's well worth it. A lot of these guys are willing to spend four or five years in minimum security prison, if they can walk away with millions of dollars for each year of incarceration. Most of them have no chance of earning that much money, legally."

"Right. Where's the deterrent?" Westlake said, his tone almost lecturing now. "If a guy thinks he's not going to get caught because there's so much graft out there that law enforcement can't keep up, and if he gets caught he gets to work out, play pool and ping pong and watch television all day on the government's tab, and then on top of that he gets paid a million plus a year to do it because the money's stashed where it can't be found, why would he not do it?"

"Since when did this sort of thing become a business plan?" Crenshaw said.

"Since the crooks figured out how much money can be made and that our sentencing guidelines treat the crack dealer and the Ponzi scheme mastermind about the same. Maybe we can put a stop to some of it. Just maybe we can deter some of the white-collar criminals. If we do something drastic," Westlake said.

"I see what you're saying," said Cunningham. "Maybe it gets them thinking. If one of the risks is our own special brand of justice, instead of Club Fed, maybe some of them won't do it."

"Right now, the punishment doesn't fit the crime," Westlake said. "It's almost a slap on the wrist to these guys. For Walker, it's likely to be nothing. But if a white-collar criminal thinks that death just might be waiting at the end of his rainbow, he's going to think a lot harder about what he's about to do. Factor the possibility of the ultimate verdict into the risk profile, you probably have a lot fewer Lyle Walkers in the world," Westlake said.

"Are we going to keep talking, or are we going to play poker?" Crenshaw said.

"Robert, we need to take a vote. It has to be unanimous," Westlake said.

"I don't hear any dissenters. Maybe we're all drinking the Kool-Aid. Maybe we've all started down the same slippery slope, but everything you say makes perfect sense to me," Crenshaw said. He wasn't sure that everyone agreed, so he expanded the argument in favor. "Sure, I like the idea of righting wrongs, prosecuting on a case-by-case basis, working within the system. But if we act on Walker, that just might prevent some types of crime. A real deterrent. And in the process, we save all the taxpayers a lot of money. Did you guys know it costs on average just over $29,000 per year to keep an inmate in federal prison? Almost thirty grand. Even if someone were to prosecute Walker, he goes away for ten years max, that costs the taxpayer $300,000, at least. And that doesn't include the cost of prosecuting him, plus appeals, plus trying to find his money while he's busy paying lawyers and bankers to hide it from us. That's easily two million. Maybe more."

Crenshaw stood up to let his message sink in. He'd brought them Lyle Walker, the biggest, most visible target the team had ever prosecuted. He took a deep, satisfying swallow of bourbon. "Anybody disagree that Lyle Walker is our next target?"

CHAPTER THIRTY-SEVEN

Ignacio Perez settled into the bushes along the fence line. He slowly brought the butt of the rifle to his right shoulder and peered through the scope. The target was in view, much closer than he would normally be. And standing still. Perez regulated his breathing. He had a clear shot. He squeezed the trigger.

Lyle Walker flinched at the impact. He reached over his shoulder, pawing at his back. He spun around twice, then fell. He writhed on the ground for just under a minute, then stopped moving.

Perez and Cunningham stepped out of the shadows and approached Walker slowly. They watched for other movement, both inside and outside of the house.

"Nice shot," Cunningham whispered.

They rolled the man onto his side. Perez pulled the dart from Lyle Walker's back.

"He should be out for about an hour," Perez said.

They drove the rental car through the quiet streets of Highland Park, heading for a rendezvous with the mobile courtroom, which was parked at a truck stop not far from the Dallas-Ft. Worth airport. Lyle Walker was in the trunk, bound, gagged and unconscious. Once they arrived at the truck stop, Perez maneuvered the car behind the rig, nearly running off into the edge of the woods that provided some cover. Together they lifted Walker from the trunk, each one ducking under one of the man's arms, and half-dragged him to the newly installed cargo lift at the back of Bravo trailer. The lift raised their package a few feet, and they strapped Walker into a metal chair bolted to the floor.

As Perez eased the rig onto the interstate, headed west, Cunningham announced to the others that Lyle Walker had been extracted. His disappearance would almost certainly hit the news sometime that morning.

"Where is he?" Crenshaw asked.

"Back there," Cunningham pointed to the rear trailer.

"How did you get him, Taser?" Westlake said.

188

Cunningham grinned. "Dart gun."

"Dart gun?"

"Tranquilizer. Went down like a big buffalo. Located him around midnight, sitting on his back patio, having a drink by himself."

"Was his wife with him?" Johnstone asked.

"Don't think so. She's back in DC, we think. No one else was in the house. But someone will come looking for him. He's got appearances lined up this afternoon."

"So where are we taking him?" Westlake said.

"West Texas. We've got a place scoped out near Odessa where we can park the trailer and have the trial. I-20 goes right through there."

"Odessa. I think that means wrathful in Greek," Johnstone said.

Cunningham nodded. "Fitting place to try a Texas oilman for fraud, don't you think?"

"Indeed it is, Marcus," Westlake said. "And after the trial, what do you have planned for the Congressman?"

"There's a plan A, B and C. Plan A, if he's acquitted, we let him go out in the desert somewhere."

Westlake smiled. "I like it. The presumption of innocence."

"Plan B, if he's convicted, is a special little punishment that will send the message you want. We haven't worked out all the details yet. Still some recon to do on Plan B. It's a little complicated. Plan C, less dramatic, Walker still gets what he deserves, message still delivered, but it's simpler and safer."

"We'll leave it to you to carry out the sentence," Westlake said. "To you and Iggy. Everyone else all right with that?"

Crenshaw and Johnstone agreed.

During the 350-mile trip to Odessa, the attorneys tried to relax on their bunks and read to pass the time. The air conditioner hummed steadily in the silence. There was little to be said. The men knew what they had to do, and they were moving toward it at seventy miles per hour. While Perez drove the rig, Cunningham watched over Lyle Walker and monitored news websites for any mention that Walker was missing. As of noon, Congressman Walker's disappearance had not yet been reported in the media.

After an uneventful drive, Perez stopped at a truck stop on the outskirts of Odessa to fuel the rig. As the others remained concealed in the trailers, he walked across the highway and bought five sandwiches from a fast food restaurant, then waited at the truck stop until the sun set. As a half-moon rose, he found the spot he and Cunningham had picked out on the map and eased the rig down a sandy road used to service the oil fields.

Perez rapped on the side doors of the trailers to signal it was safe for them to emerge. They stepped out onto the sand. Lonely lights blinked in the distance, silhouetting gray pump jacks churning the oil to the surface. The air smelled vaguely of sulfur, though a light breeze swept away the smell almost before it could be detected. The low distant hum of machinery wafted to them.

"How far away are those rigs, Iggy? There might be men working there," Westlake said.

"Two or three miles, Judge. Sound carries a long way out here. We can pick another spot, if you want to."

"Are you worried we're too close to civilization?"

"Out here? No houses within miles. Nothing but scrub. A rig like ours fits right in."

"Then I'm not worried either," Westlake said.

They ate dinner in Alpha Trailer, the meal punctuated with scant conversation. To a man, they realized they had stepped over the edge in kidnapping a United States Congressman, an irreversible decision.

"I guess we'd better get ready," Westlake announced. "You'll let us know when the defendant is ready for trial?"

"Yes, sir."

The attorneys solemnly changed into their trial attire. Each wore a dark suit, white shirt and tie.

Westlake removed the black robe from a hanger near the door. "Big fish, gentlemen," he said, zipping up the robe. "Robert, this is your show, so if you want to cross-examine this guy, go after it."

"I've got something prepared Judge, but I'm not expecting much contrition. I predict we're going to hear a lot about his stature, his high-placed friends, and his money."

"I'd like to hear a confession," Judge Westlake said. "David, you're not going to assert a right against self-incrimination, are you?"

"No, sir. I don't see the point. I'd like to hear what he has to say for himself."

Crenshaw buffed the shine on his shoes and straightened his red-white-and-blue tie. He paced back and forth the length of the confined space, silently practicing his argument, his questions. His jaw muscles bulged. He stopped periodically to jot down a note on a yellow legal pad.

Cunningham entered Alpha Trailer and announced they were ready.

The lawyers trailed behind Westlake as he entered the courtroom trailer through the side door. Lyle Walker, the accused, rose from his chair only when Perez placed a stun gun against his neck. None of them wore masks to conceal their faces.

"Be seated," Westlake said too loudly. He had forgotten how the sound echoed in the trailer, even with the sound dampening panels covering the walls and ceiling. "Except you, Congressman. You may continue standing."

"I think I'll sit," Walker spat on the thin carpet and sat down heavily in the metal chair. His face was heavy and flushed below a tangle of blond hair. "You obviously know who I am. Who the hell are you?"

Perez looked to Judge Westlake for direction. Westlake nodded, and Perez looped a cargo strap around Walker's chest, hooked it to the steel ring bolted to the trailer, and cinched it tight.

"Do you know why you are here, Representative Walker?"

"No clue." Walker looked around. "Looks like a kangaroo court of some sort. You have on a robe. Ridiculous."

"I am United States District Judge Raleigh Westlake."

"Never heard of you. If you're a real judge, how come I'm not in a real courtroom? Are we at Gitmo or something? Things like this don't happen in the United States of America."

Crenshaw turned to face Walker. "You are in the United States of America, sir, and you are going to be tried in this courtroom for operating a Ponzi scheme, bilking thousands of investors out of millions of dollars."

Walker scoffed. "That's not going to happen. The feds already dropped the investigation."

"You're wrong, sir. I'm a federal prosecutor."

"Bullshit. From where? Who's your boss?"

Westlake interrupted. "Congressman, I can see you haven't come to grips with where you are and what's happening to you, but this is real. You are going on trial tonight. Right now."

Walker strained at the strap binding his hands and tried to rock the small chair. He was a massive man, even sitting down. Though he had fattened up since his college football days, anyone could see that he would have been a menace to the defense as he tore into the secondary, bowling over defensive backs.

"You guys are so fucked," Walker said. "Let me the fuck out of here, before you do something you can't erase."

"Representative Walker," Westlake said. "We have courteously allowed you to speak, but if you continue showing disrespect to this Court, you will be gagged, and maybe worse. Is the United States ready to proceed?"

"Yes, your Honor," Crenshaw said.

"Then please proceed."

Crenshaw turned to Walker. "The United States of America has charged you with violating the national securities laws, money laundering, violating the Texas securities laws, and common law fraud. You were the chief operator of what is commonly known as a Ponzi scheme. You caused losses in excess of $500 million to your investors. You also caused several people to commit suicide, Congressman, and are charged as an accessory to homicide." Crenshaw turned back to the Judge.

"How do you plead, Representative Walker?" Westlake asked.

"Plead? Are you out of your mind?"

"If you'd prefer not to enter a plea at this time, then I will accept a plea of not guilty."

"That's right. Not fucking guilty," Walker said.

Perez delivered a vicious punch to Walker's right temple, and his head collapsed in pain.

"Representative Walker, I warned you not to show disrespect to this Court. The two men standing next to you are United States Marshals, Marines before that, and they will not countenance your disrespect any more than I will. I will give you a minute to think about that."

Walker moved his head in slow circles, trying to shake off the blow.

"You may proceed," Westlake said.

Crenshaw continued. "Through our investigation, we have amassed thousands of documents that show you solicited and accepted investor money in partnerships that were based on nonexistent oil and gas wells, as well as nonexistent mineral mines in Africa and South America. In other words, you solicited investors to put their money into limited partnerships that had no assets, and you did it willfully and knowingly. We have all of the proof necessary to convict you."

"Who is we?" Walker ventured a question.

"The federal government. The Justice Department."

Walker scoffed at this notion. "The Attorney General is not going to do anything to prosecute me, you must know that. When he finds out about this, you guys are all going to jail."

Johnstone turned to face his client. "Representative Walker, I am your attorney for this trial. We've done this before. If you want to come clean, and talk about why you did this, this will be the one and only chance you have."

"I have an attorney, a lot of attorneys. Really good ones. And you're not one of them, asshole." Walker strained against the cargo strap again, to no avail.

Crenshaw resumed. "We know that at least five people committed suicide because they lost their life savings in your Ponzi scheme."

"A lot of people made money," Walker said.

"A few did," Crenshaw replied. "Your friends and political cronies who got in on the ground floor. And you made a lot of money too, didn't you Congressman Walker?"

"You have no idea."

"We also have suicide notes from a handful of your investors who specifically named you as the reason their lives had become worthless, and the reason they were ending their lives."

"Those notes were never supposed to see the light of day. I paid good money to have those notes destroyed."

"Well, that didn't happen," Crenshaw said. "You are directly responsible for their deaths. Do you want me to read one of them to you?" Crenshaw bluffed. He had never seen the suicide notes and knew of their existence only from Caroline Bannister.

The low rumble of a truck came toward them, and the courtroom swayed gently as the truck went by on the sandy road. Walker yelled as loudly as he could, hoping to alert someone. Perez punched him in the other temple. "Dammit," Walker roared, then dropped his head.

After taking a moment to recover, Walker said, "Where are we? That sounded like a tanker truck. I can smell oil in the air."

Cunningham looked at Westlake, and the Judge nodded. "Just outside of one of your oil fields," Cunningham said.

"Odessa?"

"Precisely."

"You kidnapped me in Dallas and brought me to Odessa?"

"That's correct," Cunningham said. "This place was not chosen by accident."

Westlake allowed a tiny smile to curl his lips. "Does the United States have anything further?"

"Just a few more questions, Your Honor. Representative Walker, do you want to tell us where all the money went?"

"Not a chance. You'll never find it."

"Then do you want to tell us why you defrauded all of those hard-working people?"

Walker flipped his chin at Johnstone. "Hey you, you're my lawyer, aren't you going to object or something?"

"No. You already waived your right against self-incrimination. You should answer the question."

Walker smirked. "All right, I'll answer the question. You guys have no idea how this works, do you? It's the American Dream. You work hard, you make money, you buy things so your life will be better, you buy things so your kids' lives will be better. You buy lawyers, you buy judges, you buy influence, you buy politicians. You buy elections. You buy safety, you buy freedom." Walker paused. "In case things go south, if the gravy train runs out, you know you've protected yourself. The strong survive, the smart survive, the weak don't survive. Survival of the fittest. Law of the jungle. Whatever you want to call it. That's the way life works. That's why I did it."

"You're a predator," Westlake said. "The worst kind. You pray on the weak and take their money, sometimes their entire life's savings, leaving them with nothing. Congressman Walker, because your Ponzi scheme worked so well, you caught our attention. You became our prey. We hunted you down. How does it feel to be on the other end of this?"

Walker worked his mouth, slid his tongue over dried-out lips. "Who the hell do you think you are?"

"I'm the guy that's putting a stop to your corruption, Congressman."

"I'm corrupt? What could be more corrupt than a vigilante judge?"

"A judge who sees every aspect of your scheme and does nothing," Westlake said. "I am ready to pronounce your sentence, Congressman. Is there anything else you want to say on your behalf?"

"Yeah, I want to say that you're all a bunch of cowards, afraid to take this case to a real courtroom. Where you would lose. Fuck you."

Westlake frowned, then nodded to the marshals. Perez punched Walker in the temple again, and his head violently snapped against the side of the trailer.

"I'm afraid Congressman," Westlake said, "that will not help you. I find you guilty of all of the charges levied by the United States, and I sentence you to death, Congressman Walker. May God have mercy on you. Because these gentlemen probably won't. Gentlemen, you know what to do."

"Sentenced to death? What the hell do you mean? You can't get the death penalty for financial fraud," Walker said in a meek tone.

"You can in this Court, Congressman."

CHAPTER THIRTY-EIGHT

By the time the trial ended, much of the activity in the oilfield had abated. Most working men had gone home to sleep. The incessant wind blew sand across the plains, across the desert, across the road, and the tires of the rig were now embedded in a sand drift. The sand reached to just below the hubs. Even with 750 horses pulling, the wheels simply spun in the powder. Perez tried various maneuvers, backing, pulling and rocking, yet the last trailer, the one in which a kidnapped United States Congressman was still strapped to a chair, would not move.

They had prepared for everything, except this. They could not, for obvious reasons, call a tow truck. Cunningham reported the dilemma to the others, telling them he would guard the prisoner while Perez unhooked the cab and went to a find a shovel somewhere. For a brief time, they would be immobile. And vulnerable.

"How could you not have planned for something like this?" Crenshaw accused.

"Things happen," Cunningham said. "We improvise."

"But you've put us all at risk, stranded out here in the desert like sitting ducks." Crenshaw's face had drained of color, and he plucked at the knot of his tie.

"Hold on," the Judge held up his right hand. "We all knew going in that there would be risks. This is one of them. We've got video cameras mounted on the trailers so we can see the terrain around us. In case someone approaches."

"And if someone does come by, what then?" Crenshaw said.

"Let's hope it doesn't come to that," the Judge said.

Perez unhooked the cab from Alpha trailer and trundled out of the sand, leaving the trailers stranded. He found shovels at a Walmart that stayed open all night and stashed them in the sleeping compartment of the cab. When he returned to the trailers, an Ector County Sheriff's car was idling in the road, lights off. A deputy stood by his car, wearing a starched shirt and white cowboy hat, a belt full of tools weighing him down. Including a shiny revolver.

Perez turned around in the road and backed the tractor up to the first trailer. The deputy moved a few paces, guiding Perez to the proper spot with hand signals. The others were inside, watching through the cameras concealed in light bubbles on the top rim of the trailers. Perez felt the familiar jolt from the locking mechanism as the cab slid under the first trailer. He jumped down from the cab, one of the shovels in hand. He leaned the shovel against a tire and re-connected the wiring and air hose from the cab to the trailers.

"Got stuck, eh?" the deputy said. He was no more than twenty-two, probably fresh out of the academy and relegated to night patrol.

"Yeah," Perez said. "In deeper now than when I left a little bit ago, looks like."

"What are you hauling?"

"Oil field supplies. Gaskets and O-rings and hoses, mostly. Just dropped a shipment a while ago. Got out of center on my way out."

"Not from around here, are you?"

"No, I'm not. Back east. Not used to driving in the sand." Perez began digging.

"How come you don't call for a tow?"

Perez continued to shovel, giving himself time to think. "Tell you the truth, I'm a little embarrassed. Don't want my bosses to know."

"I got you there. Well, I'd help out if you had an extra shovel."

Perez thought about the other shovel in the cab, but he couldn't risk the deputies' question about why he had more than one shovel. "Just the one," Perez said, holding the shovel aloft. "I'll be done in a bit anyway, but thanks."

"All right, looks like you got it under control." The deputy leaned against his car and looked around. "Where you headed?"

"Over to Midland next. Got a delivery there in the morning."

"I got you. Things have gotten busy again in these oil fields. Three, four years ago there wasn't much activity. Dead as a graveyard. You'd think they'd pave some of these back roads for the trucks."

Perez kept digging. "Wish they had."

The deputy's radio crackled to life, and he pulled it from his belt to respond. Perez strained to hear whether the dispatcher was spreading the news that a United States Congressman had been abducted. Instead, the deputy was being called to a domestic disturbance in town.

"Gotta run," the deputy said, slipping into the car. "Have a good night," he said, then drove off in a cloud of dust.

After a few minutes elapsed, Cunningham emerged from the side door of the back trailer. "Everything all right?"

Perez stopped digging and leaned on the shovel handle. "Everything's good. A curious county mounty is all."

"Yeah, I saw him. He came around and rattled the door of the back trailer."

"Is our prisoner out?"

"Yeah, I gave him more tranquilizer. Should be out two or three more hours. Should we switch to Plan C? Do it right here?"

Perez shook his head. "I'm sure I'm on video. Cop had a body camera. Probably nothing to it, except now we can't do it nearby or they will check all the cameras in the vicinity. Cops and everybody."

"So, on to Sweetwater?"

"Yep."

"All right. Wish I could help you bro, but I got to guard the prisoner," Cunningham said.

"Yeah, I bet. You can't be seen out here anyway. There's only supposed to be the driver, me."

Cunningham ducked back inside Bravo trailer and locked the side door.

It took Perez another twenty minutes to finish digging out the tires, during which span he saw no one else. The sand was so fine it was like digging in sugar. When he was finished, he stowed the shovel back in the sleeping compartment, started the engine, put the truck into gear, and the trailers slipped easily out of the sand and onto the paved state road a half mile ahead.

The attorneys in the forward trailer hovered over a laptop, watching online news coverage of the disappearance of US Congressman Lyle Walker. After Walker failed to show for an afternoon engagement in Dallas, one of his assistants went to Walker's home and found the Congressman missing. No one dared call it an abduction, not yet, but the local FBI office had been notified. No doubt they were already conducting a quiet investigation and search. The vigilante team had about a twelve-hour head start, and they hoped the FBI had not yet set up roadblocks. Judge Westlake called Perez on the radio and updated him on the news.

"Any worries?" Westlake asked.

"No, sir."

"Unusual police activity?"

"Not that I can see. If the cop back there was aware that our Congressman was missing, he didn't show it."

"Good. Where are we headed?"

"Sweetwater."

"Wait, that's back toward Dallas, right? Are you sure we should be heading in that direction?"

"You've all got cars in Dallas, Judge. Don't want to leave them there, do we? Not under the circumstances." Perez said.

"Right. You're absolutely right, Iggy. I need to stay out of it, leave the logistics to you guys. Sorry about that."

"It's all right. Everybody is a little tense."

"So what's in Sweetwater?" Westlake asked.

"A fitting end for our esteemed Congressman. We're about two hours out," Perez said.

They arrived in Sweetwater without further incident. It was after two a.m. when Perez pulled the rig into a park across the street from the Nolan County Coliseum. Perez and Cunningham unscrewed the light bulbs above the license plates and placed duct tape over the DOT numbers on the truck. After putting on gloves and the black plastic masks they wore during the Elise Rutherford trial, they circled the complex, looking for signs of police or a security guard. They saw none.

Perez eased the rig into the farthest corner of the parking lot. Though unguarded, the Coliseum and outdoor sheds were surrounded by a chain link fence topped with barbed wire. They walked to the nearest gate and used bolt cutters to cut the lock. Cunningham waited inside the gate while Perez quickly conducted reconnaissance. There were several out buildings with large garage-style openings where livestock were shuttled in and out. In the building closest to the Coliseum, Perez found what he was looking for in a large round pen. There was also a front-end loader parked next to the building, with the key in it. The loader would have been easy for Perez to hot-wire, but he was grateful for the stroke of good luck. He turned the key and the loader sputtered to life. Cunningham slid the gate open as Perez eased the front-end loader through the opening and pulled up behind the second trailer.

Cunningham opened the rear door to the trailer and climbed inside. Congressman Walker was awake but drowsy. His hands and feet were still bound. A bandana gagged his mouth. Cunningham removed the hood and placed a cardboard placard around Walker's neck, fastened with a long loop of zip ties. He unbuckled the cargo strap, unbinding Walker from the chair, then spun the chair around and tipped Walker into the waiting bucket of the loader. Walker's body thudded into the steel bucket, and he groaned.

Perez backed the loader up a few feet. The Congressman rolled around in the front bucket as Perez drove the loader back through the gate and into the out building. He raised the bucket, ready to tip Walker into the pen.

Inside Alpha trailer, Westlake, Crenshaw and Johnstone watched a live feed from the remote video camera clipped to the bill of Cunningham's cap. Until now, the video had been jerky and unfocused, but they soon saw a round wooden pen, made of plywood, about fifteen feet in diameter. The camera's microphone picked up a slight buzz, but they couldn't discern the source of the distortion. Suddenly, the video angle changed, focusing down into the pen, capturing what appeared to be rumpled burlap bags covering the bottom. As the camera automatically re-focused, the picture revealed not a jumble of burlap bags, but a pit of writhing snakes. Rattlers.

Walker's body tumbled past the camera as the loader bucket tipped forward, dumping him into the pit. The snakes attacked the warm body almost instantly, and Walker began to writhe in pain. The buzz of frenzied snakes was punctuated by the man's muffled screams of agony. The rattlers, some of them five feet long and as big around as a forearm, coiled and struck, coiled and struck. Walker wriggled and threw his head from side to side in a futile attempt to evade the attacks. After a few minutes, Walker stopped moving, though the snakes didn't. The former US Congressman was lying on his side, facing away from the camera. He had squirmed halfway across the pit in his futile effort to escape the serpents.

Cunningham was on the move. At first all they saw on the jerky video was the outside of the snake pit. Then the camera steadied and re-focused, showing Walker from the front. The sign hanging from Walker's neck was printed in black ink on a white background, and rivulets of blood streaked the placard.

CRIME DOES NOT PAY
WE ARE WATCHING

The team stayed at the Coliseum complex for less than ten minutes. Cunningham re-lit the license plates and removed the tape covering the rig's identifying marks. Then he joined the others in Alpha trailer.

The attorneys sat in quiet contemplation of what they had just witnessed. On his bunk, Crenshaw bowed his head. Congressman Walker was the first victim they had seen die. The lawyers had been far away when Henry Lawter, Elise Rutherford and Tyler Becksdale expired.

Cunningham had seen it before, the shock that comes the first time you see someone die violently. A living, breathing body simply ceases to exist, the tinny ring of the bell on the ticking timer. Most people didn't handle it well. It was not something to get used to.

Crenshaw hovered near the toilet, his face blanched, looking like he needed to throw up.

"That was intense," Westlake said. "But I think it was good for us to see, first hand, the effect of what we are doing here." His voice was raspy and barely under control.

"Are you sure he's dead?" Johnstone asked.

"No one could survive that many bites from a poisonous viper," Cunningham said. "Besides, we strapped a heart monitor around his chest. I'm wearing the computer." Cunningham held up his right wrist. "His heart stopped a couple of minutes before we got out of there. Topped out at 294 beats per minute, fast-tracking the poison through his bloodstream."

"You left everything clean—is that how you guys would put it?" Westlake said.

"Iggy and I wore gloves and masks. We didn't see any cameras that far out in the parking lot. Even if there were cameras around that we didn't see, all they'll show is a tractor-trailer rig, with a very common shipping company's logo on the side. The license plates and DOT numbers were masked."

"Where did the snakes come from?" Westlake asked. "Did you guys do that?"

"No Judge. Rattlesnake Round-Up. It's a yearly tradition in Sweetwater. The Congressman was coming out for an appearance on Saturday. We just had him show up a couple of days early."

"How long before this hits the news, do you think?" Crenshaw ventured, dabbing sweat off his forehead with a towel.

"My guess is someone will be there by 5:30 or 6," Cunningham said. "Farmers and ranchers get started pretty early. Maybe they look in the pit first thing, maybe they don't. The gates open at 8:00 for the first day of the Round-Up. Any luck, we'll be back in Dallas before sunrise. We all should be on our way out of Big D by early morning, and hopefully before law enforcement can throw down any kind of a dragnet. Hard to see them stopping every vehicle on the freeway during rush hour. Get a few hours of sleep, if you can."

None of the men slept on the ride back to Dallas. The risk and excitement of their mutual endeavor coursed through their veins in an adrenaline rush. The visions of Lyle Walker writhing in the snake pit ran nonstop in their minds, a movie that could not be easily paused.

CHAPTER THIRTY-NINE

"Lyle Walker has been front-page news and all over cable news for the past two weeks," Crenshaw said.

Judge Westlake looked up from his bowl of tomato basil soup. "Did you expect anything less?"

"I can't get any sleep."

"It will calm down, Robert. It always does."

"The manhunt won't calm down. The FBI will keep searching until they catch somebody. Even if it takes years."

"Of course they will. It's their job." The Judge put down his spoon and leaned forward, cupping his tie to prevent it from dipping into his soup. "Stay calm," he whispered. "Throw yourself into your work."

"Have you seen the cell-phone video? The one somebody took when they first found Walker?"

"Of course I have. How could anyone miss it? That video is spreading our message."

Crenshaw slumped back in the booth, unsatisfied and agitated, unable to finish his lunch.

He drove to Charlotte for a regularly scheduled meeting with the other federal prosecutors in the office. He settled into a chair halfway down the table from his boss, hoping not to stand out in any way.

Caroline ran the meeting, first covering the more mundane prosecutions, then asked Crenshaw to update the team on the environmental pollution case he was prosecuting in Asheville against a public utility. The utility company had been allowing coal ash to leak from its retention ponds into a nearby river. The case was scheduled for trial in Asheville in six weeks, before a visiting federal judge from South Carolina. Judge Westlake had recused himself because he had once held stock in the corporate defendant while in private practice almost fifteen years earlier, so he would not be presiding over the case. Crenshaw told the other prosecutors he thought there was some chance the case could settle, though discussions had bogged down in recent weeks.

After all of the case reports had been given, Caroline finally mentioned the Lyle Walker investigation. "We've all, of course, heard about what happened to Lyle Walker . . . uh Congressman Walker. The White-Collar Crime Task Force is in a tizzy about it, since he was the subject of one of our investigations."

"I thought the investigation was closed," said an AUSA from Charlotte.

"Right. It was closing, if not officially closed," Caroline replied. "No one is talking publicly about the investigation. Private opinion—no names—some think Walker got what he deserved. But the FBI says we have a vigilante group out there. Their job is to hunt them down. Because I am on the Task Force, I've been asked to be the liaison with the FBI on the investigation."

"Who is tracking public opinion?" the same AUSA asked.

"Not the Attorney General's office, that's for sure," Caroline said to a smattering of laughs.

"I saw one poll indicating the public is split about fifty-fifty on whether the vigilantes should even be prosecuted," Crenshaw said.

Caroline smiled. "Of course they should be prosecuted. They assassinated a US Congressman. All right, anything else? Good. Guys, go do your jobs. Robert, can you hang on a minute? I want to talk to you about your upcoming trial."

Once the room emptied, Crenshaw followed Caroline from the conference room to one of the leather chairs in front of her desk. Caroline plopped a stack of files on the desk and sat down in her high-backed chair with a sigh. She was sporting a new hairstyle, cut shorter and less feminine. She fussed with a lock of hair behind her right ear.

"How was your vacation—wherever you went?"

"Utah. I went backpacking in Utah. And it was cold mostly."

"Glad you're back. Look, I need you to make sure this coal ash case is handled perfectly. No screw ups. Everybody on the Task Force is taking heat, including me."

"Why? That's ridiculous."

"Because even though the AG decided not to prosecute, he can't look soft. He can't come out and say the investigation had been closed, and he can't denigrate Walker for what he did without looking like an unsympathetic ass. So now we've got vigilantes on our hands. They killed a United States Congressman, for God's sake. It's unprecedented. The FBI is frantic. The Secret Service is talking about expanding protection to all members of Congress, wherever they go. The AG's getting heat from higher up to catch these guys, and you know what that means. It all runs downhill. My office, and every other US Attorney on the Task Force, is going to get a little extra heat for a while." She folded her hands on the desktop in front of her.

"Everything's ready to go on the coal ash case," Crenshaw said. "We've hyper-analyzed every opinion our new judge has ever written that even tangentially touches on environmental issues. Can't discern much. He was an Eagle Scout, if that tells us anything about his feelings toward the environment. The jury consultant is hard at work, tweaking our jury selection questions. Our experts are lined up and being prepped. They will all say that coal ash leaked from the dam because the company didn't put the time and money into maintenance like it should have, that this was an entirely predictable event given the circumstances, just a matter of time before it happens again."

"What's the damage estimate?" Caroline asked.

"That gets complicated. In the millions of dollars for water purification alone, but the main push is to get a judgment ordering the company to remove the coal ash and fill in the ponds."

"Well, that all sounds good. What do they do with it?"

"They can use it as fill to build airport runways."

"Interesting. This will be your first trial since Lawter, yes?"

Crenshaw nodded. "What does that have to do with anything?"

"Bluntly, you can't take two losses in a row."

Crenshaw clenched his jaw. "Come on, Caroline. That's not fair. What are we supposed to do when the appellate court goes off the rails like that?"

"You know better than that, Robert. Expect the unexpected. If you even had a hint that the confession was anything other than rock solid, you should have punted it to the State."

Crenshaw leaned forward, his fingers gripping the edge of the desk. "Punted to the State? Are you kidding me? You were pushing to try the Lawter case. Westlake too. Don't make me the scapegoat here, Caroline. The last time we talked about Lawter, you said it wasn't my fault."

"There are no scapegoats here, Robert. There are only prosecutors who make it, and prosecutors who don't make it. Period."

"Are you saying my job is at stake?"

She leaned forward, locking his eyes, her pupils narrowed into slits. "I'm saying don't lose the coal ash case." She kept staring at Crenshaw for a few seconds to punctuate her point. "All right, we're done here. See you in two weeks."

* * * * * *

Crenshaw and the other members of the cabal went about their normal regimens, hiding in the fabric of daily routine. There were no meetings at the lake house, no discussion of targets or reconnaissance or macabre methods of execution. Heeding Judge Westlake's suggestion, Crenshaw focused on his cases. After extensive negotiations, Crenshaw settled the coal ash suit before trial, crafting a complex resolution that required the power company to spend millions of dollars disposing of coal ash and sealing the ponds at two plants in the western part of the state. It was a good settlement for the citizens and the environment.

Caroline signed off on the deal, seemingly pleased. She convened a press conference in Charlotte at which she announced what she termed a landmark settlement to protect the environment of North Carolina for our children and grandchildren. Crenshaw made a few remarks in front of the cameras, a role to which he was unaccustomed, but he fared well and appeared composed as he read a prepared statement. As planned, he took no questions. Bannister answered questions from a few reporters, deftly deflecting those that cut too close to the inner-workings of the settlement negotiations, the answers to which might incite the other side to reconsider. Then came a question from an Observer reporter.

"You are on the White-Collar Crime Task Force, is that correct?"

"I am," Caroline replied.

"Was there any thought given to bringing criminal charges in this case?"

"Of course, all potential remedies were fully vetted, and I ultimately made a decision there was no criminal intent here and that a civil suit was the best course to protect our citizens and the environment."

"Follow up," said the reporter. "It's rumored that you are the Task Force's liaison with the FBI on the Lyle Walker investigation. The FBI appears to be out of leads. They are providing virtually nothing of value to the media."

"I can't comment on an ongoing investigation," Caroline said, giving her stock answer.

"But you are confirming that you are the Task Force liaison with the FBI?"

Caroline smiled broadly. "No comment," she said. She declared the press conference over and thanked the media, hustling from behind the lectern.

There was a small reception for office staff in the large conference room. Pastries, juice and fruit lined the table. Some of Crenshaw's fellow prosecutors stopped by to offer congratulations. A few of the staff lingered longer than they should, grabbing a final pastry to delay returning to work. Crenshaw was munching a chocolate cruller when Caroline suggested lunch, someplace out of the way.

They walked to a restaurant several blocks from the federal building, not in a hurry. The day was bright and airy, and a light wind swept away the normal detritus of the city, giving things a scrubbed appearance. The restaurant held vestiges of old days when deals were cut in back-corner booths of red vinyl, and steak and martinis were standard lunch fare. The decor had a distinctly masculine feel to it, dim lighting and remnants of cigar smoke hovering in the corners. The hostess led them to a back table in a practiced way, as if Caroline Bannister ate there every day. She did not. The budget would not allow such indulgence with any frequency, but Caroline ate there often enough to be known to the wait staff.

She settled into the booth where she could see everyone who approached the table. Crenshaw sat across from her, his back to the other patrons. A small brass lamp rested at the end of the table, casting a dim circle of light. They ordered iced tea; his sweet, hers not. When the waiter went away she raised a glass and toasted Crenshaw's success on the coal ash case.

"So, I'm back in your good graces," Crenshaw said, feeling a certain boldness from the fresh victory.

Caroline's green cat eyes darted about the room as she sipped tea, finally landing on him. "You were never out of my good graces, Robert. You know that."

"I thought . . ."

She flipped her hand as if sweeping away the past. "Motivation. That's all. You're too valuable to me, to our office. Lawter was a major screw-up for all of us, but you picked up the ball again and showed me what you can do with it. I'm thinking of moving you here to Charlotte, to be my number two."

"I thought Dan Aiken is your number two."

"Was. He's leaving to take a job in DC. Private sector. Haven't you heard?"

"I have not heard." Crenshaw paused, choosing the right words. He did not want to sound eager to leave his current post as Chief of the Asheville Division of the US Attorney's Office, nor did he want to seem eager to keep it. "So . . . if I were to leave Asheville, who would replace me?"

"No replacement. We'd no longer have a chief there, budget cuts and all, so it would fall under my jurisdiction, though it always has really. I'd have to be up there more often, which is not a bad thing. I like the mountains. Lots of hiking and climbing venues."

"I forgot you were a rock climber."

"Not quite like I used to. I'm a little out of practice. Hard to stay fit when all you have are climbing walls."

"How did you get into that, by the way? Seems a little dangerous."

"With the right equipment and support, it's not that dangerous. But you haven't lived until you've dangled from a rope a few hundred feet above the ground."

"Not for me."

Caroline cracked a smile. "So . . . back to you transferring to the Charlotte office. What do you think?" She took a long sip of her tea.

The thought of being closer to the major decisions of the US Attorney's Office, and being farther from Westlake, were appealing to Crenshaw. *If I'm down here all the time, maybe I can get more information on the Task Force and what's happening in the Walker investigation. That could be very valuable to the team. I could justify the move to Westlake that way.*

"It sounds like an intriguing proposition," Crenshaw said. "My wife is pregnant, and she's been talking about moving closer to her parents. They're in Fort Mill, you know."

"How far along is Cindy?"

"Six weeks." Crenshaw had gotten Cindy pregnant right after returning from the Lyle Walker trial. In hindsight, he viewed it as something of an act of contrition.

"Everything okay?"

"Morning sickness is starting to get bad. Otherwise, everything is fine."

"Is this your first?"

"It is."

"That's exciting, for both of you. Okay, on transferring you to Charlotte, I haven't made a decision yet. When I decide, I'll let you know."

Crenshaw understood, for the first time in the conversation, that Caroline wasn't offering him a choice. She was letting him know that he would be expected to move when she decided the time was right. He changed the subject. "So, anything new on the Walker investigation?"

"Not much," she said, glancing up at him. "No suspects, if that's what you mean. Not much forensic evidence either."

"But some?"

"Scant. The perpetrators—we know there were two—were very careful. Captured some grainy images on video at the coliseum, the place where they hold this Rattlesnake Round-Up. Old security system. Even with the FBI's technology, they couldn't do a whole lot to enhance the images. Probably men, but their faces were covered. They wore dark clothing. They wore gloves. What's your interest in it?"

He was ready with an answer, had to be. "The murder of a US Congressman. That doesn't happen very often."

"Walker was number fifteen," Caroline said. "Most of them were in the 1800s. Last one, before Walker, was in 1983."

"Fifteen, I had no idea."

"Robert Kennedy was a Senator when he was killed," Caroline said.

"Right. I'd forgotten that. Anyway, I assume every available FBI agent is on it. Just interested in how a manhunt like that gets put together."

"You said 'manhunt.' We don't know they are men. Probably are based on size and movements, but we don't know that for sure. Nothing is assumed."

"It was a figure of speech. But do you really think women could have pulled off something like that?" Crenshaw said.

Caroline pressed against the tufted back of the booth. "I do, Robert. You don't seem to have much belief in a woman's capacity for violence. Think about Lizzy Borden, and Kristen Gilbert."

"Who is Kristen Gilbert?"

"A nurse who killed at least three of her patients by injecting them with epinephrine. And don't forget Susan Smith."

"I do remember her," Crenshaw said. "She killed her own children by running her car into a lake with the kids strapped into their car seats."

"And she did it for love, Robert. We can be vicious and murderous when we want to. Do you know what they all had in common?"

"You mean other than the fact they were all women? I have no clue."

"None of them used guns on their victims," Caroline said.

"It sounds like you've been studying up on this."

"I have, ever since my sister was killed two decades ago. It's been a morbid fascination of mine. The Lawter case brought it back into my view. I've always wondered why he stabbed her with an icepick. Why didn't he use the rifle found in his tent?"

Crenshaw shrugged. "I don't know. Maybe the rifle would have been loud, would have attracted attention."

"Perhaps," Caroline said. "But stabbing is so intimate, it's so personal. It says something about the relationship, the murderer's feelings toward the victim."

"What are you trying to say, Caroline?"

"That the fact that Lyle Walker was thrown into a pit of snakes, rather than shot, tells us something about the assassins. Maybe they are women, or maybe the crime was planned by a woman."

Her tone startled him. "Well, the vast majority of murders are committed by men. We know that. I'm assuming they were men. Could be a woman involved, I guess. It's just hard to see how a woman, or even two women, could have subdued a guy as big as Walker."

"See, you're assuming again. What if it was a woman and a man? Rosemary West and her husband murdered ten young women in the 1970s. Strangled and suffocated them. Granted, that was in Great Britain, but it's still possible."

"Does the evidence point in that direction—to a couple?"

"Who knows at this point?" Caroline admitted. "It's just a theory. Eighty-nine percent of murders are committed by men, statistically. If one of the two caught on video is a woman, she has to be armed forces or an athlete. The physical movements are very . . . deliberate. Practiced. And if one of them is a woman, she probably knew the Congressman personally."

"Because?"

"The FBI thinks that may be how Walker was caught off guard. Like you said, he was a big guy, a former athlete. The FBI has uncovered a good bit of evidence of extramarital affairs. Not a surprise for a powerful politician, I guess. But in any event, maybe one of those women, a former girlfriend, decided to exact revenge. Maybe her husband or a boyfriend helped her. It's just a theory at this point."

The waiter placed their lunch orders on the table. Caroline had ordered filet mignon; Crenshaw chose the grilled chicken.

"I didn't figure you for a red meat eater, Caroline."

"Once every two weeks or so. I sometimes suffer from anemia. Red meat is the ticket."

"Does the FBI have anything to go on? Do they even know the race of the assailants?"

"No clue," Caroline said, a forkful of steak in her mouth. She chewed quickly. "If they had something, they would have made an arrest. It's been six weeks, and the pressure is still on. Everybody's feeling it. The Director most of all."

"I bet. Do they know how it was done, how he was abducted?"

Caroline shook her head. "One minute he's at home in Dallas, the next day they find him in a pit of rattlesnakes. Bitten to death. Poison stopped his heart. Get this. He had a heart monitor strapped to his chest. That tidbit has never been released to the media. You can't see it on any of the videos. I guess the perpetrators wanted to make sure he was dead, that his heart had stopped."

"Clever," Crenshaw said.

"They didn't miss a thing. Covered their tracks very well."

"My guess is Walker had a lot of enemies. All those people he bilked out of their life savings, families of the investors who committed suicide, all those enemies he must have made along the campaign trail."

"The list of potential suspects is very long. But the list of suspects who had the cunning and foresight to pull this off, much shorter," Caroline said. "Your chicken's getting cold. Eat."

They ate in silence for a time. Crenshaw chewed over Bannister's words carefully, mincing, attaching a tone to each. He set his knife and fork on his plate. "Is there a list of suspects?"

"Of course there is a list of suspects. The usual suspects. Walker got lots of hate mail, some with return addresses, some not. That's a lot of leads to run down. A lot of people to interview. Let's talk about something else. Enough business. When is your next backpacking trip?"

"August, probably. I'm thinking about hiking the Appalachian trail, the upper portion that ends in Maine."

"Interesting," Caroline said. "Solo?"

"Sure. I like the solitude, and I can hike at my own pace."

"What does Cindy think about that, you going hiking out in the forest in the middle of her pregnancy?"

Crenshaw looked down at his plate. "I don't know. I hadn't thought about that."

"Things are going to change, Robert."

CHAPTER FORTY

Caroline Bannister strolled into the Department of Justice Building in Washington, D.C. The building, named for former Attorney General Robert F. Kennedy, Jr., did not ooze the grandeur of the US Capitol, the White House or the Supreme Court building, but it displayed a respectable stolidity. She passed through nondescript wooden doors on the first floor and through security. Although a United States Attorney, she was given a visitor's badge and directed to a heavily paneled conference room for a meeting of the White-Collar Crime Task Force. She had been here before for periodic meetings, but this was the first time the entire Task Force had met in person since the kidnapping and murder of Congressman Walker.

She greeted the other Task Force members, and they got down to business. They discussed the status of a long roster of cases and investigations, much of it unchanged from the previous meeting. There were insider trading cases, a dwindling docket of investigations and indictments involving mortgage fraud, some currency manipulation, and ongoing investigation into a Ponzi scheme in California. For the most part, the Department of Justice prosecuted the criminal aspect of the cases, while other agencies, such as the Securities Exchange Commission, would pursue civil claims. The jurisdictional lines were not always clearly defined. The investigation into the Ponzi scheme perpetrated by Lyle Walker had involved both the DOJ and the SEC. The agenda for the meeting indicated the investigation of Lyle Walker's Ponzi scheme was "Closed."

After the Task Force meeting concluded, Caroline went across the street to the Hoover Building for an FBI briefing. Caroline and the US Attorney for the Northern District of Texas, Jorge Morton, were the only prosecutors at the meeting, though undoubtedly several of the FBI agents also were attorneys. Morton's district encompassed both Dallas County, where the FBI believed Lyle Walker had been abducted, as well as Nolan County, Texas, where Walker's corpse had been found in the pit of rattlesnakes. Though everyone in the room had been working feverishly to catch the Congressman's assassins, Morton was the most impatient that they had made so little progress in the investigation. The child of third-generation immigrants from Mexico, Morton had grown up in Abilene and excelled at Texas Tech law school. A sense of public duty and prevalent drug use in the barrios of Abilene had led him to the US Attorney's Office. Abilene was only a forty-five-minute drive from Sweetwater and the murder scene. Morton had shown calves at the Nolan County livestock show while in Future Farmers of America and had attended the Rattlesnake Round-Up on at least two occasions as a young man. No one blamed him for what happened to Congressman Walker, but for the slothful pace of the criminal investigation, Morton blamed himself. When the decision was made not to prosecute Walker for the financial crimes associated with the Ponzi scheme, Morton had concurred without objection. Caroline wondered why.

The lead FBI investigator, a seasoned man who had served as a homicide detective for the Dallas Police Department before becoming a federal agent, was Harry Henderson. In his briefing he first described to the prosecutors, the only two who weren't part of the day-to-day investigation, the teams he had assembled and their various tasks. Though Henderson was in charge, the amount of information that needed to be sifted was vast and deep, so he appointed team leaders to provide daily reports to him. One of the teams was tasked with the forensics investigation of Lyle Walker's townhouse in Georgetown, his home in Dallas, and the murder scene at the Nolan County Coliseum. The Texas Rangers were assisting that team in a capacity Agent Henderson did not clarify. Another team was assigned to assess and analyze evidence of a political nature, for although Lyle Walker had been in office for only two terms, his tendency to take the bull by the horns had already created a multitude of enemies. Those enemies were sometimes hard to identify. A third team was sorting through hate mail. A fourth was analyzing the list of investors who had lost money in Walker's oil and gas scheme and the voluminous pleadings in the five class action lawsuits filed against Walker and his limited partnerships. A fifth team was investigating the participants in Walker's other business dealings, many of which had gone sour. A sixth team was tasked with following the money from the Ponzi scheme itself, something in which Caroline had been involved when the Task Force was still investigating Walker. The seventh and final team was tasked with cataloguing and securing the discovered evidence. The team tasked with assessing potential suspects from the thousands of investors who lost money was the largest and most overworked. The leaders of these teams formed the committee that read all reports and summarized each day's activity for Agent Henderson.

Caroline detested the bureaucracy of it all, but she knew that over-organization of the investigation was necessary if every grain of evidence, significant or otherwise, was to be discovered, catalogued and analyzed. The evidence gathered thus far established that Walker was not a gifted businessman. He had failed at several ventures in telecommunications, retail and computer technology before striking it rich in the oil business. He was a lucky entrepreneur who ventured into the industry when the timing was right, when oil was making a comeback. With a backlog of failed ventures, there was no shortage of disgruntled ex-business partners and ruined investors, many of whom had sued Walker or were members of one of the class actions pending when Walker died. Whether those cases would continue in the wake of Walker's death was a heavily debated question.

More than two months into the investigation of the Congressman's murder, the teams had churned an enormous amount of leads, with little to show for it. After first deciding that anyone who had threatened or sued Walker would be placed on a list of prospective suspects, the list had grown so long it became unmanageable. The forensics, the prosecutors both believed, would provide the best leads, but so far they still didn't even know the gender or race of the two darkly clad figures on the coliseum video. The forensics team concluded, through analysis of the gait, movements, height, estimated weight, and approximate shoulder, head and chest measurements, that both perpetrators probably were men, but they could not yet exclude female suspects, or the possibility that a female had masterminded the abduction and execution of Lyle Walker. The grainy video also showed that one of the perpetrators knew how to use a front-end loader, and it appeared, but could not be confirmed, that the other person may have videotaped the entire affair with a camera clipped to a generic ball cap. The camera mounted near the top of the open-air barn at the coliseum caught the loader as it entered the barn, with a good shot of Congressman Walker in the bucket. Walker was alive when he was dumped into the snake pit. That was an undisputed fact. There was no video of any vehicle approaching or leaving the coliseum parking lot, and two complete canvasses of the surrounding neighborhood had turned up no witnesses who noticed any activity at all near the coliseum that night. That, in and of itself, was not unusual, given that the video camera captured the perpetrators entering the open barn at 4:07 a.m. and leaving at 4:16 a.m. To have executed the operation in only nine minutes, the FBI concluded, meant the perpetrators were well prepared. Beyond that, they did not know how Walker had been abducted, or when, or how he had been transported from Dallas to Sweetwater, a trip of more than 200 miles. And they didn't know why. No exclusive motive had emerged, though revenge was at the top of the list.

The placard hung around Walker's neck was made of standard one-quarter inch foam board. The message had been printed onto two standard sheets of white office paper, 8 ½" x 11," one sheet for each line of the message. The paper was sold at every office supply and copy store in America and had been taped onto the foam board with ordinary clear plastic shipping tape. No fingerprints could be lifted from the tape. The message itself appeared to have been created on a computer and printed on a standard laser printer, any of dozens of models. The words appeared in a 40-point Times New Roman font that every word processing program could produce.

Two profilers had been tasked with analyzing the brief message: "CRIME DOES NOT PAY—WE ARE WATCHING." One of the profilers, a trained criminal psychologist, was working under the theory that the author of the statement had probably been victimized at some point by Walker. The other profiler acknowledged that was a distinct probability, but the second line portended a broader message of vigilantism and the possibility that the perpetrators were not victims at all. Neither theory helped to narrow the list of potential suspects.

Agent Henderson told them the heart monitor belted on Walker's chest was manufactured by a company that had sold millions of them in the previous three years, both at brick and mortar stores and online. The monitor consisted of a black elastic belt with a plastic buckle, a contact area of smooth rubber to conduct the signal, and a black transmitter that snapped onto the belt. The transmitter contained model numbers but no serial number or other markings that could be traced to a point of sale. The model number indicated it had been manufactured two years earlier in a manufacturing facility near Taiwan. The monitor itself had not been found. Dead end.

The clothes worn by the assailants were dark—jeans and sweat shirts without any writing or logos on them. Both perpetrators wore black gloves and black masks, probably made of rubber or plastic. Each of the assailants also wore black ball caps that had no insignia or identifying marks. Walker had been stripped of his shirt, socks and shoes, but not of his pants. Standard zip ties bound his wrists and ankles, and a bandana had been twisted, placed in his mouth, and tied around his neck. The bandana may or may not have come from Walker's own wardrobe, but the cloth provided no clue that led back to the assailants. If the assassins had left any DNA at the scene, the FBI couldn't find it among the other debris of a county facility with thousands of recent visitors, both human and otherwise. The removal of the rattlesnakes from the pit containing Walker's body had been an arduous process in which each snake had been plucked with a pinner and placed into one of several 55-gallon oil drums. It had taken three men several hours to clear the pit before the forensics team could enter. All the while, Walker's blood-stained body had lain inside. Once they were cleared to enter, the team found the murder scene evidence somewhat compromised by the fact that the snakes had wriggled in and spread Walker's blood across the floor.

Three medical examiners, one each from the county, state, and federal governments, determined that Walker died from a heart attack caused by excessive snake venom in his system. The medical examiners also found traces of Telazol and Zoletil in Walker's blood samples. These drugs were sometimes used to tranquilize large animals. Interviews with veterinarians and zoos in the area around Sweetwater revealed no missing drugs, but meticulous records were not kept.

Agent Henderson's summary ended abruptly, as if he had come to the edge of the evidence cliff, and there were no options other than to step off into thin air.

Caroline said nothing during the presentation and now ventured a question. "Is there any evidence at all that this was even related to the Ponzi scheme?"

Agent Henderson simply shook his head, as if afraid to say it out loud. "Motive could be anything."

"So where does that leave us?" US Attorney Morton asked. "Nowhere?"

"Yes sir," Henderson said. "In the middle of the proverbial desert. We'll keep combing the evidence, of course, but the trail has gone cold. It's unlikely we'll find anything. Unless they do it again."

Caroline spoke: "You think they will, Agent Henderson?"

"Possibly, ma'am. If this was a one-and-done, there would have been no reason to leave a message at all. The psychologists think it could have been intended as a warning."

"That's no great leap of logic," she said. "Or the perpetrators could be people that Walker victimized, maybe people who lost a lot of money in the scam, and their job is now over."

"Yes, ma'am."

"But if they're smart, they'll stop, won't they?" Caroline said. "Congressman Walker was the prize."

"If they're smart, they'll stop or change the MO," said Henderson.

"So, you are suggesting that to catch the perpetrators in one of the most high-profile murder cases this country has ever seen, we need them to become active again."

Henderson nodded. "We need to bring them out of hiding."

"And how do you propose we do that?"

"The simplest way is to plant false leads."

"But that's a bit tricky, isn't it?" Caroline said. "Given that we have no idea who the perpetrators are, or where they might be, the false leads would have to be disseminated through the media."

"Yes, ma'am."

"And that could potentially send the country into a panic," Caroline said.

CHAPTER FORTY-ONE

The sensational murder of Congressman Walker dominated the national news for a few weeks, until the FBI stopped providing new information. With the FBI disclosing nothing fresh to the public, the pundits and theorists took over, tossing out wild ideas unrestrained by the actual facts. The FBI disclosed it had found an email sent to the Congressman several weeks before his death, threatening him unless he changed his position in the ongoing war in the Middle East. As a member of the House Armed Services Committee, Walker had aggressively pushed for increasing the bombing runs in Iraq and Syria to stop the spread of ISIS, even though civilian casualties in the region were on the rise. The FBI traced the email only as far as an internet server in Saudi Arabia, where the electronic trail ended. At the press conference announcing the lead, Agent Henderson did not use the word "terrorism" or the phrase "Islamic extremist" to describe the threat, but the news media and talk show hosts quickly speculated that a cell of terrorists must be operating on American soil.

Judge Westlake didn't like it at all. The message he intended to broadcast with the assassination of Lyle Walker was that white-collar thieves could no longer count on a soft justice system to escape with a mere prison sentence and a fine. That message was lost as the media focused its attention upon an alleged act of terrorism that never happened. Westlake did not, would not, consider what he and the team had done as an act of terrorism. No, they had meted out justice for thousands of people because the system was too inept or corrupt to get it done.

As he watched the media blindly climb onto the terrorism bandwagon, which soured his stomach, Judge Westlake contemplated ways in which he might re-direct the country's attention to the real reason Lyle Walker had been executed. Congressman Walker was not a hero for refusing to bend to the threats of foreign terrorists. He was a crook, pure and simple. An untraceable phone call to the FBI perhaps, or a typed letter with no return address, could get everyone refocused on the correct issue. Westlake knew any message like that would garner national attention, but could he be sure the message would be completely untraceable? After presiding over countless criminal trials, he was often amazed at how advanced the forensic skills of the FBI were, even though they couldn't find the icepick that Henry Lawter had used to murder Hannah Sullivan. And if he sent such a message, how would it be received? Would the FBI release the lead, or treat it as the unsubstantiated rant of one of Walker's victims? And if the FBI did release his anonymous message, how would it impact the rest of the country? Would it spur other vigilantes to take the law into their own hands?

Westlake invited the team for a weekend of fishing and poker at his lake house. It had been several months since Walker's trial, since they had all been together. On a bright morning in June, the team boarded the pontoon boat and headed onto the lake. Shiloh raced up and down the deck, excited by the splashing of water against the pontoons, but soon tired herself and settled at her owner's feet. As he steered the boat out to the middle of the deep lake, looking for the bottom of the V formed by plunging terrain, Westlake started the conversation that until then had been bottled inside of him.

"I see that the media has seized on our little endeavor as a suspected act of terrorism, as retribution for Walker's stance on the war in the Middle East," he said casually as he sipped a cup of coffee. "What do you think of that?"

"I think it's great they are looking the other way," Crenshaw said. "Takes the heat off us."

Johnstone agreed.

"But our message has been lost, gentlemen," said Westlake. "The potential deterrent effect has been eliminated."

"How will we ever know?" Johnstone ventured. "Has anybody really ever figured out what causes criminal behavior?"

"Poverty," Perez said. "Pervasive poverty."

"The evil gene," Cunningham chimed in.

"Poverty certainly wasn't an issue in Walker's case," Johnstone countered. "He was filthy rich."

"True, but maybe he was losing it and having only a few million looked like poverty to him." Perez laughed.

"That's a different take on it," Westlake said. "Are you suggesting that Walker's Ponzi scheme was an act of desperation and not a carefully crafted scheme that took into account all the risks?" Perhaps he had misunderstood Walker's motive and plotting.

"I didn't know Walker," Perez said. "All I know is that when we had him in the trailer, he didn't say anything that seemed to me like he had ever thought of getting caught."

"He was arrogant," Cunningham said. He took a sip of hot chocolate to let them know there wasn't any further explanation forthcoming from him.

"I had hoped for something more," said Westlake. "Some insight from Walker that would let us know we are on the right track."

"Now you have doubts?" Crenshaw asked. "If that's the case, I sure would have liked to have known about that beforehand."

"Of course I have doubts, Robert. Do you think the black robe I put on almost every day erases all my doubts? Do you believe the robe is a magic cloak that somehow makes all my decisions perfect and unassailable?"

"Don't all judges believe that?" Johnstone said. The others laughed. He looked at Westlake. "You've got to admit you walked right into that one, Judge."

"Touché, Mr. Johnstone."

"Slight change of subject," Crenshaw said. "I had lunch with Caroline the other day. You know she's on the White-Collar Crime Task Force. She's also the Task Force's designated liaison for the FBI investigation into Walker's death." Crenshaw paused for effect. "She says the FBI has nothing."

"I like that," Johnstone said. "Nothing is good."

"All they know is there were at least two assailants," Crenshaw continued. "Apparently you guys were caught on a grainy video at the coliseum. But the cameras were so old the FBI can do very little enhancement, so they don't even know for sure that the two people are men. Caroline says they're still considering the possibility that at least one of them was a woman, probably armed forces or police. They're wandering in every direction. They're still analyzing his hate mail, and apparently there is a lot of it. And now this threatening email has been discovered. I think we're in the clear."

"That doesn't mean they will stop looking before the crime is solved," said Westlake.

"Of course not," Crenshaw said. "I don't think any of us expects that to happen. But Caroline says the perpetrators covered their tracks very well.

Because of the masks, they can't get any facial recognition. Because of the gloves, no fingerprints. No DNA from the front-end loader."

"What about the heart monitor, or the poster we hung around his neck?" Cunningham said.

"Caroline didn't mention either one. Must be a dead end."

Cunningham set his cup down. "Just so you guys know, the heart monitor was purchased, by me, a couple of years ago. Over the internet. A standard model. Probably sold a million of them. I have the watch piece, the monitor. Well, had. I smashed it with a sledge hammer and dribbled the pieces out over the Gulf of Mexico."

Johnstone spoke up. "I don't mean to challenge your careful preparation, guys, but what about the truck? Could there be any video of the truck, or could anyone have seen the truck?"

"There's always that risk," Perez said. "Never been on a mission with zero risk. But here's what we did. First, we covered up all of the markings on the tractor and the trailers, except the name of the shipper. License plate bulbs were taken out. License plate covered with cardboard. Even if they got video of the truck, they couldn't trace it back."

"Except to the shipper," Johnstone countered.

"To a shipper who has several thousand trailers with the same logo," Perez responded. "We passed by dozens of rigs from the same company that same night."

"What about weigh stations? They have cameras, don't they?" Crenshaw asked.

"That time of night, almost all of the weigh stations were closed. I think the first one we had to stop for was in Mississippi. Hundreds of rigs, maybe thousands, run up and down I-20 every day. Needle in a haystack."

Johnstone spoke again. "And if someone spots the trailers now, and starts asking questions?"

"They've been emptied and re-painted. They're leased out to a trucking company over in Hickory that actually uses them to haul freight."

"Seems like you thought of everything," Johnstone said.

"Not likely. Can't let ourselves get cocky," Cunningham said. "We probably missed something. We just don't know what it is yet."

Shiloh perked up and sat on her haunches, wagging her tail. Westlake patted her large head. He eased up on the throttle, slowing the boat to trolling speed. "All right, gentlemen. Let's get those poles in the water."

CHAPTER FORTY-TWO

Robert Crenshaw officially transferred to Charlotte to serve as Caroline Bannister's Chief Assistant. The move meant a significant salary increase, more administrative responsibility, fewer cases, and an insider's view of the innerworkings of the office. It also meant a new house in Charlotte for Robert and his wife, who was now seven months pregnant. Cindy Crenshaw had been ordered by her obstetrician to stay in bed during the last two months of her pregnancy, so with her mother visiting to watch over her, she had sent Robert to Charlotte to look for their new home.

Robert had been given a list of features their new home must have, but not the permission to buy anything without his wife's approval. His charge was to spend the weekend culling the potential homes down to the three top candidates and then to return to Asheville, so he and Cindy could jointly decide whether to make an offer on any of them.

The status meeting in Caroline's office came to an end before lunch on Friday. "Have you met the realtor I recommended yet?" Caroline asked as she gathered up the case files.

"Just on the phone. We're going to start looking right after lunch," Crenshaw said.

"Sounds good. Keep me posted. I want you down here permanently as soon as possible."

"Me too, but Cindy's on bed rest and won't deliver for another two months. The doctor won't let her travel until after that."

"Understood. Make the move as soon as you can."

Robert met the realtor at her office south of the city. She had a list of nineteen properties ready to view. Some were new construction, and others previously lived in. Mara Lincoln was organized, professional and attractive. Robert felt lucky that Caroline had recommended her. Mara showed him the listings and their location on a huge laminated map in the conference room of her office, each prospective home marked with a red grease pencil.

"Seems like a lot of houses to look at in two days," he said.

"We'll have to hustle, but based on your reaction to the first few, we may be able to cull some from the list."

"My wife wants me to bring home a list of at least three for her consideration."

"Then we'll make sure that happens," Mara said with a bright smile.

They climbed into her Mercedes, the same model but newer than the one Judge Westlake drove, Robert observed, and started on their predetermined route. He rejected the first few houses as either too expensive or needing too much work. "I'm not much of a handyman," he said. "And with a baby coming, we won't have much time for remodeling."

"Oh, a baby. How exciting. When is your wife due?"

"Eight weeks. She's on bed rest until then."

"Your first?"

"Yes. And if Cindy has her way, he won't be the last."

"So it's going to be a boy. You must be thrilled."

"I am," he said. "I just don't know what to expect, you know. We've gotten advice from our parents, but the primary advice everyone has given is that nothing they can tell us will truly prepare us for it." He said this distractedly while gazing at Mara Lincoln's profile as she drove. Her dirty blonde hair was pulled behind her ears, which sported large diamond studs, tasteful and not gaudy.

She glanced over, catching his stare.

"Um, what about you? Kids?" he said.

"No kids. Not married," she said, removing her left hand from the steering wheel and showing him her ringless fingers.

"That's surprising. Well, I mean, a successful professional . . ."

"I know what you mean, Robert. My mother says the same thing. I work sixty or seventy hours a week. I love my career, but it doesn't leave much time for anything else. What about you? What do you do?"

"Oh, I thought Caroline would have told you. I'm a lawyer. I'm a prosecutor for the Justice Department."

"Putting away bad guys, huh?"

"Sometimes. I deal mostly with civil cases, but occasionally with white-collar crime. Bank fraud, stock manipulation, that sort of thing."

"Sounds exciting," she said in a tone that indicated she thought it was anything but.

"I tried a murder case a couple of years ago. That was exciting. A meth addict killed a young woman who was out cycling on the Blue Ridge

Parkway, near Asheville. Stabbed her with an icepick. Maybe you heard about the case? It got some publicity."

Mara shook her head. "That doesn't ring a bell. But I'm pretty busy. I don't read the newspapers and don't watch much television. It could have been all over the news and I would have missed it," she said. "I'm either networking, or showing houses, or researching listings, or entertaining clients."

Robert nodded. "So, the murder case. The guy confessed, got convicted, got the death penalty, but the court of appeals reversed it. They were wrong, but the guy ultimately went free because he was deaf when the cops Mirandized him."

"That seems wrong," said Mara.

"Very wrong," he agreed. "But the court of appeals said his constitutional rights had been violated, and his confession was not admissible, so we either had to re-try him or let him go."

"So what did you do?"

"Without the confession, there wasn't enough evidence. We couldn't re-try him. He was released."

"So he's out? A known murderer is on the loose?"

Robert appraised her, thinking she must be incredibly naive to think Lawter was the only violent criminal who ever escaped the system. Then he realized she was probably only making small talk, taking a minor interest in his work simply because he was a client. They pulled up to the next house, the sixth on the list of showings.

"These things have a way of working themselves out, Mara. The guy died of a drug overdose not long after he got out of prison. Call it karma."

She looked over at him. "Well, at least he won't hurt anybody else. Ready?"

As soon as he stepped from the car, he knew the house had the potential to make the top three. Tall oak trees framed the graceful Tudor, a two-story with four bedrooms and two-and-a-half baths. The light of the waning day seemed to make the house glow from the inside. "This is the best candidate so far," he said.

"Let's take a look inside." She punched in her realtor code, got the key, and opened the front door. The house was empty. "It would show better with furniture," Mara said, "but at least this way you get a better idea of the condition of the hardwood floors, the walls. It was remodeled about four or five years ago. Open concept living area. Master's on the first floor, the other bedrooms upstairs. What do you want to see first?"

"Upstairs."

Mara led the way up the wooden staircase with a darkly stained oak bannister, sliding her hand along the rail. He watched her from behind, the way her hips swayed in her tight skirt as she climbed the stairs. He followed her two steps below.

"Relatively new carpet," Mara said. "Installed last year. Bedrooms are medium-sized. Any of them could be a nursery. You could easily convert one bedroom into a study or home office."

Robert ducked his head into each bedroom, no longer solely interested in the house.

Mara stepped into one of the bedrooms and pulled open the closet door to reveal a small walk-in closet. "Walk-ins in each bedroom. Plenty of room for kids' clothes, or storage."

Two of the bedrooms were joined by a Jack and Jill bathroom decorated in a dull, bone white. He went into the bathroom and flushed the toilet. "That works."

"You'll want to have an inspection, of course," she said. "How about we look downstairs?"

She led the way down the stairs, and they toured the kitchen, master bedroom and master bath. He thought Cindy would like it. The backyard was large and shaded. "There's no pool," he said.

"No, but you probably don't want a pool with an infant. Safety hazard. Besides, there is a country club within a couple of miles, if that's something you wanted to join. They have a pool. Or you could put one in later. There's plenty of room in the backyard."

"Right." He did not see himself as a country club person, but maybe he would relent for the sake of Cindy and the kids in a few years. "Is there a virtual tour of this one on the internet?" he asked. "My wife will certainly want to see the inside of this one."

"There is. Should we put this in the top three?" Mara asked.

"Definitely. Tell me about the sellers. I see they've moved out. Are they motivated to sell?"

"They are," she responded. "In this economy, it's a buyer's market, and they know that. You never know, but my guess is that they will come off the asking price. They've owned the home for more than ten years, so they have some equity built up."

"How much will they come down? Best guess."

"We won't know until you make an offer," Mara smiled, showing almost perfect teeth.

They were standing now on the front porch, done in blue-grey flagstone. The sun was setting behind the Tudor, casting an ethereal light on her face. He wanted more from Mara Lincoln than just to buy a house. With a pregnant wife at home, he was partially ashamed of that feeling, but only partially. "Well, Cindy will have to make that decision," he said.

Back in the car, they decided to end the house tour for the day. He checked his voice mail and text messages. Nothing unusual – an expected message from Cindy, asking for an update on the house hunting.

"Where are you staying while you are in town, Robert?" Mara asked.

"At the Hyatt, downtown."

"Want to meet up for dinner?" she said.

He was surprised. "Dinner?"

"Sure," she said. "Standard protocol when I have clients in from out of town."

"Okay."

"I'll swing by and pick you up at sevenish."

Back at the hotel, Robert returned his messages. It was early Friday evening, so no one was in the office. When he called home, Cindy's mother picked up his wife's cell phone.

"She's having a bad day, Robert."

"Can I talk to her?"

"Not right now. She's in the bathroom throwing up."

"I can wait."

"She's going to take a bath afterward. I'll tell her you called. Or you can call back in an hour or so."

In an hour or so he would be at dinner with Mara. "Okay, I'll call back in a little while." The churning in his gut was almost making him nauseous. Anxiety medication usually calmed him, but he needed something else to ease the building tension. He went down to the hotel fitness center and rode a stationary bike for about twenty minutes, then lifted free weights for another twenty.

He had just stepped out of the shower when Mara called him on his cell phone to let him know she was downstairs. He thought momentarily of having her come up to the room, then rejected that idea. "Just getting dressed," he said. "I'll be down in less than five minutes."

They dined at a fusion restaurant whose specialty was Asian-Latin cuisine. The decor consisted of bamboo floors with simple, leather-backed seating. The entire place had fresh, clean lines. The clientele was young and attractive. Robert thought they fit right in. They ordered drinks at the bar while they waited for a table, then wine at dinner.

"So, tell me about your work," she said as they waited for entrees.

He realized he was being schmoozed. After all, Mara Lincoln was a saleswoman. He liked the attention. While the workout had started to ease the tension coursing through his body, the alcohol completed the job, and he began to relax. He leaned forward over the narrow table.

"In criminal cases, most of what we do is investigate and negotiate pleas," he shrugged. "We rarely appear in court, except for sentencing. In civil cases, I take a lot of depositions." He could tell her interest was waning already. "Here's a case you might be interested in. It involved real estate fraud."

The waiter brought the entrees, and they ate slowly while he recounted the prosecution of a real estate developer, an appraiser and several others who had been convicted of mortgage fraud. The developer was building a golf course community and, in order to get the loans, had recruited straw borrowers to buy lots in the development. The developer completed the loan applications for the borrowers and manufactured high-income levels so they could qualify for the loans. In some cases, the borrowers signed the applications without reading them; in others the developer and his staff forged the borrowers' signatures.

"Do you know what a light box is?" Robert asked her.

"Not a clue," she said, shaking her head.

"It's just like what it sounds. It's like an overhead projector without the projector part. A simple metal box with a glass top and a light bulb underneath. You put a signed document on it, with the document you want to forge on top. The light shines through, and you can easily copy a person's signature."

"That's what they used to forge the signatures?"

He nodded. "Amazing, isn't it. With all the new technology out there, they use a tool that's probably been around since Edison invented the light bulb."

"So you prosecuted them for forgery?"

"That was part of it. The developer had a backdoor deal with the buyers, unwritten, that he would pay off the loans while he built the homes, which would be sold to third parties to raise cash. When the homes sold, the developer would give the straw borrower a portion of the profits. The scheme worked for a while, until the real estate market tanked, and the banks began calling the loans. Without new money being pumped into the development, the developer could no longer pay the loans, the buyers defaulted on their promissory notes, and everyone sued everyone else. The banks sued the borrowers for nonpayment, the borrowers sued the developer for enticing them into the deal and failing to pay the loans as promised, and the developer evaded liability by filing for bankruptcy. But a bankruptcy does nothing to prevent criminal prosecution. The banks lost millions of dollars on the loans. In short order the banks, borrowers and appraiser provided the evidence we needed to convict the developer who masterminded the scheme. All of the targets pleaded guilty, except the developer. He stupidly opted for a trial. The jury convicted him, and he got nineteen years in prison. He's almost seventy, so for him a nineteen-year sentence is probably a life sentence."

Mara leaned forward, her elbows on the table. As a real estate agent who had sold lots in new developments, these types of scams interested her. "What about his wife?"

"He wasn't married. Divorced, I think."

"The closing attorney? Anything happen to him?"

"We couldn't prove that he knew any of the information was false, or that he knew about the forgeries. We gave him immunity. In return, he gave us all of his records and testified against his developer client." Robert savored a piece of lobster.

"Protecting one of your own?" she asked with raised eyebrows. "I'm sorry, that sounded harsh."

"Well, we didn't charge the borrowers, either."

"That's interesting. Why not?"

"Policy decision, made higher up," he said, draining his glass of wine. "The borrowers lost money too. Some of them lost hundreds of thousands of dollars paying off bank loans they never thought they would have to pay. They wound up with nothing. It wouldn't play well to the jury if we tried to put them in jail under those circumstances."

"What about the banks?" she said. "As much as easy money helps my business, because almost every home buyer needs a loan, it seems like the banks should share some responsibility."

"Well that's a more complicated issue, isn't it?" He slipped from comfortable to loose without realizing it. "The bank officer who made the loans, he was a target, pleaded guilty. Got five years or so. Other than that, the banks lost some money, but in most of the cases their losses were covered by mortgage insurance or cost-sharing agreements with the federal government."

"So the taxpayer foots the bill?"

"You and me and everybody else in this country."

He let this thought sink in while he finished his entree.

"So a lot of guilty people were never charged with anything?" she said.

"No doubt. Happens that way almost every time. You can't prosecute everybody, or no one will cooperate, no witnesses will step forward. You go after the worst offenders, and the less culpable parties cut a deal. That's the theory anyway."

They both rejected an offer of dessert, and Mara paid the bill. She drove them back to the hotel.

"Nightcap?" he said, before opening the car door.

Mara Lincoln glanced at the clock on the dashboard. It was not yet nine. "Sure," she said and handed her keys to the valet.

They ordered drinks at the rooftop bar and sidled to a bistro table at the perimeter. While he sipped a bourbon and coke, she nursed a cosmopolitan. They enjoyed the panoramic view of the lighted city.

His cell phone rang, and he fished the phone from his jacket pocket, glanced at the screen. It was Cindy.

"Do you need to get that?" Mara said.

He shook his head. "Nah. Nothing that I can't deal with later."

"So how do you do it?" Mara said. "How do you decide who to prosecute and who not to prosecute?"

"That's a great question. It can get complicated. We have a manual that sets out some of the guidelines, but it's really a matter of prosecutorial discretion. Caroline makes most of the decisions in our office, especially on the bigger cases that will involve lots of resources. On a really big case, like a murder case, the decision might be made in Washington. It depends." He had begun to slur his words slightly. He leaned toward her. "Wanna know something?"

"Sure."

"Congressman Lyle Walker, remember him?"

230

"Even I've seen that on television. It's been all over the news for months."

"Everybody knew he was under investigation. That was public knowledge," he said, thinking he was protecting himself from disclosing confidential information. "What everybody didn't know was that the Attorney General had decided not to prosecute him."

Mara took a sip of her drink and stared at him. "Are you supposed to be telling me this?"

"Probably not." He laughed and sat back in his chair. "But what does it matter, he's dead." He looked around for a waiter to order another drink.

"Who do you think killed him?" Mara asked.

He was quick with his response. "No idea," he said. "I'll probably find out when you do, when they arrest somebody."

They had come to that point in the evening, that awkward moment, when the night would either continue or it would not. Mara Lincoln was comfortable and relaxed, seemingly indifferent to how the night would end. The combination of alcohol and Xanax had made Robert almost drunk. He didn't want to make a mistake. The physical passion stirring inside him was overridden by a desire for sleep. And to remain faithful to Cindy. Mara twirled the cocktail straw in her empty glass, waiting. The breeze freshened, bringing with it a cold dash, and this was the signal that the evening was over. He paid the drink tab, then they rode the elevator down to his floor. He fumbled for his room key, hesitated as if to say something, then got off alone.

"I'll pick you up here at nine tomorrow," Mara said, her finger on the door open button.

He turned around, looking puzzled. Then he remembered. "Yes. More houses. Nine in the morning. I'll be ready."

The next day they looked at houses, a dozen more. Something more than a hangover clouded him all day. He was taciturn, showing little interest in the low-cut silk blouse Mara was wearing. He picked two more houses to add to the list of houses Cindy wanted to see.

As they made their way back to the hotel in light Saturday afternoon traffic, Mara said, "You've picked out three good final candidates for your new home. All of them in good neighborhoods, not far from the office, good schools. All in your price range. Let me know which one you want to make an offer on."

"I will," he said. "We will." He paused. "Hey, sorry about last night. I know I drank a little too much. Probably said too much. It's just you know, with everything going on, the difficult pregnancy and everything, it was nice to find someone so easy to talk to."

"I understand, Robert. No worries." She offered her hand, they shook, and then he was out of the car and into the hotel.

She drove toward her office. As customary, she would send a reminder email to the Crenshaws extolling the virtues of the homes in which they were interested and encouraging them to make an offer soon so that part of their life would be settled. Stopped at a traffic light, she clicked the phone menu on her steering wheel, then scrolled down the phone list until she found Caroline Bannister's cell phone number. She punched the call icon on the steering console. Caroline picked up after the third ring.

"Caroline, it's Mara."

"Hey Mara. How did it go?"

"Fine. We looked at about twenty houses. Culled the list down to three. He's going to talk to his wife. Very high likelihood they make an offer for one of the three. I appreciate the referral."

"You're welcome. Anything else?"

"He got pretty drunk last night. Didn't make a pass at me, if that's what you're asking. He was quiet all day today. There's something bothering him. Might be his current situation. Seems like he's under a lot of stress. Could be the new job, new city, pregnant wife. Might be something else."

"Something else," Caroline said. "Did he open up to you?"

"He talked a bit about some of the cases he's prosecuted. Mentioned a murder case and a recent real estate fraud case, nothing particularly interesting. Oh, and he also mentioned that when Congressman Walker was murdered, he was under investigation, and you guys, well he mentioned the Attorney General, had decided not to prosecute him."

"He told you that last night?"

"He did. He said he probably shouldn't have told me, though."

"No, he shouldn't have."

CHAPTER FORTY-THREE

Caroline sat down at the scarred, metal table. An attorney in a tailored suit sat on the other side, next to a prisoner in a white jumpsuit. The prisoner's left wrist was handcuffed to a steel eye-bolt protruding from the table. The colorless room was tinged with the sharp smell of antiseptic cleaner, which could not fully mask the odor of bad, rotting men.

"All right Barry, what am I doing here? This better be good for me to drive all the way out here," Caroline said.

"It's good," the attorney said, pulling a small envelope from his briefcase. He slid the envelope across the table.

Caroline opened the flap and emptied its contents onto the table. In stunned silence, she stared at the necklace and the blue opal encased in a filigreed setting. She reached out and turned the stone over, noted the monogram on the back. She pulled it closer. The letters CAB were engraved on the back of the amulet in a Balmoral font—Catherine Anne Bannister.

"Where did you get this?" she said in a sharp tone to the prisoner.

The lawyer shoved his hand in front of his client. "Not yet. What are you offering, Caroline?"

"The US Attorney's Office is not offering a thing until I know how your client got this."

"We want a deal," the attorney said. "No super kingpin status."

Caroline glared at the drug dealer, the mastermind of a southern cartel, who had been arrested a few months earlier. "First of all, Barry, your client operated his drug ring for what, fourteen or fifteen years. Raked in two hundred or three hundred million dollars over that time frame. Like it or not, he's a super kingpin."

"Take the living death sentence off the table, Caroline. Knock it down to twenty years."

"I will consider it. That's the full extent of my promise. Where did you get the amulet?"

The attorney eyed Caroline for a moment, then nodded to his client.

"It's from the personal stash of a gangbanger who turned out," the prisoner said.

"And how did it come into your possession?"

The prisoner smiled, revealing a gold tooth with a tiny diamond gleaming from it. "You want to know if I was involved. In your sister's death."

Caroline knew she could be sitting across the table from the man who murdered her sister Catherine. "That's right."

"Nope," the prisoner shook his head. "Before my time. I was like twelve when it happened."

Catherine had been murdered twenty-six years, six months and eleven days ago. "I read your file. You were sixteen. Old enough to have been involved. Old enough to know better. Old enough to be prosecuted as an adult."

"I wasn't there, lady."

"So whose stash did you take this from?" Caroline insisted.

"Not take. He abandoned it."

"I need a name."

The prisoner looked at his attorney.

"Give it to her," the lawyer said.

"Carmelo Williams."

"Carmelo Williams, the Mayor of Charlotte?" Caroline blurted out.

"One and the same."

Barry reached out and pulled the amulet toward him for safekeeping. He carefully dropped it back into the envelope. "What's it worth Caroline? It's your sister's amulet. Those are clearly her initials on the back of it. And you've got a big fish on the line."

This was the break she had been waiting for. A solid lead in the unsolved murder of her sister. A lead in a case that had been stashed in the frozen file for more than two decades. But if the man smirking at her from across the table was in any way involved in her sister's murder, she wasn't going to cut him a break, on anything. She kept her attention focused on his dark eyes. "What do you know about her murder?"

"I heard things. She didn't pay her debts. Somebody ordered to make an example of her. Carmelo did the deed."

"Witnesses?"

"There's a couple of names I could give you." A wide grin spread across the prisoner's face. "If . . ."

"I need names Jefe."

"I need you to go easy on me. I tell you what. You and my attorney work out a deal, I've got a couple of names for you."

CHAPTER FORTY-FOUR

Boots stomped across the covered front porch. Cunningham and Perez entered the lake house, one a step behind the other. It seemed they were almost always together. Westlake couldn't remember a time when he had seen one without the other. They hung up their eider down coats on the hooks beside the door. Though Cunningham was a much larger man, they both moved with a similar, deliberate rhythm, scanning with practiced eyes everything before them. They moved the same way in his federal courtroom.

"How are the roads?"

"Passable," Perez said. "Pretty clear until we got to your neighborhood. Switched into four-wheel drive for the last little bit."

"Could you have made it through without four-wheel drive?" Westlake asked.

Perez shrugged. "Might be tough."

They sat before the fire, Cunningham and Perez with drinks in hand. In the midst of his marathon training, Westlake had cut back on alcohol. He might have a beer later, but nothing now. They sat in comfortable silence, watching the fire and listening to the wind howl outside.

Crenshaw arrived shortly, and Johnstone shuffled through the front door soon after.

"He got stuck in the snow," Crenshaw said, thrusting his thumb over his shoulder at Johnstone. "No problem for my Subaru."

Crenshaw and Johnstone poured drinks from the bar, then they all settled around the poker table. After dealing the flop hand of a round of Texas Hold'em, Crenshaw announced he was moving to Charlotte. "We just signed the contract on our new house. We're moving right after Christmas."

"Congratulations, Robert," the Judge said. "I'd heard you were taking a new job as Caroline Bannister's Chief Deputy."

"Thank you, Judge. I didn't know word had spread. I don't start officially until the first of the year."

"We'll miss you in Asheville."

The others nodded.

"Well, that's another thing. With the new house, new job, new baby, I probably won't be very active with our group here. For a while I mean."

"Not trying to back out on us, are you Robert?" Westlake said with a half-smile.

"No. Of course not. I mean I enjoy our gatherings and all, but we've been dormant for the better part of a year. I was thinking maybe Walker was the final target."

"I hardly think that's the case," Westlake said. "Lots of dangerous criminals still walking around out there. Our work has barely started."

Cunningham, to Crenshaw's left, made a bet.

"And you're not worried the FBI is on our trail?" Crenshaw said.

"Worried is not the right word, Robert. Wary perhaps. Vigilant. But I fully trust that Marcus and Iggy have covered our tracks and left no leads. I am keenly aware that the FBI will never stop looking for Congressman Walker's killers, and for all other targets we go after we will have to vary the MO so there's no pattern. Right, gentlemen?"

"No doubt," Johnstone said, matching Cunningham's bet.

"That's the way it has to work," said Perez.

Crenshaw grimaced, looking like his stomach had soured.

"Robert, on a personal level, how are you dealing with all of this?" Westlake asked. "You're carrying around a heavy burden, with the new job, new house, new baby on the way. When is Cindy due by the way?"

"Two weeks. The twentieth. Or, if she's a little late, we might have a Christmas baby."

"A wonderful present, either way. That must be exciting, for both of you."

"It is."

"So how are you dealing with the stress?"

"Fine. Working out when I can."

"No offense, Crenshaw, but you don't look fine," Johnstone said. "You look like you haven't been out in the sun in months."

Crenshaw glared at Johnstone and took a deep gulp of whiskey. "You're a lawyer. You know how it is. Busy."

Perez matched the bet, as did Westlake. The pot had grown to eight dollars. "Bet's to you Robert," Westlake said.

Crenshaw tossed in chips to match the bet, then dealt the turn card.

"You see. Here's my concern," Westlake said. "It almost goes without saying that we all have a vested interest in loyalty and complete secrecy. And I'm not singling you out Robert, but by moving to Charlotte to work at Caroline Bannister's right hand, you're walking into the proverbial lion's den. She's on the White-Collar Crime Task Force, and she's the liaison with the FBI on the Walker investigation. She's as close as you can get to the FBI, without being an agent. For a lot of reasons, she'll be watching you like a hawk."

"Keep your friends close and your enemies closer," Crenshaw responded. "I'll get a lot more inside information being literally next door to Caroline. If there are any leads, I'll know about them. At least I hope so."

"That's true. But you can't probe her Robert, not even under the guise of idle curiosity. And no offense, but you don't have the best poker face. She's going to be reading you."

"I'll be careful."

"I know you will. You have to be, for the sake of all of us," Westlake said.

Crenshaw looked at the faces around the table, then turned over the river card. Another round of betting ensued, with Johnstone taking the pot.

"So, does anybody have a potential target for our consideration?" Westlake asked.

Crenshaw shook his head.

"How about you Judge?" said Johnstone. "Anybody in mind?"

"Yes, as a matter of fact. But I'm not ready to make a recommendation. If we move on this target, in some ways it will be our most difficult trial. I'll keep thinking about it and let you all know when it's the right time."

CHAPTER FORTY-FIVE

Elijah Crenshaw was born two days before Christmas. The Crenshaws moved to Charlotte the week after and were comfortably tucked in the new Tudor home when the new year arrived. Robert Crenshaw immersed himself in his new duties as Caroline Bannister's Chief Deputy. Some of his cases, most in the earlier stages of litigation or prosecution, were reassigned to other AUSAs, and his duties became more administrative and strategic. He welcomed the change. He had not fully recovered from Lawter, or Elise Rutherford, or Tyler Becksdale, or the trial and execution of Lyle Walker.

Immediately after Congressman Walker's death by rattlesnake, Robert and Cindy Crenshaw had renewed their wedding vows and enjoyed a four-day honeymoon at home, acting like newlyweds. Cindy became pregnant. Something had driven Robert, had driven them both, into a safe place entwined in each other's arms, blissfully ignorant for a brief time of the turmoil swirling around them.

For the first days of their renewed honeymoon, they watched the television coverage surrounding the assassination of Walker, including a cell-phone video taken by the person who first discovered the Congressman in the pit of snakes. Of course, Crenshaw had seen the live feed of Walker being bitten to death as he and the others perched on chairs in Alpha trailer, and he was forced to feign shock at the video of live snakes slithering around the body of the Ponzi-scheme mastermind. Then he and Cindy had turned the television off for a few days, to partially insulate themselves from the fear gripping the country. They turned to each other. The days of intimacy with Cindy had worked. For a time, anyway, he had forgotten about Walker and his own involvement in the vigilante cabal. Later, he wondered whether his decision to father a child was driven by some primal need.

Crenshaw awoke most mornings wondering what in the hell he had gotten himself into. He had always believed in justice, in battling evil, and he had been prepared to fight for it, had been prepared to fight for it with every molecule. Somewhere he had taken a wrong turn. And then it was gone. He felt it leave him when he saw the first sonogram of his son's beating heart, when he felt the first kick from inside his wife's belly.

Now, he sat with others in the conference room for the first status meeting of the new year. He wanted to be somewhere else. He wanted to be at home, with his newborn son, with his wife flush with pride, listening to the creak of the wooden rocker, the softness of Cindy's hand patting their son's back as she lulled him to sleep.

Caroline Bannister laid out the goals for the next twelve months, announced to the others Crenshaw's duties and authority as Chief Deputy, and heard status reports of ongoing investigations and prosecutions. She had let her auburn hair grow out over the holidays, Crenshaw noted, and she was wearing it longer, which reinstilled some femininity to her visage. Her suit was royal blue, and she sported a new pair of designer eyeglasses. Caroline adjourned the meeting after an efficient fifty-five minutes and asked Crenshaw to join her in her office for further updates.

After they settled into the club chairs surrounding the new oval table in the meeting area of her office, Caroline announced, "I have some news. On the Lyle Walker investigation."

"Oh?" Crenshaw said, steepling his hands together under his chin to keep them from trembling.

"There's been a break, of sorts. Some guy who lives close to the Coliseum where Walker was killed has a snapshot of a truck driving by at about four o'clock in the morning."

"A snapshot? What would somebody be doing taking photographs at that time of night?" Crenshaw said, trying to hold his voice and eyes steady.

"Came from a wildlife camera. Apparently, the guy had a wildlife camera in his front yard because he suspected the neighbor's dog was tearing up his flower beds at night. One of those cameras that is motion-activated. Anyway, turns out the culprit was a deer. Pretty good picture of the deer; fuzzy picture of the truck driving by behind it."

Crenshaw relaxed just a little, though his stomach kept churning. He attempted to quell it with a bite of the half-eaten bear claw left over from the morning briefing.

"FBI forensics is working on the photo, trying to enhance it. It's very grainy." Caroline said.

He relaxed a little more. The doughy bear claw was starting to absorb some of the acid spilling into his stomach. "They get a license plate number or anything?" he asked, trying to sound nonchalant.

"No. Nothing that definitive. Anyway, just wanted to update you on that. The investigation is still grinding on."

"Thanks for keeping me in the loop, Caroline. Is there anything else we need to discuss?"

"No. That's it. Welcome to Charlotte. Welcome to your new job, Robert. Glad to have you down here closer to the action."

He took the elevator down one floor, entered the bathroom and threw up the sour contents of his stomach. He cleaned himself up, went up a floor to his office, and swallowed two Xanax. Then he went to the bathroom, brushed his teeth, and swigged a capful of mouthwash.

"Hey buddy," said a voice from behind. "How's the new baby, new house?" It was Tom Dillingham, an AUSA hired on about a year earlier, who mostly prosecuted organized crime.

"Hi Tom. Everything's good. Some adjustments," Crenshaw said, wiping his mouth with a paper towel.

"Oh, yeah. I remember those days. What did you have, girl or boy?"

"Boy. Named him Elijah."

"Everybody happy and healthy?"

"Sure. Everybody's great."

They stood in awkward silence in the bathroom for another moment or two, then Dillingham stepped up to a urinal. Crenshaw stared at himself in the mirror. Even he noticed the lack of color in his face, the bags growing larger and darker under his eyes. He hadn't gotten a full night's sleep since the baby was born. Truthfully, he hadn't gotten a full night's sleep in months, unless it was with the aid of several stiff drinks before bedtime. He rubbed his left cheek. *You look fifty years old, and you're only thirty-seven. Jesus.*

For the rest of the day he worked in his office, attending to forms and unpacking boxes and files. He hung a framed glossy photo of himself and Caroline Bannister at the press conference where they'd announced the coal ash settlement. To date, that had been the highlight of his legal career, or at least the highlight he could talk about. He wasn't sure if his work with Westlake's team should be considered a highlight.

Crenshaw observed that the aftermath, the guilt, whatever term it deserved, had little effect on Perez and Cunningham. Perhaps that was predictable, given the nature of their training and experience. They were veterans of war and had surely seen worse. They could justify what they did as duty, merely taking orders, rarely contemplating the consequences. All of those they had killed were simply casualties of an unnamed war they had volunteered to fight.

Westlake seemed unflappable. Crenshaw was amazed at how he showed no signs of stress. He wondered how Westlake handled it. Maybe it was the running. Maybe the running somehow pounded the demons right out of him. Whatever Westlake was doing to assuage the accumulating and burdensome guilt, it was working. Crenshaw needed some of that. He needed a solution, because he was slowly deteriorating, and the pills and alcohol were no longer working. He had stopped going to therapy when they moved to Charlotte.

He wondered if he should talk to David Johnstone about what he was feeling and how to deal with it. Now that Crenshaw had moved to the Charlotte headquarters, Johnstone's office was literally just down the street. Perhaps under the auspices of discussing a case or a settlement, for surely Johnstone had some pending federal cases, they could meet and discuss what they were both going through. Even though they had developed something of a bond through their mutual endeavors and had the law in common, he was reluctant to reach out to Johnstone. Or any member of the team. It might be viewed as a sign of weakness, a sign that he was unstable. Any weakness or instability could be perceived as a threat to the team.

That night, after dinner with Cindy, he sat beside the cradle that held his son, rocking it gently with his foot. They had bought the crib with an automatic rocking mechanism, but this evening he turned it off. He stared vacantly at his son's sleeping face. Elijah, destined to be carried to heaven in a chariot of fire. He wondered whether he would be around to celebrate his son's first birthday. He could feel the FBI closing in. They now had a photograph of the truck. It was only a matter of time before they were caught.

He rolled Elijah onto his side and tucked rolled towels against his stomach and against his back to keep him in place. He could only tell the difference between sleeping and death by watching the barely visible flaring of his child's nostrils. He leaned over and kissed his son on the forehead, then stood there for a very long time.

CHAPTER FORTY-SIX

Crenshaw tried to remain calm. Judge Westlake had summoned him, had summoned all of them, to the lake house to discuss the next target. He didn't want there to be a next target. He wanted it to be over. He wanted to spend the rest of his life with Cindy and Elijah, not looking over his shoulder, not wondering when the FBI was going to show up at his home or at the office to arrest him.

"I have something to report," Crenshaw said as he walked in the door. "There is some progress on the Walker investigation." The others joined him in Westlake's kitchen. "Caroline told me the FBI has a photograph, a grainy one, showing a semi passing by on a street near the coliseum in Texas. At about the same time we killed Congressman Walker."

"Have you seen the photograph, Robert?" the Judge asked.

"No, I haven't. And I don't know what the FBI has been able to learn from it. It was apparently taken by a wildlife camera in someone's front yard. A motion camera. A deer eating roses in a flower bed set it off at the time the truck was driving by."

Perez exhaled. "Is it our truck?"

"It has to be, right?"

"That's the detail we forgot," Cunningham said. "An off-premises camera. I knew something would pop up." He shook his head.

"Yeah," Crenshaw said.

"When did Bannister tell you about this?" Westlake asked.

Crenshaw hesitated. "A few weeks ago. January."

Westlake spun around in disgust. "Two months ago, Robert. You sat on this information for two whole months?" The Judge's voice cracked the air like a slammed door. He took a deep breath. "Let's go sit down."

The men trudged into the den, but no one sat down. They all stared at Crenshaw, waiting for an explanation.

"The way she looked when she told me about it, it was clear she didn't think it was much of a lead. I've been waiting for an update from her."

Cunningham spoke with a hard edge. "Two months? This is the kind of shit that gets people caught."

"Water over the dam," Westlake said, folding his arms across his torso. "Robert, what exactly did she say about the photograph?"

"She said there was a photograph of a semitruck on a street near the coliseum. It was caught on a wildlife camera." Crenshaw sat down heavily on a leather ottoman.

"Did the photo capture any markings on the truck, or a license plate number?" asked Westlake.

"I don't . . . I'm not sure. I don't know. It caught the deer, you know, with the semi in the background. The picture was very blurry, Caroline said."

"What are the odds that anther semi was driving by at that location around that time of night?" Johnstone interjected.

They all contemplated this for a few moments. Westlake broke the silence. "We have to assume it was our rig."

"Here's the thing," Cunningham said. "Even if the photo is blurry, it probably captured some things. Like the logo on the side of the trailers. Maybe a profile of the driver through the cab window."

"And the light pattern on the cab and trailers," Perez said. "It was at night. That's probably one thing that shows up clearly on the photo. The lights."

"All right. Marcus, Iggy, where are the trailers now?" the Judge asked.

"They're at a distribution center in Hickory," Perez said.

"Are they being used?"

"Hard to say. But they can easily be traced back to the shipping company, and the company isn't going to have any record of those trailers."

"So what are the options?" Westlake asked.

"Only thing I know to do," Cunningham said, "is destroy them." The others looked at him for further explanation. "Take them apart. Sell off the metal to scrapyards."

"What about changing the light pattern on the trailers?" Johnstone suggested. "You've already had the trailers repainted, right? So if it is our rig in the picture, the trailers don't look anything like the photograph, except for the lights. If we change the light pattern, move them around, add some lights or something, our trailers won't even match the light pattern in the photograph."

"That could work," Westlake said. "While I don't want this to be about money, it's got to be less expensive to change the lights, as opposed to buying two new trailers." He'd been financing their mission, their travels, with money he had set aside from Heather's life insurance policy. The balance was running low. "What would two new trailers run us?"

"Used," Perez said, "twenty to thirty K, including furnishings."

"What about the cab? Do we know if that's on the photo too?" Johnstone said.

Crenshaw shook his head. "She didn't say."

"Well, the cab may have some things on it that are still there, even after we had it painted. Smokestacks, wind deflector, grill, shape, etc.," Perez said.

"Where's the cab, Iggy?"

"It's being used by a truck broker down in Charlotte. Short-term lease. Cab and trailers are separated."

"How much for a new cab?"

"Again, used, maybe fifteen to twenty K on the low end. We don't need anything fancy. It's not like we drive it a lot of miles."

"No, but it has to be one hundred percent reliable," Johnstone said.

"All right." Westlake looked at Perez and Cunningham. "Change the light patterns on the trailers. Do it quickly and quietly. Modify the cab in some way. Add a smokestack, a wind deflector, take something off. Just make it look different than it did when we were in Texas. Make sure you're not being watched. Could be the FBI has already found the trailers and is just waiting for someone to show up to claim them."

Cunningham nodded. "Yes sir, we'll be careful. Would have been better if we'd known about this sooner."

"I agree," Westlake said. "Robert, you are supposed to be our eyes and ears on this investigation." He put his hand on Crenshaw's left shoulder. "This little lapse will hopefully amount to nothing, but there's a lot at stake here, for all of us. You've got to let us know immediately when there's a new development. No delays."

Crenshaw nodded but didn't say anything.

"You all right, Robert? You don't look so good," the Judge said.

"I'm okay. I just need a drink I think."

"That might do us all some good," Westlake said. He walked over to the bar and poured Crenshaw a highball of bourbon with a couple of ice cubes, then pulled a low carb beer out of the refrigerator for himself. The others poured their own drinks.

"What about this new target, Judge, the one you wanted to discuss?" Johnstone asked.

"That will have to be postponed. Altering the appearance of the rig is our number one priority. Let's get that done. Then we'll see."

Soon after a dinner of roasted chicken, fixed that morning by Westlake's housekeeper, Cunningham and Perez left so they could get to work on modifying the trailers and cab. It was imperative that they expedite that operation in case the feds had made progress they hadn't been alerted to.

Crenshaw decided to stay the night, for he was in no condition to drive. He gulped another bourbon and stumbled down the hall to one of the guest rooms to sleep it off.

"I wouldn't want to have his head in the morning," Johnstone said.

Westlake built a fire to ease the chill. When the kindling caught and began to crackle, he settled into a padded chair that rocked with the alacrity of a custom-made wooden bow rocker. He folded his hands in his lap. "No. He's not right. I've never seen him like this before."

"I've run into him a couple of times since he moved down to Charlotte," Johnstone said. "Had lunch with him about a month ago, as you suggested."

Westlake merely nodded.

"I don't know if he looks worse now, but he looked bad back then, as if he hadn't slept in months."

"Did he say anything of significance?"

"We've got a small criminal case together, so we talked about that for a while. It seemed like cover though, like a prelude to something else, but he never got around to it."

"He's scared. He's not handling the stress well. I thought with the move to Charlotte, his new post at the US Attorney's Office, and the baby that he might resume something of a normal life. Alcohol is no way to self-medicate," Westlake said.

"He's on Xanax too," Johnstone said. "I saw the bottle in the bathroom, earlier."

"That's a concern. Do you think there's anything to this photograph?"

"I don't know," Johnstone said. "If they find the trailers and trace them back, who are they tracing them back to?"

246

Westlake smiled. "A limited liability company organized in Nevada owns the cab, and a Delaware corporation owns the trailers."

"That's why the license plates on the semi and the trailers are different?"

"Right. The only member-manager of the Nevada company is an Irish corporation, whose only officer and shareholder is a lawyer in Switzerland. Different lawyer in Zurich owns the Delaware company," Westlake said.

"Sounds untraceable."

Westlake nodded. "Untraceable back to anyone in the US."

Johnstone took a sip from his drink. "When did you set it up?"

"Years ago, when I was practicing law in Atlanta. You never know when you might need an arrangement like that. The companies didn't do a lot at first, sat there empty for quite a while. Then, after my wife died, I bought the rig. Never knew I'd use it for a mobile courtroom."

"Anybody else know about it?"

"Me, you and the lawyers in Zurich. That's it."

The oak logs caught, and the fire sizzled to full life. Westlake poured himself a bourbon, and he and Johnstone sat in comfortable silence for a long while, staring into the lapping tongues of flame.

When the silence of the night had fallen upon them and the tumult of Crenshaw's revelation had abated, Westlake stopped rocking. "Well David, I'm going to call it a night. I've got an early run in the morning. You're welcome to stay, of course. The bed's made up, fresh towels in the bathroom."

"Thank you, Raleigh. I think I will, then drive back to Charlotte in the morning."

Westlake spread the embers, sending sparks up the chimney. He put the fireplace poker back in the rack, then replaced the screen. He shook hands with Johnstone, and then he went to bed.

Shiloh followed him into the bedroom and hopped up onto the bed. Over the past several months she had been inching her way up from the bottom, and now she lay curled on top of the spread in the space Heather had once occupied. Westlake ran his hand along the fur of her back, stroked her head behind the ears. He went to sleep slowly, tossing around ideas of what to do about Robert.

CHAPTER FORTY-SEVEN

Judge Westlake awoke early, his mouth a ball of fuzz. He wanted to get in a twenty-mile run on trails at the Tsali Recreation Area, just a few miles from his house. He crept into the kitchen, downed two ibuprofen tablets and drank a bottle of sports drink to re-hydrate. Johnstone and Crenshaw were still asleep in the guest bedrooms. He thought about taking Shiloh with him, for she immensely enjoyed the few times he had taken her into the woods, but he didn't think she could make it a full twenty miles. She wasn't ready for that, yet.

The events of the previous night still gnawed at him. He had tried to conceal his anger at Robert's delayed revelation of the photograph of the truck. Robert was making mistakes. To the group he had downplayed Crenshaw's call to the DA about Elise Rutherford's death, but this was a bigger problem. Now down in Charlotte, Robert was no longer within his circle of control, and the trust he once had in his protege's integrity was eroding fast. There was a solid possibility that Robert had already begun, wittingly or unwittingly, to disclose clues to Caroline Bannister that would unravel the entire, carefully constructed scheme.

He forced himself to start his run slowly, to curb the urge to sprint from the gate and wear himself out so that his brain would go quiet. Over the years, he often relied on running to work out various problems, from cases to relationships, and found that a slow and steady pace ultimately allowed his subconscious to mull the problems, hone the issues, and arrive at solutions that would reveal themselves at odd times. It was a process he trusted. It was one of the few things he still trusted.

As he plodded away from the parking lot, he focused on the dirt path in front of him and the verdant surroundings slowly emerging from every corner of the forest. His footfalls were even and his pace steady. At five miles he removed his water bottle, took a couple of swigs, then stowed the bottle back in his running belt. The air had warmed above forty degrees, so he took off the red pullover and tied it around his waist, then started down the trail again.

He had not run far when he heard something rustling in the woods. He looked up from the trail. A black bear stood in the middle of the trail, at the bottom of a small swale. He and the bear detected the other simultaneously. They were about sixty feet apart, a short distance the bear could cover, were it so inclined, before he could scramble to safety. The bear stood astride the trail, perpendicular to it, and eyed him warily. Westlake held his ground. He remembered from his mother's stories that the black bear could be a spirit guide, or an omen. As a Cherokee, he was supposed to have some natural bond with this wild animal. He didn't think that helped him much in his current predicament, and he didn't want to test the theory with this particular animal.

He studied the bear, noting its dark, dull coat. The bear looked to be over three hundred pounds. For a fleeting moment he regretted not bringing Shiloh with him, for the bear might have been intimidated by a barking dog, but he realized Shiloh might not stay put, and in any encounter with a bear she would be the loser. He knew black bears were usually not aggressive animals, though the previous summer one had mauled and killed a mother and son on the Appalachian Trail, not far from where he was standing. Sows sometimes became aggressive if their cubs were nearby, but it was too early in the year for this bear to have cubs, even if it was a sow. The bear remained on the path.

He recounted the contradictory advice that when encountering a bear, a person should make himself look larger and make a lot of noise, or back away slowly without running, or curl up in a ball as tight as possible while covering the head and neck. He did neither. If this bear was a spirit guide, he wanted to know what it had to say. And while it may not have been the smartest move to stare directly at the bear, the bear was not moving toward him. The bear lifted its big head and sniffed the air.

He had no idea whether he was upwind or downwind of the bear and, now that the bear could clearly see him, he didn't know if it mattered. Keeping one eye on the bear, he bent down and picked up a small stone about the size of a golf ball. He rolled the stone in his fingers.

He could stand there for a while and see if the bear wandered off, or head back the way he had come until he returned to the parking lot, then run the other leg clockwise, which would eventually bring him back to the same spot. A part of him urged bravado, to move toward the bear in a steady, unmenacing way. *Ego* chided him for hesitating, for what kind of man sentenced others to death but was afraid of stepping onto the brink himself? The bear seemed . . . amused . . . that he had not moved, either forward or backward. And then Westlake stepped forward two strides, surprising himself. Why not just one step closer instead of two? The bear huffed and swung his head in a small arc. It was a motion he could not judge. The bear was, literally, sideways on the path, as if it could not make up its mind. He wondered whether the bear was even capable of such decision-making, whether instinct went that far, or whether the bear was just curious about this other animal, who seemed to be going generally in the same direction. Checking his watch, he noted he had been standing stock-still for the better part of seven minutes.

For unknown reasons, he felt compelled to move ahead. Somewhere within him, one of the wolves began to growl. He took two quick steps and then began to run again, down the path, directly at the burly bear.

The bear bounded into the edge of the woods, then stopped.

Westlake kept his eyes on the trail, feeling a sense of determination. He was alongside the bear, only slightly out of paws' reach, when he rolled the small stone to the bear's feet. And then he was past the bear, and he leaned into the short slope, pumping up the hill and willing himself not to swivel his head to look back. He hoped he would be able to hear the bear if it chose to chase him. He put ten yards, thirty, and then one hundred more between himself and the bear. If his past deeds had earned him death, then it surely would have come here, on this isolated trail, on a sunny morning in which the blackness itself manifested in a hungry bear emerging from hibernation.

He met no one else on the trail, human or otherwise, and the wolf that had mocked him eventually fell silent. He completed the first ten-mile loop and returned to the parking lot. There, a young woman was embarking alone upon the trail. He hailed her and walked over.

"I ran into a bear out there," he said. "About five miles in."

"You saw a bear? Out there on the trail?" She pointed into the woods. She had a long ponytail of deep brown hair and could not have been more than twenty-five, approximately the age of Hannah Sullivan when she died.

He nodded. "I did. Good-sized one. Looks like hibernation is over."

She gnawed on her lower lip.

"Look," he said, "I'm only halfway through with my run. I'm going to do another loop. If you like, I'll run with you. Just let me pop a couple of energy cubes."

She said nothing while he unwrapped two cubes and popped them into his mouth. He opened the trunk and removed a bottle of sports drink, from which he swallowed two gulps. He slammed the trunk lid. "Ready?" he said.

"I guess so," she said with hesitation.

"My name's Raleigh by the way," he said, starting down the path.

"Melanie," she replied.

"I'll lead the way," he said back over his shoulder. "If the pace is too slow, tell me to pick it up or jump ahead."

"I think I'll stay right here," she called. "If that bear is still out there, I'd prefer you be the first one it sees."

"How far you going?" Westlake called over his shoulder.

"Ten," she said. "The whole loop."

They settled into a gentle pace. He could hear her light footfalls not far behind him. She had a shorter stride, but she was steady and seemed to his ear to float with ease across the ground. Where the trail broadened, he slowed so she could pull alongside.

"This is too slow for you, I can tell," he said. He had covered almost fifteen miles, and fatigue had graveled his voice. He had lost some of his fitness level over the long winter.

"It's fine," she said. "I need an easy day. Sunday morning, you know."

He looked across at her face, at her youthful unblemished face, at toned legs emerging from a pair of spandex shorts. He allowed the images to linger. Then he pushed ahead of her, so his eyes no longer were looking there.

They came to the halfway point of the loop, where it crossed a forest road, and he stopped again for water. He offered her some. She took it, holding the spout away from her face and squirting it into her mouth across the span of an inch or two.

"Are you training for something?" she said.

There was a lilt there, but he couldn't place it. "Boston. Six weeks from tomorrow."

"Impressive," she said, stretching her quadriceps, her limberness allowing the heel of her foot to press tight against her right buttock.

"I'm doing twenty today. Three-quarters there," he said to divert his own attention.

She handed the water bottle back to him, and he stuffed it in a pocket of his belt.

"So where did you see the bear?"

"Ahead, maybe a half mile or so."

"Show me when we get there." She started to run again.

He followed. "Want me to lead?"

"It's the chivalrous thing to do."

This thrilled him, this mention of chivalry by a woman thirty years younger, whom he would not have thought would know the word "chivalrous." The lilt was soft and watery, perhaps Australian. He had challenged and beaten the bear threat, which his mind now embellished, yet he felt his resolve melting in her presence. He fought the urge to talk, to even think of her, loping along in front of him with smooth, tight legs. She bobbed when she ran, her hair swishing like the tail of a horse on canter. On a straight stretch of the trail he surged ahead of her.

As they approached the shallow valley of the bear, he slowed but did not stop, pointing to the spot where the bear had stood, noting the smooth white stone beside the trail. "It was right here, beside the trail. I ran right past, not five feet away."

She slowed as well, and he could tell without looking that she was pivoting her head around, searching for any sign that the bear was still near, both curious and wary. Cousin emotions separated by little. He charged ahead, trying to act oblivious to the danger, daringly chivalrous.

He did not hear her approach from behind until she said, just behind his right shoulder, "I guess he moved off."

He nodded, distracted by the pain that had begun to pulse within his leg muscles. Unable to distinguish the pain of longing from the pain of running long, he pressed ahead. Around mile eighteen, he began to falter. The proverbial wall. His stride came undone like an unraveling sweater, a single thread snagged on a stout, dead limb. He lurched the final two miles in a broken-down shuffle, his muscles no longer supple or responsive.

For her part, Melanie remained behind or at his side, urging him along, encouraging him with updates of the diminishing distance to the finish. "It's just around this bend," or "Just over the next rise," she said.

He both appreciated and silently cursed her presence. When they emerged finally from the woods into the parking lot, he plopped against his car, an exhausted wreck. He leaned down, bracing hands on knees, bent under the extraordinary burden. He could not catch his breath.

"Are you okay?" She bent down to his eye level.

He nodded, momentarily unable to speak. He straightened and took a swig of water. When it went down toward his lungs, he sputtered and coughed. "Maybe . . . I'm . . . not . . . ready . . . for Boston."

"You pushed through it. That's what matters." She placed her hand on his upper arm because he started to list.

When his breathing began to ease, he leaned against the car. "Thanks for hanging in there with me. Thanks for pushing me."

She smiled, then sauntered to her car without another word. As he regained his equilibrium, he watched the Tennessee license plate recede into the distance of the dusty road.

CHAPTER FORTY-EIGHT

While Westlake was confronting the bear in the forest, Crenshaw surrendered to the blackness. There was no light, no light at all. As he drove down the mountain range into a glaring sun, the dark shadows in his mind spread and deepened. The descent had begun gradually. He could not pinpoint the precise inception, for it had been with him for many years. Sometime around the first killing, the black spot within had emerged again, and with each successive execution the stain had become darker, more prevalent. The medication no longer provided any tranquility. He was spiraling into the abyss.

When he held his son and looked into Elijah's sky-blue eyes, he saw not hope but reflected bleakness. The previous night, sleeping it off at Westlake's house, he had dreamed that Elijah had been murdered as retribution for what he had done.

Depression had afflicted his mother, and her father. To cope, they medicated themselves with alcohol, using a depressant to treat depression. In the way that this happens without intention. There were vague periods where his mother would escape the house for days at a time and come stumbling home, sometimes dropped off by a friend, sometimes in the back of a police car. She rarely offered an explanation. Bitterness and sadness became her constant companions. She propelled herself through a shortened life in a blurred stupor. And then death. Both his mother and her father died of respiratory failure resulting from heart disease. These were euphemistic pronouncements from coroners who had to put words on public records. Everybody else knew they drank themselves to death.

The black gauze into which Crenshaw had awakened that morning gathered strength and pounded at him like thunder as he drove toward home. He pulled off the highway at Chimney Rock Village, went into a shop and bought a coffee and a bottle of water. He drank the coffee quickly, in his car, barely tasting the brew. He continued along the winding road and stopped at Chimney Rock. At that early hour, there were few other visitors.

He grabbed the bottle of water and decided to climb the 491 stairs rather than take the elevator to the top of the thirty-story monolith. The climb was arduous. He ascended the rock without surcease, without taking even a moment to rest at any of the landings. Even in the cool morning air, he sweated profusely, soaking his shirt. Heaving with effort, he climbed the last staircase to Exclamation Point. There, he leaned against the railing in a damp and ragged state, his mind muddled. His hands were shaking. He could not live this way. He knew it. Even the magnificent views of Lake Lure provided no reprieve.

The metal fence at the top was only about four feet high, no barrier for a man bent on self-destruction. He tested it with his hands, feeling the metal flex. He could go over the fence and take a few strides on the protruding rock before gravity became his friend. He could stop the infernal spiraling and plunge into the infinity of nothingness. It would be over in a matter of seconds.

He took a deep guzzle of water, then looked around. He was alone. He placed his hands atop the fence and prepared to vault over. Like Elise Rutherford, no one was forcing him to do it. He had a choice; Elise had a choice.

With his hands on the fence, he hesitated. The span of a heartbeat became the length of a breath. A thought wormed its way up from his subconscious, blanketed in shadow, and lit the head of another trail. He took his hands off the railing and stumbled a step backward. Another breath. Another step. A swig of water. He sat down and looked out at the view. It was stunning, stretching for seventy-five miles. As he calmed, a plan began to form.

I didn't kill anybody. I didn't kidnap anybody. I didn't physically touch any of the victims. This wasn't my idea. It was Westlake's plan. Sure, I went along with it. I didn't object. Well, I objected, but I didn't object all that strongly. I was a co-conspirator, nothing more.

His head spinning with possibilities, he descended from Exclamation Point to the elevator, then took the elevator down to the parking lot. He unlocked his car and looked around, somewhat suspecting that he was being spied upon. The parking lot was filling, yet no one was paying any attention to him. He drove fast toward home, toward his life, toward his family, piecing together the plan that might just save it all.

CHAPTER FORTY-NINE

Crenshaw approached as she was locking her car.

"Leave your purse. Bring just your keys," he commanded.

"Why? What's up?"

"Just trust me, Caroline."

She stared at him for a moment before locking her purse in the trunk. They walked in silence the several blocks through downtown to the NASCAR Hall of Fame. He scanned the faces of the other pedestrians, looking for any sign. At the crosswalks, waiting for the light, he glanced behind for any indication they were being followed. He had refused to take any calming medication that morning because he needed his head to be clear. It was imperative that he be fully alert to how Caroline reacted to every word he uttered.

They entered the Hall, which was almost empty in the midafternoon of a weekday. They began circulating among the exhibits, then stopped before the portrait of a Hall inductee. He inched closer to her.

"Caroline, I have something to tell you. This is big. Bigger than anything you've ever seen before," he whispered.

"Why all the secrecy?" she said.

"Because I need complete immunity. Transactional and use immunity."

She searched his eyes. "You need immunity? What are you involved in?"

"And witness protection. I'll testify."

"What are you talking about?"

His lips remained a tight, thin line.

"This must be really serious if you're asking for immunity."

"Dead serious."

"Okay. Look, I know you've been under a lot of pressure Robert, what with the move and the new position, new baby and all. I thought maybe you were having an affair or had a gambling problem, or something."

"No. No affair. No gambling problem."

"What is it?" she asked. "What are you involved in, Robert?"

"I have to have full immunity before I tell you anything."

"I've got to know more," she said. "I can't grant you immunity without even the slightest idea of what you're implicated in."

"There are five people involved," he said.

She did not take the bait. Her arms remained folded across her chest.

"I need immunity. Transactional and use," he repeated. "I need the full protection of the federal government. To protect Cindy and Elijah, too."

"What did you do?"

He shook his head. "No, Caroline. Not until you give me immunity. Your word. You have to trust me. This will be the biggest case you've ever had. It will literally make your career."

Caroline moved off a few steps, pretending to stare at another portrait. After a minute of silence, she nodded for him to join her.

"I can tell you this," he said. "It concerns a murder investigation. You'll want this information, Caroline. I promise. If you don't give me immunity, I'll take it to someone who will."

"Like who?" she said.

He hadn't planned to take the information anywhere else, but when she balked unexpectedly at granting him full immunity, he had to think of something to eliminate her reticence. "To the top. The AG. It's that big. I'm giving you the first shot at becoming the hero." He walked up the ramp. This had to work. He had nothing left to entice her.

She followed him. "Who's the victim?"

"Immunity first, or I'm out of here," he said. He shifted from foot to foot, looking at the exit door.

"All right, Robert."

"Full immunity? Transactional and use, derivative use? All of it?"

"Yes. You have my word. Full immunity."

"And witness protection?"

"Yes, witness protection too. For you, Cindy and Elijah."

Crenshaw exhaled, then leaned over a metal railing. He looked over at her, moisture in his eyes. "All right then. Thanks for that." He managed a thin smile. "Lyle Walker. I know who killed him."

She could not avoid turning to look at him, astonishment on her face. "Go on."

"There's a big fish. A judge."

Her eyebrows went up. "And you're involved? You and a judge?"

He nodded. "It's Judge Westlake."

"Judge Westlake—are you serious? This is not some crazy joke you're trying to play on me?"

"Perfectly serious." He had what he wanted now—full immunity from the United States Attorney and witness protection. Desperation turned to elation, and he couldn't stand still. He hurried up the ramp to Glory Road, unable to contain himself.

When she caught up to him, he told her how the scheme got underway, starting with the devastation he and Westlake both felt at the appellate court's reversal of the Henry Lawter conviction. The confession gushed from him like a flood, the power of it almost sweeping Caroline off balance. He told her everything about the Lawter case, spewing the words in a rushed whisper that left his voice dry and raspy.

"It was all in the name of justice. The trial, the sentence, everything."

"The trial? We had a trial, Robert, and he was convicted."

"Not the official trial. The second one. We have a traveling courtroom, in the back of a semitrailer. Westlake owns the rig through some shell company. There's a small courtroom. Pretty nice, considering the size. It has a small judge's bench and two tables for the attorneys. Westlake presides. I prosecute. David Johnstone defends. The result is a foregone conclusion, of course."

They gazed at one of the race cars. "We have meetings at Westlake's house on Lake Fontana and discuss the targets, vote on them. We go to them. Wherever they are. St. Augustine for Lawter. He was the first."

"Lawter died of a drug overdose," she said.

"That was us. Made to look like just another junkie who OD'd. Someone found him on the beach with a needle in his arm. Under the circumstances, who would even imagine it was anything but an accidental overdose?"

They stood in front of another race car.

"Why Robert? So the system didn't work; or maybe it did. Why launch a vigilante mission?"

"Because someone had to avenge the death of Hannah Sullivan. It felt right. It felt just. We did it for her."

"You said there were four murders."

"Four trials," he corrected her. "With sentences carried out expeditiously, efficiently. The next one was a woman over in the eastern part of the state. She was Johnstone's idea."

"I can't believe David Johnstone is involved in something like this. He's a defense lawyer for God's sake. Fights like crazy for every client," Caroline said.

"Believe it."

"I can't believe you're involved in something like this, Robert."

"Believe it, Caroline. Westlake can be very persuasive."

"So he got you into this? I mean . . ."

"I'm not saying it's his fault. I was a willing participant, but yeah, it was his idea. He's the mastermind."

They walked along for a time, side by side, both of their minds reeling with the revelation.

"The woman, what was her name?" Caroline asked.

He stopped and turned towards her. "Her name isn't important. She was some lowlife who had been part of a drug gang and pimped out her kids. Did terrible things to them. Made a video of her and others having sex with her kids. Do you understand what I'm saying? Do you know the terrible things that people do to their own children?"

She touched his forearm. "Robert, I'm a United States Attorney. I've seen these things. You're overwrought."

He leaned closer. "Hell yes, I'm overwrought. I see my little boy every night, and I can't possibly imagine anyone doing those things to him, much less his own parents. Every day that goes by, I am more and more convinced that woman deserved exactly what she got."

"What did she get?"

"One of her kids, a daughter that she molested, killed herself about two years ago. She could no longer live with what her mother did to her."

"This woman got a trial too?"

"She did. She confessed. We all heard it. Plus, we had a videotape of the home movie. Disgusting."

"And what happened to her?"

"She killed herself. Shot herself in the head; just like her daughter had done. Westlake called it death by shame."

He could see that the initial shock of his disclosure had worn off, and Caroline had slipped into prosecutor mode, carefully interrogating him and cataloguing the evidence.

"So she committed suicide," Caroline said. "No homicide, just kidnapping. When did this happen?"

"Two years ago, maybe."

"You said there were four," she said, urging him gently toward the Lyle Walker murder.

They walked over to a bench and sat down. "I can't do this," he said. "I thought I could, but I can't do this."

"You can't do this?" she said through clenched teeth. "What the hell are you talking about, Robert?"

"It doesn't feel right, turning them all in."

"This was your idea, Robert. Pulling me away from the office, making me leave my phone so nothing could be recorded. No witnesses to your confession." She leaned close to his ear. "You want your fucking immunity, you better tell me all of it. That's the deal."

He unclasped his hands and tugged his cell phone from his front pocket. He pushed a button, then held the phone close to her mouth. "You want the rest of it? Say it on the recording. That I have immunity, full immunity."

She said nothing, and he placed the cell phone in his lap.

"Have you ever been to a NASCAR race, Robert?"

He shook his head. "I'm from Pennsylvania, remember?"

"I went once. A few years ago. Out at the Charlotte speedway. It's loud. And dirty. The smell of burning rubber and high-octane fuel infuses the crowd. And, of course, we're all there to see the crashes. Six hundred miles to watch a crash or two."

"Did you see any?"

"I did. Relatively minor. It was kind of a letdown," she admitted. "Everybody wants blood, apparently."

He realized she was trying to distract him for some reason. He stood up and held the cell phone in front of her. "Say it on the record, Caroline, or we're done."

"All right, Robert. Calm down." She took a moment to compose herself. "This is United States Attorney Caroline Bannister. I am hereby granting Assistant US Attorney Robert Crenshaw transactional and use immunity for everything he is about to tell me about his involvement in four murders, or three murders and a kidnapping."

"And derivative use immunity," he stated.

"And derivative use immunity," she repeated.

He turned off the recording, then took a few steps away from the bench and leaned against a wall. He took two deep breaths, looked around. "The third one was a car accident. Sort of. Promising young baseball player down in Savannah. Got drunk and plowed into a crowd of people. Killed five or six. We took the trailer down, put him on trial. He confessed. They all confessed. Then we got him so drunk he passed out. Put him behind the wheel of his own car, then drove him off the bridge into the Savannah River. He drowned."

"I remember reading about it. That was you guys?"

He nodded. "Another accidental death. Nothing suspicious. No investigation. No connection among them. All isolated accidental deaths. We were three for three. But Westlake wasn't satisfied. Up to that point it had all been an eye for an eye. Punishing people to avenge the death of someone else. Almost biblical. But it began to seem almost petty to Westlake. It wasn't enough. He wanted to send a message, not just get rid of people who had committed some isolated crime. He wanted to deter people from committing criminal acts, to prevent crime. That's when we came up with Lyle Walker."

"Whose idea was Walker?"

"Mine, actually. I was inspired by your telling us that the feds weren't going to prosecute him. It looked like this guy was going to get away with a massive Ponzi scheme because he was rich, savvy enough to hire the right attorneys and accountants, and smart enough to make friends with the right people."

She crossed her arms over her torso. "Texas might have prosecuted him."

He scoffed. "You don't believe that any more than I do, Caroline. You were frustrated that the Task Force had decided to drop the investigation. I could see that. Westlake saw it as a huge flaw in the system. What good is the law if you can't get to the criminals who are the most guilty? That's what he thought. That's why we decided to target Walker. The other three had been lead ups to the big fish, practice I guess you could call them. People whose deaths barely made the papers because they weren't murders. Westlake wanted something more than retribution, he wanted to make a statement to see if that might stop somebody. With Walker, he could send that message. And send it to the very people who might listen: the people who plan their crimes, who assess the risks and benefits, who just might take a different tack if they thought they could get caught and the punishment could be death."

"A deterrent," she said.

"Exactly. You see it. It was perfect. Walker had bilked people out of millions of dollars, caused the deaths of maybe a dozen others who lost their life savings in his Ponzi scheme. He created tremendous havoc and costs that still haven't been fully calculated. What he did was worse than what Lawter did, or any of the others. And if we did it right, maybe, just maybe, the next guy could be stopped. We all agreed with Westlake that we needed to send a message." The sound of his own voice uttering this admission disturbed him. He stopped talking, wondering how it had come to this.

They wandered into the theater, where a NASCAR documentary was playing, and sat together near the back. If anyone was eavesdropping, the noise from the film would mask their conversation.

"We extracted him . . . well not me, but the guys on the team who do this kind of thing . . . from his house in Dallas, and drove out to the West Texas desert. Odessa. Where Walker had started his oil drilling business, where the whole Ponzi scheme had been hatched. We put him on trial in an oilfield. Odessa means 'wrathful.' Did you know that?"

Caroline shook her head.

"We brought the wrath of thousands down on Walker. He ultimately confessed. There's something about those circumstances, being put on trial in a semitrailer in the middle of nowhere, it just makes people give it up. He said . . . now get this . . . he said he did it because it was the American Dream. Can you believe that shit? The American Dream is to bilk people out of their money and cause some of them so much distress that they kill themselves?"

"That sounds like what you did to that woman," Caroline said.

"She created her own situation," he shot back.

"Who came up with the rattlesnake pit?"

"I don't remember. Probably Perez or Cunningham . . . Shit. Well, I guess I was going to have to tell you at some point, right. They're US Marshals over in Asheville. They plan the logistics, perform the extractions, carry out the sentences."

She nodded. "So, you weren't really in Utah hiking that week."

"I was actually. For part of the week, anyway. Then I drove to Dallas. We stayed in separate hotels in Dallas until they captured Walker."

"How did they do it?"

"Tranquilizer gun. Pretty easy, apparently. They shot him in his own backyard and he went down like a big buffalo. We met at the airport, got in the semi, and headed down the interstate. Oh, I forgot. There are two trailers. One is outfitted as living quarters. Bunk beds, refrigerator, bathroom, internet access. A little cramped, but not bad."

"So where were you when Walker was dumped into the snake pit?"

"Inside the trailer, with Westlake and Johnstone. We were watching the whole thing on a closed-circuit feed. Cunningham had a body camera on his cap."

"There's a video of Walker dying?"

He noticed that the sound of roaring stock car engines had abated. "I'm sure the video and the camera were destroyed," he whispered.

They sat silently for a while, listening to the background music as the credits rolled. When the documentary was over, they left the theater and wandered over to the snack bar, where they bought two bottles of water.

"So far, it sounds like you are guilty of conspiracy to commit murder, maybe conspiracy to commit kidnapping. You didn't actually participate in either one."

"Yeah, I know. But it's felony murder. The penalty is the same, even if I didn't inject the heroin into Lawter or dump Walker in the snake pit. Right?"

"Never works out that way in sentencing," Caroline said. "I'm not even sure there's a federal crime here."

"The kidnapping and murder of a sitting Congressman? It's federal. I already looked it up."

She took a big gulp of water and replaced the cap. "So why now, Robert? Why come to me with this now? Walker was killed more than a year ago. The investigation has gone cold."

"The photograph of the truck," he said. "It's gnawed at me ever since you mentioned it that day in your office."

"The photograph of the truck . . . you mean the photograph of the pickup truck?"

His face sank. A white pallor came over him. "It's a photograph of a pickup truck? Not a semi, like what we were driving?"

She shook her head. "Pickup truck. And the FBI already found it. Owned by a neighbor who was on an emergency run for baby formula in the middle of the night. Obviously not related to the Walker murder."

He found the nearest bench and slumped onto it. "I . . . I . . . I thought the FBI was onto us. I told the others about the photograph. I panicked."

"Robert, it's going to be all right." She sat next to him and draped her arm over his shoulder. "I'm the only one who has the slightest idea of what you've told me. The FBI still has no idea how many people were involved, or where they're from, or what the motive might have been. They have no idea these deaths are even linked. It's a fantastic scenario, almost unbelievable. And I had no clue, until about an hour ago."

He rubbed his face in his hands. "Shit."

"You would have told me eventually. I didn't know what was going on with you, but you haven't been right for several months. I thought it was just the stress of a new job, baby, new house. Now I know it was guilt. That's a heavy burden for anybody," she said. "You're not built for it."

He turned to her. "It was that obvious?"

She nodded.

"It was this. Lawter and Walker and the others. I thought about killing myself. Really. Almost jumped off the top of Chimney Rock a few days ago. But I knew if I did that, it would crush my wife and my little boy when they found out I was dead. And they would never know why I did it. They would probably think it was something they had done, would blame themselves. So I couldn't do it. I decided to tell you instead. It was my only way out."

"You did the right thing, Robert."

They left the NASCAR Hall of Fame and walked slowly back to the office. There was little else to say. He knew what would happen next. He had to go on the record.

CHAPTER FIFTY

Robert Crenshaw had become a man Caroline no longer knew. She left him on the sidewalk in front of the building, with an admonition to go home and not to mention anything to anyone else, not even to his wife.

"You know how this is done. I'll need a complete allocution, videotaped. Just you and me. You can't mention any of this to anyone. Not a soul. Everything must appear normal. No one in our office can suspect anything. No one in your group can suspect anything. I need time to think about how to put this together."

She went to her SUV and drove. Her mind swirled with all of it. Part of her did not believe what Robert had told her. As a United States Attorney, she was accustomed to hearing about elaborate criminal schemes and bizarre motives, but she was rocked by Robert's revelation. Such a scheme was unfathomable. How did they coordinate the logistics among five people and carry out each abduction and execution without detection? Without leaving any hints that the deaths were anything but accidental? The detective in Florida was right. Something didn't add up because, in fact, Henry Lawter was murdered. But I didn't see it. They pulled this off right under my nose. In my district. A prosecutor in my office.

She found herself in the parking lot of the cemetery. A familiar place. She turned the engine off, but didn't get out of the car. She sat there, numb, staring through the windows at blooming dogwoods, the pink and white petals drifting on the breeze like snow. Normally, visiting Catherine's grave soothed her, but she knew today it would not. She re-started the engine and drove.

Shit. I forgot to Mirandize him. Okay, I can fix this. I can do it before I videotape his confession. I'll get him to sign a complete waiver of his right to counsel and right to remain silent, then have him read it on the video.

The Charlotte traffic was just starting to build as she headed around the beltway. She drove without being conscious of where she was going. Exiting on the east side, she made a couple of familiar turns, and then drove onto a street where she had never been until recently. She parked in a row of other cars amidst houses whose driveways were too shallow to hold them all. She emptied the bottle of water and then settled down in the leather seat to wait. Two doors up was the house owned by Carmelo Williams. The Mayor of Charlotte. The man who had murdered her sister.

CHAPTER FIFTY-ONE

Robert fell asleep that night in the rocking chair in Elijah's room. He slept better than he had in months, though he awoke with a sore neck. He watched Elijah sleep for the better part of an hour before his son woke up, hungry. Elijah lay in the crook of his arm, slurping from a bottle of baby formula. Gazing down at his son's peaceful visage, he wanted nothing more than for it to be over. For almost two years he had been an integral part of a cabal that had killed four people, including a sitting US Congressman. The Judge, Johnstone, Cunningham and Perez would be arrested soon, then tried and convicted. The death penalty was on the table. He didn't relish the thought of what he had done, or what he still had to do. He had no choice. He had to maintain the facade of normalcy, keep his composure, for just another few days.

At the office, he went about his business in the usual fashion, attending status meetings and handling administrative matters. He took a pain reliever, washed down with coffee, to diminish the crick in his neck. With some reluctance, he threw away the bottle of Xanax that had been a mainstay in his desk drawer for longer than he could remember. He wouldn't need it any more. Then he waited for Caroline to call.

At midafternoon, she buzzed him and summoned him to her office, ostensibly to discuss the office budget. They settled around the oval conference table. Robert's fingers drummed the wooden surface.

"Did you sleep last night?" she started.

"Better than I have since this whole thing started. You?"

"Not much," she admitted. "I'm still trying to get my arms around it all. There's a hell of a lot to do in the next few days. How? Where? Coordinating with the FBI. Managing the inevitable fallout."

"Now you feel what I've felt for the past two years. It's an unbearable weight," he said. "I'm proof of that. When are you bringing in the FBI?"

"Soon, but not just yet."

He nodded his understanding. She didn't want to make any mistakes, and involving someone outside the room, even if it was the FBI, might wrest the matter from her control. Once the FBI learned that she had a lead in the Walker case, they would charge in. Caroline couldn't risk that, and he didn't want her to. His future, his freedom, the rest of his life, depended entirely on her keeping her word.

"So, first step, leave the office at five o'clock today and go down to the Hyatt hotel. Room 616." She slid a key card across the table to him. "That's where we'll videotape your allocution. You know how this is done. You'll have to lay out all the details. Who, when, where, how. All of it. I'm sure I'll have some questions to clear up details. You should let Cindy know you won't be home for dinner. This will take a while."

"All right," he said. "I'll be there. And have the immunity agreement ready. No allocution until that document is signed and sealed." He left her office and played his role well for the rest of the day, without furtive glances or whispered secrets in the office hallways. He busied himself with a couple of civil cases he was working on, frequently checking his watch.

At precisely five o'clock, he left the offices of the US Attorney and walked toward the Hyatt Hotel, a half mile away. He detoured into a small store and bought a pack of cigarettes and a lighter, even though he didn't smoke. To stop his hands from shaking, he lit one of the cigarettes and plopped down on a wooden bench, thinking of what he was about to do. His confession would send the others to jail for the rest of their lives, or worse. He took a couple of puffs, causing him to sputter and cough. With elbows on knees, he raked his hand through his hair. His right leg trembled. He took a few more puffs before pinching the glowing butt between his thumb and index finger. He grimaced against the pain and quickly dropped the cigarette.

When he opened the door to room 616, he entered a small suite with a sitting area. Caroline was the only other person in the room. She was fiddling with a camcorder mounted on a tripod. She adjusted the camera, then came over to him and tightened the knot on his tie. She placed a bottle of water in front of him on the low table.

He unbuttoned his jacket and sat in one of the club chairs. He had been involved in many confessions before, but never on this side of the camera.

"Ready?"

"The immunity agreement first," he said.

She handed him an interoffice envelope. He removed the contents and perused the document. It was all in order, granting him full immunity and promising to submit him and the family into the witness protection program. He smiled at the irony. Two of his co-conspirators were members of the US Marshals Service, the same organization that would be responsible for his safety and anonymity as a protected witness. He signed three copies of the agreement, then folded one and slid it into the inside pocket of his jacket.

Caroline pushed the record button, announced where they were, the date and time, that just the two of them were present. Then she recited the Miranda warning.

"Do you understand your rights, Mr. Crenshaw?"

"Yes," the word dangled from his lips.

"And do you waive your constitutional rights, Mr. Crenshaw? Your right to remain silent and your right to have counsel present?"

"I do," he said. "I waive my constitutional rights in reliance upon the immunity agreement with the United States Attorney and a promise of witness protection for me and my family, all contained in a written agreement signed in triplicate and delivered to Ms. Bannister." He didn't like creating this friction with Caroline, but it was necessary. He had to ensure that he and Cindy and Elijah were fully protected.

She began by asking him open-ended questions based on an outline hastily scribbled on a legal pad. Starting with the Lawter trial, he moved forward in the chronological order in which attorneys most often present their cases, methodically providing dates and times, names and places. He told the long story without embellishment, controlling his emotions as best he could. An octave of excitement accompanied his telling of the Walker kidnapping and assassination. Near the end, Caroline asked him why he had come forward just the day before.

"I realized that what we were doing was wrong in so many ways. Of course, I knew that from the beginning, I don't deny it, but once my son Elijah was born, I just couldn't keep living the lie. That's why. His daddy owes it to him. It's that simple."

It was late when they finished videotaping, and he left Caroline with the video equipment in the hotel suite and went home.

"Spend as much time as you can with Cindy and Elijah right now, because this is going to get harder," she told him.

CHAPTER FIFTY-TWO

They stood beneath the grandstands, munching ballpark food. Inside the stadium, the Charlotte Knights were batting in the bottom of the second inning.

"When is the next meeting of your vigilante group?" Caroline said.

"A week from Saturday," Robert responded. He swiveled his head, scanning the faces of other fans lingering beneath the stands. His eyes darted uncontrollably.

"They're not surveilling us, Robert. They don't know about this meeting. The FBI is letting me handle this without intervention, at least for now."

"So what's the plan? It's been two days already."

"The plan is to arrest all of you together. Easier for the FBI. Easier for you because it allays suspicion that you were the mole. I'm trying to protect you as the source."

"I have to wait another week?"

Caroline nodded. "You waited two years to come forward. What's another week?"

"I just want it to be over."

"I understand that. But this isn't an operation that can be thrown together in a hurry. The FBI is running down some of the information you gave me in your confession."

"Allocution," Robert corrected her.

"Call it what you want. The FBI wants to corroborate the details – verify places, times, etc. What is this next meeting for, anyway?"

"Westlake has a new target."

"Any idea who?"

"No. He wouldn't tell us."

"Do you get any sense that you're out of the loop in some way? Could Westlake be planning this next trial with the others, without you knowing about it?"

"I seriously doubt it," Robert said. "He wouldn't do that. He wants everybody to be involved. I'm the prosecutor. He wouldn't move forward without me. He thinks we need a prosecutor, and a defense attorney, for the appearance of due process."

"Plus, he wants to spread the risk," Caroline said.

"Lay it out for me. What do I need to do?"

"For now, lay low. Act normal. When the FBI has finalized the plan, I'll let you know."

"Who's in charge over at the FBI?"

"Damien Porter. He's keeping it close to the vest, for now."

"Nobody in DC is in the loop?"

Caroline shook her head slowly. "Nope. This is the way I want to play it. You came to me; it's my show."

"All right."

"Trust me, Robert."

He met her cat-like eyes. "I don't really have a choice, do I Caroline?"

CHAPTER FIFTY-THREE

Raleigh Westlake felt them closing in. The seven Cherokee clans represented in the seven walls of the church seemed to be converging on him.

It had been a long time since he had been to church with his mother. As he listened to a homily about original sin, the large stained-glass figure of Sequoyah peered down at him. He grasped his mother's hand. Joyce looked at him with an expression melding surprise and concern.

He took communion, gulped the wine, swallowed the stale cracker, and knelt on the padded rail, closed his eyes, and listened. One of the wolves within him no longer howled. He wondered if he had starved it to death.

They left Our Lady of the Guadalupe Church, and he drove his mother home. There, he stood in the living room, unable to sit or to leave.

Joyce came to him, hugged him. "What's the matter son? I ain't seen you like this in a long time, not since your daddy died."

"Nothing, mother. Just a lot going on at the court."

She tapped a finger against his chest. "There's a lot going on in there," she said.

"What? What are you talking about?"

"I can see it, Raleigh. You're in turmoil. It's all over your face."

"Don't be ridiculous, mother."

"You don't look good." She patted him on the upper arm. "What have you done, son?"

CHAPTER FIFTY-FOUR

"Why do I have to wear a wire?" Robert Crenshaw said.

"Come on Robert, you're an informant now. The FBI wants something inculpatory from all of them, in their own words," Caroline said. "It's not a wire anyway. It looks just like a wrist watch."

"What about the video we made? Isn't that enough evidence to convince them?"

"I watched it. Looks too contrived. I'm the only other person in the room, I'm operating the camera, and I'm your boss. Plus, without additional evidence, this whole story is based one hundred percent on your credibility. And it goes without saying that your credibility isn't very high right now."

"But I came clean . . ."

She held up a hand. "We have to do it this way. That's final."

"All right," Robert said reluctantly.

"Here's the plan. We drive out to Bryson City, meet at the FBI field office there, and you get the microphone and additional instructions. Then we'll drive out to Westlake's house on Lake Fontana. You'll drop me off a couple of blocks away. You'll go in alone. At the appropriate time, you drop the bombshell," she said.

"What bombshell is that?"

"That the FBI has identified the tractor-trailer rig on the Texas photograph and has traced it back to Westlake."

"Has the FBI traced the rig back to Westlake?" he asked.

"Robert, up until you came forward, the FBI didn't even know there was a tractor-trailer rig. I know the photograph is of a pickup truck. You know the photograph is of a pickup truck, but Westlake and the others don't know that."

"The FBI hasn't found the rig yet?"

"That's not the angle they're working. You're the angle. But you have to make it convincing. You absolutely must make Westlake and the others believe that the FBI has found the rig and traced it back to him. That should get them talking."

He swallowed hard. "Okay, I think I can do that."

"You *think* you can? That's not good enough, Robert. Look, you concealed these crimes from me, from everybody, for more than two years. You've become an expert liar, like it or not."

"Okay. I can do it."

"We'll practice on the ride out. Now, do any of them carry weapons to these meetings?" she asked.

"No. It's not like that. I think Westlake has some hunting rifles at the house, but nobody is standing around holding guns."

"How about Tasers?"

"No, only when there's a secret trial."

"All right. That's good to know. Keep the secret. Not a word to Cindy, or anyone else. If she asks, you're just going out to the lake house for a normal weekend with the guys. Get some sleep, Robert. It will all be over tomorrow night."

CHAPTER FIFTY-FIVE

Robert left his car in a mall parking lot, near the road, and they drove out of Charlotte in Caroline's blue SUV. As they sped along the Interstate, spring winds buffeted the vehicle as if attempting to impede their mission. In the passenger seat, Robert nervously screwed and unscrewed the cap on a plastic water bottle.

"There's no reason to be nervous, Robert. It's all going to work out," Caroline tried to assure him.

"Easy for you to say."

"No, it's not easy for me to say."

"You're going to be the hero here, Caroline."

She sighed in frustration. "I don't think anybody but you sees it that way. This scheme went on right under my nose, for two years. My Chief Deputy is a murderer, conspired to kill a US Congressman whom the Task Force that I'm on decided not to prosecute. Hero, no. Scapegoat is more like it."

He rubbed the cigarette burn on the tip of his finger, which had become inflamed and infected. Staring through the windshield, he said, "I never thought about it like that." He glanced over at her. "So, you think once I tell them the FBI has located the rig and traced it back to Westlake, that will be enough to get him to admit his involvement?"

"That's what we're hoping."

"And the FBI will be outside, in case the guys try to do something to me? Try to hurt me?"

"Yes, Robert. You're our number one priority. Our star witness. As I told you last night, we're going to rendezvous with the FBI at the Bryson City office. The plan is for them to follow us to the lake house. They don't want to set up surveillance before everyone's inside the house. The area is too remote, not much traffic. It's too risky they'll get spotted."

He nodded.

"That's the plan," Caroline repeated.

"I'm really looking forward to seeing Westlake's face when you guys come through the door."

275

"Me too, Robert."

They drove in silence for a number of miles, heading west into the foothills. Unsettled, Caroline kept switching among the multitude of channels on the satellite radio. They approached the steep grade that wound like a labyrinth up the Black Mountains and down into the bowl in which Asheville had been settled.

"Me and my family, when do we go into witness protection?"

"Once the others are in custody."

"I'll need to alert Cindy, so she'll be ready," he said, reaching for the cell phone on his hip.

"Don't. That's a bad idea. If you alert her, she's going to ask questions. She can't ask questions that you don't have an answer for. You can't let her know anything unusual is going on. What did you tell her about this weekend?"

"That I'm spending tonight and tomorrow at the Judge's house. Guys' weekend."

"Perfect. Does she suspect anything?"

He shook his head. "No, this is a normal occurrence every month or two. Cindy's used to it. Listen, when do I join them?"

"The FBI has to take you into custody, too. Otherwise, it will be obvious that you're the mole."

"Arrest me?"

She glanced his way. "Surely you realized that, Robert. This whole thing has been laid out to provide you with maximum deniability. The photograph, tracing the truck back to Westlake, you being arrested with the others, these are all part of that plan."

"I know. I know. I'm just not thinking straight."

She touched his arm. "That's understandable, Robert, but you've got to keep your head. I've already informed the FBI you've been given full immunity, but they will still have to arrest you, interrogate you, get your story, verify it. It will probably take a few days."

"A few days?"

"I'll expedite it if I can, but you know I can't be involved in the criminal prosecutions. I've got to turn this over to the FBI. The indictments and prosecutions will be handled by USAs in other jurisdictions. You guys were busy. Florida, eastern North Carolina, Savannah, west Texas. The US Attorney in each of those jurisdictions will run the cases. But I'll stand by you one hundred percent. You have the immunity agreement, right?"

"It's in a safe place."

"Good."

They whizzed through the southern side of Asheville, bisecting the Biltmore Estate, a chunk of land that at one point stretched across the mountain range to Mt. Pisgah, where Hannah Sullivan had been murdered. The event that had started it all. Caroline checked the clock on the dash.

"We're making good time. Looks like we might be a half hour early."

Engrossed in tumultuous thoughts, Crenshaw didn't respond. He was ticking through the steps he had to take, preparing himself to endure the FBI interrogation, to endure a few days away from Cindy and Elijah.

"Robert, how many criminal defendants can count on the full support of a United States Attorney? I've already started putting together a resume of the ways you've served the citizens of the United States over the past decade. Without your coming forward, these cases never would have been solved. That won't be forgotten."

He subconsciously massaged the burn on his finger, picking at the raw skin. "Okay. I guess that's the best I can expect under the circumstances."

"It is, Robert," she said, both hands on the steering wheel. "It's the best any of us can expect at this juncture."

He took a long gulp from the bottle of water.

"Not that it really matters, but I don't think you told me why you did it, Robert. Why you joined up with Westlake. You said it was in the name of Justice, but it's got to be more than that. You . . . all of you . . . took a huge risk."

He gazed off at the mountain range in the distance, dark lumps shrouded in a blue haze. "I don't really know. It's complicated. Each one was different. The Judge can be very persuasive."

"It's pretty obvious why you targeted Lawter."

"Yeah, Lawter was an easy decision. That one was Westlake's call. 'Somebody has to stand up for Hannah Sullivan,' he told us. It was the first murder prosecution for any of us. I think we were all struck by the senselessness of her death, the brutality of it. Maybe Westlake saw her as the daughter he never had. I don't know. But to let Lawter just walk out of prison to freedom? We couldn't let that happen."

"And the woman who pimped out her kids?"

"Elise Rutherford. Johnstone's idea. He represented one of her kids on a drug charge. That's how he found out about it. I was against it at first. But then I saw the video. We all saw the video. Jesus. These kids were just . . .

they were just little kids. After we saw the video, there was no doubt what we had to do."

"But you didn't kill her."

"No. We didn't kill her. Cunningham and Perez told her we were going to make her wait to learn her sentence. I don't know how long. A day, a week, maybe longer. The whole idea was to make her think about what she had done to her kids, to feel remorse."

"Apparently it worked."

"It did. We just tipped her over the edge a little bit. I think Westlake was hoping she'd commit suicide. She's better off anyway."

"And Walker was your idea?"

Crenshaw turned his head to look at her. "Yeah, as I told you, Walker was my suggestion. Westlake was pressuring me to come up with a target. When you told me the Task Force was going to punt on Walker, that was my opportunity to get Westlake off my back. Walker didn't kill anybody, but in some ways his scheme was far worse. We all thought he was a dangerous man. I think we were all concerned that as his power base grew, he would become even more dangerous. He would be able to do even more harm to more people. Or maybe even do damage to the country."

"Are you saying you put Walker on trial and assassinated him out of a sense of patriotism?" A slight smile of bemusement crossed Caroline's face.

"Maybe it's the truth," he said defensively. "Almost makes you think it's the right thing to do."

They passed a colorful billboard for the Cherokee Reservation.

"You ever been?" Caroline said, nodding at the sign. "To the Reservation?"

"A few times. Fishing. With Westlake. He's part Cherokee. Did you know that?"

"I didn't. You guys go way back."

"A dozen years. He's the reason I came to North Carolina. He's the reason I joined the US Attorney's Office."

"But no qualms about turning him in?"

"Qualms? I don't have a choice, Caroline. I'm doing this for my family."

She turned off the highway at the next exit. "I need to use the facilities," she said.

While Robert manned the pump, Caroline went inside, paid with cash for the gas and two bottles of water. When she got back to the car, Robert said he needed to use the bathroom. She watched him go inside, wondering whether he might try to make a furtive phone call while out of her sight. She knelt by the left rear wheel and, with her fingernail, let most of the air out of the tire. Robert emerged from the store a few minutes later, and Caroline watched him walk back to the car. He didn't look like a killer or a coward.

They continued west as the sun dipped below the jagged horizon formed by the Blue Ridge Mountains. As they approached the rendezvous, they remained silent in anxiety, vaguely listening to the radio. Only about an hour to go before it's all over, Crenshaw assured himself.

CHAPTER FIFTY-SIX

Judge Westlake, Marcus Cunningham, Ignacio Perez and David Johnstone were gathered around the round metal table on the back porch, poking at a meal of ham and cheese grits. On the day before Easter, Lake Fontana had already gone to dusk. Shiloh lay curled beneath the Judge's chair, her nose between his feet.

"Where the hell is he?" Cunningham asked. "I know it's Easter weekend and he's got a wife and kid. I got a wife and kids too."

"Robert will be here," Westlake said calmly.

They took their plates and cutlery to the kitchen, rinsed everything, and put them in the dishwasher. Westlake turned on the television and switched the channel to the Final Four basketball tournament. The first semifinal was underway. They watched the first half of the game without much interest. At halftime, Westlake muted the sound and walked into the kitchen. He used his landline to call Robert's cell phone. It rang several times before going to voicemail. He didn't leave a message.

"Robert didn't pick up," the Judge announced.

"Should we keep waiting? Should we go look for him?" Cunningham said with agitation.

"Where are you going to look, Marcus?" Westlake said.

"I don't know, the road from here back is two-lane for twenty miles. Maybe he broke down or something."

"If he broke down, why wouldn't he pick up my call? Maybe he'll call back," Westlake said. "Let's give him another few minutes."

The night turned to mist. The drizzle obscured the view of the lake. They anxiously played a couple of hands of poker, waiting for Crenshaw to arrive. His tardiness gnawed at all of them.

"He's more than an hour late," Cunningham said, slapping his cards on the table. "Something's up."

Shiloh uncurled from around the Judge's legs and stood up, staring at the kitchen door. Her tail was rigid.

A moment later, Caroline Bannister came through the door, without knocking.

The Judge tipped his chair back on two legs, a frown on his face, scrambling for words. "What are you doing here, Ms. Bannister?"

Caroline sidled over to the poker table as the dog stared into her cat eyes, emitting a low growl. She stared the dog back under the table, then scanned the faces of the four men sitting there, seeing barely concealed panic on all of them.

"Where's Robert?" Westlake said.

Her rain coat glistened with droplets. She peeled off her leather gloves. "Robert told me everything," Caroline said. "Down to the last detail. The secret courtroom. The trials of Henry Lawter, Elise Rutherford, Tyler Becksdale, and Walker. Especially about Lyle Walker."

Westlake's chest tightened. He lowered the front legs of his chair, folded his hands in his lap.

"Quite a little plan, I must admit," she continued. "Take out the bad ones that escape the system. Make it look like suicide or an accident, so there won't even be an investigation. Quite clever. But you got too aggressive with Congressman Walker. Decided to send a message. You thought maybe other criminals would think twice if vigilantes might come after them. Not very smart, because then you became the target. The target of the FBI, the Justice Department. And Robert's target too."

"We're not vigilantes," Westlake said.

"That's exactly what you are," Caroline retorted.

"Natural justice because the system doesn't always work." Westlake spat the words.

"So the FBI traced the trailers from the photograph out in Texas?" Johnstone ventured.

"There was no photograph of your rig," Caroline said.

"But Robert said you had a picture of our truck," Westlake said in a higher pitch.

"Not your truck. Just a grainy picture of a neighbor's pickup truck driving by."

The room stayed silent while they all took this in. "He thought you had a picture of our truck. Robert got scared," Westlake said, barely above a whisper.

Caroline nodded. "Robert got scared. So scared he almost committed suicide. Scared he would never see his baby boy again."

"He panicked and came to you," Westlake said. "That's what happened. He probably asked for immunity."

"He did. And in case you get any wild ideas, he made a videotaped confession. Laid out all the details. There's a memory stick with the recording on it in an envelope on my desk. Names, dates, places. Everything neatly packaged for prosecution. That envelope will be opened on Monday morning, if I don't show up for work."

"Sounds like you have it all buttoned up," Westlake said.

"Yes."

Westlake rubbed his chin, thoughts spinning like debris in a whirlwind. "This is a pretty big coup for you, Caroline. You'll be a hero, maybe even the next Attorney General." Westlake watched her face for a reaction.

She revealed nothing.

"Where's Robert? Is he already in witness protection?" Westlake ventured.

Caroline fingered the amulet hanging from her neck, felt the tiny pits in the soft metal, slid her thumb across her sister's faded initials.

"Is the FBI coming, or do you just expect us to get in your car so you can drive us to jail?" Westlake asked.

Caroline pulled a small, white box out of her coat pocket, then placed it carefully on the felt of the poker table. She slid it across to Westlake. "Open it."

Westlake paused a moment, looking around at the other men. The box was the size of a gift box in which a husband might nestle a piece of jewelry he intends to give to his wife on a special occasion. Westlake lifted the lid from the box. On the soft white pallet rested a bloody index finger. Westlake pushed the box away and arched his graying eyebrows. After a moment he said, "Robert's?"

Caroline nodded. She hesitated a breath as the men waited for the inevitable announcement, their fates totally in her hands. She studied them all, these vigilantes who had put four people to death, who now seemed not so brave, not so bold. Not long after Robert had revealed the incredible scheme to her, she had made a decision, one she knew would forever alter her life.

"So now what Ms. Bannister?" the Judge managed.

She placed her hands on the back of the empty chair. "Crenshaw is dead," she said. Pulling the chair out, she sat down at the table with four other killers. "Deal me in boys."

Made in United States
North Haven, CT
23 September 2023

41903081R00163